MOON-RIDERS

BY

TRACY TAPPAN

Also by Tracy Tappan

The Community Series
Award-winning Paranormal Romance

The Bloodline War

The Purest of the Breed

Blood-Bonded by Force

Moon-Riders

Wings of Gold Series
Award-winning Military Romantic Suspense

Beyond the Call of Duty

Allied Operations

Man Down

THE BLOODLINE WAR,
Book One in The Community Series
Winner of the Independent Publishers Book Awards Bronze Medal for romance

"The book starts out strong and just keeps going with the action and suspense!"
~ Snarky Mom Reads

"This book was a total hoot and a half with dashes of sexy, adventure, and humor mixed in."
~ A Little Bit of R&R

"The mythology surrounding the vampires is unlike any that I have read before!"
~ Romance Novel Giveaways

"Tracy Tappan has a hit series on her hands!"
~ Tome Tender

THE PUREST OF THE BREED,
Book Two in The Community Series
Finalist for the USA News Book Awards for Romance

"What an adrenaline rush!"
~ Bookin' It Reviews

"I guarantee you will like this book. J.R. Ward, Sherrilyn Kenyon, and the others atop the PNR mountain, watch your back, there is a fast rising star and it's Tracy Tappan."
~ Rage, Sex, and Teddy Bears

"Tracy Tappan does a grand slam in this second book of The Community Series. This is a very fast, action packed, exciting book!"
~ Sportochick's Musings

"This book is solid! Wit, humor, snark, love story, steamy romance, sexy men, secrets, intrigue, and fantastical creatures."
~ Dauntless Indies

BLOOD-BONDED BY FORCE,
Book Three in The Community Series

"I was hooked from the moment I opened my kindle."
~ The Reading Café

"I am totally astounded by what is the best novel by far in this series yet!"
~ Fantasy and Romance Book Reviews

"Intense and a roller coaster!"
~ Book Junky Girls

"This is a dark world we're diving into, but it's as gripping as the first two instalments. You just can't put it down!"
~ The e-Reader Junkie

✧ ✧ ✧

Don't miss a single story in this thrilling paranormal romance series!
Go to the link below to be notified of the next release.
http://tracytappan.net/vip-moonriders/

✧ ✧ ✧

ACKNOWLEDGEMENTS

As always, my gratitude goes out to my team of editors Jessa Slade, Faith Freewoman, and Maria Connor.

Special thanks to Cristina Garagaianu for her help with new Romanian phrases.
All mistakes are my own.

To people who think outside the box
and don't color inside the lines.
You know who you are, and you inspire me.

CHAPTER ONE

Topside
7:10 P.M., November
Sheraton Hotel, Harbor Island Drive, San Diego

HE RODE UP ON A Harley.

The distinctive, throaty grumble of that motorcycle's engine brought Charlize swinging around to watch him, along with her two chef friends, Marissa and Lara. They were in perfect viewing position to watch the biker as he pulled up to the curb, light from the hotel's portico glinting off chrome fenders and a sleek, dark helmet.

He was dressed in steel-toed combat boots, a black leather jacket, and a pair of faded jeans that hugged corded thighs...thighs that gripped the metal body of the motorcycle in a way Charlize had never seen or sensed before. Like somehow the man was more powerful than the machine. He was completely faceless, his tinted eye shield currently lowered—not the safest choice at night—which stripped him of normal human features. No expression. No eyes. Just polished black fiberglass and Kevlar.

His head turned toward the three of them.

Danger. Menace.

Charlize's next breath slid out of her on a hot rush, and something rippled through her. A shiver, maybe. Not from the cold. It was early November, but *San Diego* November, so the weather was no more than brisk. Not from fear, either...not entirely, even though the danger coming off the biker was very real. Maybe—

The engine cut off. The biker dropped the kickstand with a negligent whack of his boot and dismounted with an easy swing of a long leg. He stood for a moment, unbuckling the chin strap on his helmet, his jacket partially unzipped to reveal a navy cotton T-shirt stretched tight over a suggestively muscled chest.

Charlize ran her tongue slowly over her teeth. Mystery solved. Her shiver had been one of sexual awareness. And now...

Here he comes.

Directly toward *her*.

He moved like a big panther, sure-footed and lithe—surprising for a man who clearly wrestled bears for a living. She dropped her gaze to the bedroom roll of his hips and made an *mmm* sound. His jeans molded an impressive package in front. Her nipples pushed tautly against her T-shirt.

Beside her, Lara gasped.

Charlize dragged her attention up. She'd missed the initial unveiling, since she'd been focused so intently below his waist, but...

The biker had removed his helmet, and...

Holy yowsa.

Hot.

Hot enough to please Satan, because his looks leaned heavily toward nasty with all the darkness he had going on—shortish black hair, black goatee, and a small black ear gauge in his left lobe. Moreover, he gave off an aggressive sexual energy that from one breath to the next left Charlize's undies in need of a cycle through a clothes dryer.

She knew this type of man. Got off on this type of man. This kind of hottie snack absolutely dominated in bed. When he was done with a woman, there'd be nothing left of her. She would only be able to lie on the mattress afterward, sore thighs flopped open, vision glazed, thoughts of *thanks for the abuse* wafting through her mind.

Charlize twitched up one side of her mouth. Sounded about her speed. Her belly was already heating to the idea of getting mounted by this guy. Her last conquest hadn't been nearly as hot and dangerous as Spank Me, Mister Biker here, so she was overdue for some action of the rougher variety.

The problem was timing. Marissa's colleagues were due to pick up Charlize, Lara, and Marissa any minute.

She glanced slantways at her two friends. What would they say if Charlize asked them to hang out and wait while she bagged this guy? She stifled a snort. What would they *think* about her wanting to screw a guy on sight alone? Since the three of them mostly socialized around cooking activities, Marissa and Lara didn't know that Charlize made pretty bold choices when it came to her sex life. To her, fucking men she didn't know was a thrill and an adventure, while relationships were obligations and stress and a boyfriend who eventually got all stupid and sappy and wanted, supposedly, a closeness he would just fail to deliver on anyway, so why bother?

Yeah, no thanks. Give her a straight-up, straightforward fuck any day.

But not all women were DTF strangers. *Fine.* Others could do their thing, she would do hers, and anyone who wanted to slut-shame her for the way she lived, well…they could go party elsewhere.

Charlize took a subtle step forward. Snackilicious was almost up to her, and with no time to check in with her girlfriends, she was just going to have to do her thing and hope Marissa and Lara would be good wingwomen. Her "thing" consisted of a brazen stare accompanied by a move that always hit her a home run and got her around all the bases. She arched her spine and thrust her breasts forward.

Her breasts were her biggest asset—most obviously be-cause they *were* big. That, coupled with her being a blue-eyed blonde, with naturally curling golden hair falling in fat ringlets nearly to her waist, seemed to have molded her into every man's wet dream fantasy girl. Seeing as her nipples were still poking against her T-shirt, seducing Snacky was going to be almost absurdly easy to—

He brushed right past her.

Without even a single glance in the remote vicinity of her direction.

In fact, he shoved his helmet into her hands just before sweeping Marissa off her feet. "Riss," he growled, swinging her around. "Damn, I missed you."

Marissa laughed, her palms coming to rest on the biker's wide shoulders. "I've only been gone for three days, and *what* in the world is that thing you rode up on?"

"Just a new man-toy the warriors are testing out."

Charlize blinked. She peered down at the helmet that'd been carelessly thrust into her arms and blinked some more. Her friend Marissa was beautiful, absolutely, with green eyes, a slender, fit figure, and tarnished blond hair hanging sleekly down her back, strands of her overlong bangs fluttering in her eyes, but... Charlize had *never* been ignored by a heterosexual male.

The biker set Marissa on her feet, a pair of exceptionally glittery silver eyes nearly devouring her as he bent forward for a kiss.

"Oh, no. No way." Marissa angled away from his mouth, although she was still laughing. "I know how you kiss when you have that look in your eyes, and we're in public." She pushed gently out of his hold. "Besides, I want to introduce you to my friends. Meet Lara Klein and Charlize Renault."

The biker finally gave them his attention. "Hey," he said, his eyes slightly narrowing as he tracked his gaze over both their bodies.

Another shiver passed over Charlize. Not from sexual awareness this time. No, this man wasn't admiring her. He was conducting a surveillance, rapidly evaluating any possible threat she might pose, assessing ways to eliminate said threat. Needles prickled the back of Charlize's neck.

Marissa gestured at Snackilicious. "This is my husband, Dev Nichita."

Husband...

Shiver number three. So...

He was one of *them*.

Even without Marissa's elaborate explanation of what her husband truly was, would Charlize have known? She was guessing she would've picked up on *something* being different about this guy...the danger radiating off him, his visible super-strength, those strange, intense eyes, the definite animal vibe pulsing off him. She just wouldn't have known what it all meant without Marissa's "tell-all" with Charlize and Lara on night two of the three-day chef seminar they'd just attended here at the Sheraton Hotel.

The seminar was given once a year, every November, and the last time Charlize saw Marissa at one was four years ago. They'd waved at each other across the banquet room during check-in, but nothing else. Charlize later heard that Marissa had left the conference right after French chef Pomeroy Lefèbvre canceled his teaching gig. So when Marissa asked Charlize and Lara to come to her hotel room two nights ago, Charlize figured it was to catch up. Even though the three of them weren't party friends, Charlize had always felt a close connection with these two, and...it turned out there was a specific reason for that.

A really bizarre reason, and no wonder Marissa made a batch of margaritas before launching into it.

Taking a casual sip of her drink, Marissa told them she'd noticed Lara's and Charlize's birthmarks on night one of the seminar, when the three of them went to the hotel pool together in bikinis. This prompted Marissa to obtain permission from someone named Toni for a tell-all session.

Tell-all what?

Well… Those birthmarks meant that Charlize and Lara possessed a special gene, similar to one Marissa had, inherited from an extinct race known as "Dragons"—called this because these ancient people were born with a colorful, scaly dragon tattoo on their backs. Their human ancestors also had the dragon tattoo, but only a small, brown piece of it: a wing or a nose or a foot.

And see? Marissa lifted the back of her shirt, showing them her dragon's foot. It was just like the one Charlize and Lara had. Not *sort of* like. It was an exact replica.

Lara gawked.

Charlize tried to pretend like she wasn't gawking, but pretty much did too.

They stood, raised their shirts, and compared all around, and sure enough. Each of the brown blotches sitting low on their backs, just to the left of the spine, were identical.

Identical.

Charlize dropped back down in her seat and reclaimed her drink, taking a deep gulp.

How was such a thing possible? And how had she missed this at the hotel swimming pool? Probably because she was too busy eyeing the guy with the board shorts riding low on his hips, ripped abs on full display.

Marissa topped off their drinks, smiling benignly at their stunned expressions. Were they ready for the really strange part?

Charlize shotgunned her second margarita. You know what? Sure. Why the hell not? Not much in life ever made sense to her. Plans never worked out the way they were supposed to; people never did what they said they would do; relationships always seemed to tank for no discernible reason. She had an open mind about whack shit.

Turned out she'd needed it.

Because a lot of weird-beyond-weird was laid out in the tell-all. It took Marissa several hours to explain it all, but the main points were these:

Marissa lived in a secret underground community that was a hiding place for a subset of the human race—a species called Vârcolac. These people had a lot of special abilities and some interesting genetic differences from "regular" humans, but for now, the important thing to know was that these Vârcolac needed to get much of their red blood supply from an outside source. They accomplished this through neck-biting with fangs.

From the corner of her eye, Charlize saw Lara chug her drink.

So…

Waitaminute.

Did that mean these people were, like, vampires?

Yes, but not undead monsters or TV-hyped fiends. They're good guys.

All right.

Er… Sounded "out there," but…

So anyway, according to more of Marissa's story, the survival of these Vârcolac was in jeopardy. A long-ago betrayal by one of their own ended up killing a majority of their species. Over the years their gene pool weakened, until now they couldn't have kids together—not living ones, at least. The only way to continue the race was to hook up with the unique species of human they could successfully mate with: people with the special birthmark and the rare Dragon gene.

Seeing as Charlize and Lara were a couple of these snazzy Dragons, the crowning point of the tell-all was that the two of them were being invited to join the community. And, by the way, lucky them, they were coming in with eyes wide open. Four and a half years ago, when Marissa joined the community, she'd been told it was a top-secret research institute. It wasn't until she'd dated Dev for three months that she discovered he was a vampire.

Like…a *real* vampire…? I mean…

Community living, according to Marissa, was awesome. Charlize and Lara would be expected to contribute in some way, but Marissa was making it easy. She wanted them to be part owners of her restaurant. She had two kids now and couldn't keep the place open as much as the community needed. So basically Charlize and Lara could set their own schedule, own their own business, and not suffer a single financial concern while they were there.

Hard to find a downside.

At the core of it, they were only being asked to date any Vârcolac man who struck their fancy, go out with him long enough to see if they might fall in love, and then let nature take its course. They could leave any time they wanted, but the community preferred if they committed to at least a six-month stay. This would give them time to adjust to small-town life—and to living inside a cave—before they made a lasting decision about their futures. If they wanted to hold onto their homes topside during this time, the community would pay their rent or mortgage. They would have to quit their current jobs, of course, but weren't they both in dead-end positions right now, anyway?

Marissa followed that question with a final, *So? What do you two think?*

Charlize tried to exchange a glance with Lara, but Lara was too busy staring off into space with a dreamy look, a hand resting on her chest. Whether or not Lara believed all this vampire and Dragon stuff, Charlize got the sense it didn't really matter. Lara had just turned the maternal-clock-clanging age of thirty, and Charlize was guessing Lara was sold on the idea of joining the community the moment it was described as a place full of mega-hot men who desperately wanted to find a wife and have children. How many times had Lara been caught with her nose pressed to the window of Babies"R"Us? Lara probably would've been willing to move someplace with little green Martian men, as long as one of them wanted to marry her.

Charlize wasn't sure what she believed about vampires and the unheard-of Dragon genetics, either, although as far as convincing her of the truthfulness of some of it, the matching birthmarks went a long way. Marissa's description about how their Dragon genes set them apart from regular human beings also fit.

Hadn't Charlize always felt out of place? Didn't she have trouble making friends? Didn't she find it strange that she was a successful, beautiful woman, who a dozen men should've snapped up by now, yet she'd never been in a serious relationship? A "yes" to all of the above. Charlize had always felt wrong in life. Apparently this was because she didn't belong around regulars, but among her own people—Vârcolac and Dragons—although she wasn't going to discount her mother's contribution to her being a "wrong" end-product, either.

But, like Lara, what ultimately sold her on the idea of joining the community was the mega-hot men part—albeit for different reasons. Charlize was ripe for some new guys to play with. She'd already fucked all the cute, single guys in San Diego. Ha ha, not really. But *really*, there was nothing keeping her in San Diego, not an exciting job, not close friends, and as far as family went, living in a hideaway community would leave her readily *un*available to clean up the messes her mother and brother consistently made—an added bonus. Or maybe a *main* reason to go, take a bit of a vacay away from her old life.

So she and Lara agreed to give Marissa's community a try.

And if Biker Snack was a sample of the scrumptious offerings being put forth by this community, then Charlize had definitely made the right decision.

A giggling threesome of teenage girls wearing cheap boho fashion and trailing even cheaper perfume—like a lilac had mated with a wet dog—frisked toward the hotel.

Charlize and Lara moved farther off to the side to make

room for them. The three passed by, followed by resigned-looking parents.

"Anyway," Marissa said to her husband. "Now that you're here, I'll check out."

He raised his brows. "You haven't checked out yet?"

"No. I received a text message from the warriors saying the van has a flat tire. I wasn't sure when anyone would be here to pick us up. But don't worry, we're all packed."

Her husband started toward the hotel door.

"You'd better let me talk to the front desk, though, since I signed up for the seminar under an assumed name."

When Charlize had asked Marissa what the deal was with that, Marissa told her about a crazed San Diego detective named John Waterson who was after her husband. The last time Marissa used her married surname, Nichita, the detective picked her up and took her to a police station for questioning.

"It will just take me a—Dev! What are you doing?"

He was using his large body to block Marissa toward the front entrance, that's what, a glittery hunger back in his eyes. "The room is still available for use." The statement was made in unmistakable tones of velvet and innuendo.

Marissa scampered backward. "Stop!" she protested, but her smile was purely female. And, by the way, her breasts were heaving. "My friends—"

"Don't mind hanging out while we enjoy a little reunion time." He swiveled his head around to eyeball them. "Do you?"

Lara pressed a hand to her chest, a gesture she seemed to make whenever she was thinking, *oh, my.*

Dev's eyes were shining with such feral lust, it confirmed Charlize's initial assessment of him. He did absolutely dominate in bed. *Daaaamn, gurl, Marissa.*

Charlize tossed the two a large grin. "Of course we don't mind." She, personally, considered herself to be a great wingwoman. "Have at it, you two."

Dev smirked, then lifted Marissa off her feet with a brawny arm around her waist and stalked off.

Charlize watched them go, watched every step Dev took toward the elevators. His rear view was as spectacular as his front.

"Oh, my," did slip out of Lara now.

Charlize drew in a deep breath and let it out slowly. She tilted her chin down and narrowed her eyes. "I want one."

CHAPTER TWO

LEANING FORWARD IN HIS BLACK leather armchair with both elbows braced on his knees, an Xbox controller held loosely in his hands, Breen pulled his attention away from the TV screen long enough to check his wristwatch. He'd only just started exploring the new interface of the upgraded Xbox One S that came in the mail this morning, but he would need to disconnect now if he was going to arrive early for the morning training session.

The video imagery of *Gears of War* was unreal, but he'd have to leave in about ten minutes to be on time anyway. And ten more minutes of gameplay wasn't worth getting stuck in a locker room full of warriors busting on each other. He wasn't a big talker himself, and being around all the warriors' pre-workout bullshitting just seemed to blaze a spotlight on this fact.

On the television, an animated snipe popped out from behind a shed, and a second later red blotched across the TV screen.

Toast. Breen paused the game instead of respawning. *A good time to quit.*

"What's up?" The voice came through Breen's headset, although it was only his warrior buddy, Jeddin, one floor down.

Breen and Jeddin were two of a small group of serious gamers in Ṭărână who consistently petitioned the higher-ups for permission to join multiplayer games with people topside. But in MP battles, gamers could talk freely to one another, and Ţărână's security guidelines still didn't allow for completely unmonitored communication.

This was mostly to protect against new Dragon humans accidentally disclosing dangerous info. Unlike Vârcolac, the humans who were regularly brought into the community nowadays hadn't been raised living and breathing exposure avoidance, so someone might inadvertently mention "vampires" to an Aunt Bertha in a text message or email. Security had loosened a lot since Toni Parthen took over as co-leader of the community five years ago—travel to and from topside happened a lot more, for one—but Ţărână was still mostly a hidden community.

"You glitch out?" Jeddin asked him.

"No," Breen said into his microphone. "I just gotta go to work."

"Roger that," Jeddin said. "See ya."

They signed out, and Breen tugged off his headset and set it and the controller on the floor next to his armchair. He came to his feet and stretched, the sinews in his right shoulder popping, then checked his cell phone—it'd beeped while he was playing. His younger brother, Barbu, was wondering if he could drop by and pick up some of his Blu-ray movies.

Barbu lived in Ţărână's slum, Stânga Town, where theft was a problem, so Breen let his brother keep valuable shit here. About the only time they saw each other was when Barbu came by to grab his stuff. Otherwise they pretty much operated in different worlds. Stânga Town kids kept to themselves…or, really, they were shoved aside by a lot of the main townspeople, who judged Stânga Towners as being genetically inferior.

These kids were the last to be produced from Vârcolac-to-Vârcolac mating, born in the '80s when stillbirths among the breed had become epidemic. The deaths grew so numerous, in fact, that by 1993, Roth Mihnea—Toni's co-leader—banned all procreation.

Breen, born in 1978, just missed becoming a Stânga Town kid.

The new administration—Toni—was trying to change this attitude. Donree, her assistant, was a Stânga Towner. But it was slow going. Mostly, these fringe-born Vârcolac hung out together in their own part of the cave and tried to meet town expectations by getting into a lot of trouble.

It wasn't right for brothers to be on opposite sides of the law, but Breen and Barbu never seemed to know what to do about it, and Ungar, their father—whose job it probably should have been to fix things between his sons—didn't do anything and never would.

So Breen just texted *sure* to Barbu on his way out the door and strolled to the elevator. He lived on the fourth floor of the new Water Cliffs Apartments.

Constructed three years ago, the complex rose an impressive ten stories high, all the way to the uppermost reaches of the cave ceiling, and overlooked the Water Cliffs water park. The first story was a solid block of black-painted concrete, built for the sole purpose of adding height. This way even people who lived in apartments on the first floor, which was really the third—the lobby being on the second—would have a view of the waterfalls and geysers of the Cliffs. And, yeah, the views were definitely awesome. Every living room in the complex sported a huge plate glass window, plus a balcony.

Before the Water Cliffs Apartments existed, the warriors and single Dragons lived dorm-style in a mansion at the south end of town. Breen headed there now—the mansion was also where the gym was.

Once inside, Breen descended a short stairway to the basement floor and then went into the locker room.

It was empty.

He stood for a moment, hands shoved into his pockets,

just observing the two rows of tall metal lockers and listening to the quiet. Fragments of conversation came murmuring through the right-hand wall, probably Roth talking to someone. His office was right next door.

Breen opened his locker and started to change. Why was it he came early for the silence, then felt strange in it? He geared up in his workout clothes—black Lycra T-shirt and shorts, plus pliable wrestling shoes—then went from the locker room to the gym across the hall.

He would stretch out for about five minutes, then—

A curse *woofed* out of him as a raging hammer-pulse pounded through his nuts. He staggered backward, his knees turning to beer mash, and banged into the wall next to the door. He thrust his spine against the plaster to stop himself from sliding down the wall, hitting the floor ass-first and *what the shit nuggets?* second.

His dick was next to fall victim to the rhythmic pounding. His mouth dropped open. He hauled in breath after breath, listening to the thunder of his heartbeat...and to the insectile *whir* of one of the gym's treadmills working.

A curly-haired blond woman was running on it.

Breen swallowed hard against a sudden rush of saliva. The capillaries in the gums behind his canines began to swell. Some Vârcolac males could handle the scent of an unmated Dragon woman; Breen couldn't. Even a whiff of the hormone-drenched blood of an unmated threw him into a state of such rampant lust, he couldn't tamp it down and he could barely control it. Was his hunger stronger than others'? Did he lack some sort of tempering gene? He couldn't even guess, and right now the reasons were BFD. What mattered was that he was losing control fast—he was getting way more than a whiff of this woman.

The ventilation system in the gym was turned off, and with the treadmill runner currently lathered completely in sweat, her aroma was saturating the entire space. Breen swore his Vârcolac vision could practically see large, tasty droplets of her scent rolling down every wall. On top of that, she was all but naked, dressed only in a middy jog bra and blue spandex running shorts.

His nuts danced around some more, then a tingle ran the length of his spine, shot up the back of his neck, through his jaw, and landed right where his fangs rooted in. His instincts were telling him he needed to feed even though he didn't. And maybe this was why he couldn't handle scented females so well—it always felt like a part of him was starving. No matter how much donor blood he choked down, no matter if he'd fed five minutes ago or five days, he walked around feeling like a mass of rapacious hunger.

Yeah, and about that…he should probably pay attention. Being in the same space as a sweaty, extra-aromatic female for any length of time couldn't lead anywhere good. He needed to leave before—

"Hey!"

Before she spotted him. *Shit*.

She stopped the running machine, her eyes brightening on him as she popped out a set of earbuds. Flipping those over the treadmill's handhold, she hopped off, grabbed a towel— also off the handhold—and started toward him.

He swallowed very, very slowly. Her full frontal was amazing. Shapely hips swayed. Breasts that defied spectacular rose and fell from her labored breathing—the chest-expanding, in-breath making his eyeballs press at the edges of their sockets. Her hair was hiked into a high ponytail, creating a puffy fountain of curls on top of her head…and leaving the healthy pulse of her carotid bare.

He licked his lips. A mistake: he drew the taste of her right out of the air.

She stopped in front of him, wiping herself down with the towel. "Hi, I'm Charlize."

He clawed at the wall behind him as her aroma vibrated

through his neural pathways so hard it shook some teeth loose in his jaw. She wasn't wearing any scent-reducing mud behind her ears. Not even a smudge. That his fangs hadn't unsheathed yet was astounding.

"What's your name?" She grinned, blazing a hundred and twenty watts at him.

"You—" Speech stopped. He stared at her smile. Her canines were on the pointy side for a human's. He managed a shallow breath and tried again. "You're not supposed to be in here." Had another Vârcolac male been in the gym, Breen's low, growly tone would've snapped the man's attention over. Predators knew the sound of other predators on the hunt. "This is one of the times when the warriors train."

"Oh?" She tossed the towel toward a storage cubby on the other side of the door.

"There's a schedule posted on the wall," he told her.

"Sorry, I didn't notice. But also I'm a marathon runner, so, you know"—she shrugged—"I gotta run. First thing I do whenever I arrive at a new place is check out the gym."

Seemed kind of extreme. She'd probably only arrived here a couple of hours ago, and it had to be nine thirty at night her time—here in Țărână, they switched AM for P.M. with topside time, and vice versa. She should be in bed right now...for more reasons than tiredness. "Didn't they tell you not to leave your room?"

When a noob Dragon was brought into the community, she was required to stay in her mansion guest room until she'd read the community manual, then taken a test to prove she was completely up to speed on Vârcolac culture. Once cleared, she'd be assigned a place to live in the Water Cliffs Apartments.

"No. I was just told not to leave the mansion." She edged closer. "So you're a warrior, huh?"

His vertebrae slid together, his spine feeling like it was growing lubricated. For what activity, he wasn't sure.

"So you work with Marissa's husband, right?"

"Uh…" Only half-listening, he directed his sub-response to her breasts. Sweat had reformed and was making patterns down her cleavage, in beads and streaks, drops swelling, rivulets darting. His own sweat formed around the collar of his workout shirt.

"What kind of stuff do you do when you train?" She tilted her head toward the boxing ring. "Fight?"

"Uh…" he said again. He was getting stupider by the second.

"Do you want to work out with me before your buddies show up?"

The AC needed to go on now or—He stopped short and squinted. "What did you say?"

A smile played at one corner of her mouth, and her eyes crinkled a little. "We could spar in the boxing ring."

He stared at her. "You want me to *hit* you?"

"No." She laughed, and somehow the noise tugged straight at his balls. "I want you to let me hit you. Nothing too hard. Just something to give me a good arm workout."

Exactly what he needed: add fang-elongating aggression to what was already a serious Molotov cocktail of lust.

"Come on, it'll be fun." She upped the wattage of her smile.

He stared some more. At her smiling teeth. The sharp dig of those pointy canines at his throat would feel… His package started to burn, the throb in his dick nearly unbearable. Throttling off a moan, he tugged at the crotch of his workout gear.

The woman's attention followed where his hand went—caught! Her focus remained on his crotch for an extra-long moment, then lazily, slowly, her eyes trailed back up his body and she met his gaze again. Her pupils were dilated, hunger in *her* eyes now…

Shit-nuggets. Get out, Dalakis. Lashing his hand out sideways, he made a blind grab for the door handle. Missed it. He couldn't take his eyes off her. A force inside him wouldn't allow it.

"Or we could wrestle," she suggested in a soft, inviting voice.

He went still. His gnawing hunger made more growly noises in his ears.

"I have to warn you, though, I usually win at wrestling. 'Course I'm thinking that's because men let me." She tossed him a wink.

Getting horizontal, sweating together, legs and arms entwined, breasts that defy spectacular smashed against me... Another moan worked its way up from deep in his diaphragm. He trapped most of it in the back of his throat. But not all of it.

She heard enough.

Her blue eyes sparkling, she let out a playful whoop and jumped him.

He tried to jerk away from her, but with the wall right behind him, there was nowhere to go.

She easily cranked her right arm around the back of his neck, crossed her forearm in front of his throat, then grabbed her right wrist with her left hand, putting him in a good old-fashioned headlock. Dropping all of her weight toward the floor, she dragged down on him.

He bent over, going where she wanted him to go.

If she'd been a warrior or a man, he could've escaped her hold in a dozen different ways. But not in a way that wouldn't have caused her pain, and there was the problem. He had no idea how to resist her without hurting her. He'd never wrestled a girl before. So he just went with the flow of her body.

When she went down to her knees and twisted, he allowed his right shoulder to hit the mat.

When she pushed at him, in large part with the side of her

soft breast, he rolled over.

When she caught his wrists and scrambled on top of him, her thighs—still hot and tight from her workout—straddling him, then slammed his hands above his head, well…that's when he got into deep, deep trouble with his Vârcolac side. Because that side couldn't tell the difference between playful aggression and the canine-elongating real stuff.

"See?" Her eyes were sassy. "I win." She leaned over him, the position putting those voluptuous, sweaty tits of hers right in his face, and… It might've actually been a better idea if he'd resisted her.

His fangs punched down into his mouth, stretching longer than he'd ever felt them go.

The sass cleared off her expression. "Whoa." She stared, riveted, at his extended canines.

He watched a shiny bauble of perspiration slip out from behind her ear. He followed its progress as it slowly traveled the length of her jaw and arrived at the tip of her chin, hovering there, reflecting the light. It grew into a long, stretchy oval, quivered, then fell…fell, fell…

It splashed apart on his right fang.

He rolled his eyes into the upper reaches of his head. The taste of her was unreal: sweet, but in no describable way. Not like sugar or honey or fruit…maybe like all-over divine body pleasure. Heaven, Nirvana, Elysium, Valhalla—whatever was out there. It's what she tasted like, and he had to have her.

An inhuman, beastly sound escaped him.

Her grip on his wrists loosened. "Uh…are you—?"

He flipped her onto her back so fast the band from her ponytail flung out of her hair, sending the blond mass into a wild tumble of luminous corkscrews around her. He rough-kneed her legs apart and jammed himself between her thighs.

Her eyes flared wide.

From atop straight-locked arms, he stared down at her, his eyeballs feeling like they were burning twin holes through the back of his skull. He was growing more punch-drunk on her scent every second. *And her taste...* He smoothed his tongue over his right fang and actually grayed out for a staggering heartbeat. His arms shuddered, like his body was a thousand-pound weight he very much wanted to drop down on top of those spectacular breasts. *Get off, Dalakis*

He tensed.

She grabbed his shoulders. "Don't go," she breathed, her eyes flagging to half-mast. Whatever shock or alarm had been her initial reaction was gone now. "You've got the right idea." She slid her palms along his shoulders and down his biceps.

He gritted his teeth, his fangs squeaking against his lower bicuspids.

She linked her fingers behind his neck and pulled him down to her, her lips finding his.

Their mouths came together in a kiss and melded instantly, moving together in natural synchronicity, slanting, pressing, anticipating. He expelled a short blast of air from his nostrils. Her lips were so soft... How could a woman's lips be this soft? More taste, and *more* when she urged his lips apart and thrust her tongue inside his mouth. She went after his tongue in a way that wasn't at all gentle, but the aggressiveness of her attack was coupled with wet and smooth sensations.

Every muscle in his body knotted. Tongue-kissing was...was... He needed to stop. *But how?* Here again, he didn't have any experience. He'd never kissed a girl before. Maybe she knew it. She seemed to be taking full advantage of his dumbstruck paralysis, completely plundering him, driving him to the point where pain was starting up in his crotch, blood pounding at the closed doorway into his dick—the curse of every unmated Vârcolac.

His mind whispered the way to relief. *Bite her.* Canting his hips more tightly against her crotch, he—

A sharper discomfort speared through his crotch, and a hiss of pain helped him break the seal of their lips. He tried to move off her, but she grabbed him firmly by the ass.

"Don't stop," she panted. "I want this."

What? He peered down into her languid eyes. *What?* Had a host just told him she was willing?

Her fingers dug into his butt.

Hadn't she just said...? *I want this*: it's what she said.

Her head fell to one side, the long, fair line of her neck flaunting its artery at him.

A feverish mouthful of saliva pooled against his lower lip and fierce need rippled along the small of his back. Vocabulary scrambled. Individual words smeared into blurry syllables.

She writhed beneath him and moaned. "Come on, baby."

The edges of his nostrils flexed. His vision narrowed down to pinpoint focus, the gym disappearing from his periphery. Animal instinct reared up and took over. He came down on top of her.

"Yes." She closed her legs around his hips.

His nuts balled up into hard fists. The walls somersaulted. A hot wind roared through his ears. The ether of primal drives whited out his brain, pitching him into nothingness, and...

The next thing he knew warm skin was beneath the crush of his lips and an inebriating taste was flooding across his tongue. He groaned, a guttural sound from deep in his throat. He was being transformed. It was as if his skin was changing out for a new set with a better fit while intense energy reinvigorated every cell, and...and then his dick grew hard. He groaned again and gulped her down. Gulped and gulped and—

A strong hand fisted into the scruff of his shirt and hauled him out from between the eager clamp of the treadmill woman's thighs. His shirt collar wrenched tight across his Adam's apple.

"The fuck are you doing?" bellowed Jacken Brun, leader of the Warrior Class.

CHAPTER THREE

EVERYTHING BLEW BY IN A blur.

Charlize wasn't sure what had happened...what *was* happening. To start with, she could barely see, her eyes crossed from an intensity of pleasure she'd never dreamed possible. *Her*, who thought she'd experienced every level of pleasure out there.

Apparently not.

Weird part was that first there'd been pain. Not stinging, butt-slap pain or *oops-I-grabbed-you-too-tight-while-shooting-my-wad* pain. But nail-scratching, screaming, slapping, *stop-biting-me-you-asshole!* pain. Then just as quickly, there was pleasure. Not *oh-yeah-baby-I'M-COMING!* pleasure or even *holy-shit-are-those-diamonds?* pleasure. But a brand-new plateau of ecstasy that rocketed her vagina into geosynchronous orbit and boggled her brain.

The burly men in matching black workout gear who came pouring into the gym moments ago seemed to understand what was happening. Eyes narrowed, nostrils flared, they started cursing. And whatever the problem was, it changed her hottie-potential-hookup into a violent, wild-eyed beast.

In the second it took the black-haired man to yank Hottie off her, the two men raged into a brutal wrestling match—a *real* one—muscled bodies savagely twisting and straining, one man dominant this second, then being dominated the next. Then another edge-of-your-seat reversal. Flip again. A shot with a fist. *Wham!* The snarling going on between the two sounded like a gangland lion fight in the Serengeti. She couldn't believe the violence! Her hottie seemed like he genuinely wanted to kill his black-haired opponent, which wasn't just weird, but totally fucked up. What kind of guy changed so fast from wantonly sexual to ruthlessly violent?

It took four men to break up the fight.

From there, she and her hottie—now locked in iron shackles—were hustled to a room filled with chic décor Charlize was too frazzled to really notice. Her pulse was still racing from all the violence she'd witnessed, not to mention that her body was feeling orgasm-deprived, her clitoris a stiff, sensitive point.

Within ten minutes they were met by a woman who introduced herself as the community lawyer.

This woman, Kimberly Stănescu, asked rapid-fired questions, mostly of Charlize. Hottie—Breen, Kimberly called him—was too out of it to answer. His eyes were semi-glazed, his lungs were pumping, and he was sweating so much a small pond had formed on the carpet beneath his chair. He was also sporting a raging boner.

Kimberly did an admirable job of ignoring the tent-up, or pretending to, because there was no way she *couldn't* see it. Breen's tight workout shorts made the monster erection ginormously obvious.

Charlize herself couldn't *stop* noticing it. Breen was clearly fully equipped to see her through to her much-needed O. What she really wanted to do was *thanks-so-much-buh-bye* Kimberly out the door, then get her climax on.

It wasn't to be.

Charlize was left to field the countless questions, her head spinning like she was on a bad drug trip. Why the fuck should anyone care if Breen bit her? He was a vampire, right, so wasn't that sort of his jam?

Mid-interview, Kimberly, Charlize, and Breen were summoned to a courtroom. The space wasn't very large, just big enough for eight rows of shiny wooden benches, split down the middle by an aisle. About a dozen onlookers were scattered around the seats already—Jesus, it'd been, like, twenty minutes. Scandalous news traveled fast in any small town, but here, Charlize would guess gossip had warp capacity.

Marissa was seated in the back, a toddler girl of about one nestled on her lap. She offered Charlize a crooked, supportive smile.

Kimberly led Charlize and Breen to a bench up front and latched his shackles to a fat metal ring on the floor.

"Sorry," the lawyer murmured. "But you're not yourself right now, Breen."

As if to prove Kimberly's point, Breen did his snarly asscan act again, growling and lurching at his chain, when a man entered the room.

Black-haired and well-dressed, the new arrival was announced as Roth Mihnea. He took a seat at a rectangular head table. He was followed inside by a young woman with curly black hair who slipped behind a smaller table and flipped open an iPad, obviously there to take notes. Finally Dr. Toni Parthen entered. She was blond, or maybe closer to strawberry blond, beautiful, and elegant. Charlize and Lara had met her when they arrived at the community a few hours ago.

She sat next to Roth.

Charges were read, indecipherable phrases like "Unauthorized Bite" were bandied about, and a bunch of other yakkity-yak.

The muscles in Charlize's legs tensed. Lactic acid buildup or a case of nerves? She was used to getting into the sauce, but it had to be some kind of record for her to find herself neck-deep in it within a few hours after arriving someplace new. And how much trouble was she in, exactly? She was having difficulty telling. This town's rules and regulations were stupefying.

A masculine voice rose, and Charlize glanced over at Roth.

He was red-faced. "Breen Dalakis is guilty of an Unauthorized Bite," he accused—there was that phrase again. "If this offense goes unpunished, then every Vârcolac in the community will think he or she has free rein to do the same. This is unacceptable."

Lawyer Kimberly's gaze was iron-hard. "With the court's respect, Mr. Dalakis's guilt has not been established. It is our contention that Mr. Dalakis was, in fact, *authorized.*" Kimberly checked in with a yellow legal pad she held, then looked at Charlize. "Miss Renault, when you and Mr. Dalakis were in the gym together did you say to him, 'I want this' when his fangs were elongated?"

Charlize paused over the question, but after inspecting it from several angles, she couldn't see how answering it could hurt her. She also couldn't figure why anyone would care. Unless free love was illegal in this town or something—and, hell, if it was, she was outta here. But then…why would Marissa have emphasized the mega-hot men part of this place if a woman wasn't allowed to fuck the snacky treats to her heart's content?

"Miss Renault?"

"Um, yes, I did."

Roth pushed in. "Were you giving Mr. Dalakis permission to bite you?"

Jesus, the "bite" question again? Why the—? *Oh, crap.* Her heart tripped. Had she been "turned" by Breen's bite, was that what all this commotion was about? But…but Marissa had said her vampires weren't like television monsters. "I… No. I was just agreeing to have sex with him."

Roth turned a righteously satisfied expression on Kimberly. "Miss Renault's testimony confirms she was *only* agreeing to sexual play. We must therefore conclude—"

"Mr. Dalakis couldn't have known that," Kimberly cut in.

Roth gave the lawyer a look like, *puhlease.* "Are you suggesting that when Miss Renault said 'I want this' to Mr.

Dalakis, he wholly believed she was agreeing to a *life*-bond? After, what...?" He looked at Charlize. "How long did you and Mr. Dalakis interact in the gym?"

"I don't know..." *What's this life-bond shit?* "About ten minutes." Charlize quick-scanned the faces, expecting disapproval. She didn't find any. But then maybe everyone was just too distracted right now, both Roth and Kimberly more interested in proving their respective points rather than making Charlize feel like a slutbucket.

"*Ten minutes*," Roth emphasized. "Considering the short period of time Mr. Dalakis was acquainted with Miss Renault, your contention that he could have reasonably assumed himself *authorized* to bite her is utterly flimsy."

"Reason doesn't enter into this," Kimberly argued evenly. "In no part of the law regarding a UB does it state that a Vârcolac is required to understand the motivation behind a host's consent. He only has to *have* it. Mr. Dalakis did."

"The court disagrees," Roth shot back. "Vârcolac make these kinds of discernments all the time about the true willingness of a host."

"In normal circumstances, perhaps," Kimberly countered. "In this instance, Mr. Dalakis was in a predatory fugue."

"A what?" Roth laughed coolly. "I don't think so."

Kimberly's nostrils discolored.

Charlize glanced back and forth between the lawyer and Roth. What was up with these two?

"Vârcolac," Roth continued, "control their predatory nature all the time, Mrs. Stănescu, as they *must*—this is the very point that has to be reiterated here today. Otherwise there will only be anarchy."

Kimberly turned away and rolled her eyes.

Anarchy? Yeah, that seemed sort of melodramatic to Charlize too.

Taking a few steps, Kimberly turned back around. "With the court's indulgence, I would like to call forth Mr. Devid

Nichita to offer testimony on this issue."

"Very well." Roth gestured to the black-haired note-taker. "Donree."

The young woman hopped up, opened the courtroom door situated just behind her small table, and spoke quietly to someone in the hall. There was some murmuring—how many people were out there?—then a second later, Biker Snack Dev stepped just inside the door and—

Breen roared up from his bench and lunged at him, fangs bared, a snarl coming out of him that raised every hair on Charlize's nape. She gasped.

Breen was brought up short by his shackles, but Dev still hissed something unintelligible beneath his breath.

Kimberly leaned toward Charlize and spoke in an urgent tone. "You need to calm him down."

Me? Charlize made a face at the lawyer. "I don't know what's wrong with him." And, frankly, she wasn't particularly into this hothead anymore. She normally liked aggressive men—they made great lays—but Breen having a hairy canary every five minutes was rapidly losing its charm.

"Newly-bonded males turn savagely possessive of their mates right after bonding and subsequently view all males as rivals. Breen's in even worse shape because he's caught in a half-bond. He'll only listen to you."

Oh, well, gee, thanks for giving me the explanation in frigging Chinese. Charlize eyed Breen sideways as she edged away from him. "He's going to hurt me." The man was completely *gone*—he was salivating, for God's sake.

Kimberly squinted a little, like Charlize was a new species of kitchen fungus she was trying to figure out. "No. He's actually protecting you."

From what? Charlize huffed. *Never mind. Whatever.* She seized Breen by the wrist and tugged him down on the bench. "Be quiet, would you?"

Kimberly looked like she was going to say something

more, then didn't. She went back to the proceedings. "Mr. Nichita," she addressed Marissa's husband, "could you please describe to the court your experience of going into a predatory fugue on the night you and Marissa bonded?"

Dev's brow creased. "What?"

"It's my understanding," Kimberly clarified, "that you lost control of your predatory side on the first night you and Marissa were together."

Dev's face froze.

Behind her, Charlize heard Marissa breathe, "Shit."

Dev raised his eyes toward the ceiling. "You know what? This is when it sucks that you and Marissa are friends."

Kimberly's expression softened. "I apologize for bringing up something so personal. But it's important to Mr. Dalakis's defense for the court to understand whether or not a Vârcolac is capable of reasoning intelligibly while in such a state."

Dev's jaw hardened. "I scared the hell out of Marissa on our wedding night and almost hurt her. Does that sound like I was thinking straight?" He aimed his attention to the back of the courtroom.

Charlize followed his gaze, glancing over her shoulder at Marissa.

Marissa gave her husband a look of such loving intimacy, Charlize actually felt herself blush.

"I'm sorry," Kimberly said softly.

"Yeah, well." Dev shoved his fingers through his hair. "There were what you might call extenuating circumstances. I'd recently found out it was *my father* who betrayed the Vârcolac breed, I'd been stuck in jail for a week, and I was low on blood."

Kimberly nodded. "Those are understandable challenges." She checked in briefly with her legal pad. "And would you consider these parameters extenuating: being in an unventilated room with a Dragon woman who was sweating profusely and not wearing any scent-reducing mud, a woman who had made her sexual interest in you unfailingly clear, and who, in fact, had engaged you in a playful wrestling match? Who told you 'I want this' when your fangs were elongated and ready. Would you consider circumstances such as these extenuating?"

Dev's eyebrows rose high on his forehead, then he snorted. "Put that way? I don't see how any unbonded male could have resisted."

Roth's lips thinned.

Kimberly fought a smile. "Thank you, Mr. Nichita. You may go with the court's gratitude."

Dev looked glad to leave. But instead of exiting the way he'd come, he strode down the aisle toward Marissa. When he reached her, he plucked the baby off her lap and swung the little girl up high in his arms. The kid squealed in delight, her gaze fastened on her father in open adoration. Dev touched his wife gently on the top of her head and disappeared out the back door.

Kimberly straightened her blazer. "Taking into account the testimony we just heard, I don't think it goes beyond the bounds of reason to accept that during the time of the alleged UB, Mr. Dalakis was in no condition to stop and discuss the intricacies of Miss Renault's consent."

Roth scowled. "The court would also draw on Devid Nichita's wedding night as evidence and cite that he did, in fact, gain control of himself."

"*Only* because Marissa spoke up to stop him, whereas Miss Renault—"

"This argument is groundless, at any rate." Roth cut a dismissive gesture through the air. "Miss Renault's consent isn't valid in this instance. Just as an intoxicated woman can't give consent for sexual intercourse, the same holds true here. Miss Renault did not understand the full parameters of her so-called consent due to her unfamiliarity with Vârcolac culture, and, therefore, she was *not* capable of issuing an authorization."

Kimberly looked astounded. "*Capability* of consent is not germane to a UB."

Roth opened his mouth—

Kimberly plowed over him. "However, if the court would like to be indulged in this line of thinking, then let's pretend for a moment that Mr. Dalakis *was* capable of reasoning. Would he not have been right in assuming that if a woman was in the gymnasium she would have full knowledge of the choices she was making in regard to a bite. Because the court *knows* that Miss Renault absolutely would not have been out of her bedroom had she not been deemed fully conversant in Vârcolac culture. And so, therefore, Mr. Dalakis would have been wholly correct in assuming that Miss Renault was *capable* of giving her consent for a life-bond. Ten minutes," Kimberly concluded hotly, "ten weeks, or ten years notwithstanding."

The summation was followed by a grim silence.

Charlize blinked. *Wow*. This Kimberly woman was *Kimberly the Killer*. She might be someone Charlize could be friends with.

Toni Parthen finally spoke. "Why *was* Miss Renault out of her room?"

"Miss Renault claims she was told not to leave the mansion only," Kimberly answered. "Nothing was stated about not leaving her room."

Toni massaged her brow. Charlize didn't know the woman, but she'd guess Toni was fighting a headache. "Who welcomed Miss Renault and Miss Klein to the community this morning?"

"Hannah Crişan and Beth Costache."

The two welcome-wagon women were called to the courtroom and questioned. The old rule, apparently, had been to instruct new arrivals not to leave the mansion only, and so with some embarrassment, neither Hannah nor Beth could remember exactly what they'd told Charlize and Lara. They also both admitted to being rushed this morning.

They were thanked and excused.

Toni sat back in her chair. "Considering that no one can clearly recall what instructions were given to Miss Renault and Miss Klein, I feel the community must bear some responsibility for a woman being out in the general population when she shouldn't have been. This incident between Mr. Dalakis and Miss Renault wouldn't have occurred if they'd been kept apart until Miss Renault was cleared according to community law. Taking into account these circumstances—along with the evidence provided that consent, weak though it might be, was given—I wouldn't feel right about finding Mr. Dalakis guilty." Toni looked at Roth for his opinion.

Kimberly's eyes shone with the beginnings of triumph.

Thunder sat on Roth's brow. "Are you saying Mr. Dalakis isn't to reap any consequences for his actions? I don't like the message that sends."

"He'll reap the natural consequences of his mistake," Toni said. "Breen is stuck in the agony of a half-bond for who knows how long. Until Miss Renault can be educated about the full commitment a bond entails, she can't make a competent decision about completing it."

"At this time," Kimberly inserted hastily, "I would ask that Mr. Dalakis be taken to the hospital and sedated during the course of his half-bond. Since he hasn't been found guilty, anything less would be cruel."

Toni paused, then glanced again at Roth. "I can't think of a logical reason to deny that request."

Roth's face went tight. "I fervently disagree with allowing this misstep to go unpunished. Such negligence will have profound, negative repercussions on this community."

"So noted." Toni pushed to her feet. "Donree, please mark down Mr. Mihnea's objections for the record, then send a community-wide text warning that a newly-bonded male will be traveling down Main Street. All other males should steer clear." Toni added to Kimberly, "I'll meet you and Breen at the hospital shortly." Toni exited through the main door.

Filing her legal pad into her briefcase, Kimberly leveled a look at Charlize. "Read the community manual, Miss Renault. Quick. You have no idea the shit-storm you just landed yourself in."

Yeah? Charlize turned away and gave the wall across from her a long stare. Well, she could guess well enough. Shit-storms were sort of her forte.

CHAPTER FOUR

WALKING THROUGH ȚĂRÂNĂ WAS LIKE seeing a miniature ship inside a glass bottle and wondering how the hell it got in there. Because the same thought struck Charlize about this town.

How the hell did Happy Valley end up inside a cave?

Dark brown, uneven rock surrounded the town top to bottom and on all sides, yet the place was utterly enchanting. The main source of light came from huge, ceiling-mounted, spotlight-type contraptions, but these didn't douse the town in a wash of ugly fluorescence, rather a warm, sunny glow. All the buildings seemed to have been built with charm in mind: Aunt Ælsi's Coffee Shop looked like it was made from gingerbread with its scalloped trim, the TradeMark clothing store's window display was full of cheerful mannequins, the façade of Garwald's Pub's was rough-hewn wood directly out of a spaghetti western, and Marissa's Restaurant was fronted with a window of chic etched glass.

Inside, booths lined two of the walls while an array of tables occupied the center of the room. All were covered in white tablecloths and set with silver-rimmed china and crystal. The restaurant could probably seat between thirty-five and forty diners, more if the tables were pushed closer together. Charlize guessed it was spaced this way on purpose, to provide privacy and opportunities for romance.

Along Main Street, there seemed to be a scarcity of peo-ple...although maybe that was because all the men had magically disappeared. The women, on the other hand, appeared to be fascinated with Charlize, casting her those small-town type of looks that said they knew all the dirt about her already—which was plenty—and were eager to see what she might bone up next.

The three of them—Kimberly, Breen, and Charlize—arrived at a majestic, four-story hospital building. Just beyond, Charlize spotted a residential neighborhood, but she only caught a glimpse of it before they entered the medical building. They pushed through a set of swinging double doors, where a dark-haired woman in scrubs and a pink smock waited for them. She introduced herself as Shaston and directed their group into a room of typical medical sterility—white, clean, no frills.

Breen was released from his shackles and immediately asked to lie on an exam bed, where he was restrained again. Thick leather cuffs were secured around both his wrists and ankles, then attached to the bedrails, and, okay, even though Breen had recently turned into that guy in a bar who got into a brawl if someone dared to accidentally bump into his stool, it didn't seem right to confine the poor man. In the gym, Breen had just been trying to get some poontang, and it wasn't like he'd forced himself on her. She'd been totally willing. All this locking-up seemed kind of like an inhuman and mean thing to do to a man who wasn't even supposed to be punished.

Through it all, Breen never took his eyes off her, watching her in a way she'd never been looked at before, his chin slightly down, his gaze pinned on her through a reckless fall of black hair, like a wild cat peering through a jungle at night, sizing up a meal. The illusion was enhanced by the color of his eyes. Pure tequila gold. The hairs on her nape lifted, like she was being stalked. Like she was prey. Although she had the sense that if Breen planned to eat her, it'd be in the good way. Her sexually-frustrated vagina wasn't averse to the idea.

Toni arrived, Kimberly left, and Charlize gestured at

Breen. "Is this really necessary?"

"Unfortunately, yes," Toni answered. "Breen is going to do everything he can to try and complete the bond with you."

"Bond?" Charlize mentally stumbled over that one. *What, like, bondage and BDSM stuff?*

Toni worked at inserting an IV in Breen's wrist. "In Vârcolac biology, the combination of you being bitten by Breen followed by sexual intercourse with him would equal a marriage being formed between you two. A permanent one."

Charlize scrunched up one side of her mouth as she tried to urge her brain to comprehend what Toni had just said. It took a couple of beats for her to realize it was just more Chinese. And this was exactly why she'd hated biology in high school. It never made sense.

Toni smiled at her. "Don't worry, you'll eventually understand all of this, and until then we'll keep you and Breen apart." Toni plunged some medication into Breen's IV line.

Within a minute, his eyelids flagged to half-mast.

Toni set out an array of hypos on a metal tray, gave the nurse in the pink smock some quiet instructions, then escorted Charlize toward the door.

Breen showed them his teeth, and Toni paused.

"I'm taking Charlize directly to the mansion," she told him in a firm, reassuring way. "She'll stay there. No men will be allowed near her at any time."

Charlize rolled her eyes as she exited. Aggressive men were okay. Overly possessive ones were a drag who cramped her style. Anyone interested in doing that could consider himself excused from her life.

At the door to Charlize's mansion bedroom, Toni gave her another encouraging smile. "Just make sure to read the community manual, Charlize. A lot will become clear to you then."

Jesus. More pushiness about the frigging manual. Did the thing describe how to turn a turd into gold or something?

"I will." Charlize closed the door, sagged back against it, and released a long breath.

Freakiest three hours of her life.

✧   ✧   ✧

HADLEY WICKSTRUM'S WELCOME-BACK-TO-ŢĂRÂNĂ reception completely lacked fanfare.

Disappointment tugged at her in a niggling way when she saw only one person waiting for her in the garage. Maybe she felt a tug of worry too. Was the community upset with her for leaving so abruptly—and huffily—four years ago? Of course, she hadn't expected chilled champagne, tray-passed canapés, and a barbershop quartet, but she sort of figured she'd be greeted by more than the one man she didn't want to see.

Her ex-boyfriend, Thomal Costache.

Still gorgeous. Still styling his hair into a blond flattop. Still totally do-able. He hadn't changed much since she last saw him, except his body had filled out—and he'd been no milquetoast before—and he gave off a calmer energy. During the five months she dated him, he'd always seemed so angry...something she handily ignored, seeing as he was such a perfect specimen of arm candy.

But arm candy seemed to be a drug of choice for her, leading her to repeatedly make bad decisions. So far in her life, the glitzy type had brought her nothing but trouble and disappointment. Look at her ex-husband, Phil. He was a flashy New York attorney with a flamboyant lifestyle and magazine-cover looks—no joke, Phil had earned his way through law school as a model—and how had that ended?

In divorce.

So she was done with those types. Next guy she dated would be a regular Joe, a down-to-earth guy with dirt under his fingernails who dealt with screwdrivers and hammers rather than keyboards and iPads.

"Hey, Hadley," Thomal greeted her warmly. "Welcome

home."

Tears sprang to her eyes. *Home.* She hadn't felt like she truly belonged anywhere ever since leaving Ţărână. "Thank you, Thomal."

"Sorry no one else is here to say hi." He hefted her two suitcases out of the trunk of the Lincoln Town car that'd picked her up at the airport. "The community is in a bit of an uproar right now. There's been a UB, and an emergency court session was called."

"Oh." Well, at least it wasn't because she was unpopular. "What's a UB?"

"An Unauthorized Bite."

"Sounds dramatic," she said, just to say something. She had no idea what it was.

"Yeah. I can't remember anything like this ever happening before." Thomal set down her two suitcases, closed the trunk, then stood with his hands on his waist. His perfectly proportioned physique managed to turn simple blue jeans and a white T-shirt into haute couture. "Plus, I wanted some time alone with you first off, to work out any awkwardness between us, if there is any."

"Okay." She clutched her shoulder bag to her waist and waited.

He didn't say anything.

"Do you feel awkward?"

"No."

He wouldn't, though, would he? She was nearly one-hundred-percent certain she wouldn't have been allowed back in the community if Thomal had objected even a teensy bit. "Well, I don't either." The shoulder strap on her purse flopped down. She hiked it back up. "Seeing you now, I realize I'm completely over you."

He cracked a smile.

"No offense," she added quickly.

"None taken. But..." His smile slowly closed off. "I also

wanted to say I'm sorry about the way things went down between us, Had. I never meant for you to get hurt, although I don't regret how everything ended up working out. I would've made you a lousy mate. Fate saved us from making a big mistake."

Now she did bristle. Thomal was thanking Fate for sticking him with a half-demon degenerate for a wife rather than a *mistake* like Hadley? Gosh, could the man be any more flattering?

"And I'm really glad you're back in Ţărână. In fact, I wish you hadn't felt like you needed to leave when we broke up."

She looked away from him. Ţărână's garage was packed with vehicles ranging from a school bus—painted plain gray—to compact meh unnoticeables, to a few sporty numbers, to two Harley Davidson motorcycles. She sniffed. "We needed space from each other, Thomal. You had a difficult marriage to figure out." And she'd been in a righteous snit over being dumped for a woman who supposedly raped Thomal. The *supposedly* part might be unfair, but as she understood it, a Vârcolac couldn't perform sexually until he *willingly* bit a host. So how sex could've been forced under those limitations was something she'd never fully grasped.

Not that she even distantly cared anymore. If Thomal preferred a half-demon degenerate to Hadley, let him have her. Scrubbing her knuckles across her nose, she smiled tightly. "And I had my own marriage to go off and ruin." Had she been on an angry rebound from Thomal when she'd hooked up with Phil? Probably.

"I'm sorry," Thomal said softly. "I heard about your divorce."

She lifted a single shoulder.

"Hadley!"

She spun around at the shout.

A woman had just entered the garage, a toddler girl propped on her hip, and—*My God!* It was Hadley's dearest friend in the community! "Marissa!" she called back, and hurried over.

Even though Hadley hadn't kept in touch with anyone in Țărână, she'd missed Marissa. The two of them had been brought into the community the same harrowing night four and a half years ago, when the warriors saved them from a demon race known as Om Rău. That night they were both kidnapped and forced to witness a rape...and experiences like that tended to connect people for life.

"It's so good to see you." Hadley hugged the half of her friend that wasn't holding a baby, then ducked down to peer at the toddler. "And who's this?" The little girl was happily chewing on a teething ring, plenty of slobber on her chin.

"This is my daughter, Maylie."

"Lord, she's adorable." She was, too, with chubby cheeks and her mother's tarnished blond hair tied with ribbons into a couple of pigtails. Hadley glanced up. "So you ended up with Dev Nichita?"

Chuckling, Marissa indicated her daughter with a head nod. "Can't you tell by the eyes?"

The baby's eyes *were* a clear, vivid hue of silver, exactly like Dev's. Hadley smiled. "The rest of her is pure you, though."

Marissa widened her own smile. "You should see our three-year-old son, Randon. He's Dev's replica."

"You have a son too?" It was difficult for Hadley to arrange another smile on her face when her throat was narrowing around a soggy lump of envy. Motherhood was beginning to seem like a distant dream for her. Of course returning to the community was supposed to fix that. "Do you have children?" she asked Thomal.

Pride warmed his entire face. "A two-year-old son. Lucca."

Hadley swallowed. "H-how wonderful."

Marissa adjusted the baby on her hip. "A lot has changed

since you've been gone, Hadley. We definitely need to catch up, and I'm sorry I wasn't here sooner. My friend, Charlize, was in court a little while ago, and I wanted to be there for her."

Hadley nodded. "Thomal explained."

"What was the verdict?" Thomal asked Marissa.

"Not guilty."

"No shit?" Thomal snorted. "Hell, I thought Breen was sunk."

Breen. Hadley didn't remember anyone by that name.

"Kimberly really went scorched earth in court today." Marissa tugged Maylie's flowered shirt down her pudgy belly. "I tell you, that Dragon is a serious *dragon lady* when she's going against Roth. I get the impression there's an old animosity between those two, but whenever I ask Toni about it, she gives me nothing but vague answers."

Thomal suddenly found the clasps on Hadley's suitcase fascinating.

Marissa narrowed her eyes a bit but didn't press it. "Anyway, Breen is being taken to the hospital now. He's going to be drugged up to help him through his half-bond."

Half-bond? Here was something else Hadley didn't remember—if she'd ever known about it. But judging by the way Thomal grimaced, it was something very unpleasant.

"Can I help at the hospital?" Hadley offered. "I became a Red Cross volunteer when I was living topside, so I have some medical training now." She'd once been an event planner, but Phil insisted it was more appropriate for a high-class attorney's wife to do charitable volunteer activities.

Marissa brightened. "How great. Shaston is way overworked with her nursing duties. She'd love your help. Are you sure you want to start now, though? You must be exhausted."

She *was* pretty tired. She'd taken an evening flight from New York to San Diego, so currently it was about three in the morning according to her internal clock, making it midnight local time up top—and so noon down here, due to the time switch. But being alone her first night back would feel funny. "I'd rather just stay up for twenty-four hours straight this first night. I'll adjust right away to the time change if I do."

"All right. Let's head over then." Marissa dug a key out of her bag and gave it to Thomal. "Do you mind taking Hadley's suitcases to her Cliffs apartment? She's going to be in 4B."

"No prob." Thomal trucked off with the suitcases down a corridor painted battleship gray.

Hadley, Marissa, and Maylie followed down the same long corridor at a slower pace. Overhead, a network of pipes crisscrossed each other into a complicated maze, and it smelled like the fuel used to run the generator.

"What's this about an apartment?" Hadley assumed she'd live in the mansion again, like last time.

Marissa beamed. "I can't wait to show you the new building. I had to fight like hell to get you in right away, though. My friend Charlize's inexperience with Vârcolac culture just caused a lot of problems, so the community wasn't sure about letting you into the main town until after you prove you remember everything about how to avoid being bitten by the wrong man."

Hadley *hah'd*. "No worries on that score. Don't forget you're dealing with a needle phobic here." A while ago, she'd gone through systematic desensitization therapy to conquer her fear, but she still wasn't in any hurry to deal with a pair of sharp fangs, especially if they were attached to the wrong man.

Her string of bad luck in the wrong men department was about to change.

CHAPTER FIVE

BREEN CRACKED OPEN HIS EYELIDS.

With a systematic side-to-side sweep, he scanned his hospital room through the grids dividing his predator vision.

Center grid: open doorway.

Southwest grid: a clock on the wall, reading twelve thirty.

Eastern grid: a metal tray with hypodermic needles on a stand.

High northeast grid, on the edge of his peripheral vision: door to the bathroom.

All grids clear of people.

Finally alone, he tested his restraints—padded, steel-reinforced leather cuffs securing all four of his limbs to the bed. He rotated his wrists and ankles to gauge his range of—

His lids sank closed. Even that small bit of chafing pushed his torment to an agony that pounded at him from all directions at once, as if every artery in his body was bursting at the same instant and was now overloading pain receptors in his central nervous system. No amount of sedating drugs and morphine could prevent it. Only thing that could stop it was *her*.

He needed his woman.

He opened his eyes and glanced at the clock again. How long had Charlize been away from him? Thirty minutes? An hour? Several eternities?

She'd come from court over to the hospital with him to keep him calm while Nurse Shaston strapped him into his bindings, waiting while Toni hooked him up to an IV before leaving.

He'd watched every step of her departure, tracking her through his grids, his teeth clamped so hard it felt like he blew out several capillaries along the skin near his temples. He listened to her footsteps fade to silence down the hall, inhaling sharp grabs of air to catch her dwindling scent. When there was nothing left of her, he'd torn hunks of sheet off his bed and yowled loud enough to split a seam in his plastic IV bag.

That earned him more morphine, and Nurse Shaston's promise to pump him full of an enchanted drug if he didn't settle.

"Settling" was a joke. It felt like a million tiny fishhooks were gouged into him, urgently trying to rip off this wrong skin so that he could put the right stuff back on—the skin he'd worn when he drank from his woman.

Where was she now? Was she okay? What was she doing? What was being done to her? How many males were near her? A snarl quaked out of Breen.

Odd thing was, none of those questions had gone through his mind in actual, discernible language. More like as twisty, wormy, sick feelings. Like phantom limb pain.

Center grid: Nurse Shaston entering the hospital room, along with Hadley Wickstrum.

Breen lollygagged his eyelid halfway down, evened out his breathing, and licked some shine onto his dry lips. Not a thing he could do about his rigid muscles in order to pull off looking "settled," though.

"Why don't you take his pulse?" Shaston suggested to Hadley.

Hadley carefully picked up his right wrist—the one with the IV line—and worked the leather cuff out of the way. She smiled at him.

Breen's spine tightened on a heightened ripple of awareness. He'd always thought of Hadley as one of the prettiest Dragons ever to come into the community. Her honey-colored hair was cut Farrah Fawcett-style—the *Charlie's Angels* years—and her blue eyes were drawn into a very feminine shape. But mainly there was just something about her that tugged.

"Your pulse is racing," Hadley told him gently.

Yeah, it was. His heart was working overtime to siphon off the drugs being pumped into his body, his Vârcolac side knowing it had to keep his head clear so he could hunt down his woman.

Nurse Shaston stepped up to the other side of his bed. Dressed in light blue scrubs with a pink pastel jackety thing over it, her black hair lassoed into a horse's tail, she looked like a human version of My Little Pony—a character he unfortunately knew because the community diner played cartoons during "family hour" from five to six o'clock every night. He also knew SpongeBob SquarePants, PB&J Otter, and Teletubbies.

My Little Pony wasn't the most professional get-up for Shaston.

"Hadley is going to be a nurse's aide at the hospital," she informed him.

He ignored her, instead zeroing in on the low southeast grid of his vision: outline of a small padlock key in Shaston's right jacket pocket.

Hadley set down his wrist. "How are you feeling?"

He ran a scenario through his mind and practiced it again. He'd only get one chance to escape. Attempt and fail, and he'd be loaded up with an enchanted drug, and then it'd be like Porky Pig would say, *Tha-that's all, folks.*

Toni's enchanted drugs could sedate an Om Rău, something even a rhino tranquilizer couldn't do. On Breen, a drug like that would knock him into the back nine...and then he wouldn't be able to get to Charlize. No way could he allow that to happen.

"I've got to go to the bathroom," he told them.

Shaston grabbed a plastic jug. The opening was wide enough to fit his dick.

"Not pee," he said. "The...other."

Shaston set down the plastic jug and picked up a metal bedpan.

He contorted his face, first at Shaston, then at the contraption. "C'mon, Shaston. You're not really going to make me go in that thing, are you?"

"I'm under strict orders not to unstrap you, Breen. Not for you to go to the bathroom or to eat. Not for any reason whatsoever."

So some sessions of spoon-feeding were headed his way too? Nothing like getting a manhood-ectomy while he was already at his lowest.

Shaston pulled the sheet down, and—

Ding!

There was his massive rager.

No sense in anyone pretending they didn't see it. Stretchy workout shorts did no job at all of hiding a hard-on that refused to unharden. Not exactly the experience he would've wished for his first ever boner—to have it put on parade all during court, then also while trekking down Main Street to the hospital—but there was nothing he could do about it. The only thing that would make it go down was Charlize.

Shaston quickly pretended not to notice.

Hadley, on the other hand, practically went cross-eyed staring at it.

"Maybe, uh," Breen said, "not so many people could be around for this."

Hadley immediately volunteered to take the hint. She stepped back. "I'll wait for you on the second floor, Shaston. You were going to show me around there next, anyway, right?"

Shaston nodded. "The locker room's up there. You can change."

From jeans and T-shirt into another Little Pony, no doubt... Hadley left.

Breen grunted to get Shaston's attention before she prepped him for bedpan placement by yanking his shorts down. His escape plan would be seriously hindered by having clothing stretched around his knees.

"I can't get my butt up." He made a show of trying to lift his hips off the mattress and not being able to leverage them very high. The movement sloshed drugs up into his brain, and his eyelids went sandbag on him for a moment. "Um..." He felt his heart work in several huge, productive pumps. "You're going to have to unlock at least one of my ankles."

Shaston paused, lower lip caught between her teeth, considering. Then she plunked one hand on her hip. "Look, Breen, I know you're normally a nice guy, but this half-bond is making you act very sketchy. I don't trust you to behave."

He didn't say anything. His pulse pounded harder against the restraints on his wrists, rattling the mini padlocks. *One chance...*

Shaston set down the bedpan. "I'm going to call a warrior over here to watch while—"

"So I'll be too busy trying to kill him that I won't be able to go?"

The remark stopped her. Because it was true. Even though Charlize wasn't here to be threatened by whichever warrior Shaston called, *any* man within Breen's reach would pay for whoever was *actually* with Charlize at this very moment.

Fucker. Breen curled his lip, then brought it back down. *Be settled.* "Shaston, c'mon." He crabbed his hips sideways an inch. "Things are getting urgent."

Nibbling on her lower lip again, Shaston checked on the enchanted drug-filled hypos lined up on the metal tray. She obviously decided to find comfort in their presence because she walked to the foot of the bed and pulled out her key.

Breen targeted his center-grid focus onto the sight of her undoing the small padlock on his left ankle. She returned the key to her pocket.

In a lightning move, he snapped his left leg back, then lashed it out at Shaston, hooking the crook of his knee around her lower spine and using the leg-trap to wrench her up hard against his chest.

She *oomphed* once, then screeched and flailed.

He worked his left hand into her right jacket pocket, now hugged to her body just below his thigh, all the while keeping her secured within the hard flex of his leg muscle. A three-inch range of motion around his cuff turned out to be enough—he got hold of the key between his fingers. From there, it was a matter of bending his left wrist at just the right angle to insert the key into the small padlock. A tricky maneuver, what with Shaston struggling like she had an icy thermometer jammed into sensitive places.

He took slaps to the face, head, and neck. Lots and lots of cursing went on too.

Eastern grid: Shaston's hand reaching for the hypos.

Breen squeezed his thigh lung-crusher tight.

Shaston's arm flopped down and she wheezed.

He inserted the key.

The padlock fell open.

With blurring swiftness, Breen jerked his wrist free, snatched a hypo off the metal tray, and stabbed it into Shaston's upper arm, compressing the plunger with his thumb.

Shaston's eyes rolled up so far into her head, he lost sight of her pupils. She said, "Blerp," then slithered to the floor.

In a count of four, he had the rest of his limbs unbound and his IV needle tugged out. Springing to his feet, he paused a second to gain his balance, then scooped up Shaston and laid her on the bed. The mattress squished under her from all his sweat. When she woke up, she'd probably be pissed about that too. He hauled the tattered sheet all the way up to her face, partially covering her cheek. If someone peeked in here, they'd see a black-haired body, asleep.

Ripping a page out of his chart, he wrote on the blank side, *Hadley, Breen's asleep. I had to run out for some medication. I'll be back in 30 minutes or so."* He'd prefer longer to hunt, but more than a half hour would probably sound too suspicious. *Go ahead and wander around upstairs, and I'll find you in a bit.* He signed it, *Shaston.*

He cut off a piece of white medical tape from a roll, stuck it to the note, then dimmed the lights and opened the door. He checked the hallway.

All grids clear.

He closed the door to his room and taped the note at eye level. Barefoot, he moved in total silence out of the hospital and into the street.

Ducking behind the hospital building, he hunkered down. *Where are you, Charlize?* He lifted his chin and parted his lips, drawing air into the back of his mouth, up through his nose, and into his sinuses. Particles of her scent, clean and salty, swirled into his brain, making the merciless and violent wrenching sensation all over his skin double, then redouble. He took off at a fast lope in the direction the particles were coming from: the mansion.

The cave rock was rough beneath his bare feet as he slipped from building to building, passing like no more than a shadow behind the shops lining Main Street: the diner, the post office, the grocery store, the Teague Sisters' Dance Studio, the TradeMark clothing store, Aunt Ælsi's Coffee Shop. Along the way, his mind completely cleared of its drug soup.

At the end of Main he darted across the street, aiming for the mansion, but drifted right past the front gate. He knew the code to the lockbox. No problem there. Problem was that a camera was pointed right at the entrance. If his image popped up on the security video feed, he'd be back in his cuffs and knocked into the eighteenth hole on an enchanted drug in minutes.

Gliding along the mansion's perimeter fence of fat steel bars, he headed for the side farthest away from town, out of sight from stray, wandering people. When he came to the last bar, the one sitting nearly flush against the cave wall, he lowered into a crouch and searched his grids.

All clear.

He focused his attention on the mansion. It was a four-story structure fronted by curlique, wrought-iron balconies. The first floor was stocked with parlors and drawing rooms and fancy shit. The second and third floors held bedrooms—where Breen used to live—and the entire fourth floor was occupied by Roth and his wife. Since Roth was one of the community leaders—and before Toni came along, the virtual king of their race—mansion security was tight.

Cameras swiveled on poles in every upper grid of Breen's vision.

He carefully followed their arc, then peered straight up to the cave roof. *Okay. A plan.* There looked to be a security blind spot along this last bar. Also, at the top of the pole, a portion of the cave ceiling was eroded away. If he scaled this pole, he could mostly stay out of camera range, and there just might be enough space for him to squeeze through up there.

He hopped up and started to climb.

If he thought he had no more sweat to give, he was wrong. Scaling a smooth, steel pole was a bastard of a job. He did his best to grip the pole with his hands and feet in full monkey-mode, but his perspiration made everything slick. He periodically slipped down and lost ground. By the time he reached the top, he was huffing air from his last lung. The muscles in his thighs and across his shoulders and through his mid-back were on fire and cramping from the strain.

Worse, the eroded spot was too small for him to get

through. He clawed at the rocky ceiling to make it bigger, all the while flexing his entire body rigid to keep from sliding down the bar while he worked. Cave rubble pattered down, making a mess below. He regularly checked his grids through the haze of sweat in his eyes. He scraped his fingers raw and tore his fingernails. It didn't matter.

He couldn't give up. He couldn't stop. He couldn't leave.

His woman was in the mansion.

Finally he dug the opening wide enough to contort himself through. He slid down the steel pole on the correct side, fireman-style, and dropped into a crouch again, panting raggedly. His muscles quaked and screamed. He was hurting bad.

He allowed his heart and lungs a few moments of rest, then inhaled another open-mouthed breath. He caught Charlize's scent easily; it was so much stronger now. His fangs shivered against his gums, and the inside of his stomach itched. A bizarre sensation, feeling like he needed to feed when he'd just fed. But really it was *her* he needed. Taste, smell, touch, sound, life, *her*. More. Everything.

He shuddered. Zeroed in on her scent. *There*. Third floor up. Balcony closest to his position.

He counted seconds as the camera nearest to him oscillated on its pole. Then—*now!* He ran forward, leapt for the bottom edge of the second-floor balcony, chinned himself up, then swung over the wrought-iron onto the balcony itself. He repeated the maneuver, landing on the third-floor balcony he'd aimed for.

Her balcony.

The tang of her prickled along his tongue.

He padded across the expanse of terrace. Through the sliding glass door, he saw her.

The grids vanished from his vision, and he emitted a soft, purring growl from his chest.

CHAPTER SIX

ELBOW PROPPED ON THE DESKTOP, forehead sunk into her palm, Charlize sat at the small desk in her bedroom and forced herself to leaf through the community manual she'd been nagged to read.

Her "Bruges" room—murals of European cities were painted on all the doors in this mansion, and the rooms were named after the same—was a bunch of posh. She was surrounded by walls papered in pale blue, gold, and cream, and swanky Chippendale furnishings. There was a vast king-sized bed covered by a blue velvet bedspread, several softly glowing lamps with shades bordered in ornate beadwork, a flat screen television hidden behind the louvered doors of a tall armoire—two cushy armchairs placed in front—and a wet bar stocked with water, juice, beer, wine, tea, coffee, and carb-rich munchies. The bedroom was suitable for dukes and princesses, and was as unreal to Charlize as everything else had been so far in this community, including the ass-fuckwards time.

She knuckled her eyes. It had to be two in the morning—*her* time—and she was feeling it. For the past three days she'd averaged only about four to five hours of sleep a night. Some attendees of the chef seminar went to bed at a decent hour to make sure they were fresh for the next day's activities. Others took the opportunity to party with friends they saw only once a year. Charlize had been in the latter group.

Maybe she should just go to bed. Problem was, even though her brain was tired, her body still wanted an orgasm. Correction: her vagina wanted dick. Charlize had self-satisfied in the shower earlier, and it hadn't alleviated a damned thing. Every nerve and cell continued to hum, and it was pissing her off, because she could've had all the dick she wanted in the gymnasium if everyone had just minded their own frigging business.

Sighing and giving her eyes another rub, Charlize shut the manual. It was like trying to read Urdu, anyway. None of it made sense. Vârcolac culture was turning out to be way more complicated than she expected. *I mean, hey, they're vampires, right?* Shouldn't that be straight up? Need blood, bite a girl's neck, end of story. Why did—?

Behind her, the sliding glass door to her balcony opened. *Swish.*

She shot to her feet and spun around, her bathrobe whirling at her ankles, and—

"Breen?" She blinked a couple of good, hard times. He... Was it really him? The man was an utter horror show, all-over shiny with sweat, his eyes feral, and his hands were really messed up, like he'd gone the distance with a concrete wall, gloves off.

"How the hell did you get in here?" She was three floors up and surrounded by prison bars. And hadn't she watched him getting locked into a hospital bed? She rushed over and squinted over his shoulder outside. No climbing rope was tied to her balcony rail or—

He stuck his face in her hair.

She took a step back and hiked up her brows.

"Peppermint," he said.

It felt like every atom of his energy was aimed at her, and her belly did a funky shimmy. "There's mint in my shampoo."

He nodded. "It's under the other good smells."

"What other good smells?"

"You."

She breathed out slowly. He was back to staring at her in that intense way. He had a disconcerting capacity for immobility, his gaze able to focus on her with an unnerving feline watchfulness. Her belly danced another shimmy.

He reached for her, and she didn't step away this time. He took hold of a strand of her hair, gently pulled it until it was straight, then released it. The tendril sproinged back into a corkscrew. He observed the process with fascination.

Fascination was weird. *Lust*—it was what was right and proper. Not this soul-level, particle-deep wanting she felt coming off of Breen.

She snugged her robe tighter.

His gaze meandered down to the substantial cleavage visible at the neckline of her bathrobe, then kept going southward to her crotch. A tic jumped in his right nostril. Sweat slid down his face.

"You seriously need a shower, Breen."

"Okay." He removed his soaked clothes and splatted them to the floor.

Whoa. A short laugh burst out of her. *Howdy, naked man!* "My, that was sudden." And here they were, happily back to the good zone: sex and lust.

Never one to miss the opportunity to appreciate a fine male form, she brazenly inspected him—and this man was *mighty* fine. Not quite as tall and big as his black-haired wrestling opponent or Biker Snack, he had impossible sleekness going for him. His body was toned to the point where she couldn't find an ounce of softening fat on him—or, interestingly, a stitch of hair on his torso. Moisture glistened in crevices and grooves of lean, hard muscle, advertising that he was as much about power as agility, something she'd witnessed during his savage wrestling match. He also obviously fought for keeps; a long and shiny but well-healed scar slashed from his left hipbone to the front of his groin, where it dipped just into his pubic hair. A couple more inches and, *yikes*. He would've lost a very important appendage.

"Nasty scar," she commented.

"War."

Hmm. She would've guessed perhaps another man, feeling inadequate by comparison, had tried to castrate him. Because Breen was packing some serious heat. His equipment had seemed large in his workout gear, but she hadn't been able to tell for sure. Now...

With a lip-twist of discomfort, Breen fisted a hand around his cock. He couldn't get his fingers wrapped all the way around the circumference.

That answered that.

"This is painful," he told her. "It's been like this for hours."

"It's been—?" She jerked her attention up. "What?" How long could this guy last, exactly. "Do you mean it's never gone down?"

"No."

Ho, boy. A long time. The area between her thighs, already moist and supple from her shower antics, softened some more. She'd probably climax on first penetration with this guy, the head of his cock was so round and bulbous.

"I need you, Charlize. You're the only one who can give me relief."

She startled at the raw look in his eyes. *Wow. Freaky.* He wasn't just handing her a line. *The only one...* She released a small smile. She was always up for that kind of pressure in bed. Because she never failed to deliver, just... "Toni seemed intent on keeping us apart."

His lip-twist switched sides. "Not really her decision, is it?"

Isn't it?

"Do you really want to let other people tell us what to do?" he pressed.

Uh-oh. Gasoline on the fire. Had this guy read her personal dossier and found REBELLIOUS stamped in huge red letters across the top? One of her biggest failings was that she went after what she wanted, and to hell with anyone telling her otherwise. Probably a life spent in service to her mother and brother's fuckups—being Miz Freaking Responsible— had left her feeling somewhat entitled, like she deserved some good shit in her life too.

Breen also wasn't helping to motivate her good behavior by looking at her as if she would taste better than chocolate. She could clearly see herself squatting down neatly onto his face to show him she mostly definitely did. *That* was probably an image she needed to get out of her head, quickly. She'd already been in trouble once in this place, so maybe she should try and be good. For Marissa's sake. Charlize had been invited to this community on Marissa's recommendation, and how she acted reflected on her friend.

She blew out a breath. "I just don't know much about what's going on here yet, Breen. I haven't read the stupid manual, and it's confusing, anyway. What about the bondage thing Toni mentioned? I mean, I'm not opposed to a little tie-me-up, if that's your jam, but it sounded like…" She trailed off as humor warmed Breen's eyes.

The amused expression rolled down his face, loosening the small muscles in his cheeks, curling his mouth into a smile. Not a big one, but enough to display a chip in his left fang, and *wham*. He was *back*—the man she'd first met in the gym who was both manly and boyish and so charmingly staggered by her. She'd never encountered such an appealing combination, and how the hell could anyone expect her not to conquer something that was so conquerable? The man was standing right here with a huge, hard, naked cock, for God's sake. And hadn't she come to this community to play with some new toys? Yeah, she damn well had.

She moved forward a step.

Eagerness leapt into Breen's eyes. "There's no tying up involved in bonding," he hurried to tell her. "I swear."

She nodded slowly. "Well, I've always been a big believer

in the idea that two consenting adults should be allowed to do whatever they want as long as they're both okay with it." Besides that, good behavior was overrated. Her vagina certainly wasn't a fan of it right now. Reaching up, Charlize started to brush the hair out of Breen's eyes, but the second she touched him, he snatched her up by the waist and propelled her across the room at high speed.

Gasping, she threw her legs around him. Her bathrobe split open, making way for her wet lower region to press against the area just below Breen's navel, his hard cock jabbing her in the butt cheek.

With a hiss, Breen rammed her against the wall by the bedside table, his outstretched palm taking most of the impact. Bracing her spine against the posh wallpaper, he kept one arm clamped around her waist while the other hand jerked her bathrobe all the way open. He seized one of her breasts and squeezed it as he latched his mouth onto her nipple. Sucking the bud deeply into his mouth, he worked it over with his tongue, gliding over all the wrinkly sensitivity.

Charlize arched and moaned, her sheath throbbing frantically. The cock between her legs made an aggressive attempt to find its way inside her. "Wait," she rasped. God knew how she spoke.

Breen's head came up, his eyes widened in a clear look of panic.

"No, no—I don't want to stop. We just need a condom."

His breath was coming hard. She caught the white glint of his fangs. "We don't use those here."

She did some of her own lip-twisting. "That's insane. What about birth control?"

Sweat rained down his neck. "Are you ovulating?"

Normally she wouldn't have known such a thing, but there was a box of ovulation sticks in her bathroom, and, just for kicks, she'd peed on one. "No."

"Okay." He grabbed her waist with both hands again,

strong fingers pressing her flesh.

"But...but, diseases." The trapezius muscles reaching out across his shoulders were flexed up into beautiful formation. She was going to lose her mind. "What about—?"

"I don't have any." He stepped away from the wall, easily managing her weight, biceps visible as separate puzzle pieces from triceps in his magnificent arms.

"But...don't you want to know if I—?"

He thunked her down on his cock.

She threw her head back and screamed. "Dear God!" And *thank* God she was already so well prepared, because even though she prided herself on being able to accommodate any man, this guy was a damned crotchful. He stretched her wet lips to the limit, invaded her entire pelvis with a feeling of being over-stuffed, and definitely bottomed out against her cervix. Her clitoris quivered in a happy jig. Poor thing had been waiting many long hours for this.

Breen made a guttural noise inside his chest, and an earthquake rumbled through her breasts.

She clenched her thighs around him in anticipation of...something...something enormous about to happen.

Teeth gritted, his grip tight on her, he shot right off the mark into crazed thrusting, using his powerful hold on her waist to plunge her up and down on his cock like he was pump-priming a toy rocket for launch. His hips surged in tandem, creating beyond-belief depth to his invasion.

"My God," she panted. "My God...!" Her tits slammed into his pecs. Her hair flailed about. Her climax came without warning. No pre-orgasmic shivers. She just came. *Hard.* The strong, full-sheath spasms jarred another scream out her. Her inner muscles closed down on Breen's cock and—

His knees buckled—they must have, because he went down on them. In the resulting jolt, his cock rammed deeper inside her. She fisted her hands in his hair and kept on climaxing.

Snarling, he braced a palm on her nightstand and shoved back to his feet. Lurching sideways a couple of steps, he dropped them both down on the bed, staying tight between her thighs. His lips found hers in a passionate, tongue-exploring kiss, the rocking of his hips slowing to something more savoring.

She tore her mouth from his. "No! Keep going fast. I like it hard."

He obeyed her command and accelerated his hips back to a pounding rhythm between her thighs. His breath was a rough rasp through closed teeth. His slick chest pushed her breasts every which way. Her spine thumped the mattress.

He was going at her like a pile driver. *Holy shit.* Boyish Breen fucked like a madman! "So good," she yelled. "It's so good!" She dug her teeth into the meaty part of his shoulder.

He bellowed, then bit her in return, but not on the throat this time. He hooked his fangs into a thick chunk of flesh above her collarbone.

She yelped, although it didn't exactly hurt. It was more like a burning, stinging sensation spreading out from the area where he had her clamped between his jaws. She weirdly lost control of her body. Her muscles went gelatinous, and she lolled compliantly beneath him as he thundered toward his completion.

Bam! Bam! Two more sledgehammer thrusts, and he went all-over rigid. He yanked out his fangs and arched his neck. A husky growl rolled out of him in dangerously low octaves as he came like fuck, his cock pumping inside her in huge, eruptive bursts. His hips bucked against her one last time, jangling her raggedy-loose body, then he collapsed on top of her, fully face-planting into the wild tangle of her damp hair.

She kept her arms wrapped around him and breathed heavily through an open mouth. Breen's heartbeat bammed next to hers. His fast breathing gusted her hair against her cheek.

After she'd calmed a bit, she almost laughed out loud. *Wow.* She said she'd been overdue for some action of the rougher variety, and, *fuuuuuuck me.* The call had definitely been answered. She'd never been screwed so violently in her life.

The closest she'd come was with a criminal sort from an MC called Rhoad Rhage. Such a *ha ha* clever name for the club…except that the misspelling too accurately reflected the actual IQ level of the members. She ended up in Rhoad Rhage's seedy club bar one night after rescuing her brother from a marijuana deal going south—the bar was near the spot where she brought the rescue money. She was on her second beer when Clint sidled up to her and whispered in her ear, "I have me a cock piercing." He also wore two full sleeves of death-themed tats. So she made a one-night concession to proper English, and was glad she had, because the cock stud ended up doing wonderful things to her G-spot.

Still, Clint couldn't hold a candle to Breen in the ferocious department. Having a set of fangs no doubt helped, but it was more like—

The bedroom door burst open and slapped the wall.

Breen's head shot up, his eyes narrowing, his upper lip lifting toward the beginnings of a sneer.

It was only Lara.

He relaxed back on top of Charlize. Apparently he only got his dander up for men.

Lara skidded to a halt several steps inside the room and gaped at the two of them. She was holding the community manual, one finger tucked inside to save her place. Before rushing in here, she'd obviously been in the middle of reading it. How very studious of her. Yes, Lara Klein would make her way properly into the community: pass the required exam on Vârcolac culture, work at Marissa's restaurant, meet a man, get married, move into a house, and have two-point-five kids—everything done right and correct, accomplished with perfect etiquette.

Charlize crooked an arm beneath her head. It wasn't easy to come across as nonchalant with a lot of heavy male still on top of her—*in* her—but Charlize did her best. She smiled serenely at Lara. "Was it all the screaming?"

Lara opened her mouth.

She didn't get a chance to say whatever she planned to say because just then Breen jolted violently.

Charlize startled and peered sideways at him.

Groaning, he shoved his face into her throat and inhaled huge, almost frantic intakes of air. He shuddered again, over and over.

What the hell was going on with him? Was this some kind of secondary, latent orgasm?

Blushing, Lara whirled around and bolted from the room.

CHAPTER SEVEN

RAPID-FIRE FOOTSTEPS CLACKING ON LINOLEUM brought Hadley up from her chair. Closing the magazine she was browsing through, she quickly stepped out from behind the first floor nurses' station.

Toni, dressed smartly in black slacks, low-heeled pumps of the same color, and a lightweight cardigan in speckled heather gray, moved with long, purposeful strides down the hospital's main corridor.

Walking beside her was Țărână's largest physical being, Toni's brother-in-law, Nyko Brun. He was carrying a boy of about three. His son, obviously—the black-haired toddler was the image of his father...well, if his father hadn't been so scary-looking.

Of all the community scuttlebutt Marissa had managed to share with Hadley after court today, hearing that Nyko was married was the news that lifted Hadley's brows to her hairline. She tried to pretend her uncouth reaction was surprise over the community finding another extremely rare Royal Dragon—the only type of women the half-demon Brun brothers could mate with—but, honestly, Hadley was mostly shocked over any woman wanting to marry Nyko. With his heavy brow, anvil for a jaw, and black, arching teeth tattoos littering his entire upper body, including the circumference of his neck, he wasn't exactly the type of man a girl dreamed of marrying someday. But, also...in all fairness, if Hadley thought back to her time here, once she'd gotten used to Nyko, she'd found him to be pretty loveable.

"I gave Breen enough sedative to induce a near coma," Toni was saying to Nyko as the two of them stopped at the nurses' station. "Are you sure that won't be sufficient?"

"Definitely not." Nyko was adamant. "The half-bond will push Breen's predatory side to fight its way through conventional medication. You need to dope him up with an enchanted drug."

"*You* didn't require such drastic measures when you were in a half-bond."

Nyko snorted. "Only barely, and I'm not a Pure-bred like Breen." The toddler reached up and tugged on his father's big ear. Nyko's head skewed sideways, and he grinned at the boy, then transferred the smile to Hadley. "Hi, Hadley. Welcome back."

"Thank you," she responded warmly. "It's good to be back."

At the sound of her voice, the toddler stared at her with liquid-eyed interest.

"Goodness, I've seen so many cute kids since I've been back, I'm getting light-headed." She reached out and tickled the baby's belly. The boy broke into a smile, displaying four sturdy teeth. *Adorable!* "What's his name?"

"Mihail. It's the Romanian form of Michael, although if you ask my wife, he's named after Mikhail Baryshnikov." Nyko chuckled.

"Any more of these at home?"

"A fifteen-month-old and a three-month-old. Both boys."

"*Three* children! Already!"

Nyko beamed. "And my wife Faith is pregnant with a fourth. Although that one was an oops."

Hadley tucked in her chin. "Really? I didn't think Vârcolac couples got blindsided with those kinds of surprises." The vampire way of making babies was a pretty obvious process: when a Vârcolac male scented his mate's fertility, he was thrown into a semi-conscious "procreation mode"—a state during which he had sex with his wife, over and over, until the deed was done. Afterward he fell into an exhausted three-day hibernation period. With this kind of clear-cut activity going on, it was difficult for a woman to miss when she got herself preggers.

"Normally, that's true," Nyko agreed. "But several months ago the community received a batch of defective ovulation sticks, so a lot of women were wandering around town ovulating without knowing it. Six were taken down by their husbands and impregnated"—Nyko grimaced—"a few in some pretty awkward situations, before anyone figured what was going on. We had to segregate the town—women on the south end, men in the north—while we fixed it. Some are calling it the Great Ovulation Disaster." Nyko's smiled reappeared. "No disaster for me, though."

"That sounds—"

Toni gusted a breath. "Can we put off the baby talk till a later time? Where's Shaston, Hadley?"

"Oh. Uh..." Hadley moved her hands in a jerky way, flustered by Toni's impatient tone. Țărână's leader generally wasn't abrupt, but the topic of babies was a sore one for her. According to more of Marissa's scuttlebutt, Toni and her husband, Jacken, were fighting over whether or not to have more children.

"They've been having problems on and off for the last several months," Marissa explained as they meandered down Main Street toward the hospital. "Toni wants to have another baby, but Jacken won't consider it, not after—" Marissa eyed her askance. "That's right, you weren't here for what happened, were you? How long did you live in the community, anyway?"

"About five months."

Marissa nodded. "Well, Toni almost died giving birth to their daughter, Shaw. It scared ten years off Jacken's life."

"Jacken...*scared*?" Hadley couldn't picture it. As she

remembered the dark, hard-faced man, he never showed much emotion, certainly not anything close to fear. He was only one step down on the scary-ladder from Nyko, his forearms marked with the same arching teeth tattoos, and his black eyes capable of bringing on bouts of spontaneous fainting in others.

"In his completely rock-like Jacken-way," Marissa said, "but, yes. What pisses off Toni the most is that he won't even discuss it with her. He just shuts her down every time she tries to bring it up."

"How awful." Hadley was well-schooled in most of the pitfalls of a troubled marriage, and lack of communication was a biggie.

"Hadley?" Toni prompted, the question shaking Hadley from her thoughts. "Do you know where Shaston is?"

"Oh, yes. Sorry." Hadley cleared her throat. "She went off to get some medicine."

"Off where? We stock the medicine here."

"I'm not sure." Hadley spread her hands. "It seemed funny to me, too, but I don't know how things work around here yet." She checked her watch. "She's been gone for a good forty-five minutes."

"Look! Bear!" Nyko's son pointed to a framed picture on the wall beside the nurses' station.

Most of the pictures in the hospital were kid-friendly. This one was of a teddy bear in a bow tie.

"Very good, Mihail," Nyko encouraged.

Toni's brows started to pull together. "When was the last time anyone checked on Breen?"

"Shaston and I both did right before she left." Hadley pointed down the hall. "She taped a note on Breen's door."

Toni marched down the hallway, Hadley and Nyko following. Toni snapped the note off the door but barely glanced at it. "This isn't Shaston's handwriting." Shoving into the room, Toni flicked on the lights.

Somebody was definitely sleeping in the bed.

Toni strode over and whipped the sheet off Breen's—

Not Breen.

Shaston, drooling.

Hadley's mouth sagged open.

"Well." Toni tossed the note aside. "This can't be good."

"Oh, dang," Nyko said in an undertone.

"Daddy! Sticks!" Mihail pointed at a glass jar of tongue depressors set next to a sink.

Nyko pulled out a stick and gave it to his son.

"How is it no one reported this? Someone in town had to have spotted Breen. Or mansion security, what happened there?" Toni seemed to be throwing these questions out to anyone who would answer them.

Neither Hadley nor Nyko did.

Exhaling expansively, Toni focused on Nyko. "I take it there's no chance Charlize and Breen haven't had sex?"

"If Charlize said no and was firm about it." But Nyko looked doubtful.

So did Toni. "Yes, well, Charlize didn't exactly strike me as a woman who is particularly liberal with her *nos*, much less firm about them." She paused. "Breen wouldn't force himself on her in his half-bond state, would he?"

"Absolutely not," Nyko insisted. "But he's not capable of leaving her, either. He'll move heaven and earth to convince her to be with him."

Toni rubbed her forehead. "And he's had forty-five minutes to work on her."

"You warned Charlize not to sleep with Breen," Nyko asked, "outlined the consequences?"

"Of course. But I didn't get the sense much was going in. I didn't push it, because Charlize seemed overwhelmed and I *thought*—between the heavy sedation and the bindings—we'd keep the two of them apart." Toni swatted at one of the leather cuffs, hanging loosely open and minus Breen's ankle.

Mihail wielded the tongue depressor around like a sword, and Nyko leaned aside to avoid getting clobbered.

Toni sighed. "I guess I'd better go to the mansion. See if I can salvage anything from this mess." She didn't look too excited about the idea. She took a hypodermic needle off the metal tray, noted it was empty, glanced at Shaston, sighed again, then set it back down. The cell phone on her belt hummed. She unhooked it and checked the caller ID, then pressed the speaker button. "What's up, Alex?"

Alex...? Oh! That's right. Toni's computer geek brother.

Alex's voice came out through the cell phone's speaker. "Thought you should know a woman is screaming in the mansion. *Loudly*, since it's coming from the third floor, and I'm down here on the first at my desk and can hear it just fine." There was a weighty pause. "It sounds like, uh, sex screaming, so, you know, I wasn't sure if I should send in the on-duty warriors."

Toni's eyes closed and stayed that way for an extra-long moment. "No, Alex, no men. I'll head over right now." She jammed the phone back on her belt, spun on her heel, and left without another word.

"Bummer," Nyko murmured, although whether he was saying it over Breen and Charlize's predicament or because his son had just urped all over his shirt, Hadley couldn't tell.

✧　　✧　　✧

BREEN THE WILDMAN NEEDED TO *go*.

It had to be at least *three* in the damned morning Charlize's time by now, and considering she'd just undergone some serious pussy rammage, ho-wrecker sex, she was beyond frigging worn out. Gulp down a snack. Take another quick shower. Crawl into bed. These were the only things she wanted on her agenda right now, and at this point in her exhaustion, *all right, get the hell out*, was about all she felt inclined to say to Breen to push him to do exactly that. Plus he was—

A knock sounded at the door.

Breen snapped ramrod straight in bed and growled like a German shepherd.

Charlize gritted her teeth. Him being back to his short-fuse watchdog act was also getting real fucking old. Snatching the sheet off the bed, she wrapped it around her naked body and stalked across the room to answer the knock. Jerking the door open, she—

Great.

Toni Parthen.

Ţărână's leader stood in the doorway with an expression on her face somewhere between irritated and painfully resigned. "You had sex with Breen."

Jesus. Was this a town full of starchy assholes or what? "Yes, thank you. Anything else?"

Toni rubbed a forefinger across the bridge of her nose. "Unfortunately, yes, there's a lot more." She sighed. "Earlier I told you that you and Breen needed to be kept apart, Charlize, because he would try to complete the bond between you two. That has now occurred."

Charlize exploded air out of her lungs. "Look, not that it's anybody's business, but we didn't tie each other up, okay? We just had good, old-fashioned starchy sex." Not true, but nobody needed to hear about how Breen's pile-driver moves had turned her crotch into pudding.

Toni frowned. "Tie up?"

"The bondage part everyone seems to have their panties all wadded up about…you know, BDSM play?"

Toni's expression froze. She stood there for a three-count, looking floored. "I have no idea how to answer that." She angled around Charlize, moving past the doorjamb into the room. She strode by Breen, who was now partially zonked out on the bed, and sank down in the desk chair. "I need a minute."

Charlize closed the door and waited for ten seconds. She flung a hand out. "What?"

Toni paused another couple of seconds. "As I tried to explain earlier, the combination of being bitten by Breen and having sex with him would be like you two getting married, only the marriage would be—"

"Dammit!" Charlize interrupted. "Would the people around here *please* wake up and join the twenty-first century! Just because Breen and I had sex doesn't mean we have to get married."

"You already *are* married," Toni returned. "We call it being bonded—that's what a *bond* is. Breen's cells have now undergone a biological transformation, changing his internal makeup so he will forever be dependent on your blood and your blood alone."

Changing his internal makeup so… "What are you even talking about?" Charlize jammed a hand on her hip. "Maybe biology's not my strongest subject, but I certainly know that shit like you're saying doesn't really happen." *What does this woman think, blond hair and big tits equal a moron?*

Toni's tense shoulders moved up and down, as if she was taking a breath while counting to ten. "I realize all of this is difficult to comprehend, Charlize. When I first came to the community, it took me a while to truly understand everything too. But right now I need you to pause, draw a breath, and take a moment to acknowledge that this man"—she gestured at Breen—"has fangs. I know you know that. You've been bitten by him at least twice." Her gaze strayed over the bruises on Charlize's neck and collarbone. "You've enjoyed the pleasure of fiinţă, the elixir that comes out of his fangs. You've experienced actual, quantifiable evidence to confirm that Breen doesn't belong to the class of homo sapiens, like you and I do, but rather he is a different species of human being, in this case one known as Vârcolac." She paused to draw what seemed like a refueling breath. "So, yes, you're right, the kind of biological transformation I'm describing to you doesn't happen to regular human beings. To vampires, however, it absolutely does."

"But…" Charlize stopped talking as pieces of Marissa's tell-all rose in her memory. *These people have a lot of special abilities and some interesting genetic differences from "regular" humans, but for now, the important thing…*

Waitaminute. Charlize gaped at Toni in open-mouthed, dawning horror. *Wait just a fucking minute.*

"What I'm saying to you can and does actually happen, Charlize. You *are* permanently bonded to Breen. You're now his mate for life."

Her horror became like a physical entity in her throat, a tumorous lump, throbbing, strangling, choking. She couldn't breathe, and panic swam into her eyeballs. *His mate for life…*

"I'm not making this up to mess with you," Toni promised. "I give you my word."

Charlize clawed at her throat and found some air, but then oxygen started entering her lungs too fast. *Hish, hish, hish*—once she made this noise, Toni leapt up and grasped Charlize by the shoulders, propelling her around and making her sit instead.

Charlize bent forward in the chair, her hands convulsed around the armrests, her toga-sheet sagging low on her breasts. Through the tops of her lashes, she saw Breen upright in bed. She couldn't read his expression—he didn't *have* any—only that he didn't look zonked anymore. *You are permanently bonded to Breen.* Oh no… Oh-fucking-no. "What do I do?" she gasped out. "I don't know what to do." A sharp feeling of alarm sat at the back of her tongue like a pincushion.

Toni held out a water bottle to her.

Charlize hadn't even noticed her go to the mini fridge to get it. She took the bottle and looked up at Toni. "You probably think I'm a total idiot." Maybe blond hair and big tits *did* equal a moron. "I just couldn't…it's like the manual is written in binary code, and I'm really tired right now, and...and..."

Toni's expression turned sympathetic.

"What do I do?" Charlize repeated hoarsely.

"Why don't we discuss options for the future later?" Toni said. "For now, you have to stay constantly at Breen's side. It takes a Vârcolac a full week to go through The Change, and Breen needs you nearby during the entire biological process."

"A-a week...?" She blinked rapidly, the movement of her lashes stirring several caught strands of her hair. Then it hit her. "Waitaminute, *what?*" She tore the hair out of her eyes. "I'm stuck with this guy for a week?" She'd never spent an entire night alone with a Fuck4Fun man in her life, probably no man, much less a *week*. "No way. I'm not staying locked away with him. This guy was just supposed to be a fun lay."

Toni's expression tightened back up a little. "If you leave Breen, he'll follow you wherever you go in the community and try to kill any male who crosses your path. For the safety of the people of Ţărână, that can't be permitted."

Charlize jumped up. "Then I'll leave the community altogether." This place was falling way short on its predicted entertainment points, anyway.

Toni shook her head. "Leaving wouldn't be practical, Charlize. You'd just have to return every five days or less so Breen could feed. Remember how I said he's dependent solely on your blood now?"

"But..." Charlize stopped. There was no *but*. Toni had said that.

"And if you leave completely," Toni went on, *and on*, "Breen will go into a blood-coma within seven days and die. So, I'm sorry, but living elsewhere isn't really a viable option for you anymore." She paused. "Unless you're okay with being responsible for Breen's death."

Charlize set her mouth. "Oh, why, yes, that sounds like absolute funsies, and no fucking pressure at all—right?—

having someone's life in my hands." How well had *that* worked out for her before, huh? She fisted her fingers in her toga bedsheet as the image of the diesel truck roared across her mind, tires smoking and screeching, blood so red it was black painting the grill.

The gruesome memory stoked the heat already roiling beneath her emotions, and she rounded on Breen with a snarl. "You fucking piece of shit! You knew this was going to happen."

The man didn't say anything—*of course not!* He was a heartless drone.

"Breen wasn't able to stop himself," Toni explained in a neutral voice. "He was acting on instinct."

Charlize dragged the back of her wrist across sudden tears, streaking a long pattern of wetness along the flesh of her cheek.

Breen stared at her tears like he wanted to beat them up.

"You can move into Breen's apartment after you pass the test on Vârcolac culture," Toni offered. "There's still more for you to learn from the manual."

Of course there is!

"Then at least you'll have more space and access to a kitchen."

"Well, goody for me," she fumed. *You are permanently bonded to Breen.*

Permanently.

PERMANENTLY!

Whirling on the small desk, Charlize snatched up the community manual. She didn't sit in the chair and hunker right down to the task of studying it.

She whipped back around and hurled it at Breen.

CHAPTER EIGHT

BREEN HAD SEEN THIS KIND of thing happen on TV sitcoms.

A woman stomps around a room, banging stuff and exhaling loud breaths and acting generally T'd off.

Her TV boyfriend watches this play out for no more than a couple of seconds before he asks, "Are you okay?"

The woman snaps, "Fine."

She's not fine. The guy decodes this from her fed-up tone. It clues him in to continue with, "All right, c'mon, tell me what's wrong." He might add *honey* or *sweetie*, but will also usually attach a secret eye-roll loaded with, *I can't believe I'm dealing with another one of her moods.*

So Breen supposed when he saw Charlize still all worked up after Toni left—shoving the chair away from the desk with a rough thrust of her hip, sitting down hard enough to *eerch!* the hinges, flipping pages of the community manual with sharp jerks of her wrist and paper air pops—he should've processed all of it as his cue to ask, "Are you okay?"

Except he couldn't ask.

Right after Toni left, Charlize screamed at him, "Don't talk to me!"

So he hadn't—he wasn't.

Except now it seemed like she was just as pissed at him for following her rule. She kept cutting irate, sideways glances at him. So what was he supposed to do? What did she *actually* want him to do? Did women make a habit of saying one thing and meaning another? That was probably an essential thing to know, but he didn't have much experience with females. The only ones he generally dealt with were his mother and the waitresses at the diner. And clearly interactions like *Beer, please,* and *I'll have the number six, but with extra cheese* hadn't prepared him for figuring out if he was supposed to act on the literal meaning of what Charlize told him to do or the hidden one, whatever that might be.

Or maybe Charlize *did* mean what she said but hadn't expected him to follow through. A sitcom guy, after all, would've broken down long ago and asked her what was wrong.

But silence was sort of Breen's thing.

Charlize probably didn't realize it when she'd ordered him to shut his trap.

Being muscles-falling-off-the-bone tired wasn't helping him come up with the right answers to all these questions, either. He'd been pushed to the end of his limitations today by his savage fight with Jacken in the gym, the agony of going through a half-bond, the bastard-hard job of breaking into the mansion, then finally having sex with Charlize—who knew that would take so much out of him?

Top it all off with *not* feeling starved for the first time since coming into his blood-need eighteen years ago—*eighteen years*—and he was having a helluva time keeping his eyes open and his head from lolling off the back of the armchair he was deflated in. So being able to solve a mystery that had stumped man since the dawn of time—*woman*—was currently way outside his wheelhouse.

What he really wished was that Charlize would go to bed already. He couldn't go to sleep till she did, and along with the exhausted thing he was dealing with, his changing cells wanted the comfort of her scent. And since the likelihood of her letting him tuck his face happily into the crook of her sweet-smelling neck while she studied the manual sat at an absolute, rock-bottom zero, he needed to draw in the scent lingering on her bedsheets—her good scent from earlier, when she'd been horny and raring to go. Not how she smelled now, kind of soured from her jammed feelings.

Suppressing an exhale, he idly scratched his hip scar through his black workout shorts—the only clothes he had with him. The old wound rarely bothered him, only twinging a bit when he was really tired. He'd taken a vicious blade cut in the War of Războiul Jertfei de Sânge, or the War of the Blood Sacrifice, called this because there wasn't a single male Vârcolac who fought in it who hadn't been injured.

The war had been waged against their ruthless neighbors, the Om Rău, a demon race who'd been causing the Vârcolac problems for years by skulking into Țărână to try and steal precious Dragon women…and hurting a lot of innocent people in the process. Not much the Vârcolac had ever been able to do about it, except fight off the attacks. The Om Rău always had the advantage of being able to escape back through the long, convoluted Hell Tunnels connecting their two towns. Demons could bear the kind of heat those tunnels generated. Vampires couldn't. So the Vârcolac warriors were never able to chase after their enemy or mount an offensive against them.

Until three years ago.

Everything changed when Shon Brun—Nyko and Jacken's younger brother—gathered enough information about the Hell Tunnels to map a direct course through them. *Direct* meant less time in the heat, and so decreased the vampires' chances of over-cooking.

The warriors planned a raid, then they rampaged—along with some beefy recruits out of construction—into the demon town of Oțărât.

There, they were met by overwhelming odds.

The Vârcolac fought a helluva battle, but being outnumbered and already partially depleted from the high temp of the tunnels hadn't exactly added up to favorable odds for an all-out victory. They were forced to retreat before their main objective had been reached: to save the human women trapped in the squalor and abusive conditions of Oţărât.

It was a huge disappointment, but not, as it turned out, a complete fail.

The next day, Josnic, one of the leaders of the Om Rău, showed up in Stânga Town's Outer Edge—the barred gate leading into the tunnels—with a woman they never thought to see again.

Gwyn Billaud.

She was a Dragon female who once resided in the community...until one of the warriors screwed up her security and let her get stolen by the Om Rău.

Ragged and worn-looking, Gwyn had asked Toni and Roth for help. The war had killed most of Oţărât's best scavengers, she explained, and she didn't have anyone to send topside for supplies. Soon food and water would be gone and the residents starving. Gwyn begged the community to provide for them, and in exchange, the Om Rău would agree never to attack again.

It was an appealing offer. A truce of this sort would finally allow the people of Ţărână to live in peace. Unfortunately, the deal would abandon the trapped human women to their lives in Oţărât.

After a lot of debate, the community's Council finally agreed. The warriors were too injured to mount another campaign, anyway, and even if they could, the result of a second war might be the same—there were still plenty Om Rău left to fight. But mostly the deal was cut because it was what Gwyn wanted, and they owed her.

So the community bulldozed a chunk of cave out of the far end of Stânga Town to create an easily accessed drop-off area, and this became an agreed-upon "neutral zone." Vârcolac went in to leave supplies, then left. Om Rău went in to collect the goods, then left. One breed never saw or talked to the other.

The community was very generous with the supplies they offered to make up for the failed—

Charlize slammed the manual closed. *Bam!*

Breen peeled his eyes open wider. If he'd had any energy, he might've startled.

She thundered over to his armchair and came to a rigid stop in front of him, her hands planted on her hips.

The position bowed open the neckline of her robe, but he tried not to notice the view. He might not be a sitcom guy, but basic male instinct for doing whatever it took to calm down his woman so he could get laid again told him that ogling Charlize's tits while she was jammed up would only make her more jammed.

He met her gaze, which was glaring hot.

"You were a *virgin*!?" she hissed at him.

He blinked slowly. Now why would that piss her off? Was this another hidden meaning thing? He tried to reason it out, but his brain was a gigantic yawn.

"You fucked me like a wild man. How the hell does a virgin do that?"

He carefully studied her enraged expression. She was very, very angry. She was shouting every word at him, which he didn't mind so much. He didn't mind the fury in her gestures, either. No. It was when things got quiet—same as right before his father struck with one of his barbed remarks—that Breen didn't like. Those barbs stabbed a man like a cold blade. For all the brutal hits Breen had taken in his life, and seen others endure, he'd never encountered anything able to do a man more damage than one of Ungar Dalakis's perfectly aimed criticisms.

"Why the hell aren't you answering me?" If Charlize's voice turned any more sour, it would be sauerkraut.

He scooted up in his chair. "You told me not to talk to you."

"Oh, for God's sake. Don't be a dick."

Yeah, so…the name-calling wasn't a favorite.

Charlize's mouth tautened until her lips were a stiff, red knot. "I asked you a direct question."

He shrugged. "I don't know. I guess I've been thinking about sex for a long time."

She *piffed*. "Every man does that."

"Not like our breed. A Vârcolac reaches sexual maturity at the age of twenty-one, but because there's been no one for us to mate with for years—only you Dragons, who showed up on the scene recently—we've had to wait forever to have sex. I'm thirty-nine. That means I've been thinking about sex for eighteen years."

She gaped at him, her mouth just hanging open for a long moment, then she turned around and stomped a couple of paces away. "I don't know which number is more appalling to me. The thirty-nine or the eighteen." Beneath her bathrobe, her spinal cord was a tight stretch of bones.

Thirty-nine was actually young in Vârcolac years. He wasn't sure what to say about the eighteen. "Why does the virgin thing bother you?"

She spun back around, her glare reigniting. "Because the hell if I want to be anyone's memory." The edge of her jaw quivered. "Now I'll forever be your *first*."

First and *only*. Vârcolac mated for life. But probably he should keep quiet about it. She was already upset enough. He scratched his temple. "I'm not sure what you want me to do about it. I mean, I can't *un*do it." Virginity was one of those things.

Charlize crossed her arms beneath her breasts. The new posture was better than when she had her hands on her hips, and… No, actually, it wasn't. "No, you can't undo it, can you?" she snapped. "*Any* of it."

Breen wasn't able to stop himself. He was acting on instinct.

When Toni had said that, she'd cast him a sideways glance, and even though her expression wasn't accusatory, it wasn't exactly forgiving either. Like maybe at some point in this chain of events, she believed he should've known what the shit-nuggets he was doing.

Are you suggesting, Roth boomed in court, *that when Miss Renault said 'I want this' to Mr. Dalakis, he wholly believed she was agreeing to a life-bond?*

Sitting here now, the answer to that seemed kind of like a no-brainer. But when Breen had been around Charlize, especially during the half-bond, he was nothing but *compelled*. Driven to get the right skin back on. Desperate to escape an agony steadily turning his soul gangrenous. Determined to do whatever it took to convince Charlize to be his woman.

He sank down in his chair. So now he was bonded to a woman who was a virtual stranger. Who definitely didn't love him. Who, in fact, was giving a very convincing performance of hating him.

You fucking piece of shit! You knew this was going to happen!

Breen closed his eyes, exhausted down to parts of himself beyond the physical. Charlize or a sitcom guy, either/or, but *someone* needed to tell him what to do.

CHAPTER NINE

On Mon, Nov. 6, 2017 at 10:02 A.M. (PST) Edward Sevilli <esevilli@scrippshealth.org> wrote:

Hi John,

Dr. Edward Sevilli here. Sorry to hear about you going on medical leave from the police force. I know you've been ill for some years now, and that's exactly why I wanted to get in touch. I might be able to help you.

The United States Hematology Foundation has funded a research project for me to identify and study undiagnosed blood disorders. I think you'd be a perfect candidate.

About four years ago you were in Scripps Hospital following a gunshot wound, and your blood tests came back with an unidentifiable element. This is exactly the type of blood anomaly I'm looking to study.

I'd only need a few blood samples from you, and I've been authorized to offer you $1,000 for your involvement. I hope you'll consider participating. Maybe we could finally figure out what's going on with you.

I look forward to hearing from you,
Eddie

On Mon, Nov. 6, 2017 at 12:17 P.M. (PST) John Waterson <KCChiefsFan@hotmail.com> wrote:

Hey Eddie,

Good to hear from you. It's been awhile.

Congratulations on your research project, but I'm going to have to pass. Not really my thing.

Good luck with it.
John

On Mon, Nov. 6, 2017 at 6:11 P.M. (PST) Edward Sevilli <esevilli@scrippshealth.org> wrote:

Are you sure, John?

The results of my research could possibly cure you.

On Mon, Nov. 6, 2017 at 6:56 P.M. (PST) John Waterson <KCChiefsFan@hotmail.com> wrote:

Sorry, Eddie.

I try to steer clear of doctors. No offense to you personally.

On Tues, Nov 7, 2017 at 7:17 A.M. (PST) Edward Sevilli <esevilli@scrippshealth.org> wrote:

All right. Sorry to hear it, but I understand.

Perhaps you can help me track down another man I'd like to approach for this study. He was in the hospital at the same time you were—I believe he was a suspect of yours, in fact. His blood had a similar unidentifiable anomaly in it.

His name is Devid Nichita, but the contact information listed in his hospital record leads nowhere.

Any clue how I might get in touch with him?

On Tues, Nov. 7, 2017 at 9:04 A.M. (PST) John Waterson
<KCChiefsFan@hotmail.com> wrote:

Not really, Eddie, sorry.

I have an email address associated with Nichita, but it
hasn't been used in several years, so it's probably a
dead end.

I hate to ask a favor, since I just bagged out of your
research project, but if you unearth any new information about Nichita, could you pass it on?

I've got unfinished business with the guy.

On Tues, Nov. 7, 2017 at 3:50 P.M. (PST) Edward Sevilli
<esevilli@scrippshealth.org> wrote:

Sure, no problem, John.

On Thurs, Nov. 9, 2017 at 6:32 P.M. (PST) Edward Sevilli
<esevilli@scrippshealth.org> wrote:

John,

I received a strange hit on Devid Nichita.

A couple days ago I put this name on the site Peo-
pleFinder.com, and some man (who had an internet
alert set up for the name Nichita) wrote to me and said
he might be looking for the same person.

What's up with this Devid Nichita that everyone is after
him?

The man who contacted me is from Transylvania.
Strange, right? So I'm not sure how to respond. He
seemed especially excited about the strange blood
part.

On Thurs, Nov. 10, 2017 at 9:15 A.M. (PST) John Water-son <KCChiefsFan@hotmail.com> wrote:

Transylvania? That is strange.

Do you mind if I contact the guy?

On Thurs, Nov. 10, 2017 at 1:21 P.M. (PST) Edward Sevilli <esevilli@scrippshealth.org> wrote:

Go for it.

Here's his info:
Email: Carpathian5905@transy.ro.
He has an odd handle—MoonRiderOne. I don't know his name.

It doesn't sound like he knows anything about how to find Nichita, but if it turns out he does, please let me know.

On Thurs, Nov. 10, 2017 at 1:47 P.M. (PST) John Water-son <KCChiefsFan@hotmail.com> wrote:

I'll definitely keep you in the loop if anything pops, Eddie.

Thanks.

On Thurs, Nov. 10, 2017 at 2:03 P.M. (PST), Justice-Seeker <KCChiefsFan@hotmail.com> wrote:

Dear Sir,

I'm a colleague of Dr. Edward Sevilli, and he gave me permission to contact you regarding Devid Nichita.

I might have a way of finding this man, but if you don't mind the question, why are you looking for him?

On Fri, Nov. 11, 2017 at 1:35 A.M. (EEST), Moon-RiderOne <Carpathian5905@transy.ro> wrote:

Dear Justice Seeker,

Thank you for contacting me. I'm very interested in discussing this matter further with you.

The reason I seek Devid Nichita is a highly personal matter to me, but I will say that the situation has to do with a relative I once knew of his in Romania.

If you don't mind a question of my own, why are you contacting me if you have a way of finding Devid Nichita yourself?

On Thurs, Nov. 10, 2017 at 4:55 P.M. (PST), Justice-Seeker <KCChiefsFan@hotmail.com> wrote:

I currently lack the resources to manage Nichita and his associates on my own.

I'm hoping this isn't an issue for you.

On Fri, Nov. 11, 2017 at 4:45 A.M. (EEST), Moon-RiderOne <Carpathian5905@transy.ro> wrote:

Resources aren't a problem for me, no—I have considerable at my disposal.

If your Devid Nichita is the man I also pursue (and I think he is, because how many men named Nichita have strange blood?), I would be most eager to help you.

On Fri, Nov. 10, 2017 at 9:06 P.M. (PST), JusticeSeeker <KCChiefsFan@hotmail.com> wrote:

All right, but Nichita isn't an easy man to pin down.

He's part of a security team, and so he's never alone and usually armed.

On Fri, Nov. 11, 2017 at 11:23 A.M. (EEST), Moon-RiderOne <Carpathian5905@transy.ro> wrote:

Again, this is not a problem.

Shall we meet?

CHAPTER TEN

Topside
3:04 A.M.

THE NIGHT MELTED, BLURRED, REFORMED, and opened up, birthing forth a man.

Detective John Waterson startled so violently, his cigarette leapt from between his fingers and hit the floorboard of his Chevy in a burst of orange sparks. "Jesus Christ!" He banged his foot around to stamp out the glowing butt while his heart tried to run away from his chest.

A pair of pale hands appeared on the doorframe of the open driver's side window, moonlight glinting off stark white fingernails.

Breathing in short, croaky gulps, John glared at the hands. Considering the current state of his health, he didn't have many near-seizures like this left in him. And how the hell had this prick snuck up on him? Off the force only six months, and he was already allowing himself to be surprised. *Pathetic.* Or maybe it was because the guy was practically invisible dressed all in black: homespun tweed pants, scuffed boots, and a wool trench coat hanging past his knees. He looked like a dock worker.

"Justice Seeker?" the owner of the hands inquired, speaking with a European accent. A Romanian accent, in all likelihood, since it's where he came from.

"Yeah. Who else?" John snarked. Who else would be waiting at the top of Soledad Mountain at the ungodly hour of three in the morning, if not the person this guy had arranged to meet? "Which makes you MoonRiderOne." John yanked out a handkerchief—something he never left home without—and mopped his face. Even that small amount of cigarette-stomping had sweat flooding off his forehead and down his cheeks. But then these days, the mere act of breathing made him sweat.

"Correct." The man bent lower to peer into the car. He had a face like Pee Wee Herman's, white flesh—extra-white where a scar ran along his left jawline—with unnaturally red lips and narrow features. His hair was short, although long enough on top for his bangs to form an up-and-over swoop, like a hairdryer-exaggerated cowlick. The swoop was gray-silver while the rest of the hair was black. "You said you have a way for me to draw out Devid Nichita?"

Getting right down to business, was he? *Fine by me.* John didn't have the energy to waste on pleasantries, either. "First we have to talk about how my own justice fits into this." Or rather, *revenge*...a revenge John never would've been able to achieve had MoonRiderOne not dropped fortuitously into his life.

"Nichita travels in the same circles as a guy who has black hair, black eyes, and black teeth tattoos on at least one of his forearms." John had never seen the two men together, but it took only a little deductive reasoning to conclude that they both worked security for the same top-secret research institute. "My beef is with this second man." Because he was the one who'd kidnapped Toni Parthen, the only woman John had ever loved.

Before Toni was ripped from her life—and John's—the two of them had been on the road to dating, happiness, and then, surely, marriage and children. Teeth-Tattooed Asshole—John's not-so-affectionate nickname for the life-ruiner—had to pay for screwing this up.

"If you draw out Nichita," John went on, "there's a good chance this other guy will follow."

"And how do I draw out these men?" Back to the original question, and MoonRiderOne sounded a little impatient re-asking it.

John dug a piece of paper out of his breast pocket. "This is the email address a group of criminals used a few years ago to arrange a trade-off for some women. One gang was supposed to deliver the women to another gang at a warehouse, but Nichita and his security team showed up and saved the women. It's probably safe to assume Nichita's people monitor this email address."

How John acquired the email was simple enough. He and his former partner, Pablo Ramirez, investigated the warehouse in response to a complaint of "shots fired." A laptop was found there, and the SDPD's IT guy hacked into it, discovering the email exchange. Since then, the email had gone dark, so it was probably a dead end, like John had told Dr. Sevilli. But it was all he had.

"If you use this email address to write a bogus message," John explained, "saying that you want to turn over some abducted women or something similar, then there's a good chance Nichita will show." *Good chance* might be stretching it, but whatever. "You'll be able to set a trap wherever you say the exchange will take place."

"Very well." MoonRiderOne held out his hand for the paper.

For some reason, John didn't give it to him right away. He flipped the paper through his fingers. "When will you set your plan in motion?"

"A couple of weeks, perhaps. It will take time to organize. I'll email you."

They went silent.

Crickets sang out a string of chirps, and if John strained his ears, he could hear the low hum of traffic on the faraway Interstate 5 freeway.

MoonRiderOne dropped his hand. "Was there something

else?"

John turned to stare out the front windshield of his car. Here at the top of Soledad Mountain, eight hundred twenty-three feet up, he had an airplane's view of the town of La Jolla below. City lights looked like sparkling jewels tossed across a long stretch of black cloth, garnet, agate, and citrine for the stoplights, diamonds for the streetlamps.

It was quite a vista.

"What are you going to do to bring down justice on my man?" John asked.

"Anything you wish."

Anything. John shifted his gaze down to the hand he had resting on the steering wheel. Skeletal bone was covered only by a thin parchment of skin. His belly curled in on itself, trying to cower behind his liver. How bad did it suck that he was too weak to seek vengeance himself? How much more did it suck that one of SDPD's former finest was lowering himself to do business with a bad guy. And John had no doubts that MoonRiderOne was bad.

The reason I seek Devid Nichita is a highly personal matter to me meant that MoonRiderOne was going to seriously fuck Nichita's shit up.

Which further meant that John should have reached back into his noble core and stopped this before it went any farther. Hadn't he made a career out of incarcerating men exactly like MoonRiderOne? *Exactly.* So in response to the *anything you wish* statement, John should have answered with, *never mind, I wanna do a take-back.*

But strange things happened to a man who'd been stewing too long in regret and resentment. Amazing, too, what a man found himself capable of doing when he was on the verge of death.

And John was mere days away from shuffling off this world for the next.

Was it really so wrong that he wanted his last act on earth

to be retribution for Toni? And damn well for himself too?

John turned back to MoonRiderOne. The twenty-nine-foot Mount Soledad Cross rose up tall behind him, making it look like he belonged crucified on it. "Whatever you do to Nichita," John said, "do it to my guy."

MoonRiderOne arched a single brow high.

John handed him the piece of paper with the email on it.

CHAPTER ELEVEN

The underground community of Ţărână

THE WEEK CHARLIZE WAS LOCKED away with Breen was one of the strangest of her life.

Following her brief explosion over Breen being a virgin—which she still couldn't wholly accept; he'd clearly known where all the important parts went and how to put them together expertly—she was too exhausted to deal with anything more. She put herself to bed.

Stripping off her bathrobe and climbing under the covers naked, she gave Breen a challenging stare. "I don't care if you sleep on your side of the bed, but don't get any ideas about touching me."

"I know."

She supposed he did know. She wasn't exactly being subtle about how despicable she found him.

He came to stand by his side of the bed, dressed again in what he'd arrived in—his grungy black workout shorts—and stared at her. His bangs were hanging over the right side of his face again, semi-concealing a golden eye, his non-expression revealing nothing of his thoughts. For a woman who came from a life of chaos, his stillness probably should have been comforting. But it wasn't. She hated it. Maybe because it was so fucking strange.

"What?" she snapped. "I can't sleep with you staring at me."

"I'd like to take a shower."

"I'm sure you would." He sure as shit needed one. And

probably first aid for his battered hands too. "Go ahead. I'm not stopping you."

He smoothed his lower lip over his upper lip. "I can't go into the bathroom unless you come with me."

"I don't want to take another damned shower." Certainly not with him, especially not if he thought it was a way to sneak in another round of grabass. Even *she* didn't screw a man she was royally pissed at.

"You don't have to get in with me. You can sit on the toilet seat or something."

"You're kidding."

"No."

Yeah, he didn't exactly strike her as a kidder. She exhaled a put-out breath.

"You have to be in the same room with me."

"I'm only out *here*, Breen."

He didn't say anything.

For now, you have to stay constantly at Breen's side. "Oh, for God's sake." She sat up.

The next day, a sack of Breen's clothes appeared outside her Bruges door, along with breakfast...then lunch...then dinner. They ate together—did everything—without talking.

Breen seemed absolutely fine with her silent treatment and wasn't that fucking annoying?

The morning of her second day of confinement she passed the Vârcolac culture test, which opened the way for her indoctrination into the community. Toni gave her a cell phone coded to work in both the community and topside, a plastic card for using Țărână's "credit" system of money—no actual paper or coin ever changed hands—and a list of security "don'ts" for sending text messages and emails topside. Then...finally! Toni escorted Charlize and Breen from the mansion.

When they came to a turnoff for a place called the Water Cliffs—their objective—Charlize asked to see more of the town before she was put away. They strolled onward, and she encountered more of the charm she'd seen on her first day here while walking to the hospital with Breen and Kimberly. They passed a grocery store, a library, a diner, a clapboard schoolhouse, then finally arrived at the 'burbs, a comfy residential neighborhood constructed of carefully spaced, colorful homes landscaped with real-looking lawns, plants, and flower beds.

At the far end of this residential neighborhood, just before a large fake-grass field and park, there was another pathway, this one blocked off with yellow tape. Toni explained how the town was going to be expanded in that direction, but Țărână's engineers needed to conduct some "soundings" first to test the stability of the cave floor before construction could begin.

Beyond the neighborhood, farther along on the main path, Toni went on to say there were more buildings: an older apartment complex, a hair salon, a bowling alley, and even more, but they didn't explore those. Probably because of Breen. He was getting fidgety and squinty-eyed, even though they hadn't encountered any men.

Looping back the way they came, the three of them headed down the turnoff for the Water Cliffs, a place that was a— *holy shit*. It was a water park, with pools and slides and fountains, all decorated in a tropical jungle theme.

God, Țărână was great! Like that miniature ship inside a glass bottle Charlize had originally imagined, or an angelic snow globe town, this place felt completely outside reality— isolated from all the crap others dished up and *she* always had to deal with. The farther she toured, the more the tension between her shoulder blades eased. At least some parts of living in Țărână wouldn't be so bad.

To the right of the Water Cliffs rose a magnificent, ten-story-high black chrome and glass apartment building, four large, steel balconies stretching the width of each floor. A set of wide stairs led up to the front door, and they climbed these and went inside, crossed a silver-carpeted and mirrored lobby, then rode an elevator up to the fourth floor, where they entered 4D, Breen's apartment. The place was decorated in a masculine style, but basic stuff—a dark-colored leather couch and two chairs, plus a chunky glass coffee table—nothing overly drenched in testosterone.

Charlize zeroed in on the kitchen, located to the right of the front door and past a small dining room with a gate-legged table in lacquered black, able to seat four or expand to six. The kitchen was open, with a wide countertop that doubled as a bar, four stools set in front. It was a spacious kitchen, good for all kinds of cooking. It would be nice if Charlize's kitchen—in her *own* place—was styled the same, although better stocked. Breen only had one frying pan, one saucepan, and one chef's knife.

Before Toni left, Charlize asked for Marissa's phone number, then got on the horn right away to her friend to borrow some kitchen supplies. Charlize still had five days left of her sentence with Breen, and the hell if she was going to spend them with her thumb up her ass, nothing better to do than listen to Breen's silence.

She spent the first day in his apartment stocking up on cookware and food, then the next day she started inventing new recipes for when she would chef at Marissa's Restaurant. Since she needed a taster, she did, in fact, feed the enemy.

Breen seemed to like everything she set in front of him—*seemed* because she didn't get much more out of him than an eyebrow flicker, a twitch of the lips, or a flash of extra brightness in his eyes. Those appeared to be his high-dollar emotions.

He dressed the same way every day, in a pair of cargo shorts that reached down to his knees, black Converse sneakers, and a T-shirt with some sort of rock band on it. While she cooked and futzed around, he spent their confinement working out with weights, playing video games, and doing other mundane stuff that never took him very far from her, although his need to be near her bettered. The day she was able to pee by herself was a day to celebrate with high kicks and splits, or maybe dance around singing *Flo Rida's* "Good Feeling."

He didn't talk to her unless she spoke to him, and he never touched her.

Except once.

Four days into her imprisonment, she woke in the middle of the night to find him sucking blood from her wrist…oh, yeah, that was called "feeding." She thought she'd been having a wet dream—the onset of an orgasm was what woke her— but it was actually Breen's fiinţă elixir giving her pleasure.

When he was done, he gently laid her hand on her stomach, then turned over and fell asleep.

She stared at the back of his head, breathing roughly, teeth clenched against the unsatisfied throb in her labia. Seeing as she was no longer royally pissed at him—it was difficult to stay mad at a man who did so little to provoke her—sex was back on the table. He was a tasty snack in his own right, wasn't he? But when she reached out to him, her fingers shook, and she pulled her hand back. She rolled onto her spine and stared at the ceiling for half the night.

What was this place doing to her?

At the end of this strangest week ever, she and Breen were called into Toni's office on the first floor of the hospital at the end of a long hall. The office was expansive and bright, and decorated with large, solid-looking furniture of blond wood: a grouping of couch, chairs, coffee table, and sideboard to the right of the door, a large desk to the left. Plus, straight across from the main entrance, was a frosted glass door which led to what appeared to be a garden—difficult to tell for sure through frosted glass.

Breen and Charlize sat in two chairs in front of Toni's imposing desk.

Donree, the dark-haired note-taker from court—apparently, primarily Toni's assistant—offered them coffee. They both declined.

Charlize was in no mood to dawdle since freedom was now within her grasp. The hot topic of today's meeting had better be about her moving out. She couldn't get away from Breen fast enough. She'd lost some of her edge since being stuck with him—when did *she* not jump a guy's shit and fuck him if she wanted to? "So I can leave Breen's apartment now, right, and move into my own place?" So, okay, she might be feeling a tad impatient. "The bonding week is over?"

Breen shifted in his chair.

Charlize didn't look at him. She didn't have to; she knew what she'd see. *Nothing.* He would be blank-faced, as usual. He was the oddest man ever.

Toni slowly sipped coffee from a mug with a big daisy painted on it. "I know you and Breen have had an unconventional beginning to your relationship—and I have no idea how far you two managed to come over the last week—but if you live together as man and wife, you can both work toward achieving some kind of intimacy."

Charlize clenched her hands in her lap, even though she'd figured this was coming. She understood from both Toni and the manual—which she'd read front to back, thank you—that in Vârcolac land, being bonded meant being married.

But, *intimacy.* The word itself was a punch. The concept was a cancerous tumor. Or maybe it was a joke, because she had the strange urge to laugh. Even if she wanted intimacy—hah!—trying to achieve it with a man who showed about as much emotion as a kabocha squash would be like trying to wedge her entire fist into her mouth: not worth the pain and effort for something that would end up being all for show, anyway. Not anything deep or meaningful, because such things never were.

A boyfriend—or husband or mate or whatever—

inevitably did some kind of man thing to ruin it. She didn't have personal proof of this. She'd never had a long-term boyfriend of her own. But she'd seen enough romantic relationships bust apart—and all the reasons why—not to let herself be stupid enough to try one.

Dev and Marissa *might* have pulled it off. Charlize remembered her first day here, in court, when Marissa and her husband exchanged a look of such deep love. But Charlize was no Marissa, so settled and sure of what she wanted. And Breen the Weird-o Drone was no Dev Nichita, Harley-riding stud, dedicated husband, and clearly a doting father to his little daughter. Dev had probably delivered on every promise he ever made…until the day he wouldn't.

"A week ago," Charlize reminded tightly, "you mentioned 'options for the future.' I assumed you meant there were more than one."

Toni sat back. "The other option is for you to act as no more than Breen's blood donor. You and he would reside apart, live separate lives, and when it came to feedings, he could take blood from you when he required it, but only from your wrist. There would be no intimate contact between you whatsoever."

She jumped on it—no intimacy, *perfect*. There was more than one man out in town to be her fuck buddy. "I choose option two."

Toni paused. She took a sip of coffee. "Are you sure?"

"Yes." Charlize said the word with firm resolve, and so didn't understand why a pit opened up inside her as she watched Toni stand, stride over to a file cabinet, and pull out a key.

"Okay, this is to apartment 4B." Toni handed the key to Charlize. "You can room with Hadley Wickstrum." Toni sat. "On another matter, off topic, one of your outgoing emails was flagged by security." She picked up a piece of paper from her desk. "You responded to your mother using the term underground community. You can't—"

"Waitaminute," Charlize cut in, heat seeping into her scalp. "You read my private email?"

Toni set the paper down. "It wasn't our intention to invade your privacy, Charlize. This community just has certain security parameters regarding emails and texts. Eventually the guidelines will become second nature to you, but until then, I recommend that before you send any messages, you double-check the list of security 'don'ts' I gave you."

Charlize squeezed her crossed legs together. Toni *had* to have read the contents of her email.

And sure enough—

Toni's expression softened. "Please know that the community is ultimately here to support you. Is there anything we can do to help your mother? I can send Kimberly up to—"

"No," Charlize hurried in, "thank you. My mother's just in the drunk tank again." To her horror, tears welled. She stood abruptly. "May I go now?"

Toni took a moment to search Charlize's face. "Of course."

Charlize whirled around, clutching her new apartment key to her chest, the endless pit inside her widening, supports falling away as she rushed out, leaving Breen sitting silently, head bowed, behind.

✦   ✦   ✦

BREEN SET A COURSE FOR Garwald's Pub, the soles of his shoes scuffing the cave floor as he stumped along. He couldn't seem to pick up his feet all the way. He also wasn't sure if he was really on board with the idea of getting drunk at Garwald's—he generally didn't do that sort of thing. His mind just seemed to be stuck in unthinking, mechanical lockstep with his feet, going wherever he needed to go for a break from all the fuck that'd just happened in Toni's office.

What better place to check out than at the bottom of some nameless bottle of—?

His lower thigh vibrated.

He stopped and reached into one of the bottom pockets of his cargo pants, digging out his cell phone. He checked the screen.

Dev wanted to see him in the gym right away.

Breen stuffed his phone away, this time into a regular pocket, and kept his hand in there with it. He re-directed toward the mansion. Self-immolation sounded better than working out right now, but at least exercise wouldn't lead to a hangover.

Breen entered the gym and found Dev right inside, re-stocking the cubbies. There were about twenty-five of them built into the wall just to the left of the gym door. Some cubbies were filled with athletic gear and extra clothing, others were left empty so people could store stuff there while they worked out.

"Hey, Dalakis." Dev tossed in a last roll of white athletic tape. "How you doing with your first day back in town? You still twitchy at all?" Dev was asking if Breen still felt aggressive toward males. Some newly-bonded Vârcolac took longer than the seven days of The Change to let go of this urge completely.

He shook his head. His belly was just warped so far out of shape, it was difficult not to upchuck whenever he moved.

Dev leaned a palm on the edge of one of the cubbies. "How did your meeting with Toni go?"

Bile churned at the base of Breen's throat. He burrowed his hands deeper into his pockets. His fingernails were about to gouge through the seams. "You know…"

Dev's brows went up. Clearly he didn't know.

"Charlize is going to share an apartment with Hadley."

"Yeah? How's that going to work between you two?"

Breen shrugged, his hands still in his pockets. "She's going to be my blood donor."

"Really?" Dev paused. "That's it?"

"Yeah."

"Shit."

"Yeah." Stupid of him to have assumed it could've been more. He'd just… hell, he thought he and Charlize had come to some sort of peace accord over the last week together. So when she outright refused to give their relationship even a shot, he actually let himself be surprised. What harm could there have been in trying?

"Sorry, Breen." Dev exhaled. "We were all hoping for a better result."

"Yeah." *Me, too.* He didn't say anything more about it, though. He was never sure about how to put words to what was going on inside him. Not that Dev was Dr. Phil, anyway.

"She probably just needs to figure some shit out," Dev said. "Give her time. She'll come around."

Breen nodded. It was good advice, and Dev always seemed to have it to dole out. Dev and Breen weren't super tight—Dev tended to hang out with his Spec Ops teammates and Breen with his gamer buddies—but there weren't many men Breen respected more.

"Anyway." Dev straightened off the cubby. "Main reason I called you here is to promote you to the Special Operations Topside Team, if you're interested."

Breen shifted his eyebrows up. This was a blower. The Special Ops Topside Team was the community's elite, four-man security unit who dealt with problems topside.

These days that almost exclusively concerned the shit stirred up by Videon, a half-Răn, half-Fey psychopath who used to be controlled by Toni's long-lost father, Raymond Parthen, but not anymore. About three years ago Videon went rogue, and now he wasn't under anyone's control but his own. And considering what a demented fuck he was, that was a very bad thing. Worse, Videon had amassed a considerable force several years ago by using something called an "un-protection ritual" to steal power in the form of special warrior souls from particular Irishmen. Videon transplanted the power to his own men via amulets, leaving those poor Irish guys dead.

No one had ever figured out how Videon performed the ritual. He would've needed an active enchantment skill to pull it off, and the only way he could have switched on his Fey side was by getting loaded up with a couple shots of fiinţă. And no way had a Vârcolac female bitten that sadist. But he *had* managed it, ultimately stealing seven souls before he was stopped.

Now Videon and his group of amulet-wearing thugs were using their stolen power in some very pervy ways. Latest was that Videon had created a playland for California's depraved, offering up some pretty sick illegal activities: gambling, drugs, cockfights and other forms of animal torture, etcetera—and the worst, a rape club, where degenerate men paid exorbitant prices for the revolting pleasure of forcing themselves on an assortment of unfortunate women.

The Spec Ops Topside Team's primary goal was to put a stop to it, but whatever Otherworldly power Videon and his thugs were wielding blocked the Vârcolac warriors. Somehow Videon had been able to wrap the buildings housing his perverse activities in an invisible, impenetrable bubble. The best Dev's team had been able to do so far was save some women before they were kidnapped for the rape club.

Breen was all about ridding the world of Videon and his scumbag friends, but since when was he thought of as an "elite" warrior?

"Why me?" he asked.

The question made Dev smile. "You're a great fighter, Dalakis, and you keep your cool when the shit hits. I haven't used you before because you couldn't handle all the scents up top. But you're a bonded male now, so it's no longer an issue."

"What about Sedge or Nyko?" Both those warriors had worked Spec Ops in the past. "I don't want to bump either of them."

Dev shook his head. "Sedge has two kids at home and a wife who works full-time. He only wants homeguard shifts. And Nyko sticks out too much topside, so he's not right for this team. You fit my requirements, Dalakis, and I need a solid fourth member." Dev crossed his arms. "So you in?"

There wasn't a lot to think about, really. Nothing much exciting happened in Ţărână these days, not since the truce of Războiul Jertfei de Sânge. The occasional rowdy and delinquent Om Rău sneaked through the neutral zone into Stânga Town to carouse and party and required rousting, and there were the usual town squabbles, but otherwise, it was pretty boring. And right now Breen needed a distraction.

"I'm in."

CHAPTER TWELVE

The underground community of Țărână
6:33 P.M.
Two weeks later, late November

HADLEY HATED THE HALF-DEMON HOME-WRECKER who was Thomal's wife on sight.

First off, Pandra Costache acted very nice. The smile she aimed at Hadley when she shook her hand appeared genuine, whereas Hadley's smile felt like deformed plastic, while her eyes probably visibly bulged as she stretched her peripheral vision to its utmost in order to see all the woman without, you know, using obvious "elevator eyes."

Pandra was extremely pretty—another mark against—her hair a luxuriant golden waterfall flowing down her back, her face a Grecian sculpture, and her body overly fit in the kind of way only achieved through supernatural genes. Yes, Hadley was going with that excuse.

From her inspection, Hadley couldn't find anything to explain how a former rapist was now one of the community's elementary school teachers. Or what on earth kind of mother this Pandra person could possibly make. Hadley couldn't imagine it being a good one, although her assessment probably wasn't being helped by her first introduction to Pandra happening two days after Thanksgiving.

Four years ago, *on* Thanksgiving, Pandra had raped Thomal, her cruel act not only leaving Hadley's relationship with Thomal in a smoldering ruin, but destroying Thomal's brother, Arc, as well. Pandra also abused Arc that fateful night, and—according to scuttlebutt—he never fully recovered.

Wherever Pandra went in town, Arc generally tried to avoid the same location. So understandably he and his wife, Beth, weren't here at this taster party being given by Marissa, Charlize, and Lara for a small group of friends. "Marissa's Restaurant" would reopen in two weeks' time as the aptly named "Three Friends' Place," and this was a pre-celebration party.

Chelsea and Gábor Pavenic were among the gathered friends. Hadley met both of them more than four years ago at a cocktail party thrown in the mansion's garden parlor.

Gábor was a smart-mouthed warrior with black hair buzzed down to a mere stubble, dark bedroom eyes, and a bull skull tattoo wrapping his left bicep. Chelsea was a petite blonde spitfire who couldn't hold her liquor, and tonight they laughingly reminisced about how she got drunk at the cocktail party and claimed a vampire's fangs compensated for his small weenie. In Chelsea's defense, none of them had known they were standing in a roomful of vampires. Chelsea was one of the women who'd been caught in the recent Ovulation Disaster, like Nyko's wife, Faith, and she was sporting a pregnancy bump.

Relatively new to Hadley were Charlize—although they were becoming fast friends as roomies—and Lara. Hadley also didn't know Lara's invitees, two black-haired male Vârcolac, Kardos and Amza.

Kardos was Lara's squeeze.

According to the never-ending flow of scuttlebutt, Lara met Kardos on her first day in town. When she arrived at her new apartment, Lara discovered the garbage disposal was broken and the sink clogged. She'd called a plumber.

In walked Kardos.

Lara took one look at the man in a tool belt and went gaga.

Kardos fell equally hard for her in one glance—or one

whiff, since Vârcolac could often tell a potential mate by scent.

Lara, now soaring on the bliss of instant love and eager for someone else to feel the same, had set up Hadley on a date with Amza, a plumber buddy of Kardos's, for tonight's taster.

Instant love was not to be.

Not even close.

Amza was just...he was... God, he was a *plumber*.

Hadley winced. Even inside her own head that sounded horribly stuck up. She was having a hard enough night already without turning into her *mother*—ragging on a man for being a plumber was something Fallon Wickstrum would do, not *her*. Hadn't Hadley divorced a mega-successful breadwinner for the sake of her own happiness, something her mother would never have done? *Precisely.* Hadn't Hadley likewise resolved to date a more average Joe type, a guy just like Amza? *Yes. Exactly.* And in Ţărână, weren't the plumbers very well-thought-of, revered as engineering geniuses for having invented a system able to bring water down from one-half mile above and dispose of waste discreetly *That's, you know, super wow, right?*

Hadley secretly rolled her eyes at herself. Now she sounded lame, or like an overly-pampered princess, which she kind of was. Hadley was born eight weeks premature, and even though she'd never been a sickly child, her mother always fussed over her a lot. The extra attention made Hadley feel very cared for...except for times like now when her thoughts turned all judgy. Then she just felt spoiled.

"Okay, these are the next goodies," Lara said as she set a rectangular tray of finger food on the tall countertop in front of the partygoers.

The chefs' workstation sat just behind this tall counter, where Charlize, Marissa, and Lara stood, chatting and cooking and radiating cheer. All three chefs wore their hair pulled up and were dressed in pristine white, their outfits identical, although each sported a different style of hat: Marissa wore a French beret, Lara, a toque—the typical puffed-up popover chef hat—and Charlize, a plucky beanie.

"These are Roasted Carrot Harissa Crostini," Lara clarified. "Careful, they're a little spicy."

Everyone took a crostini except for Hadley and Breen. They were standing several feet back from the tall counter, a couple of leprosy-ridden loners, no partners to love them. If Breen was at the original cocktail party way back in the day, Hadley couldn't remember him. He was the type of man who tended to fade into the wallpaper—although now she would probably always think of him as Boner Man.

Kardos didn't take a crostini sample either, but only because both his hands were still full of other treats. So Lara picked up a crostini and fed it to him. Their gazes locked on each other with identical looks of sensual warmth.

Get a room. Hadley didn't say it, but, jeez.

While everyone made yum-yum noises, Hadley edged forward and filched two crostini. She gave one to Breen.

He un-shoved his hands from his pockets long enough to accept it with a nod of thanks. He didn't eat it.

His lips were probably too busy compressing over Charlize's laughter. His wife was being wholly entertained by something Amza just said, and the plumber was lapping up Charlize's attention. After Hadley's lukewarm reception of him—she'd *tried* to be nice—Amza's bruised pride probably needed some serious tending, and who better to give a man a lift than a knockout like Charlize?

Hadley gnashed off a bite of crostini, chewed, then discreetly spit it out into a napkin. It *was* too spicy. She took Breen's crostini back and tossed it in the trash with hers.

Breen gave her another nod of thanks.

She glanced around for her wine. She needed to pour more alcohol on this party, now.

"Here's Short Rib Ragù," Charlize said, "served on a

biscuit." She set out a small tray, and everyone reached for a sample at once. Charlize's biscuits were already legendary.

Amza was still dealing with his crostini, so Charlize copy-catted Lara and held her ragù creation to Amza's mouth for him to try, and—

And then Amza was no more.

Several women gasped.

Hadley blinked at the empty space where Amza had just been. It happened so quickly, she wasn't able to follow the exact chain of events, only that one minute Amza was wrapping his lips around Charlize's offered treat, then the next he was on the floor, rolling on his back and groaning.

Breen was standing over him with knotted fists, his fangs half-elongated.

Bright blood poured from Amza's mouth.

Oh, dear Lord... Breen had punched Amza!

Gábor snorted.

Thomal cursed under his breath.

"That's my wife," Breen said in a low tone.

Charlize's cheeks reddened. "I'm not your wife, you fuck-ing piece of shit."

Amza grimaced in pain. He was now minus a front tooth. This upped his Huckleberry-Billy-Bob number while simultaneously plummeting his potential boyfriend score down even lower than the zero it'd been all night.

Oh, God, she didn't mean to be so rude. It was just that...*I mean, Amza is...*

Come on.

He was a man who'd invented a brilliant sewage system.

Mute, Dev strode over and pulled Amza to his feet.

THE PARTY BROKE UP AFTER that.

Hadley downed the last of her wine while she watched two on-duty warriors usher Breen and Charlize off to pay the piper with Toni.

Kardos took Amza to the community dentist, and Lara went along.

The rest of them loitered in the street outside Three Friends' Place.

"Soooo," Gábor drawled, scratching the side of his face, "do you think 'fucking piece of shit' is Charlize's regular pet name for Breen, or does she sometimes go with, you know, 'cocksucking motherfucker.'"

Thomal snorted out a laugh.

"It's not funny." Chelsea scolded. "Those two are in a horrible position." She reached down to adjust the strap on her three-inch high heels. The small woman definitely needed the extra height, but her sticking-out belly threw off her equilibrium, and she bobbled the move.

Gábor steadied his wife.

"I can't imagine being bonded to a man I didn't love," Chelsea added.

"I don't know what kind of position *she's* in," Gábor said in a dry tone. "But Breen is being tortured. He had to watch his mate practically stick her fingers in another dude's mouth." Gábor flashed Marissa a look. "What the hell's the matter with your friend, anyway?"

Sighing, Marissa swept off her beret with a tired gesture. "Charlize is a bit of a wild girl."

"A *bit*." Gábor made a sound in this throat like a drain backing up. "She's off her fucking cork. No wonder Dalakis had to pull a domination bite on her."

Marissa frowned. "A what?"

From one step behind Marissa, Dev shook his head vigorously at Gábor.

Gábor scrunched his forehead at Dev but then kept talking. "A domination bite." He tapped a spot above his collarbone, the same place where Charlize had worn a bruise after bonding with Breen.

Hadley had spotted the leftovers of the bruise the day

Charlize and Breen toured the family neighborhood with Toni.

"Goes back to the old days," Gábor went on, "when vampires used to mate with vampires. It was a way for a male to get his woman under control, if, you know, she got too uppity."

"*Excuse* me?" Marissa's voice rang with outrage. "Get his woman under *what* if she got too *what*?"

Rubbing the side of his nose, Dev raised his eyes to the cave ceiling.

"Yeah...huh? What's the big deal?" Gábor shot a look at Dev.

Marissa likewise rounded on her husband.

Dev lifted both hands, palms out. "I'm going to stand here and very much enjoy not discussing this."

"Oh, for fuck's sake." Gábor gestured brusquely. "It's not like we use the bite anymore. Vârcolac females are strong as fuck and used to be prone to violence, so males needed a way to ratchet down a fight if things spun too far out of control. But you Dragons"—Gábor affectionately chucked his wife under the chin—"are soft as little lambs."

Chelsea slapped at his hand. "Is that why you've never used a domination bite on me? Because you don't think I'm tough enough to cause you problems?" She narrowed her eyes and glared.

Pandra reached over and pinched Thomal's ear. Kind of aggressively, it seemed.

"Yeah, yeah," Thomal drawled, "I see you there."

Gábor pushed his lips out as he considered his wife. "Is this one of those times when no matter what I say, I'm in trouble?"

Chelsea crossed her arms and thrust out a hip. "Maybe you're not the only one who has a domination move, smart guy. Maybe I've got one. Did you ever think of that?"

Gábor chuckled. "You don't weigh any more than a wet

boot. Well…" He smirked at his wife's belly. "Maybe not *now*."

Chelsea's gaze swept over her husband indolently. "So you're saying you don't think I can dominate you?"

Chortling, Gábor scanned the group. "Is this a trick question?"

Chelsea grabbed Gábor's hand. "We'll just see about that." She marched off toward home, tugging her husband along with her.

Gábor glanced back over his shoulder and waggled Groucho Marx eyebrows at them.

✧   ✧   ✧

"I'M IN TROUBLE AGAIN, AREN'T I?"

When Charlize asked this question, Breen didn't look at her. He sat in a chair in front of Toni's desk with his forearms resting on the armrests and his fingertips splayed wide on top of his thighs, keeping his focus on his bruised knuckles.

The timing for being called on the carpet before Toni totally blew. She just had a knock-down, drag-out with Jacken—Breen heard the two yelling at each other while waiting outside her office with Charlize—and when Donree showed Breen and Charlize to their seats, Toni looked about as unhappy as he'd ever seen her: eyes piercing, jaw held at an inflexible angle, a vein prominent between her eyebrows.

Toni's patience was clearly already sitting at a negative integer, and *I'm in trouble again, aren't I?* was answered with a firm chop of her hand in Breen's direction. "You are *bonded* to this man, Charlize. I don't know how many different ways I can tell you this to make you understand."

"I do understand," Charlize shot back. "What I also *understand* is that I agreed to be Breen's blood donor only. You said he and I would lead separate lives. I assumed this meant we could date other people."

The tips of Breen's fingers whitened on his thighs.

She…wants to date other men?

"You assumed incorrectly," Toni contradicted in a cool tone. "Being bonded to Breen means you are *his* woman. Whether you chose to reside with him or not, the biology of your bond remains an indisputable fact."

"For *him*, maybe. But I'm not Vârcolac, so I'm not restricted by a biological bond. I can fuck other people if I want to without my brain imploding."

Toni stilled.

Breen swiveled his head in a steady motion until it was turned to the side enough for him to look at Charlize. If he moved any faster, he wasn't sure what he'd do. He was barely maintaining control over the sudden jealousy and possessiveness roaring through him, his veins practically bleeding acid with it.

Technically, what Charlize just said was true. Her biology would let her have sex with another man—not that anyone would end up living through the experience.

Charlize did a quick scan of their faces. "Hey, sorry," she said, tossing her hands negligently in the air. "Just keeping it real here. I have needs, okay? And I haven't been laid in three weeks."

Toni inhaled a measured breath. "Male Vârcolac are very territorial, Charlize. To the bonded side of Breen, you two *are* married. If you sleep with another man, it would be considered an act of infidelity, and in this community, that's a crime."

"A *crime?* You've *got* to be kidding me."

"I'm being very serious," Toni answered her flatly. "The mated bond is sacred. Willful disregard of it is punishable with jail time. Any more flirtatious actions on your part will land you back in court."

"Flirtatious…? Oh, for God's sake. I was just *talking* to Amza, not—"

"You were feeding another man with your fingers. That's

flirting. Behavior even remotely flirtatious is unacceptable." Toni gave her a stern look. "There can be no touching. No coy smiles. No tossing your hair or batting your eyelashes. No conduct that could possibly be misconstrued as innuendo or seduction in any way whatsoever. I very much need you to make a special effort to understand what I'm saying here, Charlize."

Charlize's complexion turned scarlet and her eyebrows furled into a tangled knot. She sat in fulminating silence for a moment, her breathing erratic, then demanded, "So who the hell can I fuck in this tight-wad town?"

Toni gestured at him. "Breen."

Charlize blasted air. "You said there wasn't supposed to be any intimate contact between us!"

"Yes," Toni agreed. "But that's because you chose to be Breen's donor *only*. There can be no halfway within the bonded relationship."

Breen looked up.

"It's either an exclusive and intact marital union with all the attendant intimacies," Toni continued, "or the celibate life of a donor."

"What the ungodly fuck?!" Charlize went rigid in her chair. "Celibate?! Are you crazy? It didn't say anything about celibacy in the manual."

Because it wasn't true.

Once a Vârcolac couple was bonded, they could fuck like bunnies. Living together generally wasn't an issue, because most Vârcolac marriages were happy ones…although sometimes things went haywire. Dev's parents, Pettrila and Grigore Nichita, were a prime example of a married couple who'd never particularly liked each other, but fed for requisite blood and probably occasionally went horizontal. Not an optimal situation, but do-able. Breen didn't know why Toni was making it sound un-do-able, but when he glanced at her, the muscles on the side of her cheek facing him flexed, as if to warn him not to contradict her. She was probably working a plan he couldn't see.

He kept his mouth shut.

"The mistake in the manual will be rectified," Toni said coolly. "The community has never dealt with a situation like yours and Breen's before, so—"

"Then maybe," Charlize cut in, speaking in short, irritated syllables, "you should approach it with a little more leeway."

Toni eyed her stonily. "I'm afraid the natural laws of Vârcolac culture cannot be rewritten, Charlize, even for a reason as important as your sex life."

Charlize's face blazed red again, darker than before.

A soreness bloomed in Breen's chest, dead center, right where his radar was. Every Vârcolac formed a sixth-sense connection to his bonded mate, this radar-like link allowing him to pick up on her emotions. Breen's was currently telling him that Charlize was very upset...which he could see well enough for himself. Her profile was cracking, the lines at the sides of her eyes beginning to resemble fissures.

He knuckled the sore spot. Man, he felt really bad for her. Charlize didn't deserve this. *He* was the one who'd bitten her when she didn't know what was what. *He* was the one who'd relentlessly gone after her until she agreed to have sex with him. *He* was the one who'd punched Amza and got them dragged here, which was a shame on a lot of levels. A trained warrior should never haul off and hit a normal citizen, and Amza was a good guy.

"Have I made everything clear?" Toni asked tersely.

Charlize's mouth seamed into such a tight, embittered line, her lips nearly disappeared.

Toni waited.

A clock ticked, but softly, with well-oiled mechanisms. Out in the hall, Donree wished a good evening to Dr. Jess, the other community doctor, a tall, lean Vârcolac, who kept himself so neat and sanitary, he verged on prissy and—

Breen's brainwaves did an up-spike when Charlize rounded on him with savagely narrowed eyes. "You're not going to say anything about this? You're just going to sit there like a lump?"

He stared at her. And stared some more—so apparently the answer was, *yeah*. But he hadn't expected to be drawn into this part of the conversation. He'd prepped for having his balls busted for hitting Amza, not for this.

"Jesus," Charlize hissed. Rounding on Toni again, she gestured rigidly at him. "How the hell do you expect me to form a relationship with a man who shows about as much emotion as a potted plant?" Tears brimmed in her eyes, then her throat pumped and spasmed, and her jawline stretched taut.

Breen twisted his lips out of alignment. Watching her try not to cry was almost worse than her actual crying.

She lost the battle long enough for a single tear to slip onto her bottom lashes, and the look in her eyes turned childlike, as if she were a kid who just broke her mother's favorite vase and had been seriously reamed out for it.

It sent Breen's lungs collapsing to the floor, this private moment with her younger, scared, sort of lonely side. He realized then—somehow, he didn't know how—that she didn't really want to date or screw another man.

She just wanted *someone*.

CHAPTER THIRTEEN

"FINALLY, I WIN A ROUND." John Waterson swept the pile of poker chips toward him and laughed. Then stopped laughing when the movement of his lungs bumped them painfully against his ribs.

Pablo grinned. "There's a first time for everything." He laughed, too, generous enough to be happy for John's score. Probably because it happened so rarely.

What usually happened was that John took wild risks with his money and lost an imprudent amount during his weekly poker nights with his police buddies. Which was probably the only reason they still came. 'Course the excuse the detectives would've given, if asked, was that they were supporting a sick friend. But being forced to witness said friend wither and waste was sometimes visibly uncomfortable for the three men, and John knew they would've found excuses to bow out long ago if not for the money they were raking in.

A part of John would've been okay with them ditching him, even though his buddies equaled the grand total of his human contact these days. His friends were everything John wasn't anymore—successful, working men in good health— and some nights he could feel himself staring so intensely at the three, at their glowing skin and robust bodies, his eyeballs practically bled.

Right now he was all but drooling as Carlos, Pablo's new

partner, wolfed down one of the deli sandwiches John had ordered delivered—he couldn't drive anymore. Or *eat*, for that matter. His only sustenance these days was coffee, cigarettes, and an occasional carton of Ramen noodles.

How he was still upright on earth, he couldn't figure. He now resembled something that should be hanging in front of someone's house on Halloween. Probably the revenge deal he'd struck with MoonRiderOne had pissed off God, and so he was being tortured. Or maybe he hadn't switched into "acceptance mode" as thoroughly as he thought he had, but still harbored the vain, stupid, futile hope he'd go into remission again.

His last remission had been four long years ago. Oh-so-coincidentally, it happened soon after he went to Kansas to see his mother, Maggie, who he visited expressly to ask about his disease—a weird ailment called Blestem Tatălui. Specifically, he asked her about the strange element in his blood.

Were the two related?

Maggie claimed she didn't know, but she'd shown all the signs of someone who was lying: darting eyes, a fine dew on her forehead, unfinished gestures. What possible motivation would his mother have for hiding that kind of information from him? If she gave him all the facts about his disease, he could possibly get better.

He returned to San Diego frustrated, but then—*ala-kazam*. He *did* improve. The pills he took—which arrived magically on his doorstep without prescription or payment—suddenly started working again…as if, *hmm*, his mother reported John's worsening condition to someone, and that someone altered the composition of the pills.

He supposed a good detective would've gone back to his mother and asked more questions, but a superstitious side of him hadn't wanted to mess with feeling so damned good. Ask too many questions and maybe he would rattle loose what he'd gained.

He enjoyed three full years of good, if not great, health

before the rug was ripped out from under him again. And this time he went downhill with alarming speed. Within six months after his relapse, he was too sick to hide his symptoms: the shakes, an obscene amount of sweating, the rapid weight loss resulting from a hunger that clawed at his belly, but, ironically, made it impossible for him to eat.

He had no choice but to admit to Pablo what was going on, then go on medical leave.

He'd spent the past six months stewing in bitterness about the hand life dealt him. He had nothing. A few memories of the pleasant years spent as a cowboy in Kansas, plus his successful career as a cop, and that was it. No warm reminiscences of what was truly important—things like a loving wife, strawberry-blonde, sexy, and smart, and of doting children, of a house with a weeping willow in the front yard and skateboards strewn in the driveway, a dog or two underfoot.

Nothing. Nothing but a one-bedroom apartment with a leaky toilet and a refrigerator that periodically went on the fritz. He had nothing, and he *was* nothing. No more than an obligation for police buddies who would rather be home with their families instead of sitting here watching John teeter in his chair and chew the inside of his cheek raw in order to keep his constant need to groan down his—

John's phone beeped softly from where it sat facedown on the table.

No one was allowed to check their phones during play, but Frank, out of homicide, was in the middle of dealing, so John turned his cell over and checked the screen. He'd just received an email. He clicked it, and "MoonRiderOne" popped up in the *from* line. Fingers trembling, he opened it.

There were only four typed words: "All is in place."

John precisely placed his phone back in its original spot and kept his palm on top of it. If nothing else, *finally*, he would have one thing in his life.

Revenge.

Chapter Fourteen

Hands stuffed deep in his pockets, Breen leaned back against a wall in the shadow of the Teague Sisters' Dance Studio situated across the street from Three Friends' Place and watched Charlize though the restaurant's glass front. She was the chef on shift tonight for the grand reopening, and the place was packed.

Along with a lot of other people, the same couples who were at the tasting party were there—Dev and Marissa, Gábor and Chelsea, Lara and Kardos, Thomal and Pandra. Not Amza or Hadley or Breen, though. Breen couldn't be sure about the first two, but he knew he wouldn't have been welcomed.

All the diners were giving Charlize a lot of compliments, and she seemed to be really riding high on them all. Every time someone stopped at the tall counter to gush, her eyes would shine when she smiled. That was cool to see.

What blew was that he had to sneak around in order to see it.

Over the last month he'd made a habit out of spying on Charlize a lot, catching her at Cosmopolitan Night with the girls, at hip-hop dance class, at the running club she'd started. He also bumped into her here and there in their apartment building—she lived only two doors down—which had given him the opportunity to move things along with her.

Which he'd failed at miserably.

One time they met in the hallway, and he took grocery bags out of her arms and carried them into her apartment for her. Then stood by her kitchen, awkward and silent, before saying, "Okay, 'bye." A couple of other times he stepped onto the elevator at the same time she did. He said, "Hey." Then just stood there, awkward and silent, until the doors whished open, and then, "Okay, 'bye."

Big surprise that there remained nothing between them.

So how's the restaurant biz going?

Are you still planning to run marathons?

Why couldn't he have made his voice box produce shit like *that*? Strike up a casual, friendly conversation with her, be suave, make it okay for her to hang out with him.

He scraped his fingernails over the seams at the bottoms of his pockets. He wasn't a smooth talker on his best day, but lay the pressure of the future of his entire relationship with Charlize on his conversational abilities, and his tongue pretty much went into hyper-lock. He couldn't—

His cell vibrated.

He reached down and fished it out of his bottom pocket.

Inside the restaurant, Dev, Gábor, and Thomal went for their phones at the same time.

THE SPECIAL OPS TOPSIDE TEAM was called to Toni's office on an emergency summons.

They dropped everything to go—not that Breen was doing anything more important than spying on his wife—and when they arrived, Jacken, the warriors' overall boss, was already there, along with Alex Parthen.

Toni's brother, who had blondish-reddish hair like his sister, was a seer of many things by virtue of him being both a Soothsayer—his enchantment skill—and a computer expert. He was the type of guy who probably had his ass cheeks duct-taped together a lot in high school, dressing the part in tan Dockers, a plaid button-down with a pocket protector, and a pair of wire-rimmed glasses. Alex was bonded to Dev's sister, Luvera, and they had a son, named after his father, but in the Romanian tradition, Alexandru. They called him Alec.

Dev, Thomal, and Breen lined up in front of Toni's desk, while Gábor plopped down on the couch.

Breen glanced over his shoulder at him.

Gábor stretched out, lacing his fingers behind his head and crossing his feet at the ankles. "Just tell me who I need to kill."

"What's up?" Dev asked Toni.

Toni held out a piece of paper to Dev. "An old email account Alex monitors just reactivated. It's the one the Topside Om Răul used four years ago when they kidnapped Marissa and Hadley."

The Topside Om Rău were a relatively new faction of bad guys run by Raymond Parthen, Toni's uber-powerful father. For clarity's sake, the community referred to these guys as the "Topside Om Rău," and Ţărână's nasty neighbors living in Oţărât as the "Underground Om Rău." Usually the two demon races had nothing to do with each other, but four years ago, the Topside Om Rău arranged to give Marissa and Hadley—and another woman named Kendra—to the Underground Om Rău. The Spec Ops Team stuck a pin in the plan by saving the three women before the handoff could be completed.

Dev looked up from reading the message. "They're planning another exchange?"

Toni gestured at the paper. "It appears so."

Thomal's eyebrows shot up. "Doesn't that break the truce?"

"Not necessarily," Jacken stepped in. "The Underground Om Rău agreed not to steal our women from *down here*. There's nothing in the contract preventing them from going for women topside."

Dev rubbed a hand over his goatee as he reread the email.

"It still doesn't make sense. The Underground Om Răuˇ don't have the resources for that kind of shit anymore, not since the war."

"Agreed," Toni said. "I don't like this."

"Me either," Alex said.

Dev glanced at Alex. "Any visions about it?"

Alex sighed thickly. "No."

As a Soothsayer, Alex could sometimes see the future, but only if the future involved the Vârcolac. Alternatively, a lack of visions didn't mean the Vârcolac were free and clear of trouble, just that the spiritual world was staying out of it.

"I could ask the Underground Om Răuˇ about the authenticity of this message," Toni suggested, "see if it actually came from them. But that would entail me leaving a note in the neutral zone, waiting for them to obtain it, read it, and answer. *If* they even responded."

Thomal was peering over Dev's shoulder at the message. "This handoff is going down within an hour after the sun sets topside. *Tonight.*"

Toni checked the clock on her desk. "We have nine, ten hours to get an answer."

Dev shook his head. "According to what Jacken just said about the fine print of the truce, the Om Răuˇ are under no obligation to tell us dick about what they get up to when they're topside."

Toni made an open-handed gesture.

On the couch Gábor burped.

Dev's mouth tightened. "Are we just going to ignore this?"

Thomal growled low in his throat. "Not sure I could live with myself if we did, brother."

Toni looked at her husband. "Jacken?"

"No, we're not going to ignore this," Jacken clipped out. "Have your team head to the address listed in the email and *observe only.* Get dialed in on what's really going down with this bullshit, and don't act unless fully warranted."

Dev set the paper on Toni's desk. "I can live with that."

"Be careful." Jacken crossed his arms. "I don't like this, either."

CHAPTER FIFTEEN

BREEN PLUGGED HIS LEGS INTO his black cargo pants, hitched them over his hips, then buttoned, zipped, and belted. Next his shirt went on.

The other Spec Ops Team members geared up for the mission ahead around him, clattering at their lockers.

"What's the difference between a drug dealer and a hooker?" Dev asked, tugging his shirt down his torso.

Thomal planted a booted foot on the bench and started to lace up. "What?" he asked, already laughing.

"A drug dealer can't resell his crack."

A louder laugh burst out of Thomal.

Gábor cracked up too. "So we're going with butt jokes this morning?" He rooted around inside his locker. "All right, I got one. What did the cannibal do after he dumped his girlfriend?"

Nobody said anything.

Gábor grinned. "Wiped his ass."

Dev groaned. "Fuck, Pavenic."

Thomal stomped his boot to the floor. "That's not a dirty joke, douche-bucket."

"Hell if it's not," Gábor defended. "It's the ultimate in dirty."

"Dirty *gross*," Thomal countered, "not dirty sexy. You want gross? How about this: chick drops off a dress at the dry cleaners. Shop lady says, 'Come again!' Chick says, 'No, just toothpaste this time.'"

Dev's shoulders shook.

"Not bad," Gábor approved, laughing harder. "Not bad at all. But, hell, I can be grosser."

"Do *not*," Dev ordered.

Gábor found a stick of deodorant in his locker and applied it. "You're up, Dalakis."

Breen lifted his eyebrows. "What?"

"Whenever we have a holy-shit-o'clock call," Gábor explained, "we tell dirty jokes to wake up our sorry asses."

"Dirty *sexy*," Thomal clarified.

Breen shrugged. "I'm just stoked to finally be going on a real topside mission."

For the past month he'd only been patrolling Videon's regular hunting grounds with the team, looking for trouble and not finding any. He'd used the time to familiarize himself with being topside again. Last time he'd been in the city was four years ago, back when all the warriors went up to deal with an exchange Raymond Parthen arranged of Marissa—who he'd kidnapped—for Toni. A *fake* exchange, considering Jacken wouldn't let Toni get within spitting distance of her messed-up father. But a month was plenty for re-familiarizing. Now it was time for action.

Dev pulled two extra ammo clips out of his locker and jammed them into the leg pocket of his cargo pants. "Little girl says to her dad, 'How are babies made?' The dad answers, 'Daddy plants a seed in Mommy's tummy.' Girl asks, 'Oh, does she swallow the seed?' Dad says, 'Only if she wants new shoes.'"

Thomal hooted. "Oh, that's fucking bad, Nichita. I'm so telling your wife."

"Ha!" Gábor raked a gesture at Dev. "See, Dalakis?"

Breen moved over to a table where a spread of guns and knives had been brought in from the armory. He snapped a Browning .32 automatic in a holster on the right side of his belt and a drop-point knife, specially crafted for the warriors, on the left.

Gábor narrowed his eyes. "You have to be able to talk bullshit to be a member of this team."

Breen picked up a clip and started loading it with bullets, pushing them in one at a time with his thumb.

"Speaking of talking bullshit," Dev said. "Did Chelsea ever make good on her promise to dominate you?"

Gábor gave Dev a blank stare. "What?"

"Two weeks ago," Dev reminded, "after the tasting gig at Three Friends' Place. Your wife marched you off to pull a domination move on you."

Thomal chuckled. "Shit, I'd forgotten about that."

Breen looked up from his clip. "What's this?"

Thomal cut a never-mind gesture at him. "You were busy getting into deep sneakers with Toni for punching Amza."

Gábor chortled. "Oh, yeah. Chelsea pulled a move on me, all right. And you guys definitely don't want to know what it is."

The spring came tight in the magazine, and Breen put the clip in his lower pants pocket. He started to load up another.

Thomal crossed his arms over his chest and gave Gábor a pointed glare. "Spill, Pavenic."

Gábor continued to chortle. "The only thing I'm saying is that it had to do with my ass, and it was *awesome*."

Dev, who'd just grabbed a set of car keys out of his locker, froze in the act of putting them in his pocket.

Breen likewise stopped loading the second clip.

"See?" Gábor gestured at their faces. "Told ya you didn't want to know."

Thomal's mouth slanted. "Oh, I think it's just the opposite, Pavenic. I believe you have everyone's undivided attention."

"Here's what I'm thinking." Dev slipped the keys into his pocket with a rattle. "Pavenic has been dominated by a *pregnant* woman. Maybe he needs to resign from the team."

Closing his locker door, Gábor kept his hand pressed to

the front and gave Dev a bored stare.

"Now, see," Dev continued, "Costache here is married to a half-demon who's strong as fuck. We all understand it when his wife dominates him."

"She does?" Thomal stroked a thumb over one of his fangs.

Eyes bright with amusement, Dev started for the door. "Pavenic still has to pony up details about what Chelsea did to him, but he can give those in the car. It's launch time."

The rest of them followed.

As they exited into the hall, Breen asked, "What's the difference between peanut butter and jam?"

They all stopped and looked at him.

"What?" Dev obliged.

"I can't peanut butter my dick up your ass."

Dev's goatee split into a wide grin, and Thomal guffawed.

Gábor snorted. "Fuck if I want your dick anywhere near my ass, Dalakis."

Breen hitched a shoulder. "Based on the story you just told about Chelsea and what you like going on down there…maybe not."

Gábor gave him a narrow stare.

Dev exhaled a laugh from his nose. "Hey, you're the one who said Dalakis has to talk bullshit."

Topside
8:45 p.m.

THE HOUSE WHERE THE HANDOFF was supposed to take place was in the boonies of Lakeside, separated from any neighbors by an acre of forested landscape. The large A-frame structure was built of dark-paneled wood in an alpine rustic style, rising two stories high. It *should* have been an upper-middle-class home, but unkemptness added a layer of cheap. Open window shutters sagged, the lawn out front was dotted with a scattershot of crabgrass, and bird-of-paradise plants had been left to grow to the size of pelican heads.

Breen crouched behind a bush, a shadow among shadows. The night was still and nippy, with a dark blue sky, stars like glowing buttons, and an almost-full moon. He steadily watched his side of the house—the east—while the other warriors observed the north, south, and west sides.

Gábor's voice crackled through Breen's earpiece. "Anybody else *not* feeling all bunnies and rainbows about this place?"

Breen certainly didn't like what he was seeing. No lights on. No smoke wafting from the chimney. No signs or scents of human occupation. No movement. Nothing. Only a reflection of the pale fist of the moon hanging suspended in the glass of the upper window pane.

Breen pushed the speak button on the throat-mic he wore like a choker necklace. "I agree. Something's off. Nice place, but feels deserted."

Thomal weighed in. "I'm beginning to get a distinct wild-goose chase vibe here."

Dev's snort came through as a short burst of static. "Who the fuck would send us on a wild-goose chase?"

Valid point. "Any texts from Toni?" Breen asked. Maybe she'd heard from the Underground Om Rău.

"Zero," Dev answered.

They waited some more.

"Anyone picking up signs of life?" Dev asked.

"Negative," Breen said.

Thomal and Gábor responded the same.

They'd been "observing only" for close to an hour now.

Dev exhaled over comms. "Not sure I feel comfortable leaving the scene without confirming absolutely that no one's here. We need to recon inside."

The flesh on Breen's nape crawled, although why, he didn't know. Strong likelihood was this place was as abandoned as it appeared.

"Pavenic and Dalakis," Dev directed, "take the upstairs windows and meet in the middle. Costache, you head for the front door. I'll go in the back. Be the night, gentlemen."

Breen left the cover of his shrub at an easy lope and did exactly what Dev said—he sucked in the power of the moon, turning his body into organic blackness, and putting wings on his feet.

Gliding soundlessly and invisibly up to a bougainvillea straggling along the east wall of the house, he grabbed hold of the trellis underneath and started to climb up through the gnarly tentacles, hand over hand. The bougainvillea's sharp thorns scratched his cheeks and arms. He arrived at the second-story window and, keeping his head low, reached up to test it. He gave the frame a prod. It nudged up.

The window was unlocked.

Cold sweat drizzled down the channel of his spine. He wasn't bunnies and rainbows over that, either.

Shifting to the right, he eased higher and peered through the window from the corner of the pane. Sheet-covered furniture. Dust and grime. No people. No strong Dragon scent, either, although that could be the result of him having a "bonded male" nose now.

He waited. There was an unearthly quiet to everything. No wind, even. He swept the room once more. Everything remained the same.

With one thumb, he raised the window all the way open. The air inside met the air outside and didn't change temperature. It smelled like the interior of an unplugged refrigerator, sour Chablis and old, tart baby food, like mashed mangoes, and…something familiar.

He waited again.

No gutter punk gangsta jumped out at him.

He edged over to a center position, chin-upped through the window, his belly passing the frame, and landed lightly on outstretched palms. Somersaulting, he came smoothly to his feet, his hand on the butt of his pistol, adrenaline swelling in his bloodstream.

He panned the room.

No one.

He waited for a "clear" call through his earpiece. None came.

Outside, the trees murmured.

He moved a single step forward, and—

Then there was someone.

A man floated down from the rafters and landed without a single breath of sound several feet in front of him.

Breen froze.

The guy wore black pants, black boots, and no shirt, leaving exposed the interlinked circles of a strange tattoo. Almost supernaturally black in color, the geometric shapes marked his left arm and the left side of his chest. He had strange eyes, too. The irises were thunder-gray and surrounded by what looked like a string of tiny black pearls.

The familiar scent was stronger now—the man had brought it with him. Blood filled Breen's muscles as his body prepared to strike.

The guy hard-stared Breen, and the dots around his irises began to spin like well-oiled miniature ball bearings in a roulette wheel.

What the *hell*?

Breen unholstered his Browning just as shouts erupted from the first floor. Next came the basso sound of gunfire rolling up the stairs—only a quick, one-two punch of shots before the noise was cut off. Then more shouts, different voices, and Breen was pulling his own trigger.

The guy's tats spun, and the bullets from Breen's gun veered around him.

Wood pulp chunked out of the wall behind the guy.

Breen's heart thumped a couple of extra-violent beats.

The shirtless guy grinned nastily—clearly enjoying Breen's shock—and what Breen saw in that smile rooted him in place.

He could only stand there stupidly, staring at the man's mouth, not doing a single damned thing to prevent it when the guy whaled a vicious uppercut at him.

The inhumanly strong fist met the underside of Breen's chin and threw his head back. He saw the ceiling through a splintered matrix of pain right before the shutters on both eyes slammed shut.

WHEN BREEN WOKE UP HE was lying with his nose pressed to a dirty wooden floor, smelling a mixture of brambly woodsmoke, trampled bougainvillea, and Red Man or maybe Copenhagen chewing tobacco. Each of his eyelids weighed an even ton. His bruised jaw thumped. His brain was an inert blob.

He managed to scan around a little with just his eyes. He was in the house's living room, next to a pile of smashed cell phones and comm equipment, and maybe he was seeing double, because it seemed like there were a hundred bad guys around. Every one of them had hair as black as tar and were wearing dark pants and boots, many of them shirtless, like Breen's attacker had been, most with geometric tattoos on their bodies, but on different parts of the anatomy. They carried knives, some had swords—*freaky*—and Breen couldn't understand a word they were saying. Maybe his hearing was off.

Maybe he'd woken up inside *Assassin's Creed.*

A couple bad guys bent over him and roughly bound his wrists with duct tape. They hauled him to his feet, a trip he made woozily, then dragged him outside.

A fleet of rental cars had magically appeared in front of the house.

Breen was tossed into the trunk of one, trussed up—his

ankles now duct-taped too—but not gagged.

The drive to wherever they went took about twenty minutes, long enough for Breen to Humpty-Dumpty his brain back together. When the trunk lid finally opened, he was clear-headed.

A bad guy slashed the duct tape free of Breen's ankles, yanked him out of the trunk, and set him on his feet. Breen was steered through nondescript woodland, and his mind shifted into overdrive, thinking of escape options, but almost immediately discarding them. Because, *hell*, he hadn't been seeing double before—there *were* a hundred bad guys. And all the training in the world couldn't overcome the kind of problems four warriors against a C-note of inhumanly strong shitbaggers would bring on.

He saw his teammates, their bodies vague, shadowy figures interspersed among tall trees that were sparse at first, but growing thicker. Breen tried to meet their eyes to silently come up with a plan of action, maybe a coordinated assault, but even though he could see in the dark well enough with his Pure-bred eyes, the bad guys were keeping the four of them too far apart to communicate.

The crunch of multiple pairs of boots through dead leaves was the only sound. Meager darts of moonlight penetrated the snarl of bare branches overhead, and the dimness turned the landscape threatening.

If this was foreshadowing, Breen wasn't a fan.

They walked for a good ten or fifteen minutes, then finally came to a clearing where the sky opened up to a canopy of icy stars. The glade was about fifty yards across and was lorded over by a giant oak tree, its long-shafted, knobby limbs spidering across the pale moon. Two strong branches grew at right angles about twelve feet up the trunk, and several bad guys began securing chains to them: three sets on the left-side branch, one set on the right.

Dev was muscled over to the right-side branch, and

Breen's mouth went dry when the bad guys ripped Dev's shirt off. Dev quick-shifted, managing to step back and land a few kicks. But there were just too many to fight. Dev was overpowered. His wrists were bound in chains, then he was hoisted up, booted feet dangling, his bare back aimed toward the clearing.

Thomal, Gábor, and Breen were likewise stripped of their shirts and bound in chains. Breen exchanged a glance with his teammates, and silently they all agreed to stay cool. Fighting this many men was pointless, and Breen's head had already taken enough abuse tonight. It'd be stupid to risk getting his wits rattled again. He needed them.

The three of them were strung up, side by side, on the left-side branch, but facing the clearing.

A bonfire was lit in a center pit, illuminating a collection of half a dozen log cabins about seventy-five hundred feet beyond, embedded in the woods. The cabins appeared to be simple, saggy, one-room structures, all with boarded-up windows.

As the bonfire roared to full inferno, flames whipping at the darkness, a group of men whooped and hollered and danced around, their undulating bodies casting tormented shadows across the backdrop of trees.

This was bad.

"So, Dalakis," Gábor drawled, "how do you like your first real topside mission so far?"

Breen shifted on his chain with a *clink-clank* and looked at Gábor and Thomal.

Thomal had a fulminating glare trained on the bonfire. "That whole be-careful thing?" he gritted. "We should've done that."

"We *were* careful," Dev argued. "These men cloaked themselves, and they're strong as fuck. *And* there's a shitpile of them."

Gábor sneered at the savage, cannibalistic display by the

pit. "You think these assholes plan to put us in a cauldron?"

There wasn't time to figure it out.

A man strode forward importantly, and the others murmured in excitement, speaking in a foreign language.

Maybe Breen had woken up inside of *Halo*.

The important man was older than the rest, with a white skunk streak at the front of his black hair. He wore more clothing than everyone else, including a long trench coat. He had an aura of power about him, and when he aimed for the oak tree, a hush fell. The other bad guys leaned forward intently, attention pinned on him.

The leader came to a stop right next to Dev, and, with cool haughtiness, looked up at the warrior.

Dev looked back down at him, his gaze flat and dangerously calm.

"Son of Grigore Nichita?" the leader asked in accented English.

The name made the entire length of Breen's spine lock straight, his chain *clanking* louder. Holy shit, this man knew who Dev was.

Dev said nothing. The name of Dev's father, Grigore Nichita, was loathed.

The skin on Breen's nape began to crawl again.

This was very bad.

The leader chuckled darkly. "No need to answer. You are practically the man's replica, especially your eyes." His chin rose another notch. "Are you prepared, Son of Grigore Nichita?"

Dev still didn't answer.

Because who the hell knew what Skunk Streak was asking? *Prepared for what?*

The leader tut-tutted. "Must I elucidate?" He asked the question as if Dev was an especially stupid child. "You carry the foul blood of Grigore Nichita in your veins, and thus we have brought you here to answer for your father's wrongdoing.

Grigore Nichita betrayed his own people in the most despicable manner possible, and for nothing more than selfish greed. His heinous actions resulted in many deaths. Everyone here"—the leader made a massive sweep of his arm—"lost loved ones because of *your father*. So, I ask again: are you prepared, Son of Grigore Nichita"—his glare flared brighter—"to pay for you father's sins?"

Dev matched Skunk Streak's glare with one of his own.

The fire crackled. Embers spat and sizzled.

"Very well." Imperiously, the leader held out a hand toward his men.

One of the bad guys hurried forward and placed a coiled bullwhip across his palm.

A rush of adrenalin nearly blinded Breen. *Oh, shit.*

Skunk Streak let the bullwhip uncoil.

It slapped the ground, and muscles along the wide breadth of Dev's back twitched.

Thomal released a low growl, a sound so ferocious that even the hairs on Breen's nape prickled.

Dev stared at Skunk Streak for a long moment, the sweat on his body glistening in the firelight. "Why the hell not?" he said through tight teeth. "Go for it."

"What the *fuck*?" Gábor barked.

One of Skunk Streak's brows lifted a fraction of an inch—in surprise?—then he gestured someone forward, still all righteous and royal.

A thin man stepped out of the crowd, his black hair rising at odd angles from his scalp. He accepted the whip and positioned himself behind Dev.

Breen's temples pounded with the rushed throbs of his heart.

The skinny guy's eyes darted over to his superior.

Skunk Streak nodded. "*Începe.*"

The thin man flipped the working end of the whip behind him, then struck out, yelling the name, "Cezar!" as the stinging tip lashed Dev's back.

Dev hissed and jerked. A red welt rose along his flesh.

"Dammit to fuck!" Gábor yelled. "What the hell is this!? Back off, you cockburgers, or I'll shove my boot so far up your asses, you'll choke on your own shit!"

Another name yelled. "Stefan!" Another lash.

Another welt. Dev's hands clenched into fists at the top of his chain.

The thin man scurried back over to Skunk Streak and returned the whip to him.

The leader slowly wound the long length of leather around his fist. He moved closer to Dev. He peered up. "Uncomfortable?" he inquired blandly.

Dev stared straight ahead, his breath coming hard, his jaw rigid.

"I would think so," the leader said in a musing tone. "But *uncomfortable* isn't really payment for a betrayal of the kind your father committed, is it?" He did the annoying tut-tut again. "No. I would say it isn't." He gestured another man forward.

This guy was shirtless, with geometric tattoos covering thickset shoulders. Long-haired, sharp-eyed, with a grim block of a mouth, he looked tough, mean even. He took the whip from Skunk Streak and lined up on Dev in an angled-body position. He let the whip dangle in readiness, the tip dancing near the earth.

This fucker knew what he was doing.

"Dorina!" he bawled and slashed out.

The whip *crack-snapped* against Dev like super-charged lightning. A long strip of flesh tore off Dev's back, the ribbon of meat flailing out then flopping down past his belt.

Dev arched and yelled.

Thomal, strung up closest to Dev, flinched aside as blood hurled across his face.

Roaring, Gábor kicked and thrashed and thumped on his

chain, his cheeks gorging bright red.

Breen sagged motionless as a corpse on his cable, his armpits stretched painfully taut from bearing his entire body weight. His heart dropped like a stone sinking deeply into still water.

CHAPTER SIXTEEN

The underground community of Ţărână
6:33 P.M.

CHARLIZE GAVE THE BOLOGNESE SAUCE bubbling on the stove a light stir and checked the linguine boiling in the stock pot. She was going Italian at the restaurant tonight, and everything was looking ready for the doors to open for the dinner crowd at seven o'clock, just half an hour away.

Her assistants bustled behind her, rolling out fresh dough for the mini pizzas.

Marissa strode into the restaurant, a clipboard tucked under her arm, her daughter, Maylie, propped on the other hip. "Last night's opening was a smash success," she announced, smiling brightly. "You ready for a repeat performance tonight?"

"You bet." Charlize returned her friend's smile.

Marissa had been a saving grace during Charlize's first month out in the community, making sure Charlize was introduced around to new people and got involved. Her life was pretty good because of that. She had friends, a rewarding career, shared hobbies.

Just no man.

And no sex.

Yeah, *her*, every guy's wet dream, was living the life of a nun. She'd never been so lonely for a man in her life, and, frankly, she was doing a damned poor job of dealing with it. Who the hell was she if she wasn't big, bold, bawdy Charlize who could fuck whoever she wanted, whenever she wanted?

She gave the sauce another stir, more vigorous this time. See? She didn't even know who she was anymore...what kind of way was that to deal?

Maybe she should join a mah-jongg group. No, she should take up knitting, then she could sew her vagina shut, useless thing.

Masturbating to her heart's content wasn't working. Those orgasms were minus the warmth, smell, and feel of a strong male body, and in the long run did little to lessen her stress and nothing at all to relieve the loneliness. At this point, she was so desperate to heat up her sheets, she was actually considering—*considering*—hooking up with her only option. The major hold up, of course, being that she couldn't just make Breen her fuck buddy like she wanted. She'd have to try and have a relationship with him, and, *barf.*

Although...

Breen was a good guy, right? Whenever they'd run into each other, he was always completely and absolutely nice to her. He never uttered a single word of complaint about her refusing to be with him, even though a mate's rejection was incredibly brutal for a bonded male to take—she was coming to understand this as she learned more about Vârcolac culture. She kept waiting for him to trip up, drop the nice guy con-job, and lay into her with all the resentment he *had* to be feeling. But so far...he just continued to surprise her by being steadfastly quiet.

Did that make him a kabocha squash?

She was starting to think *no.*

During her brief encounters with him, she'd come to discover that his minimal responses actually conveyed a lot. He wasn't unemotional. He just expressed things several layers down. When he got on the elevator at the same time as she did, he would look at her with deep curiosity stirring in the depths of his pupils. Nothing prying. Just a desire to know her better. When he carried her bags into her apartment, he paused to look at her for a long moment, the intensity in his eyes speaking of how much more he wanted to do—provide for her, protect her, be her man. After he fed from her, he was at his most intense, staring at her with dark, sensual eyes, his lips parted, a warm tension rolling off him. The soul-level, particle-deep wanting would be back...and that's what always threw her.

It reminded her that *there can be no halfway within the bonded relationship.*

But *all the way* could only end badly. If she went *all the way* and threw in her heart *all the way*, she'd just end up getting hurt. Breen being a vampire was supposed to—hypothetically—make him different. His physical bond to her, according to the almighty manual, created some kind of a special closeness between them. But she just couldn't believe it *all the way.* She was unable to push past her deeply held belief that all men were really the same, vampire or not, biological bond notwithstanding. At their core, men were insecure—oh, the famous fragile male ego—and so unreliable.

And unreliable equaled a bad end.

Caring for people hurt, and she was done being hurt. Period. Done.

She cleared her throat, dislodging the sudden lump there, and told Marissa the restaurant was reserved solid from opening to closing.

"No surprise." Marissa beamed, then added, "By the way, I'm putting in a supply order with the Travelers." She waved the clipboard. "So I need to know if you want anything."

"How fresh can you get fish?" Charlize was eager to try some nouveau American cuisine. "And I'm talking, off the docks fresh."

"I can probably arrange that. Here—" Marissa held out her daughter to Charlize. "Take Maylie for a sec."

"Uh..." But apparently the sight of a slobbery pudge-face and the puppies-made-out-of-rainbows smell of a baby had the power to bring latent maternal seedlings out of dormancy even in Charlize. She took the kid and naturally propped her on a hip. The lump in her throat returned with a vengeance. She hadn't held a little girl since her sister was young.

Marissa scribbled notes on the clipboard paper.

Charlize gazed into Maylie's long-lashed silver eyes. "Hi," she said.

The one syllable greeting produced a toothless grin on the baby that fireworked a burst of sunshine in Charlize's chest and, oddly, also made her feel like she needed to pee. Probably just the inner workings of her nethers becoming confused over the sudden rush of maternal warmth down there. She'd never thought about having a baby of her own. But then, she'd never really figured she deserved one, not after…

Charlize stomped her foot on the nasty grub of a memory that was trying to dig its way up and out.

"Okay." Marissa finished her notes. "So I've put you down for—"

Jacken pushed inside the restaurant.

Charlize automatically took a step back.

A large man with rocks for fists, Jacken was the type of guy who seemed to have baggage hanging from meathooks in the dark closets of his mind. Even in one of Charlize's vilest moods for rough 'n' nasty sex, she would never have gone for a man like Jacken. She had a completely adequate supply of her own baggage—*thanks, Mom!* Although she could bend enough to give him major brownie points for having a great bod.

Marissa didn't look glad to see him either. She pointedly checked her wristwatch. "It's dawn topside."

"Yes," he said.

Marissa set down the pen on top of the clipboard, her movements deliberate. "Dev always texts me as soon as he's on the elevator platform heading home. I haven't received any messages from him, and now *you're* here." She held Jacken's gaze for a long beat. "The team didn't make it back, did they?"

"No."

Marissa crossed her arms. "What else?"

A muscle moved back and forth in Jacken's jaw. "They never showed in the topside safe house, and we lost the signal on their tracking devices."

"*All* the signals?"

"Yes."

Marissa's throat bobbed.

Charlize looked between Marissa and Jacken. She wasn't exactly sure what was going on.

"I'm sending up Wilson and Ty to search for the men now," Jacken said. "I don't want to wait till sunset for answers."

Wilson and Ty were two Dragon males who'd given up their work as topside cops to live down in the community with their Vârcolac mates. Charlize forgot what their main jobs were down here, but they helped out the warriors with security issues up top during daylight hours when needed.

"Okay," Marissa said quietly. "Have you told Chelsea and Pandra?"

"Yes. As soon as I know something more, you wives will." Jacken paused. "Sorry." He left.

Whey-faced, Marissa turned toward Charlize. "Are you okay?" she asked in a scratchy voice. "Do you want to close the restaurant tonight?"

Close the restaurant? "I…" Charlize floundered. She didn't know what to do. Or think. Or feel. "I'm not sure. What did all that mean?"

"Well." Marissa cleared her throat. "Maybe the team simply didn't have time to get to the safe house, so they're shut up somewhere else…someplace where their tracking devices don't work. This could all be nothing."

"Okay."

"In fact, it *is* nothing." Marissa conjured up a brave smile. It was pretty sad, how fake it was. "You should keep the restaurant open."

"Okay."

Little Maylie patted Charlize's cheek and said, "Maaaaaa."

Marissa reached for her daughter.

It was one of the hardest things Charlize ever had to do, but she gave back the kid.

BY THE RESTAURANT'S CLOSING TIME, Wilson and Ty had returned from the topside Lakeside house, reporting on evidence they found indicating the Spec Ops Team's presence there: earpieces, microphones, and cells had been left in a crushed pile in the middle of a living room floor.

The situation was no longer being considered as *possibly nothing.*

IN APARTMENT 4B, CHARLIZE STOOD in front of the large plate glass window in her living room and stared down at the Water Cliffs. Now at midnight, the upper pools were dark and still, their glassy surfaces reflecting the ferns and palms above them, but the large, ground-level pool was tinted with colored lights.

Charlize watched as green faded and blue took over. A moment later lavender appeared.

Her chest felt shredded from tiny piranha teeth of panicky worry nibbling steadily at her heart. Her husband-who-wasn't-really-a-husband was missing and probably for a very bad reason.

Charlize slammed her eyes shut. Damn her. Was she learning impaired or something? Because, really, how many times did life need to bash her over the head for her to get it?

People let you down.

No one ever did what they said they were going to do.

It didn't matter if people fouled up because of doing some man thing or the special closeness turned out to be a big lie. Whatever the reason, if people said they were going to stick around, they didn't. They walked out the door on a mission, then didn't come back. They took off on a bender and didn't return for three days. They ran out into the street, then didn't come back, *ever.*

This was exactly why relationships were a pot of piss. *Stress.* Charlize wrapped her arms around her waist, hugging herself. *Fuck it. Let 'em all not come back. See if I care.*

Below her, the pool bloomed red. Like blood.

Her spine pulled taut as a rubber band stretched toward snapping. *Blood so red it looks black painting the grill...* The nightmare that stalked her. She put a hand over her eyes, blocking out the view. *No more.*

No more caring. No more hurt.

No more thinking about the nice guy with a chip in his fang.

Chapter Seventeen

Topside
Pre-dawn

NICOLAE LAZĂR THREW HIS DAGGER. It flipped end over end, sparks of moonlight leaping from the metal blade, and found its target. The haft bonked the jackrabbit on the skull, and the animal plopped over dead.

Nicolae strode over and picked up the limp body, adding it to the others—he had eight—then navigated over to the camp cook fire with his kill.

At a large, flat stone, he made neat work out of skinning the beasts, filleting flesh from bone, then chopping the meat into chunks.

Andreea came up to him and gave him a quiet look.

He nodded to the un-woman.

She scooped the meat into a bowl and took it over to the stew pot.

Nicolae strode to the water pump, still functional even though this tourist vacation site of log cabins had long ago gone bankrupt—according to information found on an internet site called Yelp. He cranked water into a bucket, then crouched down and cleaned his knife of blood and fur, first scrubbing, then caressing his fingers over the blade. Perfectly crafted for both fighting and the meaner tasks associated with hunting, this knife was an extraordinary weapon. He used it with all the reverence it deserved, although he would've surrendered it in an instant and carried some fossilized dirk instead if it meant getting his father back. If Lucien was still alive, *he* would be the one wielding this blade.

Ten years the man had been gone, and Nicolae still hadn't put his feet all the way back on the ground.

But then, the center of Nicolae's world—his older brother's, too—had been his father, a big, dark, smiling man who could knock a charging boar senseless with a single blow from his fist, dodge a lightning-fast strike from one of Zalina's Amazon-sized warriors, and make a longsword sing on its way to carving flesh.

Nicolae and Vasile had loved their mother, of course, missed her dearly, too, but she'd kept herself on the fringe of the men in her life. Cătălina married Lucien only to save herself from becoming an un-woman after her first mate died. She never loved him, so there'd been no place for her among the tight-knit Lazăr men.

Fathers and sons weren't supposed to be so close. According to American television—and other men's conversations—sons were *supposed* to be plagued by competitive distance, struggles to please an impossible-to-satisfy man, and disillusionment when the son learned of his father's imperfections, the discovery sending the father toppling from his lofty and heroic perch down to the earth of mortals.

Nicolae and Vasile never knew any of these troubles.

Distance? Never. To survive the prejudice of others, the Lazăr men banded together and depended on each other.

"You'll always have to be twice as good as everyone else in order to achieve one quarter of their regard," Lucien told his boys.

And so he taught them to be the best—the greatest protectors against the enemy factions of the Patru Puternic, the most skilled hunters and providers, the strongest in moral character. Lucien set difficult tasks before his sons to train them, ones Nicolae and Vasile worked tirelessly to conquer. And whether they succeeded or failed, Lucien was always proud of their efforts. He was *never* impossible to please.

How could a man like this topple from his valiant status? He never did. Lucien had forever been their hero: large, unstoppable, invincible...until the day he wasn't. The day the Lazăr men decided to go outside the safety of the ward to hunt—food had been scarce for several weeks—and Savatina appeared from nowhere, just *nowhere*, her longsword already swinging downward in a lethal arc.

Savatina's blade cleaved Lucien nearly in two, slicing him from the left shoulder in a diagonal cut down to the lower right side of his body, and in the next blink, she skewered Vasile through the side of his waist.

Flung back onto his butt during the half-second melee, Nicolae threw his dagger from where he sat, missed Savatina, crawled over to his dead father, jerked the knife from the belt-sheath, then thrust upward with the blade right as Savatina was bending over to deliver a death blow to Vasile. Nicolae drove the steel straight into the witch's black heart, although Savatina didn't die. A pierced heart couldn't kill one of Zalina's daughters. It only sent her into a Sleep.

As the warrior witch dropped to the ground, then disappeared under one of Zalina's protective spells, Nicolae hunched over his father, covered his face with his palms, and wept.

Vasile didn't die, either, but almost. The puncture wound missed his important internal organs, but both Nicolae and Vasile never recovered as quickly as others did. Once Vasile did finally heal, he ceremoniously gave Nicolae Lucien's knife. Vasile, as eldest, had familial rights to the weapon, and the blade had become even more exceptional the moment it touched Savatina's blood, for it gained a mysterious power.

But Vasile said Nicolae saved his life with it. He would hear no arguments otherwise.

Nicolae dried the special blade now on his pants leg, then slowly sheathed it. The knife often brought up memories of his father, but more so at present, what with everything being done in the glen this night. A man was being tortured with a bullwhip, and not because of any personal failings of his own, but in the name of his father.

It was vastly unjust.

Nicolae knew *exactly* how unjust from personal experience. He himself had spent his whole life paying for having the blood of his forefathers in his veins, and not a single day of it had been fair. A man should be judged on his character, not on the happenstance of his birth. But what could Nicolae do about it?

They were all under the control of *Şef de clan*, or Chief, whose decisions were uncontested law. And Nicolae possessed even less power than the other men due to who he was, as had been proven long ago when he failed his mother. Despite Nicolae's passionate argument to Chief on Cătălina's behalf, she was made an un-woman after Lucien died, the very fate she'd always fought to escape.

If Nicolae spoke out about the brutal, undeserved whipping of Son of Nichita, the only change he'd bring about would be getting himself fired from guard duty and sent to clean the shit pots. And even worse, he would go back to being shunned.

"Nicolae!"

At the shout, Nicolae straightened from the water pump and turned around.

Răzuan stood at the head of the path leading to the clearing. "<Go tend to your prisoner,>" he told him in Romanian, gesturing toward the large oak tree. "<They're being taken to the cabin now.>"

Nicolae nodded and set off. When he arrived at the tree, the only prisoner remaining was the one with black hair drooping in his face. The man wasn't showing any traces of pain, even though his arms were blue from wrists to armpits.

Nicolae strode over and unhooked the chain, releasing him to the ground.

As the man dropped in a heap to the earth, his expression broke, his lips pulling back into a tight spasm, exposing savagely locked teeth. It had to be unparalleled agony having blood and feeling rush into those dead limbs, although the man obviously wasn't going to make a sound…not when Son of Nichita had endured so much worse.

At some point during the brutal whipping, Nicolae hadn't been able to watch anymore. He'd faded into the shadows of the trees and bowed his head. Crouched only about twenty meters away, though, he'd still heard everything.

Bending over, Nicolae checked the duct tape binding his prisoner's wrists. The chain had eaten through some of it, so Nicolae grabbed the roll from near the tree trunk and taped a few more strips on. The man's teeth gritted harder. Nicolae tried not to wrap it too tight.

"Come, come," he said, gesturing toward the prisoner's cabin.

When the man didn't get up, Nicolae helped him stand, then led him by the arm inside the shelter.

Son of Nichita was already lying belly-down on a pallet, looking nearly unconscious. The other two men were seated on the floor at Son of Nichita's feet, their backs propped against the wall.

Nicolae sat his prisoner down by the wall across from these two.

Nicolae had thought meeting these men would be like reuniting with long-lost cousins, but they were more different than expected. Son of Nichita wore a beard, and he was way too young for that! Another man had whiskers, too, the one with a tattoo on his arm. Not like the warding tattoos Nicolae and Vasile wore, but an evil-looking beast. The man's left eye was bluish-purple from the ambush fight.

Out of the same battle, the man with light-colored hair had earned a puffed, split lower lip. His body was also splotched with crusted blood, but this blood belonged to Son of Nichita. The curious part about this man was his hair. Nicolae had only ever seen light color of this sort on television or on the Şarpe Pursânge breed. And, yes, this man *was* giving off a whiff of Dragon, but that would be impossible. A Dragon would never be allowed among these other three men. The hair had to be fake.

Nicolae's brother, Vasile, entered. He was a tall, strapping man with long, thick black hair, the strands lacking the natural waves that created the tangled mess of hair on Nicolae's forehead.

Vasile ushered in two un-women, Céline and Eugenia.

These two both knelt beside Son of Nichita, and Céline began to attend to the injured man's back with the medicinals from the basket she carried.

Son of Nichita groaned.

The one with the tattoo sneered. "Fixing him up so he'll be healthy enough for more abuse tomorrow, is that the plan?"

Nicolae didn't care to answer the question. He hunkered down in front of the light-colored one. "Hair?" He tugged on his own hair and pointed at the other man's. "How?"

The light-colored one looked him straight in the eyes. "My dick in your ear."

Nicolae opened his mouth, then closed it. *Huh?* "What?"

The light-colored one said something else. He spoke in a conversational tone, but Nicolae didn't quite catch the words. *Go…what? Go duck yourself?* He sat back on his haunches and ran a hand over his chin. He'd studied English in the manor school as a child, along with the others, but lack of daily practice meant none of them spoke it well—some, like his brother, not at all. Many of them didn't understand much more than a simple syllable or two. Nicolae understood a great deal because he watched so much American television. But the words this man spoke didn't make sense at all.

"<They speak nonsense,>" he informed his brother.

Vasile scowled. "<Don't talk to those two, Nicolae.>" He

indicated the prone man. "<Son of Grigore Nichita needs to feed. Tell him.>"

Nicolae peered closely at Son of Nichita's ragged face. "<I don't think he'll hear me.>"

"<He won't heal sufficiently if he doesn't feed.>" Vasile gestured impatiently at Eugenia.

She stuck her wrist under Son of Nichita's nose.

The man didn't react.

"He's bonded," the tattooed one growled.

Nicolae spun around. *What? How…?*

Vasile closely observed Eugenia, a towering presence, his customarily stern expression growing darker as nothing continued to happen between Nichita and the un-woman. "Eugenia—!"

"<They say Son of Nichita is bonded,>" Nicolae cut in. A bonded male could only feed off his mate, but that was—

"<Impossible.>" Vasile's brows bunched into a more sharply-drawn vee.

Nicolae shrugged. Why would they lie?

Andreea entered, bearing a tray with four bowls of rabbit stew. She passed these out to the prisoners—Son of Nichita's was set beside him—then left.

Nicolae shook his head at the tattooed one as he pointed at Son of Nichita. "Bonded. *Imposibil.*"

The tattooed one rumbled a noise in his chest. "Listen, cracker—"

Nicolae made a *stop* gesture with his hand. "No discuss."

The tattooed one leaned over and scooped up a spoonful of stew—he couldn't pick up the bowl with his wrists duct-taped together—and shoveled it in his mouth. He chewed, then said, "Duck you."

Nicolae frowned. "<They keep talking of ducks.>"

Vasile waved dismissively at the bowls of stew. "<They will eat what we give them.>"

Exhaling, Nicolae pointed a stronger finger at Son of

Nichita, then transferred his finger to Eugenia. "*Feed.*"

"He *can't*, you twat." The tattooed one glanced at the light-colored one. "Was I unaware that I'd switched to Greek when I said it the first time?"

The light-colored one didn't answer this question. He concentrated on his stew, his movements rigid and overly precise, as if his arms still weren't functioning properly. Blood had returned to all the prisoners' arms, but this didn't help the appearance of these limbs. From elbows to armpits to ribcage, all four men were marbled with bruises.

Nicolae inspected Son of Nichita again. The man definitely didn't look like he could feed, but whether from being a bonded male or from his injuries, that remained the question. "What is twat?" Nicolae asked the tattooed one.

He snorted, then curled his upper lip. "A coward."

Nicolae flushed. "<This one calls us cowards,>" he tattled to Vasile.

Storm clouds lowered onto Vasile's brow. He stalked over to the tattooed one and loomed over him, his long black hair framing a fierce expression. The circles around his irises spun with his anger, and he made a hammer fist.

The tattooed one set down his spoon and braced himself.

"<He's right, you know,>" Nicolae said quietly.

Vasile whirled on him.

Nicolae averted his gaze. "<We are cowards.>"

Chapter Eighteen

Dawn

Birds twittered with the arrival of the morning, and far off some human pull-started a lawn mower. The camp was quiet other than those noises, everyone having settled down to bed. No guard had been left behind to watch the prisoners in their quarters. Why bother? Right outside the door was sunlight, and there was no surer way to contain a vampire. Plus the four of them were shackled.

Breen shifted with a *clank-clank* of his manacles and grimaced. The weight of the chains was no fun for his sore arms. His blood-need was also rapidly—He cut off the thought. His discomfort and blood-need were nothing compared to Dev's, so he should just shut up about it forever.

Sweating, he peered across the expanse of floor at Thomal and Gábor. By the light of a single lantern, he could see that neither of them looked sleepy either. *Tired* was another matter. Pissed, too, seeing at their plans to lay out their captors had just been shit-canned.

A few minutes ago the two warriors had been exchanging silent, collaborative glances while being "put to bed" by their guards. *You head-butt my guard while I wrap my bound wrists around his throat, then you steal the knife off his belt...*

Then two more guards entered the cabin, one carrying a fistful of shackles, the other, a stick about the size of the fat end of a pool cue. One end of the stick was on fire, and as the man brandished it, he spoke in a threatening tone.

Breen's guard translated in broken English, the gist being:

fight while you're being shackled, and you can count on me burning one of your eyeballs out.

There went Battle Plan A.

Now each of them wore chains on the wrists and ankles, secured to another chain around the waist. Dev was shackled only at the wrists and ankles. But he was in no state to fight.

Breen moved his feet, catching back another grimace. It felt like a belt sander had been let loose inside his stomach. He could probably drink his own body weight in blood right about—*Oh, yeah, don't think about it.*

He should try to focus the bilious gray matter of his brain on the job of figuring out an escape plan. But about as many ideas were coming to him now as when he'd been hanging all night with purple and inflamed arms. He didn't see how they could get their asses out of this mess without help.

The lawn mower coughed to a stop. Wind hissed through the slats of the boarded-up window.

Breen dredged up some saliva to speak. "How do we contact the community in a situation like this?"

"Beats the shit outta me," Thomal retorted. "The tracking devices in our cell phones were our only backup communication." He showed his teeth.

Yeah. Destroyed. "So there's no other way of contacting anyone?"

"Other than telepathically?" Thomal said dryly. "No."

"Dammit to fuck." Gábor rubbed the center of his chest. *Clank-clank.* "Chelsea's totally freaking out about my no-show." His radar was obviously acting up.

The entire community had to know by now that the team's mission had gone tits-up. It was dawn, the four of them had never checked in, and they were now AWOL. Elements such as those generally added up to the obvious. But the community knowing what was going on and being able to do something about it were two different things.

Gábor growled. "These asswipes are already dead, but if

anything happens to my unborn kid because Chelsea got too upset…" He didn't finish the thought.

He didn't have to.

"We need to steal a cell phone off one of the guards," Breen said.

Thomal passed a hand over his bruised lip. *Clank-clank.* "I haven't spotted any cells. And even if someone was wearing one and we managed to swipe it, how the hell could we make a call? It's pretty impossible to dial while dangling from a tree like bait in a trap."

"We could stash it in our pants and call from here tomorrow," Breen suggested.

Thomal cut a glance at Dev, sprawled unconscious on a floor mat.

Tomorrow… There was going to be a *tomorrow* of this.

It was unbelievable that this was happening to Dev. To all of them.

Breen's voice dipped down into his throat. "Did either of you know about these guys?"

"Fuck, no," Thomal came back. "And if they weren't so effectively stomping mud holes into our asses, I'd say we were hallucinating them."

A suspended silence followed while no one looked at Dev.

Breen slid his focus in slow-motion over to one of the wooden walls, pitted from neglect, weeds struggling up from cracks in the corners, cobwebs sagging from the low rafters in elaborate weavings of gray.

"Our shit-nozzle guards all wear blades," Thomal said tightly. "We're just going to have to make a grab for one."

Gábor chuffed his disgust for the idea. "That ain't happening, Costache. You saw them—they're not taking any chances with us." His upper lip rose, showing part of a fang. "We look too mean."

A funereal silence descended over them again. They all just sat in it.

Breen supposed they were all plotting, but, down to the nuts and bolts of it, there really wasn't a lot to figure out.

They were screwed.

CHAPTER NINETEEN

Night two

SOMEWHERE IN THE MIDDLE OF the second night of violent torture, vomit started dribbling uncontrollably past Nicolae's lips onto his chest and belly.

Was it because Son of Nichita started hollering loud enough to shake the night from the sky the moment the first lash fell onto a back already so raw and bloody?

Was it that Răzuan, after finishing his turn, greedily licked blood from the whip?

Was it when an extra-vicious lash from Mircea made blood shoot out of Son of Nichita's nose?

Yes, this.

Nicolae faded away from the clearing back into the shadows of the trees, hiding from the spectacle of a man being brutalized as much as concealing that he was a sympathizer. He slid down the tree trunk and hunkered immobile on his haunches.

It began to rain. Droplets fell lightly through the trees, clicking on the old, dead leaves scattered across the woodland floor and spattering on the cabin roofs.

The torture was suspended, some men seeking shelter, others moving about, eating and drinking. Nicolae stayed by his tree, the rain wetting his hair down to the roots. The air began to smell of moss, toadstools, and freshened blood from where Son of Nichita drooped unconscious on his chain, his head lolled to one side, a long string of saliva trailing from his mouth. He'd just been left to hang there beside his companions, who weren't pleasant sights either.

The light-colored one looked like he'd taken ill. His lips were white while the rest of his flesh—except for his arm bruises—was yellowish. He squirmed regularly on his chain, probably trying to keep some trace of life in his arms.

Nicolae's prisoner showed very few signs of life. He stared at nothing with the gaze of a fish on ice, rain rolling off him. His mouth was now framed in stubble, too, like the one with the tattoo, who Nicolae would not care to approach at this point.

He'd been hung closest to Son of Nichita for this round, so he might enjoy being sprayed with his friend's blood, and at about the time Nicolae started puking, the tattooed one turned into the embodiment of pure rage. He held his chin very low, and his eyes burned with a constant low, fury-filled light.

Doubtful that tonight Laurenţiu could handle the tattooed one on his own.

Gică drew a twig out of the fire and strode up to Son of Nichita, touching the hot end to the man's waist.

Nichita came back to the living world with a sharp intake of breath.

Chief stepped forward, the whip coiled around his fist, the gray streak in his hair silvered by moonglow.

Nicolae's stomach sank as the horrible words that would restart this obscenity were spoken yet again.

"Are you prepared, Son of Grigore Nichita, to pay for your father's sins?"

Son of Nichita's throat moved. "Yeah," he choked out. "Sure. Go for it."

The light-colored one closed his eyes and held them closed.

The tattooed one's pupils flared with white lightning.

The quiet one remained still. His over-stretched arms looked two inches longer than they had yesterday.

Nicolae stared at the wet polish on the trunks of the trees and listened to leftover rain dripping through the branches.

"Nicolae Lazăr."

He startled so hard, he snapped a bootlace. Standing quickly, he rounded the tree trunk.

Chief was holding out the whip to him.

The earth unbalanced beneath his feet. *My turn?* He shot a look at his brother.

Vasile met his gaze once, then wouldn't.

A clammy sweat broke out over Nicolae's body. He swiped the wet hair off his forehead. "<Um…no relation of mine was wronged by Grigore Nichita's betrayal.>"

"<Your great-uncle, Costi, was on a ship sunk in the Constanța Harbor.>"

When Nicolae didn't budge, Chief's eyes narrowed and his grip on the whip tightened.

Every eye bored into Nicolae, severe and disapproving.

A familiar shame flushed up the back of his neck. Wiping his wrist across his grimy mouth, he started forward. His legs felt like half-snapped stilts. The closer he came, the more his shame deepened.

What am I doing?

He was about to participate in an act that went contrary to everything he believed in—punishing a man for no more than the sin of having tainted blood—and he was going to do it out of fear. Fear of being shunned again. Fear of returning to the days of being "accidentally" elbowed, tripped, and jabbed by the other men because he was unclean. Hateful acts to be avoided, yes, but…at what cost? If he committed an act of unconscionable torture because he was afraid of the snubbing of others, who would he be afterward? What kind of man?

Nobody his father would be proud of, that was certain.

No one *he* could even be proud of.

He stopped in front of Chief, and his stomach recoiled at

the sight of the blood-slicked whip.

Be the greatest protector, the most skilled hunter, the strongest in moral character.

He'd already allowed his father's teachings to slip once, back when he hadn't stopped Chief from deciding Cătălina's fate. Letting down his mother was the worst failure of Nicolae's life, and he still remembered how horrible it'd been watching her at slave work, how horrible he'd felt. Like he was an insect. A powerless, weak little nothing of a creature. He didn't think his heart could bear it if he disappointed himself again. The organ would rot and shrivel inside his own chest.

"<No.>"

There was a heavily stunned silence.

Chief glared at him.

A tic bounced at the edge of Nicolae's eye, but he set his shoulders. Better to deal with the ostracism of hundreds than be stripped of who he was.

A man was no man if he couldn't decide his own character.

"<I won't participate in this,>" he said.

"<You will,>" Chief ordered coldly. "<Or you disgrace your people.>"

The men stirred.

Heat needled Nicolae's cheeks, and his nerve endings felt like they were being burned by one of Gică's lighted twigs. He swallowed. "<I won't harm a man I do not know.>"

The men buzzed louder, like wasps poked in their nest.

Nicolae raised his voice. "<How do any of us know if this man lacks honor, just because his father did? Search within yourselves for the answer.>" He stepped back and scanned the crowd. "<Who of *you* are your fathers? Marcel>"—he picked out the man's face from the others—"<your father paid someone to kill your mother so he could be free of her. Are you the same?>"

Nicolae heard Vasile hiss.

Recklessly, Nicolae went on. Or tried to. "Horia—"

Chief struck him full across the face with the whip.

The blow made a loud *thunk* as the handle met Nicolae's jawbone. His dark hair flung across his eyes. Pain collapsed the entire left side of his cheek, and blood rushed out of his nose.

"<How *dare* you speak of other men in such a manner,>" Chief fumed, "<when you are naught but a worm?>"

Nicolae straightened. He was no worm. His days of being a powerless, weak little nothing of a creature were over. He was a fool, that's what he was, to have believed he'd managed to obtain a measure of acceptance among his people.

Because here it was, gone.

In a blink.

A snap.

If what he previously gained was so easily lost, he never actually had it in the first place.

Working his jaw, Nicolae gave Chief a flat stare. Warm liquid crawled onto his upper lip from his nose. He didn't wipe it away. He sniffed burning blood up into his sinuses. "<I won't participate in this,>" he repeated.

Chief's complexion stained red, the scar cutting along his jaw standing out paler and rigid against the darker hue.

Nicolae's look of defiance was probably worse for the man than the insubordinate words themselves. Because it spoke louder than the words.

No more.

Nicolae turned away and melted into the shadow of his tree.

CHAPTER TWENTY

BIRDS SANG IN AN UPLIFTING chorus, joyously announcing the day. A vehicle drove by a few miles away with a muffler-heavy sound, then faded into the general hum of life at a distance. Another day dawned.

Leading to another night…

Breen sat slumped against the cabin wall, his useless arms tucked in close to his sides. Sweat sheeted over his eyes. The long hours of hanging by a chain with limited circulation two nights in a row had repeatedly torn the muscle fibers in his arms. And now that his blood-need was somewhere out in the far reaches of the next galaxy over, his accelerated healing powers weren't really fixing things up so well anymore. At least he wasn't like…

He glanced at Dev, and an epileptic violin started playing inside his head, the bow wrenching across the strings in shrill shrieks and whines, rising to its highest note until a string would break on a hyper-discordant screech. The noise would dip, then rise once more, beginning the process again. There weren't many undamaged strings left.

Sanity was a funny thing, wasn't it?

His was effectively being eroded by watching Dev slowly die.

Because here was the thing about death, it meant *gone*. Forever. No coming back. An inarguable absolute in the cycle of life…yet Breen's mind couldn't grab hold of it.

How could there be life without Dev?

The man was too much of a solid presence in community

life, too much a part of Breen's world ever since he'd joined the Spec Ops Team. Before then, Breen and Dev had worked a lot of years together dealing with Om Răus problems, fighting side by side, watching each other's backs, but now Breen was part of an even tighter, more cohesive brother-hood—and Dev was the glue. It just wasn't possible for Dev not to be around anymore. It just wasn't.

He rasped a breath and choked on his words. "We have to do something."

Gábor didn't respond, didn't even move. Not exactly a problem-solver on a good day, he was currently lost in a terrible place.

Thomal cranked his head up. His eyes were hot and red, so red it looked like lesions had ruptured along his optic nerves. But then Dev was his best friend, and if watching Dev being skinned alive by a bullwhip was making Breen's brain squeal like a violin played by an untrained hack, he could only imagine what was going on inside Thomal's mind.

"Do you think," Thomal said evenly, "I've just been sitting here tugging my dick about this? I've analyzed this from every conceivable angle, and all I can see is nothing's changed since yesterday. We're still minus weapons and comms, and we're *never* left unbound. No. I take it back. Something has changed since yesterday—we're weaker." He leveled a stare at Breen. "If we managed to steal a knife today, do you have the arm power to fight with it?"

"Maybe with a shit-ton of adrenaline."

Thomal glanced aside, jaw tight, and shook his head.

Okay, maybe not. Which meant night three was coming their way… Breen closed his eyes as the violin in his head whined. "Dev's not going to make it through another night." He kept his eyes closed. Whatever expression was going to come over Thomal's face over that, Breen didn't want to see it.

"I don't know what the fuck to do," Thomal croaked.

"We need help, but unless you have a means of comm tucked up under your nuts, we're still at yesterday's telepathy option."

Breen opened his eyes, but looked down, staring at the duct tape binding his wrists under the shackles. Threads were fraying off the borders, and some of the sticky stuff was gummed up in spots along turned-back edges.

"Dammit." Thomal massaged his radar. "On top of everything else, Pandra is very much not a Jolly Rancher right now."

Both Gábor and Thomal's radars had been paining them on and off during the—

Breen bolted his eyes up. "Holy shit." *Pandra.* "That's it."

Thomal frowned. "What's it?"

"Telepathy," Breen breathed out. "That *is* the answer."

✧   ✧   ✧

The underground community of Ţărână
5:17 p.m.

CHARLIZE RAPID-FIRE CHOPPED CELERY AT Marissa's kitchen island, helping her friend prepare Dev's favorite soup for "when Dev comes home."

Yeah.

Sure.

For when Dev comes home.

Charlize would go along with it if that was what Marissa needed to believe in order to survive her terror. Cooking was providing Marissa with a much-needed distraction, and maybe busy hands would also help Charlize not think about everything she didn't want to think about. How Jacken, Nyko, and Arc scoured the streets of San Diego every night, Wilson and Ty every day, and none of them had found a single clue about where the Spec Ops Team might be. No warrior had ever gone missing this long, and the unspoken opinion was now—

"They're dead." Chelsea swung her juice glass around the group of them. "You all know that, right?"

Chelsea and Pandra were sitting at the kitchen island, Pandra drinking wine, Chelsea, juice, both of them solemnly watching Marissa and Charlize cook.

Marissa whirled around from the stove, tight-lipped and defensive. "I absolutely do *not* know that. Our husbands are highly trained warriors, and they know how to take care of themselves. I personally believe in Dev's abilities."

"Gimme a break." Chelsea blurped her lips together, making a raspberry noise. "Da Nile ain't just a river in Egypt, Marissa."

Marissa scowled. "Would you please not be negative, Chelsea?"

"Why the fuck not? If there was ever a time to get real, it would be now, Gábor lying dead in a ditch somewhere." Tears gathered in Chelsea eyes. "God, but I wish I was like *her*"— she flung a gesture in Charlize's vicinity—"Little Miss Couldn't Give Two Shits About My Man."

"Chelsea!" Marissa rebuked.

Charlize exhaled sharply, her body temperature spiking. Last thing she needed was to be made to feel like more of a freak of unwifely nature than she already did around these three real wives. What she needed was Breen and the calm assurance he always brought with him.

Yeah, somewhere along the way, his stillness had stopped being strange to her and turned into something comforting to be near. Ironic, wasn't it, that she needed Breen to get over Breen? Pathetic, too, that her resolve not to think about him was such a total fail.

Pandra picked up a piece of celery and crunched it. "People deal with stress differently, Chelsea. Not everyone's a saddo about it." Her voice darkened. "I'm not."

"*You've* been going to the gym every day and demolishing a punching bag," Chelsea countered. "That shows you at least feel something."

Anger formed a ball of hurt in Charlize's chest. "You know what, Chelsea, maybe you're right. Maybe I don't give two shits. And if not, then good for me for not sitting around slurping wine and making myself crazy imagining Breen in a ditch, hurt and bleeding..." Her throat jerked her sentence to a stop. *Bleeding...* The mere thought of blood let slither out of her mind the image she hated most, the one that curled her soul into a fetal pretzel and stripped her down to a bare, vulnerable framework.

The diesel truck.

Tires smoking.

Locked-up, shrieking brakes spewing splinters of metal.

Blood smearing across the sky as if by giant, unearthly fingers...across the grill...the windshield, the road... The kind of dark purple blood that still stained the asphalt when a friend's mother accidentally drove by the same spot a month later...

Charlize tossed her chef's knife onto the counter. "I used to spend all my time worrying about the people in my life, like my mother and my brother—who are a couple of bona fide bunny boilers—and it just about ruined me. So I stopped caring. And if that makes me a bag of dirt in your opinion, then so be it. I've also never been in a relationship before in my life—hell, I'm not even really in one now—so I have no idea how—"

"What, never?" Chelsea's mouth twisted in a look of disbelief. "Not even a high school boyfriend?"

"Never," Charlize returned flatly. "I use up men and throw them away like trash."

Pandra's brows arched. "My, my, my," she drawled. "This is beginning to feel like peering into a long-ago mirror."

Charlize glanced at Pandra. A lot of rumors flew around about this woman, the gossip describing her in shades of both black and white. What was true and what was legend?

Charlize didn't know, having avoided Thomal's wife out of loyalty to her roommate, Hadley. But the more she found out about Pandra, the more she wanted to get to know her. She sensed a kindred spirit in her.

Marissa scooped up the chopped celery. "You can't just throw away Breen, though," she said to Charlize, dumping the celery in the soup. "I know your situation is complicated, and I don't pretend to understand what you're going through. But maybe this is your chance to reevaluate your relationship with him, make some changes."

"Why?" Charlize countered. "Because Breen might be dead? Because if he's not, I've had a good scare, and I should realize what I've got and grab it?" She started to shake her head, but Marissa just gave her a steady look.

"Yes," she said. "Breen is perfect for you." Marissa set the lid on the soup pot. "His calm nature is an ideal counterbalance to your wild side."

Charlize's jaw went earthquakey on her. *Perfect for you...* What the hell was she supposed to do with that concept? Back when Breen was a kabocha squash, the thought of pulling off a relationship with him had been a joke. Now that he was actually a man of depth, the thought of a relationship still made clawed beetles crawl up her spine.

Poor guy was damned if he did, damned if he didn't, and Charlize had no idea why she was so intent on setting him up to lose. It probably had something to do with what she just said to Chelsea. She'd stopped caring.

Charlize went back to shaking her head. "It sounds good, Marissa, but it's the kind of stuff that only happens in books and movies. I'm too fucked up to make those kinds of changes for real." A pampered and sheltered woman might've been able to indulge in the fantasy that with dedication and discipline, marital bliss was possible. But Charlize's view of the world was too realistic for her to have faith in positive outcomes.

Pandra chuckled. "This is becoming right uncanny." She cocked her head at Charlize. "Has anyone ever suggested that you have a gab with Karrell?"

"Who's Karrell?"

"The community therapist."

"Therapy?" Charlize made a face. And have a stranger crawl around inside her private thoughts?

Pandra's mouth tipped into a half-smile. "I know, I know. I wasn't too keen on the idea at first, either, but therapy turned out to be a bloody corker for me. The work I did with Karrell allowed me to take on roles I never would've been able to do well if I hadn't found peace—wife and mother and teacher. It gave me—Shite!" Pandra flung her hands up to her head, knocking over her wine glass as she clutched her temples.

The glass shattered, spilling wine.

"Pandra!" Marissa exclaimed. "My God, are you okay?"

"I'll be buggered," Pandra breathed. "I think I just heard Thomal's voice inside my mind." She massaged her temples with her fingertips. "His *actual* voice." She grimaced at the mess she'd made. "Sorry about your goblet. But hearing that startled the bleeding pants off me."

"Forget the goblet." Marissa threw a dish towel over the broken glass. "What's this about Thomal?"

Pandra dropped her hands, and small frown lines appeared between her brows. "For lack of a better way of putting it, the doorway into my Fifth Element was rattling. I think the hubby is trying to communicate with me along that pathway."

Marissa's eyes widened. "Can he do such a thing?"

"We've never done it before. But he was with me when I performed the ritual to stop Videon from stealing souls, so I'd wager he and I are connected along that realm to some degree."

Fifth Element? A ritual to stop soul stealing? Charlize thought back to the manual—none of those things were in it.

"So our men are alive?" Marissa asked, speaking fast with excitement.

"It's sounding like it, but..." Pandra rose. "I need to go home, get into a trance, and see if Thomal and I can do this. Would it be all right if I leave Lucca here?"

"What? Of course, of course." Marissa flapped her hands. "He's fine having a sleepover with Randon. Just *go*."

Slumping on her stool, Chelsea rested her palms on her swollen belly and cried quietly.

Charlize took over the job of raking up the broken glass. *So our men are alive?* Was that even remotely possible? Was Breen about to pull off a miracle and actually come back?

Charlize's hands shook, and she cut her finger.

CHAPTER TWENTY-ONE

Night three

THE DAM BROKE ON EVERY sweat gland on Breen's body when a new guard started to lug him toward the clearing. Just imagining what was coming next made instinctive animal fear fire on all nodes in his brain—the feel of tendons detaching from bones in a painstaking inch-by-inch process, blood clotting into a violent throb around his wrists, his armpits spearing out multiple stabs of pain as they stretched beyond normal human limits…and all the while his ears being battered with the steady *whizz* and *crack* of the whip.

The sprawling oak tree came into view, and Breen locked his spine.

His guard tried to tow him over to the spot next to Dev—*his* turn to get drenched with the byproducts of his friend's torture—but Breen dug in his heels and threw his head back like a balking horse.

Another bad guy arrived to help, the one who'd punched Breen at the abandoned Lakeside house. He aimed a disapproving frown at Breen and bound his wrists, the now-familiar *rattle* and *clank* of the chain spiking through Breen's teeth.

He tried not to make a sound when he was winched into the air. No complaints allowed when a person wasn't being filleted by the lash of a bullwhip. He knew Thomal and Gábor felt the same way, but all three of them grunted and growled the moment their boots left the earth.

It couldn't be helped.

Breen bit his tongue, drawing blood as he forced a collateral scream so far down his gullet, it bunched in his groin. The torment of having unhealed arms re-stretched was worse than he'd even anticipated. If it wasn't for Dev, he would've given his lungs evacuation orders and howled them up his throat and out his mouth.

Dev was hoisted on his chain. A noise came out of him, agonized and low, like an animal dragging a trap.

The violin in Breen's brain screeched. Snapped strings gnarled together into a ball of steel wool.

Bad guys gathered around the fire pit, tossing wood onto a growing blaze. The fire sent up sparks that fizzled out almost before they really lit.

"Thomal." Dev's voice was weak as tissue paper.

"Yeah, brother. I'm here."

"Listen… I need you to… Marissa…" Dev's dangling feet jerked. "Tell her…t-tell…"

"Stop." Thomal made a weird hitched-up guttural noise. "I'm not telling your wife anything, Dev. Do you hear me? We're not doing this last words thing."

More bad guys crowded around the pit. A black cloud of smoke billowed up, smelling faintly of eucalyptus.

"God, please…" Dev tilted his face toward the moon. "Tell her…tell Marissa she's the last thing I thought of, okay?" He wheezed. "I love her so much."

"Fucking tell her yourself when we get out of this." If Thomal was trying to come across firm and determined, he'd failed. He sounded scared and desperate.

The bad guys passed around a jug of something. Some of them ululated at the moon.

"My kids… I also need you to… Ah, Jesus…" An exhale shuddered Dev's large shoulders. "I really wanted to watch them grow up."

"Nichita, *shut* up." Panic was raw in Thomal's tone, like a man who saw where this was heading and knew it was inevitable and unchangeable. "You need to hang on. Help may be on the way, okay? I'm not sure, but just *hang* on."

"I…can't." Dev's voice was a thin thread. "Sorry, man. This is my…my last night. I think you know that."

"Fuck if I know that."

They all knew that. Dev was as tough as a man came, but he was Vârcolac. He needed his mate's blood to survive injury and stress, and he wasn't getting it. A violin chord ripped out of Breen's brain.

"Randon and Maylie…look out for them, Thomal. Promise me."

Breen's throat squeezed and closed up tight. The violin chord was now wrapped around his neck.

Skunk Streak wended his way through the rabble of men. The clamor rose. Bloodlust throbbed.

"Just one more night, Dev," Thomal begged, hoarse and crumbled. "All right?"

Skunk Streak separated himself from the crowd, the bull-whip snaked around his fist.

Breen was still suffocating from the violin chord, but now the arm of the instrument was beating him over the head.

It's going to happen.

Again.

"P-promise me," Dev struggled in an ashy voice.

Skunk Streak stopped next to Dev. He looked up at the battered man, his expression as unemotional as the unfeeling bastard was himself.

A yell strained up Breen's throat. *Promise him, Thomal, you no-load shitbird! Promise him!* But the words got choked off below his violin neck-wire.

"Are you prepared, Son of Grigore Nichita," Skunk Streak asked, "to pay for your father's sins?"

Breen's breath came fast and hard. His gut went loose.

Dev swallowed several times. He rubbed his temple against his upraised arm, wiping away sweat. "Yes," he whispered.

Breen flashed Thomal the edge of his teeth. *Do something! Promise him!*

Thomal's eyes were stark, wide, horrified. No assurances came out of his mouth.

Gábor was no help.

Skunk Streak called forth the first man. "Radu."

A guy with scabs in his hair came forward and took the whip.

This was *it*.

The whip uncoiled. *Slap.*

Dev was going to die.

Sorry, man. This is my last night.

Breen arched on his chain, accidentally setting himself to swinging. The agony in his arms smeared black jelly across his vision. *No. This can't happen.* Ţărână without Dev was an impossibility. The man was everything. He was someone Breen depended on, like a big brother, like the big brother Breen didn't have, but really needed.

Like the big brother he wasn't for Barbu.

He saw it so clearly now.

Suffering, desperation, hopelessness, tottering insanity: all these things had a way of stripping a man of his filters. How he'd come to fail so badly at the role of big brother, he wasn't sure. It wasn't like he consciously set out to leave Barbu to tackle life alone, or that he didn't consider himself worthy of the role because he bought off on all the "worthless piece of shit" comments his father loaded on him. Although…those criticisms were to blame in some way. He'd grown so sick of hearing crap, he just stopped listening. He'd ghosted out.

And a nonentity, by definition, didn't exist. So now shit seemed to happen *to* him rather than him making shit happen…like with Charlize. No thought went into biting her; he'd merely done it. No decision-making had been behind having sex with her; he just went where his body took him.

And now here he was once again. A rock in a pail being sloshed around by a hand not his own. Doing nothing.

He saw what that made him. Weak. Someone who, by ghosting out, had avoided life's toughest challenges, and now when the shit was really hitting, he couldn't hack it. He was weak, and he was failing, and it was an embarrassment. And the hell if he was going to continue. The consequences of doing nothing were too severe: desert Dev…keep letting down Barbu…never claim his rightful mate. And *die*, like Dev. Here in the middle of nowhere, alone…alone in the ways it counted the most.

Unless he could wake up.

Make decisions.

Decide a course.

Act.

The kid with the scabs in his hair swung the whip back.

The screws keeping Breen together sheared smooth. Pieces fell apart, and then—a bellow tore out of him, a huge, echoing, tree-felling sound, a cross between Tyrannosaurus Rex and Mount Vesuvius.

Everyone in the clearing froze.

Everyone stared at him: the shy one. The nonentity.

Make decisions.

Decide a course.

Act.

He took in two hard breaths. "Nicolae!" he shouted. That was the name of his former guard, wasn't it? That's what Breen had heard the bigger, long-haired guy call him, right?

He sucked in another lungful of air. "Nicolae!"

CHAPTER TWENTY-TWO

THEY WASHED DISHES IN SILENCE.

Nicolae was in no mood for conversation, and the un-women clearly didn't know what to say about a man being made to do women's work.

Sullenly, he fished out a bowl from the bin of soap suds and scrubbed it, his hands cracked and red—the least of his complaints. His jaw was still sore from Chief's blow with the whip, his shin smarted on the spot where Răzuan just so happened to kick him, his ribs ached from an "inadvertent" collision with Tudor's elbow, his tailbone throbbed from landing on his butt on a rock after "accidentally" being pushed down by Marcel, and there was a pounding in his ear from when, *oops*, Noni's elbow caught him with a solid, pointed jab.

Everyone's opinion of Nicolae refusing to punish Son of Nichita was more than clear.

No one's opinion—or their cruelty—was a surprise.

Nicolae thrust the washed bowl at Otilia for rinsing and drying, then snatched up another, glaring down at the dirty dish. He was so sick of feeling unclean. He—

"Nicolae!"

He startled and stumbled around, looking down the path leading to the clearing. The shout had come from over there...

Within the throng of men gathered around the oak, faces started to turn searchingly.

"Nicolae!"

He jerked his eyebrows up. It was his prisoner who was calling for him. Or he should say, his *former* prisoner, since Nicolae had been taken off guard duty and given the job of a washerwoman. He hadn't been made to clean out the shit pots, at least, although being ordered to work with un-women was about as humiliating.

Otilia slipped the bowl out of Nicolae's hand, as if giving him a cue to walk forward. He approached the crowd.

Grumblings passed through their ranks, but the men parted to make a path for him.

He walked through and stopped at the edge of the clearing.

"Please stop this," Nicolae's former prisoner said frantically. "This man"—the prisoner nodded at Son of Nichita—"this man is not 'Son of Grigore Nichita.' His name is Devid Nichita, and he's a good man. A *great* man. He is a father and a husband. He has two children and is considered to be one of the best dads in our town. He has a wife who loves him, and...and..." He seemed to struggle with the direction of his thoughts. "He's...good."

Nicolae's arms hung at his sides. Soap dribbled off his fingertips and softly ticked onto the earth. What was he supposed to say or do? Chief was watching him through meanly slitted eyes, and Nicolae's pulse was coming apart. He didn't need to be punished and shunned any more than he already was.

"I know you don't agree with what's going on," the prisoner went on. "You didn't hurt Dev yesterday, so, *please*, do something to stop this. Dev Nichita doesn't deserve to die."

Vasile came to stand next to Nicolae. Some of the tension eased from Nicolae's shoulders, but only some. Nicolae wasn't sure how much support he could count on from his brother. Vasile wanted to be a man of strong character, same as Nicolae, but he had worked tirelessly to gain acceptance, too, and didn't want to lose his hard-won position, as he'd seen happen to Nicolae as a result of yesterday's defiance. "<What does the man say?>" Vasile asked him quietly.

He translated a summarized version.

Vasile lowered his voice. "<Stay out of it, Nicolae.>"

He had planned to but hearing his brother say it made him bristle. Those words came from a wrong, fearful place. "<Is that what Father would've wanted me to do? For *us* to do?>"

Vasile's cheeks stained rust red. Uncertainty still raged across his face, and even though Nicolae's gut hollowed out with a feeling of vast isolation, he couldn't fault his brother for hesitating. The cold outskirts were an extremely difficult place for a man to live his life.

Nicolae glanced again at Chief.

He was observing them both with glittering pupils.

Nicolae told his brother in an undertone, "<Step back. I'm already destroyed, but you're not.>"

Vasile's jaw knotted.

Nicolae hadn't meant to make Vasile feel like the big brother being rescued by the little brother, but it's obviously what he did.

With temper churning in his eyes, Vasile lifted a staying hand to Chief. "<This will end.>"

Chief began to seethe something at them, but whatever he'd planned to say wasn't allowed to gather full steam.

Four unknown people rampaged into the clearing.

Not just any sort of people—*fighters*.

Dressed all in black and strapped with weapons, two were well-built, dark-haired men with black teeth tattoos on their forearms. The larger one also had these marks ringing his neck, and he wasn't just larger, but *huge*. The third male fighter possessed that strange, light-colored hair, and the last one was... Holy heaven. A *woman*. Her light hair was gathered into a streaming tail on top of her head.

Each fighter was armed with about twenty-five knives in

crisscrossed body holsters. But despite the numerous blades, they also carried pistols, drawn and ready. No talk. They scanned the scene once, then started shooting, as fast as they could, it seemed.

POWPOWPOWPOWPW.

The cacophony of gunfire got trapped in the small clearing by the surrounding trees, raising the acoustics to something close to multiple neutron bombs going off.

"Bullets don't work on them!" The light-colored prisoner was yelling this from his chains even as Nicolae's warding tattoos spun into activation—everyone else's too.

The bullets flew wild, pinging into tree trucks in sprays of bark, dimpling cabin walls, kicking up dead leaves.

The fighters paused.

Gunsmoke wafted like a halo of mist around them.

The one with just forearm tattoos scowled, his jaw hardening into chiseled rock. "Go, Arc," he commanded the male light-haired fighter, "Get the bus."

The man hesitated.

Then Rock Jaw snapped something confusing. "Half-Răus only for this."

The light-haired man cursed, but turned and sprinted back through the woods.

Rock Jaw issued a low order to the other two, and all three formed into a tight, defensive circle, back to back, knives in their hands. They breathed more rapidly, their eyes panning about in calculated threat-scans.

They looked like loaded destruction, set to erupt.

Not a group anyone should laugh at, but Mircea did laugh, deeply and darkly as he pulled a long sword from a sheath on his back and brandished the superior weapon at them.

Metal hissed on leather in staccato bursts all over the clearing as more blades were freed, daggers and swords.

Nicolae drew his own knife, his heart racing fast enough

to hurt his veins. His muscles filled with energy as they always did before a fight, but this time something felt different. Wrong or worse. He scented how dangerous the tension was. Three enemy fighters compared to their one hundred and two, yet… He could feel the nearness of death.

He remained cautiously back while his countrymen stole forward, converging on the three, slowly and stealthily. There would be no headlong charges for predators who enjoyed stalking a meal. Wind whispered, and the wispy filaments of a lone cloud curled around the moon like a shredded shroud.

Rock Jaw snarled, a lethal set of fangs stretching down into his mouth.

More laughter erupted, stupidly demeaning.

"Go Rău!" Rock Jaw bellowed, and red light glowed from his eyes, then from the other two, and—

And then unholy hell was unleashed.

Nicolae shouted and stumbled backward as bodies began to fly, tattered flesh flapping, blood pinwheeling. One body hurled into him—Horia!—and knocked him down.

In the second it took him to scramble back to his feet, he was engulfed in the reeling chaos of combat: steel ringing against steel, blow and counterblow pounding in accompaniment to ragged breathing, shouted curses, the moans and the screams of the injured and dying.

Nicolae barely managed to form the thought that he should swipe out with his knife, and he was already on the ground.

The threesome had completely mowed him down.

Panting in high-pitched gusts, he peered down at his belly. *By holy night.* His gut was pared open, the wound vomiting blood like a grimly-stretched mouth. He felt a sensation of ice coating his intestines…then the pain came. The shearing agony ripped his eyesight in two. He clutched shakily at the gash. Blood gushed through his fingers and coated his hands in wet, red gloves.

Eyes watering uncontrollably, Nicolae glanced around for Laurenţiu. The man knew something of medical treatment…

And across the clearing, he saw Chief.

His face was purple with rage—well, one hundred two of his men against three of theirs, and his men were losing. Chief roared and charged at Son of Nichita, dagger held high. He brought the blade down, yelling his sister's name.

Nicolae's prisoner—who was hanging next to Nichita—swung his lower body up, shouting at the terrible wrench that must have given his arms. Wrapping his legs protectively around Son of Nichita, he took the blade hit. Chief's steel sliced a deep gouge into a spot above his knee. Blood spilled out of a long rip in his trousers.

Chief raised his weapon for a second strike, and—

Thunk! A knife hilt appeared in his right shoulder blade. Chief's body torqued. His own knife spilled out of his hand, and he fell.

Son of Nichita convulsed, jerking on his chain like a disemboweled animal would do.

Nicolae's prisoner dropped his legs and yelled something at him.

Words were forming bubbles on Nichita's lips, too quiet to hear.

The threesome was still fighting like a whirling knot of death, the thunder of their destruction rising to a deafening bedlam.

Son of Nichita's chest expanded, his shoulders inflated, and then he somehow managed to holler, "STOP, JACKEN!"

In the acoustics of the clearing, the two words boomed like a command sent down from Mount Olympus.

The threesome stopped…although by this point there wasn't anyone much left for them to massacre.

The clearing was a sea of the dead and dying, all with nauseating knife wounds, some bodies writhing, others completely still. Nearby, Mircea watched Nicolae with blank eyes. Răzuan's slashed throat smiled gruesomely at him. His brother—*Arahh!*

"Vasile," Nicolae groaned.

A bloody trench cut a path across his brother's chest. He lay scarcely moving, white-eyed with pain.

Nicolae's lungs heaved. He was swallowing convulsively.

The three fighters stood in place for a long moment, breathing noisily, blood hazing the air around them and feeding the earth at their feet. They looked like they'd been birthed from a butchered cow.

Rock Jaw was the first to shake himself out of whatever held him. The red light dimmed from his eyes.

Next, the huge fighter returned to himself. He stared dazedly at the bloody knife in his hand, the puppy-dog curious look crinkling his brow at odds with the two savage fangs thrusting down into his mouth.

The woman fighter seemed stuck. She snarled and quaked.

"Pandra," the light-colored prisoner called to her from his tree. "Pull out of it, baby. Okay? I need you to come back to me."

Her eyes blinked several times, then cleared...except when she got a better look at the light-colored prisoner—yellow-skinned, his arms a vision of bruised abuse. Red trembled around the edges of her dark irises again. She started for him—

"Everyone *stop*," Son of Nichita wheezed. "Stop killing them."

Rock Jaw sheathed his blade with a forceful *swap*. He stalked toward the tortured man, not particularly careful about who he stomped on along the way.

Nicolae would guess not much emotion ever showed on such a rigid man. But as Rock Jaw drew up next to Son of Nichita, his eyes became unmasked, his face turned into over-stretched pigskin, and his lips contorted into a grimace of abject horror.

Yes, well…Son of Nichita's back looked like cherry pie filling.

"Dev," Rock Jaw growled on a low breath.

"You have to…stop killing them." Son of Nichita's head drooped in Rock Jaw's direction. "Jacken, they… You have to stop. They're Vârcolac."

CHAPTER TWENTY-THREE

THE BUS RIDE FROM LAKESIDE to the community's main topside entrance took forty-five minutes and added a layer of near-suffocating, crammed-in torture onto Breen he could've done without.

The max load for a school bus was seventy-two, and they were over capacity by at least sixteen. In addition to nine community members, four from the Spec Ops Team—Dev, Gábor, Thomal, and Breen—and five rescuers—Jacken, Nyko, Arc, Pandra, and Dr. Jess, who had stocked the bus with medical supplies, but not enough to deal with *this*—there were seventy-nine bad guys: fifty-two injured—a decent portion, gravely—seven uninjured—who managed this feat by running off and hiding in the trees—and twenty women, nearly identical in appearance, with dark hair and block-like, masculine features. Almost half of the bad guys—forty-three in all—were killed outright in a slaughter for the history books.

The rest Dev refused to leave without. *They're our people, and we take care of our own.*

So now bodies were stacked, in some cases literally, on top of each other, while Dr. Jess hurried among the wounded, tending to them as efficiently as he could.

Jacken and Nyko assisted, Pandra, too, but reluctantly. She hadn't wanted to leave Thomal's side, although he refused to feed until the rest of his team could.

With so many people sharing the same oxygen space, Breen could barely breathe. He was also nauseous from all the blood flowing from wounds. Not from the sight, but because the cloying scent had pasted itself onto the mucus membranes of his nostrils.

There was so much blood, a red tide of it had gathered in the center aisle. It steadily flowed toward the front of the bus, where it waterfalled sluggishly down the steps, then oozed out from underneath the door's rubber flaps, becoming a red spray as soon as the wind hit it. Any highway patrolman who spotted that would absolutely pull them over, and then they'd find themselves in the very sticky position of having to explain a busload of carnage. And, really, how was that explainable?

Arc was more than a little tense as he drove the bus.

When they finally drove onto Țărână's elevator, tucking themselves safely away from unwanted scrutiny, a communal gust of relief was released. And then they could also open the bus doors and unload many of the injured onto the huge platform.

Breen climbed off the bus as fast as his lame leg would allow. Shakily clutching the IV bag Dr. Jess had attached to him, he hop-stumbled down the stairs, sucking in huge mouthfuls of air, and collapsed against the bus's rear wheel.

More of the wounded were unloaded, and within five minutes the platform was a lake of blood.

The butt of Breen's pants got soaked, which was just another discomfort to add onto others: near-useless arms, plus a knife wound in his leg that was rapidly sending his blood-need toward a dangerous point of no return. The interior of the elevator regularly orbited around him, and a viscous quicksand kept trying to pull him under. Only a twisty fear—of never waking out of a blood-coma if he let himself go unconscious—kept his eyes open, if just halfway.

Through the slit of his eyelids, he was vaguely aware that the bad guys on the platform were unnaturally quiet for men who were hurt as bad as they were. They should've been moaning, but they weren't making much of any noise. Some rapid breathing was going on, and that was about it. Probably they were scared, figuring a bunch of *a whole lot worse* was heading their way after what they'd done to Dev.

The long-haired guard and Nicolae were slumped side by side against the rear wall. Dr. Jess had judged their wounds bad enough to warrant scarce and valuable bandages and IVs—same as Breen got—but the two men had already soaked through several layers of gauze. Their complexions were as white as new bathroom caulk.

About halfway through the twenty-minute elevator ride down, Breen started to heave. He didn't stop until he was pretty sure he'd turned his stomach inside out and barfed it partway up his throat. It now sat like a wet flap at the back of his tongue. Finally, thank Christ, after what seemed like the length of an episode of *Glee*, the elevator came to a stop with a small lurch and a winded gasp.

The large door chugged open.

Toni was revealed, standing directly in front, Charlize, Marissa, and Chelsea hovering a step or two behind her. Beyond the anxious wives, the rest of the Warrior Class was waiting near a stack of stretchers and medical supplies.

Not much rattled Toni, but when the opening elevator door released the lake of blood, that did. She gaped as the red tide oozed lava-like off the platform and blub-blubbed around her low-heeled shoes. "My God," she breathed.

Little Chelsea gasped.

Marissa cried out.

Charlize took one look at all the blood, and her knees bent sideways. She collapsed to the garage floor in a dead faint.

"Shit," Breen croaked.

Sedge rushed over and knelt beside her.

Jacken splashed to the edge of the elevator platform.

Toni's eyes stretched wider on her blood-drenched husband. "You texted me 'plan for incoming wounded.'" She was astounded. "That's all you said."

He gestured behind him at the carnage. "I didn't exactly have time for more."

A clattering noise came from inside the bus.

Jacken checked over his shoulder, then barked, "Marissa."

Marissa rushed forward, her expression stricken.

"Prepare yourself," Jacken growled.

Dev was lugged out of the bus, Nyko and Arc each manning an arm. Dev's head lolled back and forth on his shoulders as if his neck was no more than a flower stem, and—

Marissa's hands flew to her face, and she shrieked.

Well, how could anyone really expect her to prepare for how Dev looked right now? He wasn't even fit for a chum bucket.

Arc gestured her down. "On your knees, Marissa."

Sobbing, she kneeled.

Dev was placed on top of her, and she toppled over under the weight of his limp body.

Nyko held Dev up by the back of the belt to keep his full weight off Marissa—God knew Dev couldn't do it himself.

Dev latched onto his wife and fed greedily.

Marissa kept weeping.

The scene was both messed up and a heaven-sent relief.

Toni watched it all with searing blue eyes. "What the hell is this?" she snapped, glaring down at Dev's back.

"I have no idea," Jacken answered her. "No one's been able to give me the full story—just that these people are Vârcolac."

"*What?*" Toni exclaimed. "How is such a thing possible?"

Jacken chopped at the air. "That's the current *what the fuck* of the hour, isn't it?"

Dev moaned, and Breen's own fangs pressed down. Hunger shuddered up his spine, and he checked on Charlize.

Sedge had placed a rolled towel underneath her head. She

was still out cold but looked comfortable.

Gábor trudged out of the bus.

His wife, Chelsea, blinked a couple of times as she took in her husband's appearance—arms like swollen plums, savagely bright eyes, and an expression locked into homicidal rage. "Uh oh," she said on a low breath.

Thomal and Pandra exited the bus next.

As Thomal passed by his brother, Arc, he clasped fists briefly with him, then he stepped off the platform and came to stand next to Gábor over Dev.

Nyko helped Dev shift to Marissa's side.

"Both of you, go home," Dev said hoarsely, propping himself unsteadily on his elbows. "Be with your wives and heal. Gábor—" He reached out sideways and wrapped a hand around Gábor's ankle. "Let Chelsea fix you, man. Do you hear me?"

Gábor glared across the room at a wall hung with a wide selection of tools, a couple of fan belts, sparkplugs, a grease gun.

"That's an order." Dev let go.

Chelsea slipped her palm in her husband's and led him away.

Pandra urged Thomal to leave, too.

"Where's Breen?" Dev asked.

Dr. Jess came to the edge of the elevator platform. His suit was totaled, although his black hair was still miraculously neat. "I'm sending him to the hospital right now." He gestured to a couple of homeguard warriors, Jeddin—Breen's X-Box buddy—and Kasson—owner of a surfer boy cowlick.

The two picked up a stretcher.

"Take extra good care of him," Dev said. "He got that leg wound saving my ass."

Breen peered down at the IV needle in his arm, the veins under his skin looking kind of shrunken. Dev's voice had been filled with a lot of pride, and Breen fiddled awkwardly with the IV tube. He didn't know how to take it. He'd never been complimented before—besides, *Dank move!* for an exceptionally skillful Xbox kill or, *Nice way to bust it!* following an extra hard training session.

Kasson and Jeddin brought the stretcher onto the platform and set it down next to him. "Hey, man," Jeddin said, flipping his white-blond hair off his forehead, "you look like you came outta someone's ass."

"Toni," Dev said, sounding like he had a fistful of sediment congesting his larynx.

Toni crouched down next to him. "Yes."

"Promise me you'll take care of the others."

Toni's eyebrows pressed together. She glanced up at her husband.

Jacken made a *yeah, I know, can you believe it?* gesture.

She transferred her attention over to Dr. Jess.

"I've already triaged them," he told her quietly. "About fifteen need major surgery, while the others can probably be treated with suturing."

Several short, measured breaths left Toni's lips, then her mouth screwed up tight at the corners. "Dev, do you have any idea what you look like?"

"I'll be okay. I just need Marissa and sleep and pain meds and… But the rest of them…they've been chopped into fajita meat."

Toni didn't speak. She shook her head.

Marissa carefully caressed her fingers through her husband's hair.

"You're the leader of our people," Dev kept on, "and *these* are our people."

Toni dragged a hand over her mouth. She shook her head again.

"These are people who…who shouldn't even be alive because of what my father did." Dev angled his head up to look at Toni. "I need you to think as a leader right now, not as my friend. Okay?"

Toni's jawbone stuck out against her flesh. With a biting sound, she thrust to her feet and marched to the edge of the platform. "Do you see the man you hurt?" She glared at the bad guys. "He's fighting for *your* undeserved survival."

The accused sat, sprawled, and lay in frozen terror. No one really understood English, but Toni's expression and her tone got her point across extremely well.

Jeddin and Kasson hefted Breen onto the stretcher, setting the IV bag on his belly.

"Charlize," Breen squawked. He was pretty sure he couldn't go another second without her blood.

She was just now swaying to a sitting position. As soon as she saw all the blood again, she blanched.

Toni swept another incensed gaze over the bad guys. "Who's in charge here?" She enunciated the question with steely precision. "*Who?*"

"I am."

Toni whipped her attention over as Skunk Streak struggled to his feet from out of the bloody mass.

He walked forward stiffly. The wound from the knife he'd taken to the back still leaked, but somehow he managed to put a decent amount of rigidity into his spine as he faced down Toni. "I am Octav Rázóczi, ruler of these people," he said in a cold, ruthless voice. "In the name of the entire Vârcolac race, I have led my people to exact a rightful and just blood debt against the son of Grigore Nichita, betrayer of our people."

"*Look* at this man." Toni made a slice motion down at Dev. "This isn't the image of a blood debt. It's murder."

"As it should be." Skunk Streak's chin went up, his tone turning as superior and snide as his posture. "It is mere unfortunate happenstance that Son of Grigore Nichita isn't dead. Grigore Nichita's actions led to the death of thousands. The level of the blood debt exacted on his son is in accordance with the laws of Danturǎ Pravilǎ."

"Dantură Pravilă," Toni said through set teeth, "is no longer followed. The Străvechi—"

"A *human*," Skunk Streak spat, "would have no knowledge of such matters."

Toni gave Skunk Streak a thousand-yard stare.

Not the smartest tone for a guy to use when his nuts were currently poised in a vise of her choosing—although Skunk Streak obviously didn't know that.

"And you don't speak for the entire Vârcolac race," Toni corrected coldly. "The people here"—she made a town-wide gesture—"are of that race, and every one of them takes exception to what you did to Devid Nichita."

"Then the people here have not endured the loss of family, nor suffered the near-extinction of the Vârcolac way of life, as we have." Skunk Streak sneered. "My only regret is that I myself did not have the chance to apply the bullwhip to Son of Grigore Nichita in the name of my sister, who was killed in the siege of Constanța Harbor along with so many others." Fury blazed from his eyes, and there was malice in his voice. "May the son of Grigore Nichita always bear the scars of those deaths. May my sister, Pettrila Rázóczi"—he shook a clenched fist at Toni and elevated his volume—"finally be avenged!"

Skunk Streak's melodramatic declaration echoed off the walls of the garage and faded by degrees into a *holy shit, say what?* silence.

Breen's brain wasn't working at full speed, but even he could compute what that name meant: Pettrila Rázóczi was the maiden name of Pettrila Nichita.

Dev's mother.

Releasing a wet snort, Dev lowered his forehead to the garage floor. His shoulders quaked.

Skunk Streak frowned at what looked like a show of laughter.

"You imbecile," Toni hissed.

Skunk Streak's attention swung back to her, and he gave

her an incinerating glare.

"You utter and complete idiot." Toni exhaled down her nose, a condescending sound that actually outdid Skunk Streak. "You just tried to kill your own nephew."

CHAPTER TWENTY-FOUR

BREEN WOKE INTO INSTANT, FULL-BODY awareness. There was a twinging pain in his right leg, an IV needle in his arm, several small, round sticky pads on his chest, and he could smell rubbing alcohol.

He licked his lips in an instinctive gesture of hunger. He needed more of Charlize. He'd fed on her right before being wheeled into surgery, but by the time she'd arrived at his side and offered him her wrist, his brain was the consistency of a gooey omelet, his hearing obstructed by a high frequency whine, and his stomach long ago dropped into his colon. He only dimly recalled feeding on her—his lack of being dead right now was the only reason he knew for sure he had—and he needed more. For health's sake, but also so he could enjoy her.

The sound of breathing caught his attention.

He lifted his eyelids open and turned his head to check out his roommate. Too many wounded meant Breen couldn't have a private room, even as a community warrior, but still. What a bummer to be saddled with Skunk Streak.

The blinds on the window by the man's bed were slanted low, letting in only a little light. The light was dim. Evening time in Ţărână.

Breen squinted, but, no, it wasn't an illusion.

Pettrila Nichita stood next to Skunk Streak's bed, her hands clasped at her waist and her posture erect. She was the type of woman who always appeared ready for a White House dinner, her clothes and hair flawless. At one hundred and sixty years old, she was in her Elder Phase, her black hair streaked with some gray. Her figure was still slender as a young woman's, though.

She stared at her sleeping brother for many long minutes.

When she turned to leave, Breen closed his eyes. And slept again.

✧   ✧   ✧

NICOLAE HAD NO AWARENESS OF time passing. He just woke in a hospital bed, woolly-headed and partially sedated, a tube running out of his arm that was attached to a fluid-filled bag, and a monitor silently streaming information about him with neon-green, bouncing lines.

What was he doing on the TV show *Grey's Anatomy*?

It didn't make sense for him to be on television, but where else could he be? This was clearly a hospital room, everything spotless white—sheets and painted walls—and as a vampire, he would never end up in a real hospital in Transylvania. And no room in the manor house looked like this.

Maybe he wasn't on TV. Maybe he was dead, and this was a strange antechamber to heaven. His knife wound had been severe, after all, and Laurenţiu only knew the rudiments of medical care. Doubtful Laurenţiu had been able to save Nicolae, and even if he had, Nicolae would be suffering far more pain than he was now. He was without energy, true, but he should be feeling like his belly had been triple-trampled by a team of oxen, not merely this dull ache.

Footsteps approached.

He turned his head, and his tired brain sloshed inside the bowl of his skull.

Two doctors in long white coats entered his room. More *Grey's Anatomy*.

One doctor was the man who'd attended them on the bus. The other was the scary lady who yelled at them in the garage and stood up to Chief.

Chief had accused this woman of being human. She was, but also…not. Nicolae was catching a whiff of Dragon coming off her, although stronger than usual. Plus she had the light-colored hair of the Dragon breed—a color that was proving to be common around here.

Why would Vârcolac be mingling with Dragons, though? This was very non-*Grey's Anatomy*.

The bus doctor pulled a clipboard out of a slot at the end of Nicolae's bed, saying, "Still no improvement," to the scary one. "For either of them."

Either? Nicolae turned his head, more carefully this time, toward the other side of the room. Lying in a bed near a window was Vasile, also hooked up to a tube and a monitor.

Dark night. His brother looked terrible, his flesh washed out, his features sunken in, and his lips dry and cracked from his high blood-need.

"<How do you feel?>" Nicolae croaked.

Vasile didn't glance over. He probably didn't want to move his head, either. "<Like a goat's butt.>"

"Their blood won't clot," Bus Doctor continued to Scary Doctor, "and their pressure is still down."

Scary Doctor accepted the clipboard and read papers on it. "I think they're hemophiliacs, Jess."

Bus Doctor nodded. "They do show signs of it, but Vârcolac don't contract hemophilia, so it has to be something else. We're just missing it."

Scary Doctor looked up from the clipboard. "Have they been feeding adequately?"

"Yes," Bus Doctor answered. "But on the donors they brought with them, and I suspect the blood of those women is weak. They don't give off a scent."

Scary Doctor's brows rose. "*No* scent? At all?"

"They smell like Vârcolac, but otherwise, they only exude the minimum to indicate they're female."

"That's odd."

"Very," Bus Doctor agreed. "I took a blood sample of one of the women earlier to see what I could determine." He checked the time on a wall clock. "The results should be ready by now." He picked up a phone tacked to the wall by the door and spoke into it. "Hadley, could you bring me the latest blood test results I ordered from Mekhel? I'm in Room 210. Thank you." He hung up.

Nicolae scraped his tongue across his lips. All this talk of feeding and blood was making his mouth go dry as newly sheared wool. He needed to feed again. Very much. He'd even put up with the leather-like flesh on Eugenia's throat right now, he felt so empty. He coughed once, then somehow managed to speak around all the glue in his mouth. "May I feed?"

Surprise flashed across Scary Doctor's features. Her brows rose again, soaring higher. "You speak English?" She put the clipboard away and moved to the side of his bed.

His heart did a funny skip when she came close. Her face was very pretty, especially compared to the coarse, blunt features of the un-women he was used to being around. Maybe he shouldn't think of her as scary anymore. "Some," he answered. "Understand lots."

"Well, okay." She smiled warmly. "I'm Dr. Toni Parthen, Nicolae. Dr. Jess and I are trying to figure out why you and your brother aren't improving."

Yes, he'd heard their conversation.

"In the past," she asked, "have you and Vasile ever had trouble getting better?"

"Yes," he answered. "Both."

"*Both* of you have had trouble?" This answer seemed to please her. "All right. That's helpful to know. Do you have a medical condition that would account for your difficulties?"

Medical condition? He didn't know. The only condition he and Vasile had was…something he wasn't going to say. He and Vasile didn't need to be shunned by a new set of people. Nicolae was no kind of fool to bring that down on them.

In answer to his silence, Dr. Parthen rephrased her question with simpler words. "Do you two have a special illness?"

He shrugged his shoulders.

This answer didn't please Dr. Parthen. She sank back on her heels and expelled a thick breath.

Footsteps approached from down the hall, then someone else entered the room. A feminine voice spoke. "Here are the blood test results you—"

Woof! Air detonated out of Nicolae's lungs as an aroma barreled into his brain that he'd never smelled before. Something compelling, captivating, hypnotic. Something that filled him with urgent impulses: to claim, to protect, to possess, to attack, to shelter, to devour. Things he *must* do. His teeth slammed together, his fangs shivering in their sockets. What the ungodly hell was happening to him?

"Thank you, Hadley." Dr. Jess accepted a sheet of paper from the newly arrived woman.

Nicolae stared wide-eyed at this light-haired woman called Hadley. Her... *She* was the one doing these strange things to him.

Stars in the sky, she was so beautiful, she belonged in a story book, with her fairy-shaped blue eyes, full pink lips, and soft and dewy flesh. She all but sparkled. And, stranger still, the sight of her body—especially where the front of her shirt pushed outward—was rousing a foreign place inside his mind, awakening pleasure where before there had only been...nothing.

Who on earth was this woman? She gave off a Dragon scent, yes, but also that compelling aroma of hers, an ethereal barrage of sensations. The kind of scent that made a man into a man.

Be the greatest protector, the most skilled hunter, the strongest in moral character.

But more. Much more.

Realize untapped strength, revel in drives of the utmost power, fulfill a primitive sense of the self. It urged him to scale impossibly high mountains, start wars, murder friends. Kill *anything* for her.

Nicolae shook his head. Maybe to deny these thoughts. Maybe to clear his head. It felt like he was going mad. He rasped out a sound to Vasile. "<Are you smelling this woman? Is she doing things to you?>" The moment he asked the question, fury boiled up inside him. He grabbed the bedsheets in fists that he would use to pummel his brother should the pile of pig shit dare to smell this woman the way Nicolae did.

He blinked a few times. *Would* he do that?

The Hadley woman cast a glance his way—no doubt feeling his gawping stare—and smiled. It was a fake smile, tight and brief, no more than civilly polite, and it still undid him. A pulse of raw sensation went through his penis. He fast-inhaled a couple of breaths. *Never* had he felt anything like that in his penis.

It was fantastic.

Dr. Jess showed Dr. Parthen the paper Hadley had given him. "Look at this. Those donor women don't have hormones."

"You're kidding? How have these men lived on blood like that?" Dr. Parthen accepted the paper, read it, then glanced up at him. "How often do you feed, Nicolae?"

"One, two times day."

"A *day*?" Dr. Parthen made a *tsking* sound. "No wonder those donor women look so glazed. They're completely drugged out on ființă."

Dr. Jess put his hands in his coat pockets. "I think we should have the Lazăr brothers feed on our donors. A healthy dose of hormone-rich blood could only help improve their condition."

Hadley offered to fetch one. "I saw Zerenity downstairs a

few minutes ago. I'll get her for you." She started for the door, and as she went, she walked close to Dr. Jess...too close.

Nicolae's spine went so rigid, the stitches on his gut tugged painfully. *Too close!* Snarling, he bared his fangs and lunged at Dr. Jess, seizing the man by the coat collar. The tube ripped out of his arm and whipcorded strings of blood around.

Hadley yelped and stumbled backward.

Nicolae felt his pupils heat as the rings around his irises began to spin violently. He cranked back a fist, aiming at—

Dr. Jess seized him by the shoulders and pushed him back down on the mattress. "It's all right, young man. Calm down. I won't get near your woman again."

Hadley squeaked, "*His* woman?"

Dr. Jess glanced over his shoulder at Hadley. "He's reacting to you." Turning back around, Dr. Jess pried Nicolae's fingers loose, then pressed a bandage over Nicolae's seeping wrist.

Flushing, Hadley shoved some hair off her face. "I...I have to go get Zerenity." She left.

She *left*.

Everything was wrong and bad now. Nicolae's knuckles ached, his jaw burned, his spine throbbed; he was fisting the sheets too tight, clenching his teeth too hard, holding his body too stiff.

"His belly wound is bleeding again," Dr. Parthen remarked.

Dr. Jess glanced down.

Dr. Parthen exhaled. "Something is still bothering me about these brothers, Jess. All the other injured men have improved from feeding off their own donors." She pulled out the clipboard again and fastened the blood test results onto it with the other papers. "Every hematologist bone in my body is telling me the Lazăr brothers are hemophiliacs." She looked at Nicolae. "Do any of the other men speak English?"

"Bujor," he answered. "Some."

Dr. Parthen dropped the clipboard back in its slot. "I'm going to talk to him."

Nicolae frowned. *What?*

Dr. Jess worked at reattaching the tube to Nicolae's arm. "I believe the young man Bujor is two doors down on this side of the hall."

Nodding, Dr. Parthen strode out the door.

Nicolae's dry throat closed over. Why had he said anything to her? He flopped his head to the side of his pillow so he could peer at his brother. "<She's going to speak to Bujor. He'll tell her about us.>"

Vasile exchanged a look with him, a quick look, but long enough for Nicolae to see the dark blot of unease there.

After Dr. Jess re-secured the arm tube, he re-bandaged Nicolae's stomach, then made notations on the clipboard papers.

Dr. Parthen returned, striding inside with sure steps.

Hadley came in just behind her.

Dr. Parthen drew up to Nicolae's bed and leaned over him. There was a bright look in her eyes.

He swallowed hard.

Dr. Parthen grinned triumphantly. "You're part *human*."

CHAPTER TWENTY-FIVE

NICOLAE CLOSED HIS EYES. AND now the shunning would begin.

"Your humanness means you and your brother *can* have hemophilia." Dr. Parthen's voice was higher in pitch. She seemed excited about this.

Nicolae didn't know what hemophilia was, but it didn't sound like anything to get excited about—not for him, at least. Although whatever the ailment, it was distracting everyone from Vasile and him being half-breeds. That part was good. Although maybe his humanness didn't matter here. Dr. Parthen was human, after all, and so was Hadley.

"Well done, Toni." Dr. Jess gave her a small bow of his head.

Beaming, Dr. Parthen picked up the clipboard and wrote swiftly on it. "I'm prescribing the Lazăr brothers a clotting promoter."

Hadley nodded. "I'll start them on it right away."

Another woman came inside. Her hair wasn't light and wasn't black. She was attractive enough, but she was nothing.

"Thanks for coming, Zerenity," Dr. Parthen greeted her. Putting away the clipboard, the doctor spoke to him. "Even though I'm going to give you medicine to help you, Nicolae, I agree with Dr. Jess. You should take in the blood of one of our community donors." She gestured at the brown-haired woman. "I'd like you to feed on Zerenity here."

Her? But she was nothing. Nicolae slid his attention right back over to Hadley. It was *her* perfume saturating his brain and blood with pleasure, *her* aroma that was sending sensations swirling from his lungs, into his belly, down to his crotch. "No." He pointed at Hadley. "Feed. Her."

"Oh, my." Hadley laughed, the sound coming out in chugging pockets of air, as if it wasn't a laugh at all. "Haah, haah, haah."

Nicolae's face burned. Maybe it did matter that he was a half-breed.

Dr. Parthen's mouth curled upward into a slight smile. "I know *her*, but I'm sorry. Hadley isn't a donor."

What is all this talk of donors? Nicolae's eyes found the tender spot on Hadley's throat where her heartbeat fluttered. The burn inside him to sink his sharp teeth into Hadley's sweet artery and drink her down was volcanic. His fangs stretched down farther with a longing ache, and his hunting vision snapped into place: little squares of hyper-clarity where Hadley was the focal point of the center square, everything about her crisp and clear.

He growled low. The inside of his veins itched and the emptiness in his belly yawned wider. He felt the rings round his pupils start to spin. "*Her*."

❖   ❖   ❖

THE SMILE HADLEY PASTED ONTO her face was forced and stiff and hurt her cheeks, and...*good God.* Did she have a tattoo printed across her forehead, *wrong men, please apply here*, or some other phrase which would explain why this kind of crap kept happening to her?

In the little over two weeks since her bombed-out date with Amza the plumber, she'd gone out with Shanelon—boring—Ruarc—arrogant—Istvan—a total mama's boy—Ninza—obsessed with football—Cavan—clueless about women—and Llawell—still hung up on his dead wife, Candace, who he talked about the whole date, and since Candace had been killed by Videon—the sadist who'd kidnapped Hadley and so regularly took up residence in her worst nightmares—Hadley begged off with a migraine real quick.

And now this scruffy manure-shoveler was getting his shorts in a knot over her. All right, so maybe that was too harsh and unfair, but she was so sick of these wrong men, and this guy was the worst yet. A savage who'd been raised on the side of a mountain. Grime behind his ears and in the creases of his wrists, roughly callused hands, and hair that looked like a dog had slept on it—he'd probably never seen the light of civilization. Clearly, no one had taught him manners. Like, hey, it's impolite to *stare*.

Hadley was used to dealing with a lot of gawking from the men around here—Thomal once told her she exuded some kind of magnetic essence—but this guy's stare wasn't the appreciative or enthralled type she was accustomed to seeing. It was too intense. Too hungry. Too *much*.

Too damned rude.

And hadn't anyone ever taught this guy to respond when spoken to?

Zerenity just said, "Look, pal, I know I'm not your favorite pick here, but you need to get some blood in you."

And Mountain Boy still wouldn't look at the donor.

"Hey!" Zerenity snapped her fingers in front of his face.

Mountain Boy finally switched his gaze over to Zerenity. He peered at her like she confused him.

"It's either me or no blood at all," Zerenity warned. "So let's go." She stuck her arm toward him, her wrist pointed upward toward his mouth.

Mountain Boy glanced at the arm Zerenity had volunteered, then returned his focus to Hadley.

She took a step back and shook her head.

His lips screwed tight. He sighed, but then grabbed Zerenity by the wrist.

"Wait a moment," Dr. Jess tried. But—

It was too late. Mountain Boy was already using his grip on Zerenity's wrist to yank her forward. He lunged off his pillow, his other hand clamping around the back of her neck, and latched onto her throat with a bite hard enough to flex up all the muscles in his face.

Zerenity screamed.

Mountain Boy released Zerenity at once, but not, evidently, because of her scream. "*Abominabil*," he hissed, spewing blood from his mouth. It sprayed all over Zerenity's face.

"You jerk!" Blushing furiously, Zerenity slapped Mountain Boy across the face.

His head jolted to the side.

Hadley's heart and lungs stopped.

Dr. Jess lifted a hand. "Everyone, stop. Please."

Mountain Boy came back around, his eyes spread wide. "She putrid," he told Dr. Jess, pointing at Zerenity. "Blood spoilt."

"Fuck you!" Zerenity pressed her palm over the twin puncture marks on her throat.

Hadley gaped at the blood seeping between Zerenity's fingers. *An animal.* Worse than a savage, this man was a low, base animal.

Vasile watched the scene from beneath scowling black brows. He was as crude-looking and uncouth as his brother.

"Zerenity, please," Dr. Jess said in a calm voice. "Nicolae didn't mean anything by what just happened. He's not used to the taste of the hormones in your blood, is all, and also this is how these men feed on their own donors. You have to teach him how we do—"

"The hell if I'm teaching this penis-head anything," Zerenity snapped. "Let another donor take him on." She stomped out.

After the noisy pounding of Zerenity's strides faded down the hall, Dr. Jess cleared his throat. "Well. Perhaps Ruxandra is available to—"

"Hold on a minute," Toni cut in. "You're saying these men always feed like that? So forcefully?"

"Yes," Dr. Jess said carefully.

"How else do they treat their women?"

Dr. Jess tipped his head a little. "From what I've observed, not particularly well. But now that I know their women don't have hormones, I understand why this is the case."

Toni's brows lowered. "What does that have to do with anything?"

"It's difficult to explain. It's as if...their women aren't *women* to them."

"What are they, then?" Toni's tone was sharp. "*Things?*"

"Please, try to understand, Toni, this is a biological construct, not a social one. The Vârcolac male needs the scent of female hormones around to activate certain areas of his brain. Without this scent, his mating instincts—the fierce desire to protect his woman, for example, or the urge to procreate—will remain inactive. Plus other important drives. In fact, Breen told me that Nicolae was shocked when he found out Dev is a bonded male—he even said it was impossible. I'd warrant Nicolae and his generation have never bonded, not if the only women they've ever been exposed to are hormone-less ones. I wouldn't be surprised if these men have a very limited understanding of male-female relationships, and perhaps little to no knowledge of sex."

Hadley lifted her eyebrows. A man, *any* man, not knowing about sex? *Hah*, she'd believe that when she saw it.

Toni turned to Nicolae, a thoughtful look on her face. "I'm sorry to ask this of you, Nicolae, but"—she gave him an encouraging smile—"do you know about sex?"

Mountain Boy's forehead scrunched, then cleared. "Ah. Sex...yes. Yes. Seen things on TV." Mountain Boy's storm-gray eyes latched onto Hadley's lips. "Kissing."

Hadley ground down on her teeth, fighting back the urge to shout, *Quit staring at me, you cabbagehead!*

"Yes." Toni nodded. "And?"

Mountain Boy's forehead scrunched again.

Toni exchanged a look with Dr. Jess.

Uncertainty washed over Mountain Boy's expression. "Not kissing?"

"No, there's kissing," Toni assured him, patting his arm.

And here he goes again. Back to staring. "Then *why*," Hadley asked, "does this guy keep reacting to me? To the point where he even attacked you, Dr. Jess? If the manly side of him is dormant, then he shouldn't be doing that."

"Well." Dr. Jess offered her a kind and patient smile. "There's always been something different about you, Hadley."

CHAPTER TWENTY-SIX

A FAMILIAR, INTOXICATING AROMA FLOODED into Breen's nose and slammed him awake. He popped his lids open and gulped a breath, his blood-need instantly propelling into a full, voracious hunger.

Charlize.

She was standing at the foot of his hospital bed, dressed in a form-fitting white T-shirt and a pleated gray miniskirt that showed off the sexy length of her runner's legs. The morning light coming in through the blinds highlighted her abundance of glossy blond curls.

His fangs reacted instantly to her, looking so beautiful and exuding the best scent in all the world. And he'd thought he needed more of Charlize last night, when Pettrila was in his room. The sensations he just woke up to—his pale green hospital pajamas soaked with sweat and his tongue feeling like poster putty—signaled a screaming blood-need.

"How are you feeling, Breen?"

Charlize's lips hadn't moved. She wasn't the one who'd spoken. She was just staring at him, mute and motionless. Was the sight of him in a hospital bed, one leg bandaged—his right pajama pant cut away to make room—reminding her of the lake of blood she'd seen in the garage, a sight she'd found so upsetting she fainted.

Please don't do that again. He hadn't liked it.

"Are you hungry?"

He recognized Toni's voice. She'd asked the question—this one and the one before.

"Um…" There wasn't much in his head that was currently fit for out-loud speech. Not with thoughts of feeding on Charlize waking up other parts of his body. He lived in a constant state of horny these days, but when he fed on Charlize that got jacked to teeth-shivering heights of lust. Anticipating her taste was giving him a serious case of morning wood.

Something squeezed Breen's arm, and he glanced over.

Hadley was at his bedside, taking his blood pressure. He hadn't noticed her, either. He was *really* zeroed in on Charlize. He gave the room a quick scan. No Nurse Shaston, which was good. She still hadn't forgiven him for all the shit he'd done to her to escape his half-bond. No Dr. Jess.

"One hundred twenty over eighty," Hadley announced. She removed the cuff while keeping her eyes averted from the area below his waist.

Man, he was going to start giving poor Hadley a complex if he kept popping boners around her.

Toni nodded, apparently satisfied with his blood pressure numbers, and wrote it on his medical chart. Strands of hair had escaped a disheveled topknot on Toni's head and lay in straggly threads around her face. Exhaustion circled her eyes in raccoon black, making her look totally beat up. She'd probably been working around the clock—all the medical staff had—considering the number of wounded that cycled through Țărână's hospital yesterday.

He pressed a button on his bed frame. A motor *hummed*, and he rose with the bed into a sitting position. "How's Dev?"

"Good," Toni answered. "Sleeping a lot. Feeding a lot. It'll take several days for him to reform all the skin on his back, but he's getting there. Marissa, of course, is relentlessly pampering him."

"He's already home?"

Toni snorted softly. "He went straight home from the garage. He didn't want to tie up a hospital bed."

"Can I go home?" Last time he'd been in the hospital, he was shackled to a bed and going through a brutal half-bond. Not good memories.

"Probably later today." Toni glanced over at the other bed.

Skunk Streak was stirring.

"Hadley," Toni said, "please let Pettrila know her brother is waking."

"Of course." Hadley headed for the door, rolling the blood pressure cuff into a ball as she went.

"I'm going to order you a post-surgery liquid breakfast." Toni wrote on Breen's chart again, flashing him an amused look when she added, "That means Jell-O, broth, and tea are in your future. Yum."

"Uh, yeah, I'm hungry, but, you know." He cast a sideways glance at Charlize. "Not necessarily for food."

Toni slotted his chart. "Of course." She gestured at Charlize. "That's why she's here."

Pettrila arrived, Hadley reentering behind her.

The room went quiet, full only of the whoosh of a heater.

Brother and sister stared at each other. Both of them had dark amber eyes.

Skunk Streak *hummed* his bed up, too, and finally broke the silence, his voice weighted with emotion. "*Pe toți sfinții! Cum e posibil să fii în viață? Nu pot să cred—*"

"I don't understand Romanian anymore," Pettrila interrupted.

They stared at each other again.

An orderly strolled by out in the hall, whistling tunelessly.

Breen shifted in his bed. Even his feet were sweating.

"My dear Octav…" Pettrila's gaze darkened. "How on earth are you alive? I saw your ship sink."

Octav's lips slanted. "That is what I just asked you in Romanian." He exhaled softly. "I wasn't *on* any of the ships, Pettrila. A group of us never boarded in Constanța Harbor.

We refused to be driven from our homeland by the Vârcolac Vânător."

Both of Pettrila's perfectly plucked brows went up.

The Vârcolac Vânător, or vampire hunters, were groups of civilian fighters organized in Romania in the 1800s to protect the population from the "evil" of vampires. Vampires had lived in peaceful obscurity in Romania for centuries before that, but sentiment changed when an overly ambitious Russian general invented horrific rumors about vampires so he could obliterate them for his own benefit. Eventually the Vârcolac Vânător proved so lethally effective that in 1887 all Vârcolac were forced to evacuate the country of their birth...or so everyone thought.

Four nights ago, in the abandoned Lakeside house, when Breen saw another person with a set of fangs—impossible for anyone outside of Țărână—he'd been shocked immobile.

Pettrila drew herself up and gave her brother a critical look. "You never said anything to me about your plans."

"It was a profound secret. Only one man knew of our intentions. Stanislav Lazăr. He was to be our emergency liaison in England, should we have needed one. By fate's good fortune, Stanislav was onboard one of the two ships that survived the Russian attack. But—" Octav's upper lip curled—"he ended up forging off on his own and so proved useless. We were never able to contact anyone of our own kind again."

Pettrila stood in silence.

Maybe if Breen said *this convo would be* so *much better outside* they would go.

Octav's expression softened. "I also didn't want to risk interfering with your future plans, Pettrila. You were set to go to England with Ștefan Dragoș, marry him, and start anew."

Color rose in Pettrila's cheeks. She looked away.

"But...you..." Octav's tone thickened. "I don't understand...did you truly bond with Grigore Nichita?"

The blush on Pettrila's face darkened. She said tonelessly, "Grigore convinced me it was Ştefan Dragoş who betrayed our race."

Octav's brows flashed down. "And you believed him?"

Pettrila's chest moved. "Right before we were due to set sail on the armada, Ştefan sent me a letter, tossing me aside for another woman." The smile Pettrila brought up was brittle. "After that, I'm afraid it was quite easy for Grigore to manipulate me into viewing the evidence his way. Only a mere four years ago did I discover Grigore forced Ştefan to write that letter. For the rest of nearly a hundred years, I thought Ştefan never loved me."

Octav's eyes went back and forth across his sister's.

Pettrila clasped her hands at her waist, the skin across her knuckles stretching taut. "I was injured in the Constanţa sea battle during our escape and needed to feed. No blood donors were on my ship. Grigore was. I bonded with him." Her nostrils quivered almost imperceptibly. "Ştefan had thrown me over, *you* were dead—I watched your ship sink—leaving me without any family. So what did it matter?"

The lines at the corners of Octav's eyes lengthened. He slumped back on his bed and turned to stare out the window. "It hasn't been a good life," he said quietly.

"No." The hands Pettrila had clasped at her waist switched positions, top to bottom, bottom to top. "I lost four daughters to a cave collapse some years ago. And now I almost lost a son to…"

Breen looked down and fiddled with the strings on his pajama bottoms. Now his fingers were sweating.

"What you did to Devid, Octav…" Pettrila trailed off again and shook her head. Apparently, the mother had feelings for the son she was estranged from.

Octav turned toward his sister again, the tendons on his neck flexing. "It hasn't been a good life for me, either, Pettrila. Too many enemies to contend with in Romania, too much fighting, so much death."

"The Vârcolac Vânător—"

"We had troubles with them, yes, but, mostly we have suffered from constant war with the three other factions living within the warded lands."

Pettrila frowned. "Warded lands? We always brushed those aside as being no more than a legend."

"They exist," Octav corrected. "Ştefan Dragoş led us to the special area in the Carpathian Mountains after those of us who decided to stay in Romania helped him fire cannons at the Russian frigates attacking the armada—and we helplessly watched *your* ship sink. Dragoş couldn't bring himself to stay in Transylvania without you, so he remained only long enough to help us lure several Solomonori to our side, then he moved to New York."

Breen snapped his focus away from Charlize's legs when Toni tried to exchange a glance with him. *Warded lands...Solomonori...* Yeah, the conversation between brother and sister was off-roading into the bizarre, but...Charlize had really cute creases behind her knees.

"For these many long years," Octav went on, "I have tried to keep my people sheltered from the outside world, but it came to pass that our own small corner of the mountains proved the most devastating. The Creaturi Care-şi Schimbă Forma, Dragoni Autentici, and the Vrăjitoare Războinice—"

Pettrila raised a hand. "Now you're not making sense, Octav."

Octav smiled vaguely. "The three other factions: The Shapechangers, the Pure Dragons, and the Warrior Witches. Otherwordly beings, like Vârcolac."

Toni jumped in now. "Pure Dragons? I thought that race had gone extinct."

Octav gave her an unfriendly look before answering. "They still exist in the warded lands, although Vârcolac don't interbreed with Dragons anymore." He assessed Toni critically. "Not like you people clearly do."

"Of course we do," Toni countered. "The Dragon blood-lines helped to stabilize the vampire population when Vârcolac first started having genetic problems. Why would you stop interbreeding with them?"

"They became enemies," Octav answered simply.

"Has it affected your genetics?"

Breen nearly crossed his eyes. Now he had to listen to a discussion on *genetics*? This was so damned ridiculous, he was starting to imagine himself sticking his thumb in his mouth and straining real hard until he exploded all over everyone. They'd get the fuck out of his room then, right?

Octav's mouth turned down. "I suppose so, yes. Most of the men have re-assumed more ancient, purer traits: they grow facial hair late, have a different activation to their Pure-bred eyes, and possess hunting vision. Unfortunately, all of our women are infertile." Octav smoothed the blanket over his lap with a rough sweep of his hand. "We have become the weakest faction, second only to the Shapechangers."

"Shapechangers?"

"Were-creatures. Wolves, bears, various large jungle cats, living in packs. Ever since Zalina stole their ability to change from their human shape to their animal form, they have suffered greatly."

"Who's Zalina?"

"She is leader of the Războinic Vrăjitoare, or Warrior Witches. This is the largest, wickedest, and most powerful of the factions. After we Vârcolac arrived, the Patru Puternic, or the Mighty Four, was created. The original idea behind uniting was for us to help each other against our common enemy: regular humans. But Zalina's lust to conquer us all has kept us struggling to outdo one another. Creaturi care-şi schimbă forma, Şarpe Pursânge, Războinic Vrăjitoare, Călăreţii Lunii—we all do nothing but fight."

Faint lines creased Toni's brow. "Călăreţii Lunii? Who's

that?"

"Vârcolac." Octav patted his chest. "It is the title the others have given us due to the vampire ability to harness and control the power of the moon." Octav scanned everyone's faces.

Everyone stared back blankly.

"Călăreţii Lunii," Octav repeated then clarified, "Moon-Riders."

CHAPTER TWENTY-SEVEN

THERE WAS A LENGTHY PAUSE.

Perfect time to tell everyone to go do other things and do them somewhere else so Breen could get to feeding already—the inside of his stomach felt like it'd sprouted stubble. But Toni was too intrigued by the topic.

"All right," she said, "go back to the beginning for a moment. What is a warded land?"

"It is a land within a land," Octav explained. "A place where *two* lands exist while there appears to be only one, the second land lying hidden from normal human perception beneath a magical warding cloak. If a regular strolls through this area in the Carpathian Mountains, he will see one view of existence—of trees and hillsides, maybe the odd shack or two. He won't see what exists right on top of it—many buildings and streams and whole populations of people. Unless, of course, he can pass through the ward into the secondary world, but he can only do this if the ward has been coded to allow him through."

Toni paused, a thoughtful frown creasing her brow. She glanced at Breen when she finally spoke. "This warding system sounds like how Videon is keeping you warriors out of his depraved playland. Jacken described being blocked by an invisible, impenetrable bubble. He says he's seen people disappear into thin air in certain parts of the city, but when he goes to the same spot, nothing happens. Doesn't that sound like a ward?"

Breen didn't answer. *Just fuck me dead already.*

Octav looked skeptical. "If so, this Videon would have to wield the powers of a Solomonori."

"What's a Solomonori?"

"Mages or wizards. The wards are created and controlled by them. There are only eight Solomonori total. When we Vârcolac first arrived in the warded lands, Zalina was in one of her Sleeps, so Ştephan Dragoş was able to gain us two. The Pure Dragons also have two, and the Shapechangers used to have two, but Zalina stole one. She wants all of them, you see, and this is a great source of strife among us all. There is an antidote for every spell Zalina casts, *unless* she controls all the Solomonori. Should this apocalyptic turn of events ever occur, she would have ultimate power." Octav looked toward the heavens. "Then woe betide us all."

"Moreover," he added, "Zalina seeks to breed with the Solomonori. Through them, she creates the most powerful of the Nature Spirits as her daughters: the Iele. The Solomonori understandably don't want Zalina to have their offspring. She trains them to be Warrior Witches like herself. Whenever possible they hide their girl children. But this isn't an easy endeavor. Every Iele who is spawned of a union between Zalina and a Solomonori is born with an identifying symbol: a Z."

"For Zalina, I presume?" Toni asked dryly.

"Exactly. Except the Z is written in the Cyrillic alphabet, so it will resemble a 3."

Hadley, quiet until now, exhaled a loud gasp. "Oh, my God! I have a birthmark like that!"

Breen stared at the wall across from his bed. *A new topic to discuss.* How fucking great was that?

Octav transferred his attention over to her. "Indeed?" he drawled, clearly doubting it. "Although..." He surveyed Hadley from head to toe. "The Iele are beautiful and voluptuous women who exude great seductive powers over men. You fit those parameters." He made a casual gesture at her body. "Might I be so bold as to ask to see your birth-mark?"

Hadley hesitated. "Yes, all right." She angled to the left and tugged down her scrub pants just enough to reveal a lopsided "3" on her hip.

Octav intently studied the mark, then slowly raised his gaze to Hadley. His eyes glittered. "That *is* it."

Hadley yanked her scrubs back up. "But that's impossible. My mother is…my *mother*. You know. I mean…" She tinkled out an awkward-sounding laugh. "My mother isn't Zalina the Warrior Witch, right? Hahahahaha."

"Child," Skunk Streak asked quietly, "were you perhaps born early?"

Hadley choked off her laugh and swallowed audibly. "I… Yes. I was eight weeks premature." Her lashes were moving very rapidly. "How did you know that?"

"Because *you*, specifically, weren't born early. Another baby was, and that premature infant actually died."

Hadley whitened. "What?"

"The Solomonori who is your father put you in the child's place to protect you from Zalina." Skunk Streak folded his hands in his lap. "You, my dear, are a changeling."

✧   ✧   ✧

BREEN STARED DOWN AT HIS lap and messed with the IV tube trailing out of his wrist.

Hadley had just hotfooted it out of the room, and soon after, Pettrila wheel-chaired Skunk Streak out to the hospital courtyard to "take air."

Finally. Time to feed.

When everyone was gone, Toni turned to Charlize and said, "Due to the severity of Breen's wound, he's going to need to take in more blood than usual. He'll have to feed from your neck instead of your wrist this time."

And that's when Breen discovered a fascination with his

IV.

Because Toni was making shit up about Vârcolac culture again, same as she'd done when Breen and Charlize met with her after Breen punched Amza.

Truth was, Breen could get all the blood he needed absolutely fine from Charlize's wrist. Her throat was just way better, the skin softer there, her blood especially aromatic, the contact more intimate, and… Saliva flooded his mouth. Yeah, *way* better.

Now, as before, Toni was probably trying to force Charlize's hand when it came to getting closer to Breen.

Now, as then, he kept his mouth shut about it.

Toni folded her stethoscope in half and stuck it in her lab coat pocket. "Okay?"

A tendon flexed once in Charlize's neck, like maybe she'd swallowed. "Yes, okay."

"I'll give you two some privacy, then." Toni left.

Charlize went back to standing at the end of Breen's bed and just staring.

What was she thinking? That she wouldn't be able to handle the closer contact of the neck feeding? Or was she wondering what it'd be like to face down two feedings in a row, something they'd never done before? He didn't know what the extra ființă would do to her, but he could reasonably predict that his dick—always pissed at him these days for subjecting it to nothing but beating off—would substantially up the volume of its complaints over the lack of follow-on sex.

"So, uh…" Charlize's tongue smoothed across her lips, and blood rushed into Breen's groin. *Shit-nuggets.* Yeah, he was going to hear extra grief from his dick, for sure.

Without another word, Charlize moved woodenly to the side of his bed, bent over, and stuck her throat in front of him.

Her long, curly hair tumbled around his head, and her scent exploded through his sinuses, aerosoling his brain with such intense pleasure that both his fangs and his dick reared—fangs down, dick up.

Shoving her hair aside, Breen gripped the back of her neck, pushed his face into her throat, and inhaled deeply. He growl-groaned and nuzzled her, savoring what might be his last time in this special place.

She released a muffled, urgent sound, and the stiff appendage between his legs grew more adamant about finding its way inside her. His fangs gave a huge, painful, *stop-fucking-around* throb. He plunged in and groaned again as her rich blood flowed over his tongue and glided down into his stomach, washing a drugged contentment through him and filling his body with life at its purest. Much better than when he'd fed on her yesterday, half gone to a blood-coma.

Snarling softly, Breen sucked hard, squeezing his fingers rhythmically around Charlize's nape. The rapid beat of her heart pulsed against his lips, and the aroma of her arousal bombarded the room. He swayed back against his pillow. Grids momentarily uploaded across his vision as the predator within him stretched into muscle and sinew, its nostrils flared wide, as if scenting a female in heat.

He drank until he was forced to stop—when his fangs retracted—leaving him no choice but to pull back. He stared at her with hot eyes while he licked the residue of her blood off his lips. He was breathing heavily.

So was she, her cheeks pink, her lips wet and parted.

His sex bucked.

She lowered her eyes to his crotch. His jutting dick was straining the fly of his pajamas open.

Her jaw flexed once, then she hissed. "Fuck this screwed community and its sphincter-tight rules." Hiking up her skirt, she dropped her panties to her ankles and flicked them aside with one foot. "I can't stand it anymore." Climbing onto his hospital bed, she straddled him.

He grabbed her hips, aiming her into a rapid entrance

position.

A bell in his brain banged a sideline warning.

Wasn't he supposed to be following through on something Toni set him up for? But...but, he couldn't seem to get the picture of it clearly in his mind now that Charlize's panties were off, releasing more of her clean and salty scent. The aroma struck him on the brain with a hammer. His next breath caught in his lungs.

Charlize darted a quick glance down at the bandage on his leg. His wound was near his knee, far enough away from his lap that she wouldn't hurt him if she planned to give him a good trouncing.

Which she clearly did.

Not even bothering to tug his bottoms down, she fumbled his engorged dick through the fly of his pajamas, then propped him up and lowered herself down. Her wet opening met the head of him.

His fangs pounded down again, and a guttural sound broke from his throat.

She started to sit.

He snapped his fangs together. She was only a quarter of the way down his length, and the suctioning power of her inner muscles was already staggering.

She lowered her lips to his. "I fucking love your cock," she whispered against his mouth. "It's so big and thick and powerful. It feels so good."

His dick kicked so hard, he wouldn't be surprised if he'd just jacked some pre-come inside her. *Feels so good.* Understatement. He squeezed her hips and tilted her forward, putting her in a better position to—

He stopped.

Feels so good.

What the hell was he doing?

He was letting himself get overwhelmed again by how fantastic Charlize felt, that's what, once more just being led instead of doing the leading himself. No thought was going into having sex with her. Again. And how great was it that he was ignoring death's door epiphanies to keep messing up the same shit in his life? He exhaled slowly from his nose. Not great at all.

It took him two hard swallows to get the one syllable out, but he finally managed it. "No."

She startled. Her eyes opened all the way, her gaze looking puzzled for the length of two heartbeats. Then her lids narrowed. She snatched up his face in a strong, one-handed grip, her fingers stretching over one cheek, her thumb extending high across the other. "You want this," she gritted at him.

Yeah, he did, more than he wanted to breathe, but there was something he wanted way more than sex. *Her.* And the only way he'd even come close to getting her was to stop doing more of the same stupidness.

"And *I* want this." Her blue eyes fierce, Charlize flexed her powerful runner's legs and tried to force herself down lower onto his shaft.

Damn, she was strong. And determined. And he was in for the fight of his life, because his dick throbbed out its own opinion on this battle, and his predator entered the fray, making Breen's grip go slack on her hips—for two more inches' worth of descent.

Make decisions. Decide a course. Act. Bracing his jaw, Breen got his shit together and held Charlize off with strong hands. "I just want you to be sure about us before we do this. That's all."

There can be no halfway within the bonded relationship.

A wild panic darted across Charlize's face. She shook her head at him.

He showed her gritted fangs. His balls were eagerly pumping semen up his shaft, creating a painful back-jam at the exit portal. "Then we probably shouldn't."

Tears leapt into her eyes—angry, frustrated tears. She uttered a low growl and flung herself off him.

He winced, her sudden departure tugging his dick out of her painfully fast. *Not* the response he'd been hoping for. Grimly, he tucked himself into his pajama bottoms.

She stomped away two paces and whirled around. "Why does it have to be this way, Breen? Why can't we just fuck? Would it really mess you up so bad if I don't act like your bonded mate? Explain it to me."

And join in on Toni's white lies? Bad enough that he was going along with the setup. He didn't need to compound his involvement further. He countered with his own set of questions. "Why can't we be in a relationship, Charlize? What's so awful about the idea of being married to me? I've never understood it. I mean, it can't be about *me*, because you've never bothered to get to know me."

Her complexion flooded red.

"Is it because our hooking up was a colossal mistake? Okay. I get that part. It was a huge fuckup. But here we are stuck with each other anyway, so why not give us a chance? What harm could *trying* do?"

"The *harm* is that I don't want obligations and worries and stressors. And that's what relationships are. A bunch of crap."

He heard the slight tremor in her voice—a thread of fear beneath the anger and disgust—and searched her eyes for more. What stupid son of a bitch had made her think that? "Maybe I'll be different. But you won't know it if you don't—"

"Oh, shut up, would you?" She stomped back to his bed. "You're no different from anyone else."

What? "How am—?"

She leaned so close to his face her shout stirred his hair. "You disappeared for three days!"

He slowly shut his mouth. His stomach waited, clenched so tight it hurt.

Her lips trembled. Just once, and then she was glaring at him. "When I was six years old, my mother disappeared for three days. Do you have any idea what that was like? Struggling to take care of my little brother and sister, running out of food but knowing I couldn't ask anyone for help because Mom would get busted and then I'd be in trouble and probably taken away from her. For three days I thought my mom was *dead*." Tears dampened her eyes. "I thought *you* were dead! *Three fucking days* you were gone, Breen, and when you finally came back, you were covered with so much blood it was…it w-was…"

His tongue gnarled up. Not in the way of his usual silence, not purposeful or watchful or careful. He also wasn't just lost for the right response. He was utterly dumbfounded by what he was hearing her say…by what he was seeing in her expression.

Immersed in the horror of her memories, Charlize's defenses had fallen away, allowing the real woman to peek out through slim cracks. And this was more than a glimpse of Charlize's softer, scared and lonely side. This was a revelation of the most profound vulnerability he'd ever seen, an unveiling of the self-hatred that lived at her core.

His heart began to beat in a funny way. "I didn't know, uh… I didn't think you cared. Thomal and Gábor's radars picked up on their mates' worry while we were in the forest, but I never felt anything from you."

She moved a wobbly step back from him. "Because I don't care."

He studied the muscles twitching all over her face. She was trying to harden herself up, but she couldn't do it this time—her eyes remained bewildered and too young. Haunted. "You do care," he told her in a soft voice. "You've shown it to me, Charlize. You can't take it back now."

Her hands balled into rigid fists. "Then let me rephrase. I *won't* care. Not when you could die at any second."

That one tripped him up. How could he assure her he wouldn't get hurt again? He was a warrior. He couldn't promise her that, but…but, hell, she obviously needed to hear something comforting. Moving his tongue around inside his mouth, he searched for some fancy words to tell her, but as per his usual MO, he didn't find any.

Why hadn't he paid better attention to females in his life, gained more XP points? Then maybe he would know the right things to say and when to say them. He just never figured he'd have a woman of his own. What woman would pick him when there were so many other great men in the community to—

He bowed his head. No woman *had* picked him.

"Look," she said, exasperated. "I'm going to go. We're obviously not going to fuck."

He pinched the bridge of his nose and rubbed it. He didn't know what to say to stop her from leaving. He just didn't. But the hell if he could give up, either, not after the deeper glimpse she'd given him. He'd seen someone inside her he could really love, a woman who wasn't all about the sex, like she acted—

He brought his head up. Holy shit, that was it.

This guy was just supposed to be a fun lay.

I'm going to go. We're obviously not going to fuck.

He needed to focus on what she wanted—sex—not what she didn't want—permanence. He finally knew what to say. "We *can* fuck, Charlize. You just have to agree to try to be in a relationship with me. Just *try*. It doesn't matter if we succeed."

She stilled.

His heart thudded. He had her attention.

"So you're saying if I try with you, we can fuck? No matter the outcome?"

"Yes."

"How do we try?" Her eyes narrowed in suspicion. "Because the hell if I'm moving into one of those white picket fence houses and playacting Mr. and Mrs. Beaver Cleaver."

"We won't do that." *We're really talking about this!* "Just throwing ourselves together probably wouldn't work out so well. We need to iron out some rough edges first."

"Okay. I repeat—*how?*"

"Well…" He hadn't exactly cracked that specific nut yet. "I don't know how."

"Great." She sniffed. "It'll be like the blind leading the blind."

"So, we get help." Maybe Toni would be willing to sit down with them every day to—

"Oh, I see where this is going." Charlize crossed her arms, although it looked more like she was hugging herself. "You're talking about couples counseling with that Karrell woman, aren't you?"

Uh… He sat up straighter. That was actually a great idea. "Yes. That's what I'm saying."

Her crossed arms tightened. "I don't want some stranger poking around my private business, Breen."

"Do you have another idea?"

Her chin stiffened. She paused for a long moment. "So if we go to couples counseling together, we fuck? That's the story?"

"Yes."

"Fuck regularly?"

"Yes."

"Like…starting right now."

The muscles around his hips flexed. "Sure, why not?"

She hesitated another second, then put her hands on her hips. "You'll have to talk in therapy, Breen. You can't just do your usual and sit and say nothing."

His face heated. "I know."

"I'm not going to do all the talking."

"I'll talk."

She moved her lips together. "Okay."

Okay. The word sucker-punched him. What exactly did she mean by it?

She climbed back on the bed and moved to straddle him again.

"Wait." He stopped her. "So you agree?"

"Yes. Jesus. I agree. Can we stop talking about this now?"

Astonishment or triumph? He didn't have the chance to experience either. Charlize was rooting around inside his fly.

His dick had lowered to half-mast during their negotiations, but the moment her hand curled around his length, he reared back up to full power.

She drew him out into the open, straddled him again, then—no giving him another chance to stop her—just, *pow-whoa!* She sat down hard on his dick, encasing him completely in her wet heat.

A growl barked from his throat as a shattering tide of pleasure rushed through his pelvis and along his thighs. His fangs shot down.

What followed next wasn't a good trouncing. It wasn't in the realm of fucking, and probably couldn't even be defined as rough sex. It delved too far into animal barbarity to be anything but a pummeling, plunging, grinding act of violence that hammered her body into his and jolted the bed so hard that the locked wheels screeched in metallic hysteria and the frame thundered up pieces of plaster dust from the wall.

Breen hung onto her ass with everything he had.

Without warning Charlize climaxed, her sheath convulsing around him aggressively and with impossible flexibility.

His legs went rigid as her inner muscles milked ecstasy up from the very root of his shaft. He squeezed his eyes shut, just letting himself be taken by her orgasm. His spine bowed. His hips strained. A guttural shout exploded from him, and his whole body shuddered with the power of his orgasm, his dick jerking and pumping against all of her soft inner tissues. He shuddered again. And again—*damn*—then finally sagged back into his pillows.

Charlize collapsed on top of him, her hair spraying all over his chest, a few strands tangling around one of his biceps. Her hot breath streamed across his pajama top. Her breasts surged in time to his own labored breathing.

He worked at evening out his oxygen intake while his leg wound throbbed along with his nuts, one irritating, the other throb pleasing.

"Well, Costache," Gábor drawled. "You were wondering if Dalakis was okay. Guess we have our answer."

Breen angled his head toward the door.

Thomal and Gábor were standing just inside his room. An amused shine was in Thomal's eyes. Gábor was smirking.

"Shit," Charlize hissed. Scrambling off Breen's lap, she snatched up her panties and darted by the two warriors, performing some fancy footwork to maneuver around Octav, who was being wheeled back inside.

So much for taking time to savor a post-orgasm high. Breen quickly stuffed his dick back in his PJs.

Jacken was coming in right behind Octav, shouldering past Thomal and Gábor to get inside the room. He cut a swift glance at Breen, long enough to see he was okay, then stalked over to the foot of Octav's bed, waiting while Pettrila helped her brother settle under the covers.

Jacken observed Octav with a dark look in his already very black eyes.

Octav pursed his lips at Jacken. "What kind of creature *are* you?" He elevated his nose, as if Jacken was a pile of excrement left behind in a bedpan, his scent offensive to more delicate sensibilities. "Not a pure Vârcolac, that is for certain."

"What I *am* is head of security here." Jacken's voice held the kind of razor edges that suggested very little control was being maintained over his temper. "You fucked with the safety of my people, Rázóczi, so now you and I are going to talk. I ask questions. You answer them."

"Sounds scintillating." Skunk Streak gestured Jacken onward, like a king granting audience to a simpering plebian. "How might I assist you?"

Jacken crossed his arms. "How did you get the email address you used to set your trap for Nichita? That's a private account."

"Someone gave it to me."

"You don't say." Jacken showed the tip of a sharpening fang. "Who?"

Octav looked pointedly at Jacken's forearm tattoos. "Oh, someone who very much wants *you* dead."

Jacken uncoiled. Leaning forward, he braced his palms on the rail at the end of Octav's bed, then leaned forward some more, his jaw jutted. "*Who?*"

Chapter Twenty-Eight

THE DOOR EXPLODED OFF ITS hinges with a thunderous crack and flew into the room, chunks of wood spewing across the living room carpet.

John Waterson shot up from his chair on strengthless legs, stumbling, then worsened his equilibrium by whacking his knee against the Formica table.

Poker chips rolled this way and that like Barbie hubcaps.

John's police buddies Pablo, Carlos, and Frank, leapt to their feet and shouted.

Three huge men poured through the gaping hole of the doorway, although only one came forward. He approached with the muscled stealth of a fighting professional and—

John's heart stalled out.

Teeth-Tattooed Asshole.

A kick to the head.

A punch to the temple.

Pablo and Carlos were out.

Frank made it as far as yanking his service revolver from its shoulder holster.

Teeth-Tattooed Asshole arm-blocked the weapon snout-up toward the ceiling while his other fist made a line-drive into Frank's forehead, connecting brutally enough to lobotomize the detective. Frank hit the kitchen floor like several pounds of liver into a waste bucket and drooled.

John stood in place, shaking. Three seasoned police officers, neutralized in seconds. By one man. He would've been embarrassed for his friends if he wasn't so busy being embarrassed for himself.

Teeth-Tattooed Asshole was looking him over now, and clearly he was appalled by what he saw.

"*This*," scoffed one of the other men, "is the infamous Detective John Waterson?"

John's face flamed. If he'd thought his poker buddies were men to be envied for their health and vitality, these three had physiques to inspire steaming jealousy. He clamped his teeth together so hard a couple of molars leaned sideways inside his gelatinous gums. Standing here in front of his enemy, feeling so blaringly inadequate, gouged a stick into his soft underbelly about as deep as it could go. "What the fuck do you want?"

Teeth-Tattooed Asshole's lip lifted into a sneer. "One of my men almost died because of the deal you cut with Rázóczi, Waterson."

Almost. So MoonRiderOne—besides *obviously* welching on his agreement to kill Teeth-Tattooed Asshole—had hosed up his own revenge against Nichita. *Christ.* How was a dying man supposed to fulfill last wishes when forced to deal with rank amateurs?

He gave his enemy bland. "I beg your pardon?" One act he definitely wasn't performing from his deathbed was offering this man more information. He didn't know how much Teeth-Tattooed Asshole knew about John's plans for justice, but he sure as hell wasn't going to fill in any gaps.

Teeth-Tattooed Asshole exhaled a blast of air. "Don't try to pull any shit, Waterson. The techie guy who works with us could find a hymen on a whore, which means it took him less than ten minutes to discover you're Justice Seeker."

John started to spread his hands in an *oh, well* gesture, but his fingers were shaking badly—adrenaline was not his body's friend these days—so he just shrugged.

If there'd been any humanity in Asshole's dark eyes, white

fury now incinerated it. He stalked forward, his boot sole leaving a geometric print on the back of Frank's shirt on his way over to a nose-to-nose position with John. "You think you can get away with messing with one of my men?"

This close, the absolute power of Teeth-Tattooed Asshole was immense. John could almost feel his marrow curdling. One punch. That's all it'd taken from this man to lay John out on the floor of Scripps Memorial Hospital the last time they'd gone nose to nose. That's what John just saw happen to his police buddies.

Suddenly it felt like he was breathing at altitude. After a 10K. He edged a step back, his chest constricting further when he nearly tumbled off his teeter-totter legs. Weakness absolutely fucking sucked. The only thing worse was the impotence his illness—He flushed.

The two men by the door watched him curiously.

"Time to settle your account with me, Waterson." The black hell on Asshole's face would have made most men lose bladder control.

John was going to blame his immediate need to urinate on his illness.

The apartment across the hall began to spew the Bossa Nova. Too loud. *Mr. Palmeiro, you deaf fuck.*

The fist just *arrived*.

Out of nowhere.

It carried the weight of a pallet of bricks, and John's head snapped completely around, cranking his entire body with it. He spun a full three-sixty, his legs braiding together like a Rainbow Twist Lollipop. No way could he stay upright like that. He fell. His hip, then his shoulder struck the linoleum one after the other. Then his chin connected, knocking his jawbone against his skull bones, thundering a pain through his head unlike any he'd ever known. Manic Ferris wheels. Demented Teacups. An air horn blaring in his ears. Barbed spears stabbing down from his brain into his upper teeth.

He clutched his temples and screamed.

Teeth-Tattooed Asshole made a rude noise. "Chrissake, Waterson, I barely tagged you."

Unbelievably, the pain got worse, as if his cranium was fissuring apart and poking sharper shards into his waxy brain while his jaw rent in two, crowbarring an upper molar out of his mushy gums. He spat it out. A crippling, endless chasm of hunger opened up inside his stomach and boiled over into a searing agony, like having Hell's furnace for an ulcer.

He raised his screams to shrieks.

"Holy shit," one of the other men cursed. "Would you get a load of this guy?"

"Let's fucking roll. All this racket, cops'll be here in a heartbeat."

John's face was grabbed and maneuvered over until Asshole's scowl came into view. "Something's not right with him."

"Ya think? Dude's half-a-corpse."

"No. It's something else." Asshole was closely examining him. "I don't like it. We need to take him to a hospital."

"Jesus. All right. Which one is closest to—"

"Not a topside one. *Ours.*"

"Shit."

And then someone must've switched off the lights.

Chapter Twenty-Nine

JOHN WOKE TO AN INNER foreboding and went limp, fighting to stay hunkered down in the mire of unconsciousness. His senses were coming back online with slow waves of input, and the info he was receiving wasn't reassuring—he heard the hefty tread of footsteps generally associated with large men and smelled the sour antiseptic reek of his least favorite place on earth: a hospital.

The reality waiting for him on the other side of his closed eyelids wasn't one he wanted. Better just to hang out in the dark. But the veil of blackness obstinately grew thinner and lighter, the electrical impulses in his brain increasing, and full consciousness arrived despite his best efforts. His eyes unstuck themselves on their own.

And as suspected, it was bad.

The most off-putting face imaginable was right above his: Devid Nichita's.

"Welcome back to the living, Waterson," Nichita sneered, his drawling voice grating against John's flesh, his nerves. His mood. "Not very much fun, is it, waking up cuffed to a hospital bed?"

He was? He rotated his wrists and felt a padded restraint on one. A tic twitched in his eyelid.

A nasty smile split Nichita's goatee.

John's breathing roughened. No brain surgeon license required to figure this one out: he was about to be handed a

load of retribution for having cuffed Nichita to a hospital bed
years ago, the incident happening right after a shootout
between the two of them. John had needed to interrogate
Nichita, damn well get some straight answers about the
strange shit always surrounding the guy. During the questioning process, John *might* have been somewhat of a bastard, so
he supposed it made sense that now he'd come full 'round to
the proverbial *payback is a bitch*.

He heard some scuffling movement and craned his neck
up, quick-scanning the room. The two men who'd been with
Teeth-Tattooed Asshole earlier in John's apartment were
there—one with a blond flattop, the other with black, buzz-
cut hair. John sank his head back down. Way too much power
for him to deal with, even on his best day with both hands
free. His knees jolted, then his feet, as if his "flight" reflexes
were gearing up his body for a run that no way he could
manage. Even if he had the energy and the strength, he was—
as Nichita was savoring—trapped.

"Although you're no longer much of a worthy adversary,
are you?" The flare of satisfaction in Nichita's expression
dimmed. "What the hell happened to you?"

Boy, it was just so much fun for men who didn't have
more health worries than the occasional zit to keep pointing
that out.

"He's obviously very ill."

John dropped his eyes shut at the sound of the voice
that'd been haunting his dreams, and a good deal of his
waking thoughts, for years.

Toni.

His long-hoped-for reunion with the love of his life was
finally here, and it was so far from the myriad fantasies he'd
entertained about this very moment, it was pathetic.

His favorite fantasy was of him charging in—cape flying,
of course—to save Toni from the men who'd kidnapped her.
She would be dressed in the same clothes he'd last seen her

wearing, especially the wraparound blouse that had done things to her breasts no woman should have a right to do. It just wasn't fair to the male population. John would vanquish her abductors, then sweep her into his arms and stride off to the safety of his apartment. There, he'd peel her slowly out of her wraparound blouse, and after a lot of tangling up the sheets, she'd agree to marry him and have his babies.

Another favorite fantasy was of her showing up on his doorstep—like she'd suddenly reappeared at Scripps Memorial Hospital four years ago—and moonily confess that her recent harrowing experiences had given her a new perspective on life. She knew what was really important now…and would John please marry her and grant her the esteemed honor of bearing his children?

None of his fantasies—not a single one—included his current reality: Toni looking sterile in a white lab coat, him lying before her as the skeletal remains of a man who was no longer worthy of her.

Toni peered down on him with sympathetic eyes. God, and what eyes. He'd forgotten what clear blue skies they were. "How are you feeling, John?"

Oh, just a couple of railroad spikes still jammed in my skull. No biggie. The mere act of shifting his focus over to the other two men who drew up to his bed—across from Toni—hurt like fuck.

One was Teeth-Tattooed Asshole. Nichita stepped back to make room for him, moving kind of carefully, it seemed.

The second guy had black hair, too, but he looked like he'd just stepped out of a Hugo Boss sportswear ad.

Toni set a gentle hand on John's forearm. "Can you tell me what's wrong with you?"

He didn't say anything. Being gravely ill in front of Toni was probably only marginally worse than discussing it with her.

Soft lines pleated Toni's brow. "I've given you some

morphine for your pain, but I don't want to prescribe anything else until I know what's going on. What have you been diagnosed with?"

He licked his dry lips and sweated some more. Was she even more beautiful than she'd been four years ago, her skin more youthful and vibrant, her hair more luxurious? He didn't see how it was possible, considering she'd been held against her will this whole time. That had to be hard on a woman. Then again...she did appear pretty exhausted.

"John, I can't help you if I don't know what's wrong."

"You can always *dissect* him to find out," Nichita suggested nastily.

Toni flashed an admonishing look in the direction of Nichita's voice.

"This man isn't our concern, at any rate," the Hugo Boss guy said. "He shouldn't even be here."

Toni shook her head. "Jacken was right to bring him."

"John Waterson is a topside *police officer*," Hugo Boss countered hotly with this not-completely-accurate statement. "I would think Jacken, of all people, could appreciate the dangers of having such a person here."

John's nemesis crossed his tattooed arms. "Something about what's going on with Waterson is getting under my skin, Roth. He doesn't belong at a topside hospital until we've figured it out."

"Where am I?" John croaked.

Toni gave him a reassuring smile. "It's okay, John. You've been brought to the hospital at the top-secret research institute where I work."

The lie clutched at John's insides. No such "institute" existed and hearing Toni offer up such a bullshit answer only confirmed that she was still in trouble. Although, weirdly, she wasn't giving off any of the behavior subtleties he'd expect from a woman who was under duress but trying to hide it. No secret pleas buried in her eyes. No tension lay around her mouth, like the muscles were constricted from holding back the truth. Probably his disease-rotted brain was just missing the signals. It also didn't help that his skull was currently crushed in on itself.

A dark-haired woman wearing scrubs entered the room. "Here are the films you ordered, Dr. Parthen."

"Ah, good. Thank you, Shaston." Toni patted John's forearm. "Hopefully I'll be able to figure out what's going on with you now. I took X-rays of your head when you first arrived."

The nurse tucked a couple of X-rays under the clips of a viewer, then turned on the light. A skull materialized on the screen—apparently his—at two different viewpoints.

Toni walked up to the viewer and examined the pictures. A frown tugged her mouth down. "Odd," she murmured.

"What?" Teeth-Tattooed Asshole moved up next to her, so close he brushed shoulders with her.

She didn't pull away.

John chewed his teeth.

"I'm not entirely sure what I'm seeing. I…" Toni stepped closer to the X-ray and squinted. "It appears that John has extra bone matter traveling up from the top of his canines into his cranium. Here." She pointed them out. "I don't know what would account for—"

"Holy night," GQ Roth hissed. "*Fangs.*"

Toni whirled around, her eyebrows startled high.

"Those are fangs," Roth insisted.

"What? That's imposs—"

A hard exhale from Teeth-Tattooed Asshole interrupted her. "*This* explains what's been bugging me about Waterson…what I'm seeing in his eyes." He pointed at John. "*Hunger.*"

Toni's whole expression went wide. "Are you completely off your rocker?" She looked back and forth between Roth and Teeth-Tattooed Asshole. "John doesn't have fangs."

"I'm afraid he does."

This announcement came from a different doctor, who'd just stepped into the doorway. He was slender and black-haired and meticulous in appearance, a real Madison Avenue type in a dark gray suit under his lab coat. He looked like the kind of man who wouldn't lift a hand to swat a fly, much less deliver a statement that carried enough damning heft to fell an entire room.

But he did.

"John Waterson," he said, "is my son."

CHAPTER THIRTY

AN INTESTINE-FREEZING HORROR FLUSHED THROUGH John's bloodstream.

The flabbergasted silence gripping everyone in the hospital room was not of the *somebody lock up this loon for spouting a bunch of hoo-ha nonsense* variety, but rather the much less preferred *holy shit!* alternative. It was as if everyone thought this might actually be true.

As if.

People, chill the fuck out, okay? My father was a rancher in Kansas, not loony Mr. Meticulous here.

This was the statement John wanted to make, *should* have made, although, truthfully, at this point in the proceedings he wasn't sure if he could've pulled it off without laughing hysterically, thumbing his nose at his fellow bedlamites, and calling them names.

It was never put to the test. No words made themselves available to him. Because... John had extra bone stuck up inside his head and these were fangs, and some anally hygienic man was really his—?

No.

Nope.

No, no, no.

Ha ha, that *was* hysterical.

The silence pounded against his eardrums. An icicle bored into his chest, his forever empty stomach shriveled into a rotten prune, and the bane of his existence, his infernal sweat glands, went into overdrive.

Mr. Meticulous walked two steps inside the room and stared at him.

Blinking through sweaty eyes, John did the man the courtesy of staring back, curious about him despite his need for all of this to be a bad dream. Mr. Meticulous's face was currently drawn and pale, but otherwise he was a good-looking guy. His black hair was combed back neatly, giving way to the authority of a wide brow. He had the aquiline nose and finely-drawn mouth of a man who came from money, and he was relatively young. He also had... John tore his attention away. He didn't want to see that the man also had the same unique blue-green eye color John did.

The fancily dressed Roth finally broke into the silence—testily, angrily. "What the hell are you talking about, Jess?"

Mr. Meticulous Jess swallowed, his throat moving. "Yes, I...I should explain, of course." He clasped his hands behind his back. "It happened on the night of April 30th, 1980. I went up to San Diego to attend a seminar on in vitro fertilization. This was when I was still struggling to find a solution to our race's procreation problems, and I was hoping this technique might provide inspiration. According to security protocol at the time, I couldn't go topside alone, so two men accompanied me: Grigore Nichita and Dake Costache."

Jess darted a glance over to his audience, primarily at Devid Nichita and the blond guy with the flattop. "Most of the other doctors brought nurses with them, and three lovely women were at our table. We all established an instant rapport, and..." He shifted his weight. "That night Grigore, Dake, and I had romantic liaisons with these women."

"*What?!*" Blondie blasted.

Jess cast Blondie a regretful look. "I'm sorry, Thomal. Please don't think your father didn't love your mother. He did. But Dake was a rare offshoot of male who had a wandering eye—I believe you know that. As for Grigore, there was nothing to hamper him. He and Pettrila were eternally unhappy. And I…I myself had been a widower for many years and was very lonely."

"Hold on," Toni cut in. "I'm confused. In 1980, both Grigore and Dake were bonded males. They couldn't have had sexual intercourse with anyone besides their mates."

John ground the heel of his palm into one eye, struggling to make sense out of what Toni had just said. His thoughts jumbled disjointedly, in no particular order, and after a moment he realized there was no making sense of it.

"Normally, yes, such would have been the case," Jess agreed, "but the three of us were operating under the power of a Lună Zână."

Whatever that meant, it was gargantuan.

The air left the room.

The temperature dropped.

Fancy Roth hissed out a long breath.

Toni glanced around. "What's a Lună Zână?"

"Lună Zână," Jess explained, "is a full moon on Beltane Night, a phenomenon that occurs only every nineteen years. In the Celtic tradition, Beltane is a celebration of the harvest and fertility, and so a full moon—already a source of extreme power for us—on such a fertile night gives a Vârcolac special abilities. It is the one and only time we can have sexual relations outside of a bond."

Roth leveled a pointed stare at Jess. "It also gives a Vârcolac almost supernatural potency."

"Yes." Jess cleared his throat. "All three of our liaisons bore live issue."

If an entire room could clench tight, it just did.

The slope of Toni's brows steepened. "How is that possible? These were regular human women you had affairs with, weren't they? Vârcolac can't successfully procreate with regulars."

Jess unclasped his hands and stuck them in the pockets of his lab coat. It seemed like a fidgety gesture. "As a part of the supernatural potency Roth just mentioned, Otherworldly protection is offered to babies conceived during a Lună Zână. A Zână is a fairy from Romanian mythology. She possesses the power to give life to fetuses in utero and to act as a Guardian Angel to children." Jess smoothed two fingers across a single eyebrow, flattening it down. "Dake ended up having a daughter. Grigore and I had sons."

"What?!" Nichita came roaring off the wall, his silver eyes on fire. "Are you shitting me? I have a *brother*?"

Jess startled back a step. "You…did. But he…the pain of suppressing his Vârcolac nature eventually became too much for him to bear. I tried to change his medication, to help him, but… His Pure-bred side was too strong."

John squinted. Things were really sounding—

"I'm sorry, Devid." Jess's gaze clouded. "The boy took his own life several years ago when—"

"You fuck!" Snarling through gnashed teeth, Nichita seized the front of Jess's shirt in knotted fists. "For years I had a brother, Costache has a sister"—he rammed the doctor against the wall—"and you never bothered to say shit about it?"

Bug-eyed, Jess wrapped his hands around Nichita's wrists.

Blondie Thomal watched the scene with incandescent rage.

"Grigore, Dake, and I," Jess wheezed, "vowed never to speak of it. I couldn't say anything."

"Grigore and Dake," Roth reminded coldly, "have been dead for many years now."

Jess strained his eyes over. "A vow is a vow. A man of honor cannot break his word, no matter the circumstances."

"You think you're a man of honor?" Waterfalling sweat, Nichita dropped the doctor and lurched backward.

Rasping for air, Jess fumbled to loosen his shirt collar.

"Where," Thomal seethed, "is my sister?"

"I don't know." Jess's voice sounded clotted, like he was

speaking around a swollen epiglottis. "A couple of years ago she stopped collecting her medication from her PO box and disappeared."

"So you don't know if she's alive or dead?" Thomal ground out.

"I...don't, no."

John's heartbeat hitched out of rhythm. The cold icicle in his chest bore deeper. All this was starting to seem...horrifyingly true.

"You're a shit, Jess." Nichita collapsed into a chair, violent agony storming across his face. "You let people die to cover your ass."

"That's a rather simplistic summation, Devid." Jess jerkily ran a hand down the front of his tie. "There were many, many layers of complexity of this problem to consider. First off, were we even to tell these children about their unique bloodlines, and if so, what were we to do with them? Bring them *here*, to live in a community which at the time was rife with suspicion of regulars? Heaven knew how half-breeds would have been treated. And logistically, how would we have moved them here? Ever since landing in California over a hundred years ago, no Vârcolac has ever ventured beyond the state lines. Yet only Dake's girl lived in California. My boy was in Kansas, and Grigore's was in North Dakota."

My boy. The two words brought gagging bile surging onto John's tongue.

"And what about the mothers? We couldn't just take their children away from them. We would have needed to give the mothers in-depth explanations about our breed in order to bring them into the fold, and this was back when Roth had everyone battened down so tight with security none of us could move an inch without bumping into a rule."

Roth's expression turned prickly.

"Or are you suggesting we should have ripped them away from their lives, do to them what we did to those poor

Dragon women when Roth first initiated his procreation program? I think all of us can agree *that* was not our finest hour. Would you have liked to answer for more of the same?"

Tension was mounting, jaws growing stiffer, expressions flattening.

Something about this part of the conversation was stirring John's suspicions. *Ripped them from their lives...* He'd bet his right nut this had to do with the case of the serial kidnapping of blond women—women just like Toni—John had investigated for years.

"On top of all that," Jess added, "Grigore, Dake, and I couldn't agree on whether or not to confess our sin and even *deal* with all these problems. Grigore desperately wanted the boy in his life, so he was all for a full rendering, but Dake knew his affair would have crushed Livy. He was adamantly opposed. Then the two of them died, leaving me to bear the oppressive burden of the vow of secrecy alone. The only thing I could do was scramble to develop a drug to suppress the Vârcolac blood-need of the three children. So I invented a disease called, Blestem Tatălui, and—"

John jerked his eyes wide. *Blestem Tatălui!*

"—informed the mothers that when their children reached the age of twenty-one, they would develop certain symptoms for which they would need to take medication in order to live. I religiously sent the pills, but..." Jess turned sad eyes toward John. "I... Stars in heaven, John, I'm so sorry. I've been trying to keep you alive by bettering your medication, and I thought... I had no idea how ill you'd become."

There was such parental concern in the way Jess gazed at John, it sent wretchedness oozing up from John's feet, spreading over his shins, knees, thighs...into his heart. This couldn't be true. This *had* to be a lie.

"Margaret didn't tell—"

"Maggie," John spat out. "My mother's name is *Maggie*." Desperation was turning his words into hard punches. "And she wasn't a nurse. Your story is total bullshit." He really, really needed this to be bullshit.

Jess's throat worked. "I knew her as Margaret," he said quietly. "And no, she wasn't a nurse. She worked the front desk for a Dr. Holland. His nurse, Amanda, came down with the flu that week, and so Margaret...uh, your mother traveled to San Diego in her stead."

John's face flushed so painfully hot he felt sick from it. Christ, the man knew everything he shouldn't know. "You could've Googled that information."

Jess's brows shot up. "I could have?"

No. Dread foamed in John's stomach. He'd always thought his eye color was really strange, and here was Jess with the exact same shade. How could something like that happen coincidentally? John curled his hands into fists, his wrist bones chafing against the padded cuff. Had everything his father taught him, how to rope and ride, how to be a good man, to tip his hat to ladies and provide for a family—was it all a lie now?

"Did he know?" John choked out. "My father...did he know I wasn't his?"

Jess gave his head an adamant shake. "No, absolutely not. Your mother diligently kept the secret. Robert Waterson thought you were his own son."

John believed it, and that was something. On his last trip to Kansas when he'd asked his mother about a strange element in his blood, she hadn't embraced the question as a prime opportunity to inform him that he might have a different genetic situation going on. If she hadn't fessed up then, when confronted with a dying son, she sure as hell wouldn't have told her husband and risked ending her marriage.

And what, exactly, was his different genetic situation? If Blestem Tatălui was a made-up disease, then what did he actually have? Would Jess answer the questions Maggie never had? "I have something in my blood doctors don't recognize.

Did I get this strange element from you?"

Jess inhaled air in a long, steady stream. "Yes. But the element is merely a genetic marker, considered *strange* by the doctors you've dealt with thus far only because they don't understand it."

John started to nod, then frowned. He'd expected a more complicated explanation for something that'd been causing him so many problems for so long, including him being knocked out by an ex-girlfriend so she could steal his blood for this element. "If it's just a genetic marker, then why would someone want it...*need* it?"

Jess looked taken aback. "I beg your pardon?"

"Several years ago my ex-girlfriend's sister was kidnapped, and *my* blood was the ransom demanded." John glanced at Nichita. "The same psychotic fuck who showed up the night of our shootout was the one who snatched my ex's sister."

Nichita nodded grimly. "Yeah, we know the shit-stain. Videon."

"Well, my ex said this Videon needed the element for something."

"For what?" Nichita demanded.

"How the hell should I know?" This stupid element had been baffling him for years.

An expression of concentration tugged at Toni's features. "I remember that case. It was Elsa Mendoza who was kidnapped, right? And about the same time Videon became 'The Symbol Killer.' He was murdering certain men of Irish descent to steal their souls through an un-protection ritual, and...remember what Aunt Idyll told us?" She surveyed the group. "Videon would have needed supernatural powers to perform the ritual."

John grimaced. He was normally pretty open to weird-ness, having once worked in Occult Crimes, but the conversation had just off-tracked into the super weird, and it was giving him a case of the heebs. Maybe because Toni was involved. He didn't want to think of her as being heebie-weird.

Teeth-Tattooed Asshole nodded. "We all guessed Videon somehow acquired his enchantment skill, but he would've needed fiinţă to—"

"Fiinţă," Jess exclaimed. "Yes!"

Everyone turned to give Jess a questioning look.

Jess explained himself in an eager voice. "Fiinţă is normally only accessible through feeding, right? *Normally*. But an exception occurs during the stasis state between pre-blooding and full-blooding. At this time, a Vârcolac carries a special form of fiinţă in his or her bloodstream—a raw form of the elixir. It would have been ingestible."

"Ingestible?" Teeth-Tattooed Asshole's eyebrows hiked up. "So you're saying Videon drank Waterson's blood in order to—?"

"All right," John barked. "That's enough." This conversation was now officially gross. "Somebody needs to explain what the hell you're talking about. What's a Vârcolac? What's fiinţă?" He looked at Jess. "Is this fiinţă shit what's making me sick?"

"No, John, no," Jess assured him. "You're ill because your body has been forced into an unwanted dormancy, that's all. Once you realize your true nature, you'll be healthy and fine."

Healthy and fine. God, that sounded fantastic, if beyond comprehension. "But…true nature…what do you mean?"

Everyone in the room suddenly found other things to look at.

"Well." Jess smiled uneasily. "Here is the part I'm afraid will be difficult for you to accept."

Now what? A sticky feeling compressed John's throat. *Christ, am I still dying?*

"You asked what a Vârcolac is," Jess went on. "It's the name of the race I hail from, and since you're my son, you're also Vârcolac."

"Of all the people…" Nichita muttered, scrubbing a hand over his face.

"The pills I invented to treat you," Jess continued, "were meant to suppress this true nature because…well, who you are isn't accepted in today's world. But the Vârcolac side of you is just too strong, and the pills aren't working anymore. The more years that have passed, the more this part of you has tried to take over, and so the sicker you've become. If you don't let this side come out, then you'll eventually die."

John tried to moisten his lips but didn't have any saliva. "How do I do that?"

"You need blood."

Blood… Hell, was that all? What an idiot he was for never having gone to a doctor all these years. "If it's as easy as a transfusion, then—"

"A transfusion won't help you at all," Jess overrode him. "You need to take in blood using the fangs stored in your head and ingest it with the elixir we've been talking about called fiinţă."

"I need to…?" John stopped talking. This couldn't be right. Jess was making it sound like John was a…

"A Vârcolac is a vampire, John."

John shook his head. "No, it isn't." He shook his head again. He was *John Waterson, humanoid.* That's who he was.

"*John.*" Now it was Toni who said his name, very firmly. Probably trying to make sure he was really listening.

The look of shock on his face had to be astronomical. His heartbeat ricocheted off his ribs, bruising them. He shook his head again. How many times had he done that now? But Toni's next words barged into the room like unwelcome houseguests.

"You're a vampire."

JOHN HAD NO MEMORY OF blacking out. One moment he was alert and awake, and the next moment he was the same, but he had the sense of time having passed. Words were streaming by his ears, for one, as if Jess had been talking for a while.

"...not an undead monster," the doctor was saying, his features coming back into focus. "That's just a fable. You're a human being. A different species of human, yes, but still..."

"Stop," John croaked. "I can't... I don't want to hear any more."

Jess sighed. "I know this is incredibly difficult to grasp," he said, *not* stopping. "But the sooner you come to terms with who you really are, the sooner you can transition."

"No." This also seemed like something John was intent on saying over and over again.

"These symptoms you've been experiencing," Jess *kept* on, "are proof of your Vârcolac nature. You show all the signs of a vampire suffering from a voracious blood-need: sensitivity to light, profuse sweating, insatiable hunger, yet the inability to keep down food because what you actually need is blood—"

ShutupShutupShutup! A shout was building inside John's head.

"—and you've probably lost your sexual functioning by now, along with—"

"Shut *up*!" John bellowed. *Fuck and shit!* An entire roomful of people just heard he was impotent—*Toni* heard that! "Let me out of here." He banged his handcuffed wrist against the bedrail. "Unlock me right now!"

To his shock, they did. 'Course they had to be pretty damned confident in their ability to stop him from fighting his way to freedom.

Once the cuff was off, John crashed down the bed rail and tumbled off the mattress. As his feet hit the floor, he discovered the linoleum was bucking and rolling with a sickening, nautical motion. He made a grab for the back of the bed, only managing thin morsels of indrawn air. The level of his sweating belonged in *Guinness*.

Everyone stared at him.

Nobody looked crazy-eyed. There were other expressions: resignation, concern, wariness, mild disgust. But not clinical insanity.

John shook all over, his muscles contracting with epileptic vigor. His mind started spitting out unwanted facts.

After the shootout with Nichita, he'd ended up at Scripps Memorial Hospital, where Dr. Edward Sevilli dropped a bombshell on him about his blood test results. *A strange element popped up in your blood work, John...nothing identifiable as strictly human.*

Now Jess was telling him, *You're a different species of human, yes...*

And Nichita had warned him back at Scripps, *Leave this case alone, Waterson. I'm telling you right now, you're in way over your head. You have no idea what you're dealing with.*

John, you're a vampire.

Cold descended on him. Blackness soaked into the sides of his vision.

This explains what's been bugging me about Waterson...what I'm seeing in him. Hunger.

John's knees decided to go on vacation. He firmed his grip on the back of his bed to keep from falling. A near thing.

Toni's gentle voice intruded on his unraveling thoughts. "John, maybe you should sit down."

"I want to get out of here." His lips felt long and rubbery around the demand. "Right now."

"Okay." Toni looked at Jess. "What happens if John stops taking his pills?"

Jess's eyebrows lifted briefly. "He'll leave behind pre-blooding and move into his full blood-need. His fangs will finally descend, and he'll need to feed shortly thereafter."

"How long will it take to make the transition?"

Jess turned his palms up. "I have no idea. Hours. Days."

"Very well." Toni addressed the dark-haired nurse. "Shaston, go and quickly pack a bag. I'm sending you up with John. You two stay in the safe house, since we've equipped it with metal shutters. Make sure John doesn't take his pills. As soon as he drops his fangs, give him a sedative, then text me. I'll send up a transport to bring you back down here so he can feed on a donor."

The nurse nodded, then shifted her attention over to Jess. "Will John immediately go totally vampiric? He'll, uh…acquire many new senses, and, you know, it could be a shock to his system."

Jess shook his head. "Due to his prolonged stasis state in pre-blooding, I would say no. It will take several months for him to change completely into a Vârcolac."

"Okay." The nurse nodded. "I'll keep an eye on it."

Toni glanced at Teeth-Tattooed Asshole. "Take him back up."

Asshole gave her a dubious look. "You sure about this?"

"He needs time to process." Toni focused solemnly on John. "And without his pills, he'll find out soon enough that everything he's just learned about himself is very true."

CHAPTER THIRTY-ONE

THE THERAPIST'S OFFICE SMELLED LIKE cinnamon and cloves and something else sweet…maybe apple dumplings. Or a basket of kittens—*insert eye-roll here*—to go along with how happy, go-lucky the pictures on the walls were: sailboats on a bay, leaning gently into a sunset, a winding mountain stream, trickling magically through twin banks of vibrant green ferns.

Did anyone else besides Charlize think it bizarre that the artwork should be so cheerful when the people coming here most likely weren't?

Guess it doesn't matter. The pictures would be gone soon, anyway. Any minute her nastiness would melt them off the walls. *He he.* She smirked wryly, then immediately wiped off the expression when Karrell asked, "So who wants to start?"

The therapist was sitting in a small, padded chair across from Charlize and Breen, who were sitting in two similar chairs. The grouping of three was set in front of Karrell's desk. Behind the desk bookshelves took up the entire wall and were filled to capacity.

Karrell's legs were crossed, and she held a pen poised over a pad of paper. She'd just finished a spiel about how these sessions were confidential, how she ran them unconventional-ly—sometimes they lasted ten minutes, sometimes an hour and ten minutes—and a bunch of other blather. Now she was looking between Breen and Charlize, regarding them pleasantly. No wonder she'd been able to successfully maintain a practice topside, undetected. She had the most petite fangs ever.

Charlize glanced at Breen.

He was wearing his usual cargo shorts, the bandage on his knee visible, and a rocker T-shirt, this one of the *Grateful Dead*. His elbows were set on the armrests, his fingers spread wide on his knees, and the carpet's Berber rating appeared to be fascinating him.

Despite his promise to talk in session, he didn't appear to have any intention of starting. She could hardly blame him. She was nervous too.

Why the hell she'd agreed to go to couples counseling, she didn't know. Well, she supposed she did know: hormones. She damn well wanted regular bootie calls, and if trying to be Breen's mate—*try*, mind, she didn't have to succeed—was what it took to do the tube steak boogie whenever she wanted, then so be it.

You can't throw away Breen, Marissa had said.

So, if you can't beat 'em, join 'em, and Charlize knew when she was beaten. The limiting realities of Vârcolac culture had kicked her horny little ass, so here she was, ready to put enough window dressing on this "relationship" to get what she wanted. But that was it. Nothing profound was going to get discussed here. *Hell, no, and fuck that.* Bad enough she'd slipped up yesterday at the hospital and blurted out stuff about her mom disappearing for three days. Now Breen had all kinds of sappy notions in his head about her "caring." Yeah, she *cared* all right—cared about her vagina.

Karrell flipped to another page on her pad. "Why don't I start by telling you what I know from your files." She checked on some notes. "Charlize Renault, chef and marathon runner. Breen Dalakis, warrior and gamer. About six weeks ago, you two had an incident in the community gym. Breen bit Charlize and then bonded with her via follow-on sex. Due to the fact that the bond was a misunderstanding, Charlize subsequently decided to act as Breen's blood donor only. Now, however, you're both here, and I'm assuming it's because you'd like to change the dynamic of your relationship. So how about we kick it off there?" Karrell folded her hands over the top of her notepad, the pen sticking up between her fingers. "What don't you tell me what your goals are?"

Charlize thought about what to say. Why the hell not the truth? "I'm here for the sex."

"Oh?" Karrell looked over. "How's that?"

"As you said, I've been Breen's donor, and in this weird-o community, I can't have sex with him unless I'm his actual mate."

One eyebrow lifting, Karrell glanced at Breen, but he still wasn't giving her anything.

"So my goal," Charlize said, "is to see if we can work out some kind of…regular sheet wrestling, if you get my drift."

A smile tugged at Karrell's mouth. "I think I understand, yes." She probably did. She was a real free-love-looking Karma Mama type, with long, straight gray hair—a mixture of white and steel colors—hanging well past her butt. A braided leather band held back strands at the forehead. She wore simple cotton drawstring pants and a loose shirt, both in earth tones, the long, flowing garments more suited to yoga class. Maybe she wanted to stay ready to break into meditation at any moment, perhaps whip up a roll or two of sushi. "Sex can be a place to start, if it works for you both."

"I'd say it works." Charlize laughed deeply. "We've only had sex twice, but both times were great." At least *she* had climaxed like her vagina's rocket boosters were hurtling her off the planet.

"All right. Super. It's always useful to find out what *is* working in a relationship." Karrell gave her attention to Breen. "And for you, too, Breen, the sex with Charlize has been good?"

Good. Charlize almost snorted. Sex with her was generally described with more bells and whistles than *good*.

"I, um…"

Charlize blinked once at Breen, then bolted upright. *What?!*

Head down, Breen was still inspecting the carpet.

"What the hell does *um* mean?" Charlize demanded.

He didn't answer.

She crossed her arms firmly beneath her breasts and set her mouth. "You know what, pal, no one's ever complained to me in the past, but if you don't want to have sex with—"

"I'm not complaining. It's just, uh…the sex is always…" He cleared his throat. "Violent."

"Vio—?" Charlize rolled her eyes. "Oh, take a chill pill, will you? I just like it rough sometimes." She snapped her attention over to the therapist. "Don't analyze. It doesn't *mean* anything. I'm just a passionate woman."

"Of course."

Charlize slung a gesture at Breen. "I thought a Vârcolac, of all people, could handle the rough stuff."

"I can handle it. It just seems too… I don't know. Not like sex should be."

Charlize huffed. *Like you would know.* "Look, I can do the slow ride, if that's what you want. Just—"

"Perfect," Karrell piped in. "Then you two have your first homework assignment. Between now and our next session in three days, you are to have sex together, but gently. Absolutely none of the rough stuff." The therapist smiled. "Sound good?"

Sounded stupid and boring. "Sure." Charlize curled her lips. "Sounds great."

CHARLIZE COULDN'T FUCK BREEN THE first night after therapy because she had to work at the restaurant, but the next night she arranged for her roommate, Hadley, to be gone for a few hours, and for Breen to arrive at seven o'clock. Around six-thirty, Charlize slipped into a slinky lavender baby doll nightie, going commando underneath, white lace trimming the plunging neckline.

She inspected herself in the full-length mirror and smiled at her reflection. Things might start out slow tonight, but they sure as hell wouldn't stay that way. Driving men to ferocious feats of sexual insanity was a proud forte of hers.

At seven o'clock on the dot, Breen knocked—well, the man *did* live only two doors down.

She flung the door open and posed, leaning one shoulder seductively against the jamb. "Hel-lo."

Breen examined every inch of her. His eyes flashed.

Ooooh, a high-dollar emotion.

He had dressed up to the extent that he was wearing pants instead of shorts, although still of the multi-pocketed cargo variety. His T-shirt was dark brown *Fleetwood Mac*. The scruffy five o'clock shadow he'd sported in the hospital was now shaved off.

"What's with the wine?" She nodded at the bottle in his hand.

He held it out to her. "I thought we could have dinner first and talk for—"

"Why would we want to do that?" She fishhooked her index finger into the collar of his T-shirt and pulled him into her apartment. The door banged shut, and she continued across her living room and into her bedroom.

Plucking the wine bottle out of Breen's grasp, she set it on her dresser, then came to stand right in front of him. Peering up at him through her lashes, she smoothed her hands along his pecs, over his shoulders, then up the back of his neck. God, his body was so yummy. "It's been ages since I've seen you naked," she purred, then did a kittenish arch against him, pushing her ass outward while pressing her breasts to his chest. "Strip for me," she moaned, then took a step back to watch.

He just stared at her.

She saucily slanted a brow. "Undress."

He pulled off his shirt in a single motion and tossed it across the room. Efficient and expedient.

She laughed low in her throat. "No. Sexy-like."

He looked at her again.

"You know, get naked slowly, maybe dance for me a bit."

He thumbed open his pants, then walked his legs out of them, along with his shoes.

Quick and down to business. "No?"

"I don't know how to do that."

She smiled. *Well, it doesn't matter.* She had what she wanted. Breen, without clothing, looking so survival-of-the-fittest masculine with that physique of his. Naturally built from hard work and real-life fighting, his sinews and tendons were delineated under smooth, taut flesh, his chiseled abs a beautiful symmetry of hills and valleys, rolling down to... She drew a nostril-widening breath. *Long time, no see, Big Boy.* Day-um, she'd forgotten how nice his equipment was. Hanging down over a full, potent sac, his cock extended several inches past it, soft now, but as she stared, it started to rise.

A sliver of wanton heat slid from her belly into her loins, making her ache to be filled by him. *Not yet.* She still had ferocious feats of sexual insanity to inspire. Wrapping her hand around his impressive organ, she swept her thumb back and forth across the wide top. Tension rippled through Breen. The smooth crest became slick, and the scent of sex rose up between them. She licked her lips. It was going to be a challenge to suck off all of this monster, but she was always ripe for these kinds of challenges. Dropping to her knees, she grabbed his cock firmly by the base and steered him toward her mouth to—

He bent over and caught her by the elbows, urging her back to her feet. "Not this time."

"But..." She blinked. "I..." How could she drive him to ferocious insanity of sexual feats if she—No, she meant...

He slipped his fingers underneath the thin strap of her lingerie and, lifting the nightie a bit, tugged the silky material back and forth across the crest of her breast. Her nipple poked up against the cloth, and a small gasp floated past her lips. *Okay, this is actually very good.* The frustration that had begun to build inside her stopped its ascent, and she sagged her lids half-closed. Her sex melted, and a quiver of pleasure fluttered along the flesh of her belly.

Breen tugged the strap off her shoulder, baring her breast, and bent his dark head to her nipple. His tongue flicked out. He wet the erect point, then glossed his thumb over the dampness, and did it again. Heated lightning burned from her breast to her core. She shivered. His tongue, velvety and attentive, swirled around her nipple, languidly exploring in one direction, then circling in the other. She tangled her hands through his hair, tightly, then tighter still as she was nearly overcome with the need to have him powerfully inside her.

Clutching his shoulders, she raised one leg until she'd wrapped her calf around his hip, then angled her bare crotch against his fully erect cock.

With a sharply indrawn breath, Breen captured her around the waist with a corded arm and pushed her backward toward the bed, moving her where he wanted her to go with his muscular chest and his prowling animal energy. Her lowered foot skimmed along the carpet, then the back of her knee bumped into the mattress. Suddenly she was flat on her back.

Breen brought the full length of his body down on top of her, locking them pelvis to pelvis, pressing her against the unrelenting strength of his thighs, the flat boards of his belly. His erection was an iron rod prodding the area between her vagina and her anus. Her labia pulsed at his nearness. Her breasts ripened, and her womb quickened, and, *God*, she had to have him.

She flung her legs around his waist, dug her heels into him, and in a move of sheer, crude possession thrust her hips upward.

His cock jammed into her lower butt cheek.

She opened her eyes.

He'd shifted out of the way.

"There's no rush," he said softly.

She scowled. *What the fuck?* He was stopping again?

Resting his weight on one elbow, he touched a finger to the small hollow at the base of her throat, then stroked across the ridge of her collarbone.

She took in air while anger burned a scorching path through her hair follicles. She ground her molars together, the pressure burning her gums. She did *not* like to be *stopped*. Things wouldn't go the way she wanted if she wasn't the one in charge here.

He turned his attention to her other breast, cupping and massaging it, then ducking his head to her nipple, pulling it deeply inside his mouth. The sensations of wetness and heat and animal hunger sent more unstoppable wetness rushing to the area between her thighs. Every suckling swirl of his lips and tongue was making nerve endings all over her body come alive with quivering sensitivity, but even though what he was doing felt great, the gentle awe with which he was doing it was rapidly becoming irritating. He was going to ruin everything by taking the no-rough-stuff edict too seriously.

You do care. You've shown it to me, Charlize. You can't take it back now.

The sap was trying to make this more than it was. She squirmed. "Do you think maybe we could actually screw, you know, sometime this year?"

His head came up. His lips were moist and full, his fangs showing in pointy glimpses between them, the cords in his neck visible. A question surged forward in his eyes, but met a sandbar of uncertainty there.

Oh, God. "I like what you're doing," she rushed to say, an automatic, verbal stroke of his ego. No matter how much of a pain in the ass she could be in everyday life, in the bedroom, she never hurt male pride. "I'm just eager to get to the main event." She slid her hands down to the hard contours of his buttocks and gave him an encouraging squeeze-pull. "Please?"

His nostrils went wide and hard. He changed the position of his hips, and then she felt the crown of his cock prodding her, solid and wide. Her quivering nerve endings lit up. He started to breach her. There was pressure. She stretched around his girth, and he shoved in, finding the deepest part of her.

A raw groan escaped her. She pushed her head back into the pillow, arching her neck. *Oh, Lord. Okay, all is forgiven.* He felt so damned good. Who cared if he was a sappy dope, as long as he could make everything else go away.

He got his boogie on right away, and everything became even better. He sank and withdrew, sank and withdrew, moving with the power and grace that made him a fighting man.

Her sheath opened more fully to him, blossoming, milking nectar to the mouth of her core.

Breen hissed from what sounded like the back of his throat. His eyes glowed molten gold.

Winnowing her fingers into his hair, she urged him toward her and claimed his mouth in a kiss, taking things deep and penetrating right away, angling her jaw and parting her lips. She suckled his tongue inside and played with it.

He joined eagerly in the kiss, his mouth slanting hard toward hers, claiming, possessing. Heat came singeing off his body, and if she'd been an old-timey damsel, she might've swooned from that...from that and the steely male scent of him. From everything. Every square inch of her tingled. A potential orgasm burgeoned into a demanding throb between her thighs, a nearly frantic desperation to lose herself.

She fastened her legs around his rocking hips and pounded her crotch up into his in rhythmic unison. *Yes. Yes. Yes.*

Harder! She dug her nails into his shoulders. *Oh, God, it's so—*

He lurched to a halt and pulled his lips from hers. "Charlize," he panted. "You're not supposed to get rough, remember?"

"What?"

He reached up and unlatched her fingernails from his shoulders.

"I…I didn't…" she stumbled.

"Let's just pause a sec, okay?"

She shut her mouth. Her lungs moved in a strained way. Perspiration trickled between her breasts.

Just enough light was coming in through the open bedroom door for her to make out the boyish spill of black hair on Breen's forehead, his golden eyes and the depth of feeling in them—everything he wanted to give to her. Everything he would expect in return. Soul-level, particle-deep connection. Her esophagus narrowed down to a thin pipette.

He slipped his fingers along her cheek, so gentle. So loving.

Pain completely drenched her, like an auto-immune rejection of her own innards. She tried to get angry over him stopping again, but couldn't summon the emotion. Trapped in the cocoon of warmth his body created—in the warmth he clearly felt for her—emotions stirred in her that she didn't want and couldn't handle. Destructive things eating in patterns of wormwood through a woman's uncomplicated need for sex and burrowing into her heart. She gave his chest a panicked nudge. "I-I can't do this anymore. Please get off me."

Right away he push-upped onto straight arms, his cock sliding out of her. He sat back on his heels between her spread thighs.

She scooted toward the headboard, dragging the sheet over her breasts as she sat up. Tucking her legs underneath her, she stared stupidly at him…at the scar on his leg, spigot to so much of his blood, the scar dipping into his pubic hair she knew nothing about but should know about, *would* know about if she wasn't such a freak of unwifely nature. Her throat pumped a couple of times from her efforts to stop tears from coming. "I don't mean to leave you in a state." She gestured at his erection. "I can give you a hand-job, if you want, to finish—"

"Charlize," he said softly. "No. Come on. That's not what this was about." He got off the bed and tugged on his pants, then came back over and sat down next to her. "You hungry?"

God, be anything but nice *to me right now.* "Breen…"

He took her hand. "I only want to be with you, Charlize. I don't care how."

She looked at him through blurry vision. "I don't know how to be with you like this."

He quick-squeezed her hand. "Easy. Let's watch a movie together."

Her heart beat loudly in her eardrums, noisier than it ever had before. Or maybe it always beat this way, but she was more aware of it now, with this man sitting next to her, his soul reaching out to hers, wanting to connect with her beyond simple fleshy pleasures…wanting to peel away pieces of her that could never be replaced. "I can't be with you like this." She reclaimed her hand. "I'm sorry."

He gazed at her in his calm, still way.

Maybe she was a freak of general nature. A sick tremor rattled through her chest. "You should probably go."

CHAPTER THIRTY-TWO

Topside
3:23 A.M.

A SUNSET STRETCHED ACROSS THE landscape of John's dream, streaks of orange and gold staining the sky, just like in real life about a half-dozen hours ago, when John had sat on the front porch of the safe house, holding a beer—he hadn't been able to drink—propped on his knee. He watched the sun sink into the horizon; maybe the last sunset he'd ever see, according to Nurse Shaston, who'd shooed him out there.

'Course she'd said the same thing the last four evenings in a row, and here he still was, John Waterson, Humanoid.

John, you're a vampire.

Yeah? Really? Sooooo…. Was he a nice, Muppety vampire, like Count Von Count, or a real nasty character, like Lestat? Or a version of Dracula? He hoped he wasn't that, 'cause, gee whillikers, he would hate to be something so cliché. Or, golly, even worse, what if he was a teeny-bopper bloodsucker like Edward Cullen? He might have to kill himself if he actually sparkled. Although wasn't he already dead 'n all?

You're not an undead monster—that's just a fable.

Huh. Interesting. How about him being something that actually *existed?*

Jesus Christ. The whole bogus thing belonged up his ass. If he was really and truly a vampire, then why hadn't he changed over yet? Although—there was always an *although*, wasn't there?—he'd never come up with any other reason to explain his bizarre cluster of symptoms.

You show all the signs of a vampire suffering from a voracious blood-need.

He brought the beer to his lips, then just set it back on his knee. *Insatiable hunger yet the inability to keep down food...* Great. He let his focus stray from the beautiful gold ball of the sun down to the stretch of street in front. Turned out this safe house was Toni's old place, and so that curb was where he would've parked his car had he ever come to pick her up on the date they planned.

One night after working a criminal case together, he'd stolen a kiss from her, a *tongue* kiss, her body fitting sinuously against his, her welcoming warmth fulfilling a huge fantasy of his. After the kiss he finally convinced her to go out to dinner with him.

It was the date-that-never-was, because...

Because, why?

A lot of conflicting variables seemed to be going into making that an impossible question to answer. But maybe it didn't matter anymore. Maybe what mattered was that Toni was back in his life. He could finally fix things between them. He'd be returning to her—she said she was going to send a transport to bring him back to her oddball town—and when he did see her again, he was going to make sure—make damned sure—they got their shot this time.

Exhaling, he returned his attention to the sunset. He probably *should* look at it, since it might be a monumental last or—

He startled as the sky suddenly turned gory, red liquid dripping off bloody clouds and the Pacific Ocean heaving into a viscous, sluggish stew. His heart lurched into a hard thud, and his head pounded. The sky boiled over into a stormy hell, silvery webs of lightning streaking across dark thunderheads. An overlarge face pushed between two black clouds. Gray-skinned, the creature had fangs. Twin bolts of lightning shot out from its sharp teeth, hitting John high up on both temples, right above the eyebrows. He choked on a gasp, his head pounding harder, like his skull was taking a serious bludgeoning from a police baton. More lightning, more painful, silvery whiplashes. He jerked in his bed, becoming vaguely aware of the cotton bedsheets beneath him.

The pain was waking him up…

The ocean went black.

Another lightning strike sent pieces of John's cranial bones flying in all directions.

Seal-barking in terror, John spine-locked himself straight upright in bed, his eyes widened as far as he could stretch them. Shaston had left the nightstand lamp on dim, but even that small amount of light was agonizing. Nausea crackled like old parchment paper in his empty stomach. He clutched his head, hard, harder. It felt like his skull was sucking inward, then bloating back out, bulging, straining. *Something's about to…*

His head burst out at the temples. The towers and pillars that made up his canine teeth crumbled like an epic Armageddon, chunks of enamel raining down on his lap. He made a waffling sound of panic and cupped his hands over his mouth, scrambling to the side of the mattress. Blood roared through his fingers.

Aaaahhh!

Hysteria engulfed him in a feeling so deep and drowning and black, he could only scream. And scream and scream.

Nurse Shaston exploded into the bedroom, her long, black hair flying, a pair of cotton shorts twisted sideways on her waist. She took one look at him, then whirled back around, returning a second later with a dark blue hand towel.

"Here." She gave it to him, crouching down at his feet. "It's okay," she had the audacity to add.

He jammed the towel to his mouth, an action which thankfully shut up his screaming. He sucked air in and out of his nose. The smells of detergent and lint—and blood—blasted through his sinus passages. He stared at Shaston over the top of the towel, his eye sockets feeling overstretched, as if his eyeballs were pregnant slugs.

"I know this is bizarre and scary, John." Shaston set a palm on his knee. "But it's okay. We all go through it when we drop our fangs for the first time."

His continuing gall over her failure to properly lose her shit over this apocalypse helped to substitute irritation for some of his panic. *He'll leave behind pre-blooding and move into his full blood-need. His fangs will finally descend…*

Descend? This was way beyond mere fucking *descending*. A little more warning would've been nice.

"Do you want to see them?" Shaston asked. "Your fangs?"

Fangs. *Fangs…* He crept his hand underneath the towel and eased his fingers inside his sore mouth, exploring the area where—

Holy shit.

"Come on." Shaston caught him underneath the arm and helped him to his feet. "I think you need to see them to truly believe." She brought him into the bathroom and placed him in front of the mirror.

He lowered the towel, and—Jesus, his face was a mess. He looked like a two-year-old who'd just gone hog wild on a plate of spaghetti.

"Smile!" Shaston chirped.

He fixed a glare on her.

Her mouth tilted. "It's okay."

"Quit saying that," he snarled, and, *whoa.* He'd never heard himself sound like that. He shot his attention back to the mirror. His eyes appeared brighter, sharper, more feral. He started to peel back his lips, then hesitated. *Please. Just…don't… Don't let me have…* He grinned.

And a beast was born.

He rocked back on his heels, dizzied by the strange sensation of his soul tripping and falling, tumbling away from himself.

The John Waterson he'd always known was gone.

The image in the bathroom mirror was officially his—same facial structure, familiar brown hair, those one-of-a-kind turquoise eyes. But he recognized the man staring back at him merely in form, cerebrally only. He couldn't relate to or connect with the image emotionally, because...

The man in the mirror had canines stretching several inches down into a blood-smeared mouth.

Maybe he was hallucinating. A new symptom acquired.

John ran his tongue experimentally over one of his canines. The tapered tip was extremely sharp. No way could the thing be explained away as anything other than a fang.

He had fangs.

He fell forward against the sink, gripping the porcelain rim to keep from going down.

"Hey." Shaston's hand came to rest lightly on his shoulder. "They look great, John. Really. They're quite a pair."

He glowered at her. Bile rose. Accusations formed. He needed to blame someone for this, vent his overstock of horror. But all the things he wanted to spew stuck to his tongue.

He was snared in a net, trapped by the sudden, shocking honing of his vision as his eyes dropped to the veins in Shaston's throat. He focused on her in a way he'd never done before, never knew he could do. It was a riveted, shallow-breathed, laser lock onto her carotid, and, *holy crap*, he could actually *see* the blood pumping through the light blue trail of it.

The sight pulsed into primitive parts of his brain. His canine teeth throbbed, not painfully, but with a wanting so deep, it was pre-evolutionary and...kind of sexual. His nuts throbbed, too. He was just getting into those sensations when his stomach chose that moment to be done with all the years of bullshit. It howled at the moon. For blood.

John doubled over in pain, feeling the seismic vibrations of agony in his pelvic bones. "Shit on a brick."

"You need to feed," Shaston told him.

He cranked his neck back up to peer at her.

She had the kindly Nurse Nightingale expression down pat, mouth curved into a soft smile, brows marred with a little stitch between them. "You'll feel fine once you do."

Fine… Healthy and fine… *Healthy and fine!* He stared at her vein, riveted…that vein… Drool drizzled over his lower lip—his mouth had just flooded with saliva.

"I'll call Toni and tell—"

"I want you," he growled. Straightening, he made a fumbling grab for her.

She came into his arms at once, pressing up against his blood-drenched T-shirt. An animal gleam darted through her eyes "I want you too," she whispered. Her fingers threaded into the back of his sweaty hair and urged him toward her throat.

He sank his face into the crook of her neck—it fit perfectly—and hauled in a chest-swelling breath. She smelled of mint toothpaste, Vitamin C, body lotion with too much glycerin in it, and the granola cereal she must've eaten for breakfast this morning, and… *Good God.* How did he know such things?

"It's okay," she moaned, encouraging him on.

Some distant voice in the back of his head warned him that this "okay" should be just as galling as the ones before—for some unknown reason. But little voices were easily being out-shouted by big ones: calls of the wild, cellular-level drives to finally fill the massive void inside him, to find himself. Yes, he sensed it…no, he *knew* consuming Shaston's blood would also make him feel whole and complete—like the *real* John—for the first time in his ever-loving life.

Once you realize your true nature, you'll be healthy and fine…

He didn't know what the hell he was doing, and yet, somehow…he did.

Instinct took over.

His jaws pried apart.

His open mouth shifted in micro-movements over Shaston's flesh until his fangs suddenly thrummed. *There!*

Synapses fired, and he bit down. He felt a liquidy *pop*, like squeezing a grape between his teeth, then something wet was on his tongue.

Every kid who's ever bonked his thumb, then stuck it in his mouth to suck the pain way, knew what blood tasted like. It was the taste John had expected. It wasn't what he got, not by a long shot.

He couldn't even say there was a taste to the thick substance coating his tongue, not according to conventional expressions of that concept. More like a host of sensations—of rightness, of strength, of energy, of healing, of ease and relief. And, somehow, of life shifting onto a correct path at long last. How could he verbalize those as *tastes*? Not possible.

Overarching everything he felt a peace he hadn't in years, maybe a lifetime, and he hugged Shaston closer, trying to gulp more blood down his throat. Amateur that he was, he made a mess of it, blood leaking past the inadequate suction of his lips.

It spilled down Shaston's neck and onto her shoulder. She didn't seem to mind, especially not when the muscles around his canines flexed and a vague pumping sensation started up in his fangs.

Shaston writhed and moaned.

She felt extra squirmy-good in his arms…sexy.

When he finally lifted his head and peered down on her, her eyes were gauzy. He blinked. The room came fully back to him, the drawn borders of the medicine cabinet, toilet, and sink, redefining themselves.

In the kitchen, the ice maker activated, the sound of cubes

dumping into the freezer tray like a bin of billiard balls spilled onto ceramic tiles. He could hear it so clearly, it was as if the refrigerator was right next to him.

He felt so different now. One bite, and here he was...

Bite.

He focused on the two small holes in Shaston's throat. *He* had made those.

Holy crap.

He was a vampire.

CHAPTER THIRTY-THREE

IT WAS FUNNY HOW LOUD silence could be when it was unwanted—a first for Breen. He was used to silence offering him a welcome invisibility, a place he could go to keep attention off him while he made calculated observations, got the lay of the land so he could decide what to do.

But sitting here next to Charlize in Karrell's office—practically able to hear his hair growing—the silence wasn't about him getting his bearings. It was a reminder about how he never knew what to say to make it okay for Charlize to be with him.

Easy. Let's watch a movie together.

He'd obviously needed to say more on the night of their date…or homework assignment…or failed date. But hell if he knew what. So he'd gone with his standard, "Okay, 'bye," when Charlize asked him to leave, and then he left, trudging back to his apartment to sit in his living room with an empty head. And heart. And now, as always, there remained nothing between them. *Decide a course. Act.* Yeah, he got that already. He was all about doing something. He just needed to know what.

"Good morning," Karrell greeted them as she settled into the chair across from theirs. "So how did the homework assignment go?"

The silence that followed was complete enough to hear the low moan of air through one of the cave's wormholes outside, where oxygen entered the community.

Charlize smoothed her thumb across her fingernails,

keeping her eyes down.

Breen tapped his fingertips on his thighs. His knife wound didn't need a bandage anymore, but the scar was still pretty red. Maybe Karrell should've tried a little warm-up small talk to get things going first.

Karrell un-crossed then re-crossed her legs. It was an easy, relaxed movement that said she had all the time in the world.

The silence stretched to Buzz Lightyear's infinity and beyond. Breen finally filled it. "We weren't able to do it."

"Okay." Karrell didn't sound very surprised. "What happened?"

"It was a stupid homework assignment, that's what," Charlize accused. "I felt choreographed the whole time, like I wasn't free to be myself." She crossed her arms in a blockade of bone and muscles over her chest. "I *told* you I'm here for the sex. It was the one thing I wanted, and I didn't get it."

"I'm sorry to hear that," Karrell said, sounding sincere. "I'm confused, though. You said doing the slow ride was okay for you."

Charlize paused, then her chin firmed. "It is."

"All right," Karrell went along. "So why do you think you felt choreographed this time, with Breen?"

"Well, for one, he kept looking at me."

Breen lifted his chin. Blinked once. Glanced over at Charlize. "I'm not supposed to look at you?"

"Not all lovey-dovey-like. Jesus. I'm *so* sick of everyone trying to make sex into some ridiculously intimate act, like it's supposed to involve all this barfy caring. That's not a social construct I buy into, okay? Sex is physical pleasure. That's it. It's a cock in a cunt, going at it with mad-ass friction until orgasm is achieved. That's *all*. I don't need you"—Charlize jabbed a finger in Karrell's direction—"or you"—now toward Breen—"ruining it for me."

Karrell nodded slowly over this answer. "Okay. So just to confirm, sex for you is the pleasure of the physical act *only*. If feelings become involved, you don't like it."

"Exactly."

"Why do the feelings bother you?"

"They don't *bother* me, necessarily, just... Well, shit, I don't know."

Breen had an idea, but saying it would piss off Charlize. He was supposed to talk in therapy—he'd said he would. It'd just be a lot easier to talk if Charlize wasn't so mad all the time. He picked at a frayed spot along the hem of his shorts, waited another second, then cleared his throat.

Karrell and Charlize looked at him.

"I think caring about me scares Charlize."

"God, not *this* again." He could hear the eye-roll in Charlize's tone.

He kept his focus on Karrell. "She once told me she wouldn't allow herself to care because I could die at any second. And when I came home from the botched mission covered in blood, she got really upset."

"The blood was gross," Charlize countered in a surly voice.

"You fainted."

"All right, so it was *really* gross."

Karrell reached behind her to the desk and picked up a water bottle. "Is Breen right, though?"

Charlize's brows narrowed. "About what?"

"About caring for him being scary for you?"

Charlize's tone cooled. "I told him before, and I'll tell you now. Relationships are a bunch of obligations and stress. *That's* what I don't want."

"Fair enough." Karrell unscrewed the water bottle cap. "What kind of obligations are you trying to avoid?"

"All the usual stupid crap that goes with having a boy-friend." Charlize made a snap-wrist gesture at the room. "Being required to constantly text the fucking sap so he knows you're thinking about him. Having to check with him before you can go out with your girlfriends. Having to...to, I don't know. *Crap.*"

"Having to build trust?"

Charlize vented a loud sigh, like dealing with incompetent therapists was such a ball-ache. "*That's* the route you're taking? Really? 'Trust issues.'" She wrapped these last two words in air quotes.

Karrell shrugged. "It's actually a reasonable question to ask someone who doesn't want anything to do with feelings. Avoiding intimacy is a great way to protect yourself. You cut your losses." Karrell took a sip of water. "'Course you cut your gains too."

Charlize *tsked*. "I'll believe the gains when you show me the money."

"It's not something I can show you, unfortunately." Karrell put the cap back on. "You have to experience it for yourself."

"I guess that's an okay-thanks-buh-bye for me, then. I'm not going to form a relationship just to have it turn into the inevitable shit-show. So, yes, I guess you're right—I am all about cutting my losses." Charlize rounded on Breen. "I'm offering you sex, Breen, that's it. Take it or leave it."

The muscles along his belly twitched as he thought about how to answer her, thought hard. He turned away, his eyes pulling taut around the edges. He was already feeling the loss. Scanning the shelves behind Karrell, he read the book titles, though none of them really made sense to him: *Reviving Ophelia* and *Identity and the Life Cycle* and *On Becoming a Person*... How was that last one so difficult?

Charlize gripped her armrests. "Were you ever going to answer me?"

"I don't know what you want me to say, Charlize."

Karrell turned to set down her water bottle back on the desk. "This isn't about saying what you think Charlize wants to or needs to hear, Breen, but sharing your own thoughts."

The High-Conflict Couple, How to Be an Imperfectionist—huh?

"Charlize can't read your mind," Karrell went on. "You'll never have your needs met if you don't let her know what they are."

"I don't really have needs. I just want her to be happy."

"Everyone has needs, Breen. For example, what is it you want out of your sex life with Charlize? Is engaging in the physical act only okay with you?"

"It's not a matter of what's okay, but what I can do. I can't turn sex into nothing the way she wants." He looked at Charlize. "I like you, and when I'm inside you it's kind of impossible to ignore."

Charlize froze. Then her cheeks colored. "You do not," she bit out, "like me. I've never done anything to make you like me."

But she had. She'd gifted him with those glimpses of her soft, scared, lonely side, her vulnerable core.

"What do you like about Charlize?" Karrell prompted.

Impossible to answer *that* and not get his balls handed to him. "Charlize'll get mad if I say." He went back to the bookshelves. *EMDR Toolbox: Theory and Treatment of Complex PTSD and Dissociation.* What the hell was this stuff?

"I think she needs to hear."

He messed with the fray on his shorts again, tugging out a long thread. "Charlize works hard at being tough when she's actually soft. I think she believes her soft side makes her weak, so she'll get pissed hearing me say she's soft, because she doesn't want to be weak, though really, that side just makes her...I don't know. Sweet and nice."

Charlize's chest started to rise and fall. Because she was, yeah, getting pissed off.

He should probably just shut up. But shutting up had gotten him exactly nowhere with her so far. Even if he said all the wrong stuff, he had to say it, or he'd never figure out anything about her.

Charlize ground out a curse. "You know what, Breen? You don't know jack shit about me."

He slid his attention over to another shelf. *4 Essential Keys to Effective Communication*, *Breaking the Chain of Low Self-Esteem*… He focused on this last title. "I don't think you like yourself very much."

Charlize hissed.

Karrell jumped in. "Why's that?"

He tried to take a deep breath, but the air hurt his lungs. "The first night we had sex, Charlize got really upset because I was a virgin. When I asked her why she was so mad, she said she didn't want to be the memory for my first time, like…I don't know…like maybe she wasn't worthy of being that memory." He bounced his leg a couple of times. "And now I'm sitting here listening to her say she doesn't want me to have feelings for her during sex, and I can't help wondering if it's because she thinks she doesn't deserve them."

Charlize glared at him in fulminating silence, her eyelashes spiked out from her lids.

Karrell waited. "Does any of that fit for you, Charlize?"

Charlize rotated her jaw a couple of times. "Who doesn't hate themselves sometimes?" She sharpened her glare on Breen. "Do you think you're mister hunky-dory all the time?"

"No."

"Yeah? See? It's normal."

"Not," Karrell contradicted, "when it interferes with a person's ability to form relationships."

Charlize's face pinched. "I form relationships just fine. How *I* want to form them. Not how all your stupid books"—she made a panoramic gesture at the floor-to-ceiling shelves—"say I'm supposed to form them."

"Yeah. About that." Karrell shook her head. "I'm not buying into this whole social anarchist role you're trying to sell, Charlize. See, the thing is, sex *is* intimate. I believe very strongly that you know that. In fact, I would argue that the reason you have so much sex is because you desperately want closeness. Problem is, you never achieve the intimacy you truly want and need because you ruin it for yourself.

"Why do you ruin it?" Karrell folded her hands in her lap. "I suspect Breen is right: caring for someone scares you. So when the tenderness of sex grows too intense, you turn the act into something violent in order to strip away the intimacy. You protect yourself, yes, but you end up always leaving these encounters feeling dissatisfied, so you go back for more, then do the same thing again, and... Well, do you see where I'm heading with this? You're stuck in an unhealthy loop of pull-push with the men you're with."

Charlize's face was a translucent white. The whole time Karrell was talking, the flesh across Charlize's facial bones had been steadily thinning.

Karrell continued. "I see this happen with people who didn't experience healthy parental bonding. Makes sense, right? If you never had a good model for forming relationships as a child, how do you know how to manage intimacy on your own as an adult? It would also explain self-doubt."

Charlize gave the therapist a rigid look. "I know you're the one with all the diplomas on the wall and all, but you're way off the mark on this one. I experienced perfectly healthy parental bonding."

Breen bolted his head around. "What? No. You didn't. I mean...you told me your mom disappeared on you for three days once. That doesn't sound like—"

"It was nothing," Charlize snapped, her eyes taking on a weird glitter. Either from tears or something maniacal and tragic, he couldn't tell.

He glanced aside once—*Parenting from the Inside Out*—then pushed on. "I saw the look on your face when you told me the story, Charlize, and it wasn't nothing. I think you—oh, shit." He went back to Karrell. "One time when Charlize and I were in Toni's office, Charlize found out her mom was in the drunk tank again. I think her mom's an—"

"Shut up!" Charlize screamed at him, shouting so loud the corners of her eyes squeezed down into thin lines. "Stay out of my fucking business, Breen. You want to talk about families, talk about your own damned family, not *mine*."

He closed his mouth and turned away. *Handbook of Philosophical Companionships, Psychiatric Pharmacogenomics.*

"Maybe it would be a good idea to let this subject rest for a bit," Karrell agreed. "So, yes, let's find out a bit about you and your family, Breen. Why don't you talk about your parents?"

He swung back around to stare at Karrell. What? How would talking about his parents be useful here?

"What's your relationship like with them?"

"Um…" He felt Charlize's gaze boring into him, hot and challenging. "Pretty normal, I guess."

"Does that mean you're close to them?"

"Yeah…I mean, no. I don't know. Not really, probably."

"Why's that?"

"We're kind of a family of loners."

"Both your mother and your father?"

He looked down, his bangs sliding over his right eye. "My father mostly."

"Ungar Dalakis is your father, right?"

"Yes."

"What's he like? Other than being a loner."

"Like all fathers are." Breen squinted at his lap. How did he get a mustard stain on his shorts?

"Which is…?"

"You know." He reached around his neck and scratched his shoulder blade. "Impossible to please."

"Ah." Karrell nodded slowly. "That can be rough on a kid."

He shrugged. "He just wanted more for his sons than he

ever had." The mustard had to have come from a burger, but he hadn't eaten one for at least a week. When was the last time he did a load of wash?

"More, how?"

"I suppose for us not to be working class. Ungar hated that he came from simple people. In Transylvania, our ancestors were hay farmers, and in England, the Dalakises grew wheat. When the Vârcolac race escaped to this community, my dad figured he'd finally leave behind the agricultural business he inherited—here we are, *underground*, right?" Breen studied a book tipped over on its side. It had a multicolored cover. *When Art Therapy Meets Sex Therapy: Creative Explorations of Sex, Gender, and Relationships.*

He scratched his temple. "Roth saddled Ungar with sanitation disposal. Honest work in my mind, but nothing that raised the status of the Dalakis name. My father resented the hell out of it. Still does. He always believed the Dalakis family was better. He even thought we were above the race's procreation problems. He kept trying to have kids after Roth banned breeding among the race. So Barbu was born when he shouldn't have been and ended up as a Stânga Town kid, and the baby after Barbu was a stillbirth. My mom refused to get pregnant again after that."

Karrell's lips bent sympathetically. "I'm sorry."

Breen lifted a single shoulder. "It's our race's cross to bear, right?"

Charlize was quiet now—a quietness different from not yelling or not speaking. It was more like the defensive hostility rolling off her had toned down. He glanced quickly at her, but only caught a glimpse of the shadow of her long lashes against her cheeks before Karrell was asking him more questions.

"So you and Barbu are the only children?"

"That's right." Breen scraped his thumbnail over the mustard stain. He didn't want to talk about his little brother. He was still figuring out how not to be a nonentity when it came to Barbu, and all the details weren't straight in his mind yet. Although, actually, it probably just took more *doing* than thinking.

"And how did your father show you and your brother he wanted more for you?"

Breen looked up. "What?" *No Barbu?*

"You said that Ungar wanted more for his sons than he ever had. How did you know?"

"Know?" *Dialectical Behavior Therapy Skills Training with Adolescents.* He scrunched his face at the therapist. *Dialectical…?* "What do you mean?"

"For example, did your father try to give you everything he never had?"

"Give us stuff?" Breen caught back an expression of shock, the skin along his cheeks stretching. "No. Um… No. Ungar tried to make Barbu and me better than everyone else."

"Ah. How?"

How? How did the carpenter who built that bookshelf make it so none of the nails showed? Did the trick affect its load-bearing capacity?

"How did Ungar try to make you and Barbu better than everyone else, Breen?"

He went back to the mustard stain. He flaked it up and swept the particles away. "Any time we didn't act like men, he gave us static about it."

"And what does it mean to act like a man—according to Ungar?"

"Don't cry, that sort of thing." There was probably more to it, but Breen was starting to feel tired. Funny, though, how words just kept coming out of his mouth. He'd never thought about any of this before, but the answers seemed to be there.

"How did you measure up to Ungar's expectations?"

Breen used the toe of his right Converse to scratch his left heel.

"Earlier you mentioned your dad is impossible to please.

I'm going to guess this means you didn't measure up so well."

10-Minute Mindfulness, Relaunch Your Life…

"Breen?"

"No." The back of his neck felt tight. "I didn't."

"And since Barbu is a Stânga Town kid—and so probably, unfortunately, considered incapable of much—I'm also going to guess the lion's share of pressure for fulfilling your father's hopes and dreams fell onto your shoulders."

The tightness in his neck moved into his throat. "Maybe." He'd watched Barbu take a lot of crap.

"Would it be fair to say that you've endured a great deal of criticism from your father?"

"Yeah. I mean…" He couldn't come up with a way to defend his father for that. "Well, yeah."

From the side of his vision, he saw Charlize's chin sink toward her chest.

"And how do you deal with your father's criticism?" Karrell asked.

A dull ache was forming behind his eyes. He was losing track of why they were doing this.

"Does it make you feel bad?" Karrell asked.

"No. Not really."

"No?"

"I ignore what he says."

"Ignore it?" This clearly surprised Karrell. "Really?"

"Yeah. I learned to."

"So that kind of stuff doesn't bother you anymore?"

"No."

"Not from anyone?"

"Not much."

"So when Charlize called you a 'fucking piece of shit' after the food-tasting gathering at Three Friends', it didn't bother you. You were able to ignore it."

The backs of his ears warmed. Everyone knew everything about everybody in this stupid town.

The side of Charlize's face he could see quivered and clenched.

"Everything's just A-Okay with you," Karrell pressed. "Is that it, Breen? You don't have any needs?"

"It bothered me," he admitted, "when she said that." His voice felt far away.

Charlize's lips did something. He couldn't tell what.

Karrell pressed her fingertips to her mouth for a moment. "Do you know how I experience you, Breen? As very thoughtful in the way you answer questions. At first you seem almost slow about it. But, no. What's actually going on is that your father trained you to search for landmines in everything people say." Karrell leaned toward him. "And, no, Breen, Ungar is *not* like other fathers. No kid should have to endure constant criticism."

A book in the far corner of the top shelf had a partially ripped spine. A piece of the fabric was flopped down, covering the first part of the title.—*Introverts. Master Your Personality.*

"I'm sorry." Charlize's voice was squeaky and raspy, nearly unrecognizable.

Breen looked over at her. His eyes felt strained and over-worked. It was a weird feeling.

A tear was dangling off the end of her nose. "I know what it's like to feel like you can't do anything right. Ever since I was eight years old, I *haven't* done anything right, and it's the worst feeling ever. If I…I-I-I…"

Breen's chest ripped in two like a soggy newspaper. *Don't cry, Charlize*, and *Don't worry about it*. He didn't say those things, though. As bad as he wanted to let her off the hook, he had the sense that if he did she would just feel worse.

"If I contributed to you feeling awful about yourself by calling you names, I'm so sorry. It's just the way I vent anger. I-I mean, I'm not trying to make excuses. There is no excuse. I just… I want you to know I didn't mean anything by it, and…and…" She looked at him.

Her eyes were extra-shiny with tears, and even though he'd rather eat half-decomposed roadkill than see her cry, her eyes were the most beautiful he'd ever seen them. And he was no longer lost about why Karrell had done this. By bringing out his own family mess, the therapist took away Charlize's anger at him and replaced it with understanding and kindness. Charlize saw him differently now, as someone she could relate to, who could sympathize with her and *her* mess. And whether she liked it or not, or realized it or not, now there *was* intimacy between them.

She dragged the back of her wrist across her cheek. "I won't ever call you names again."

"I believe you," he said, and his heart tumbled in his chest. He couldn't be sure, but he thought the thing might've been doing a hoo-yah fist-pump.

CHAPTER THIRTY-FOUR

AM I A FIEND?

John didn't know, couldn't think about it, because right now he felt like a pharaoh on high, exultant, godlike, arms spread wide with rays of divine sunshine beaming out from his chest.

He was alive, truly *alive*.

He filled his lungs with a gigantic breath of air—new air, in a new world, where… He paused and cocked his head, as if listening. Something was missing. All was quiet. Complaints silenced. The constant, horrific, nails-on-a-chalkboard whine vanished. *The damnedest thing.* It was…

Satiation.

That's what this was. His hunger was gone.

No. Not exactly. He was hungry, but in the normal way. For *food.* He let out a whoop. "I can eat!" Swiftly sidestepping Shaston, he bolted from the bathroom and raced into the kitchen, skidding to a stop in front of the refrigerator. Flinging open the door, he went down on his knees in front of the deli drawer and tore it open. *Yes!* There was a salivating variety of lunchmeat and cheeses—black forest ham, roast turkey, Havarti cheese, Swiss, cheddar. He ripped open packages and shoved the contents into his mouth. He couldn't chew and swallow fast enough. He was eating. *Fuck me, I'm eating!*

Shaston moved to hover over him. "Careful, John," she warned. "You'll make yourself sick."

Orange juice? Yes! Side door. He chugged it, head back,

juice streaming down the sides of his mouth onto his neck. He came to the end of the carton on a gasp and tossed the container aside. He pointed at the pantry cupboard. "What's in there?" Chips, maybe? Cookies…wait, there were tortillas in the fridge. He could make himself a quesadilla or a taco.

"John." Shaston hunkered beside him. "Take it easy, okay?" She took him by the wrist.

He glanced sharply at her, prepared to wrench free, then…didn't. There was something about her now. The shape of her eyes was so…and the thickness of her hair like… Had she always been this pretty? He zeroed in on her chest, where the simple cotton T-shirt she'd worn to bed clung to the firmness of her breasts. He undressed her with his eyes, and—

He grew erect so fast he toppled over backward onto his ass.

Chuffing a breath, he sprawled on the floor in ungainly shock, gaping at the huge swelling at the front of his sweatpants…his dick. *My dick!* It was no longer an unresponsive tube of loose flesh. No longer the half-flab-half-firm thing it'd been even when he was in remission from his "illness." This was a man's cock, fully erect and ready to conquer.

Scrabbling onto all fours, he sprang at Shaston.

She threw her arms and legs around him in a death-lock embrace, and they tumbled onto the linoleum together. He came down hard on top of her, landing solidly within the cradle of her spread thighs. Grunting, he hooked a thumb into the back of his elastic waistband and tugged his sweatpants down. Her cotton shorts came off in one hasty, seam-tearing yank. *God, yes.* Naked on naked, cock to crotch. He moaned and ground against her, his rigid sex sliding along her soft thigh. His brain waves shorted out.

"Wait," she panted. "I have to bite you first."

He caught only a glimpse of her elongated fangs and the vitreous brightness of her eyes before she roughly twisted a hand in his hair and cranked his head to one side, then—

OW! Whore-ass-bitch-sleazewad-cumsucker. He fought to get away from her, away from the agony searing his throat in half.

He couldn't.

His current muscle mass equaled the exoskeleton of a cockroach, and Shaston was unnaturally strong. The only thing he managed to do was cycle his legs through the litter of Boar's Head wrappers on the floor. He barked at her in his authoritative police voice. "Stop!"

She didn't.

Fucking fuck. He was going to—

"AH!" His world super-novaed into an explosion of sharper scents and brighter colors, rainbow lights zipping around behind his eyes. "Holy crap, don't stop!" The length of his spine convulsed in ecstasy, his hips juddered, and—he ejaculated everything he had onto the floor between Shaston's legs. *Aw, shit.*

He pushed out of her hold and slump-rolled off her, panting, tingles of warm still racing all over his body.

He didn't know how long he lay there, staring at the ceiling, before he glanced down at himself. *Jesus.* He looked like he should be passed out in a gutter after a bachelor party gone wrong, food crumbs trapped in some of his belly hairs, his sweatpants bunched around his knees, and his naked cock flopped across his hip. His shirt, for all appearances, had been used to clean up a murder scene.

He sagged his head back down. "Not one of my finer moments."

"Oh, don't worry about it." Shaston caressed the backs of her fingers across his arm, a tender gesture that made him flinch away.

He covered the movement by tugging up his sweats. Not to be rude about it, but Shaston wasn't the woman he wanted, and now that sexual tension had been fully—if embarrassingly—relieved, he just wanted to move onto other things.

"I can get you erect again," she said.

Nice of her to think it of him—and herself—but that would way overestimate the capabilities of his exoskeleton and additionally fail to recall he'd been hovering near death for months.

And yet...

Weirdest thing.

As they cleaned up, changed clothes, and waited for a transport to arrive to take them back to the community—and, presumably, to the donor Toni had mentioned—he kept eyeballing Shaston. A compulsion of some sort seemed to be driving him beyond the utter neutrality he felt for her and on to wanting to screw her. *Needing* to. It was an itchy, antsy feeling steadily growing inside him, as if he no longer was the cockroach but was inhabited by millions of them, their prickly leg spines scraping under his skin as they scurried about. What was it about *Shaston* calling to him as the answering scratch to that itch?

His jaw was clenched to the throbbing point by the time a Lincoln Town Car pulled up to the safe house. He climbed into the back and hunkered down sideways in his seat, staring at Shaston with ultra-clear vision. An iron band of tension wrapped his chest. His mind kept trying to figure out what was going on. Then there was no figuring. Just doing.

Either fight or fuck...

He jumped her.

Once again, she hugged him fiercely to her, as if she were as itchy and needy for some grind as he was. Leaning back on the car seat, she aimed her crotch at his, making things easy for him. Her skirt bunched around her waist, also paving the way. He fumbled his flaccid dick out of his pants. Once things got going, the appendage would hopefully—She bit his neck, and... Hell, he did get erect again.

Snorting air down his nose, he jerked Shaston's panties aside and pushed inside her. He bit her too—a move requiring

Upper Level Advanced Vampire Neck-Maneuvering skills to
do at the same time she was biting him, and, *hah*, newbie that
he was, he did it. Sucking, grunting, panting, he pounded into
Shaston's body, and then his world super-novaed again,
rapture spurting from the top of his dick like a Roman candle.
Unbelievable.

Lungs working, he sank back on the floorboards between
Shaston's legs.

Christ, he'd never orgasmed like that before. Ever.

Shaston flipped her skirt down.

He reclaimed the seat beside her, hiked up his jeans and
buttoned them, then lounged back, eyes half-shut, marveling
at how good he felt. *Healthy and fine* couldn't even begin to
describe the rebirth he was going through right now.

When the Lincoln finally came to a stop and the car door
swung open, GQ Roth and Toni were waiting for them.

As John exited the car, he gave Toni a smoldering look,
one that hopefully projected plenty of *I'm not impotent
anymore.* It probably made him the un-coronated king of
DicksVille to give Toni a look like that minutes after balling
Shaston. But Shaston was—for lack of a better term—a
transition girl. Sorry for how crass it sounded, but it was true.
She was nothing, and Toni was the substance making up his
heart.

A suited-up woman with blond hair cut short started
forward, aiming to take their place in the Town Car.
"Congratulations again," she was saying over her shoulder to
Toni, "on Jacken being in hibernation. I'm glad you two
finally worked out the kid situation."

The suit was talking about Teeth-Tattooed Asshole, but
John had no idea what it meant for the guy to be in "hibernation."

"Thanks," Toni said, although her smile was strained.

The suited-up woman continued forward, intending to
pass him... Hell, he knew her. Her name was Kimberly

Stănescu, and she was the fierce lawyer lady who'd showed up at Scripps Hospital to release Nichita from John's clutches.

She stopped abruptly and stared at him, gaped, really, but not *at* him, as in, at his face. She gawked at his throat.

John was sporting an ugly bruise there from Shaston's bite, Shaston the same, and for some reason—he saw when he glanced around—these bruises held everyone's frozen interest.

For a moment John felt like he'd just stepped into the middle of a wax museum.

Toni tipped her chin up, inhaled a breath, then gave Shaston a solemn look. "Did you have sex too?"

"Yes."

Dammit! Don't admit that to Toni. "Look," John began, "it was..." He stopped, stumped over how to tell Toni *it was nothing* and not come across sounding like a total lowlife. Women didn't like to hear that a man could screw someone and have it mean nothing, even when it was another woman. It probably pecked at the back of their minds that if he could be robotic with one, what would stop him from someday reducing her to a nothing lay? *As if,* with Toni. But he needed time to explain it.

And right now Toni was wholly focused on Shaston. "Does John understand what's between you two now?"

Dammit, there's nothing between us! He wanted to shout it.

"No." The cords in Shaston's throat stretched into tense, stringy lines.

"You didn't explain it beforehand?"

"No. I didn't."

Roth's complexion turned a choleric shade of crimson.

"Why?" Toni asked, although she looked like a person who didn't expect to receive an answer she would understand.

A single bubble of moisture formed on Shaston's tear duct. "I want a baby."

A...? John's lungs shut down for two strangled seconds. A *baby*! Holy shit! That's right, they hadn't used a condom.

He'd been too single-minded-of-purpose in the back of the Lincoln, but, but…*dammit*, wasn't the woman supposed to see to birth control when the man became a sex-crazed dunce? Sure she was… Unless, of course, she was *trying* to get pregnant.

He just might throw up all the awesome food he'd eaten.

Toni spread her hands, because, yeah, Shaston's answer clearly went beyond her comprehension. "I don't get it, Shaston. Vârcolac can't procreate with other Vârcolac."

"But John's *not* Vârcolac, not a full one yet, anyway. Dr. Jess said it would take time."

"Shaston." Sharp now. "John still isn't someone you can breed with. His human side isn't Dragon, it's regular."

"But…no," Shaston argued. "There's something more to him. I've sensed it. I mean, look at all the years he suffered in pain, but he survived."

Toni shook her head.

A tear splashed down. "I-I just…I can't wait any longer to have a—"

A low growl overrode her. It reverberated behind John, and then he was being shoved aside as Roth crashed by his shoulder.

Shaston squeaked and scurried away, but Roth wasn't aiming for her.

He marched in a straight line for the lawyer lady and stopped mere inches from her. His eyes were icy steel, and his voice a tight snarl. "What do you say about this, Mrs. Stănescu? Shall we make a note in the record that yet *another* Unauthorized Bite has been committed in this community? Yes!" His voice was rising. "Let us indeed write it down, along with how *shocked* you surely must be. Whereas I," he was outright shouting now, "most definitely, *am not.*" These last two words where bellowed directly into the lawyer's red face.

Stănescu inhaled a huge, fire-in-the-hole breath, but Toni cut in before the lawyer could retaliate.

"Why don't we convene later to discuss the ramifications of this infraction? For now, John needs to be made aware of the drastic turn his life has just taken."

Drastic? Come on. What just happened didn't have to be seen as drastic. If Shaston wanted to go off and have a baby, let her. It didn't have to interfere with Toni and him finally getting their shot, the shot John had been waiting years to have. If Toni would just give him a minute, he'd explain it all to her.

Toni finally did look at him. "Why don't you come upstairs with me to one of the mansion's parlors." She swept some hair off her forehead with her fingers, slender, elegant fingers that damn well would be his soon. He was going to figure out the right thing to say.

"You're going to want to sit down for this, John."

CHAPTER THIRTY-FIVE

The underground community of Țărână
Noon
Three days later

THE SHANK TOOTH BAR IN Stânga Town was one of the seediest dives Charlize had ever been in, low-ceilinged and dark, several walls missing patchy bursts of plaster, probably either from water damage or the result of body slams—nightly bar fights were no doubt a showcase event in a place like this.

The occupants were slitty-eyed and slash-mouthed from being mean, dangerous, suspicious, or just plain high—take your pick—and in general made Clint and his Rhoad Rhage pals look like Cabbage Patch kids.

Just her type of crowd.

She was in no mood for apple dumplings and baskets of kittens today. Or any day in the past three, which she'd spent dodging Breen and his damned calm face, his deeply layered eyes, the chip in his fang that peeked out only occasionally but was a total heart-melter, and his stupid affection for her.

I like you, and when I'm inside you it's kind of impossible to ignore.

She made a face. Soul-level, particle-deep jackhole had then gone and made things worse by forming a deeper connection with her in their last therapy session, showing her that he was as much of a survivor as she was.

And how do you deal with your father's criticism?
I ignore what he says.
Ignore it?

Yeah. I learned to.

Charlize tossed back her drink. She was done with bull-shit.

Everything she couldn't deal with. *Done.*

Breen. A relationship. Sex.

She was shutting it all down.

A guy entered the bar, pausing long enough to look at her like she was harboring a new troubling form of STD. Or maybe it was her hair he was staring at. Her curls stood out like a glowing gold beacon in this joint. If there was another blond head in here, it was covered by a hat.

Giving her a final, unfriendly glare, the guy clumped to the right toward a scattering of tables and chairs that had seen better days. Up at the front of the bar there was a stage for live performances, although right now alternative rock droned from several cheap, wall-mounted speakers, tinny and garbled. The long wooden bar where she sat was directly across from the entrance. The top of it was covered in wet ring stains linked together in patterns that made her brain go psychedelic if she stared at them for too long.

She wiggled her fingers at the bartender, Anatol.

He'd never spoken to her. She only knew his name because when the young man first arrived for his shift about a half hour ago, sloppily dressed and with uncombed black hair, the other bartender complained, "What the farks, Anatol? You're late."

Anatol simply replied, "No I'm not," then hadn't spoken again. He'd wrapped a carnage-ridden apron around his waist, strode over to her, leaned both palms on the bar, and looked at her. She'd ordered a shot of tequila.

In answer to her summons, he did the same thing now.

So did she.

Anatol sloshed tequila into her glass.

A ripple of heightened awareness rolled through the crowd. Faces turned away. Shoulders hunched.

Someone sat on the stool next to Charlize.

She turned to look. She stiffened as a craving ache opened up a hole in her heart. She turned back to her drink. Her face probably showed too much of the pain ripping through her.

Anatol looked at Breen.

"Just a Bud," he ordered.

Anatol nodded and went off to pull the draft.

"Hey," Breen said to her.

She stared down into her drink, the tequila a rich gold color...like his eyes. She pressed a hand to her belly. Her stomach hurt. She was pretty sure it had been for three days straight. Why, just *why* couldn't she be someone other than who she actually was?

Anatol dropped off a foaming mug of beer.

Breen tugged his wallet out of his back pocket. He found his money card and pointed it in Charlize's direction before handing it to Anatol. "Hers too."

Yeah, well, Breen probably had money to spare. The Spec Ops warriors were the highest paid workers in this town, second only to the leadership.

Anatol ran the card then set it in front of Breen on the bar before meandering off.

Breen didn't pick up the card. He didn't sip his drink. "You maybe shouldn't be in a place like this."

"I like it here. It suits me." Face forward, she lifted her upper lip. "Dark and nasty and fucked up."

"Charlize—"

"I'm thinking about making it my new hangout."

Breen picked up his money card, tapped it a couple of times on the bar, then put it back in his wallet. "We're supposed to be in session with Karrell right now."

"Please pass on my regrets to her. I'm never going back there." She moved her shot glass from one ring stain to the next to the next. A board game for the barfly, for the sad and pathetic and hopeless.

Breen hung the tips of his fingers on the rim of his beer mug and paused a long moment. "So we're done? You and I?"

Emotion jammed in the back of Charlize's throat. Oh, God, she was already on the verge of crying.

"I know I've let you down—"

"Stop!" She whirled on him—on him and his eyes, the corners of them squeezed down in pain. Because *she* was hurting him. "You haven't let me down, dammit. *You* have done nothing but be nice. It's me!"

From down the bar, Anatol glanced up from the stereo knobs he was fiddling with.

"I can't do it anymore, Breen. I can't keep h-hurting people." Charlize wedged her palms against her face and wiped away her tears. *Shit.* "Karrell was right. I ruin everything, and when I do, I ruin everybody nearby."

Breen's brows sagged down.

She sniffed hard. "Consider my departure an early Christmas present." She looked away and clenched a fist around her shot glass.

Deep inhale. Long exhale. "You're stronger than this," Breen told her quietly.

She closed her eyes and moved her lips around. No, her lips moved on their own, trembling. "Don't," she returned. "You don't know who I am."

"For the last few days," he said, "I've been researching what it's like to be the child of an alcoholic."

She swallowed, but only succeeded in lodging the lump of emotions more firmly in her throat. He'd done that for *her?*

"It's…messed up. But you were strong enough to make it through a fucked-up childhood, Charlize, so you're strong enough to kick the ass of whatever it is scaring you. And…I don't think it's me you're really scared of. Or us."

"Well, I am." People didn't stick around, and it was her fault they didn't. She couldn't live with it anymore.

"Then there's a reason for it, and you can face it."

Ear-splitting guitar noise squealed from the speakers, and people in the bar turned and *boo'd* at Anatol. The sound quality was the worst ever in this place.

Breen cupped her elbow and eased her off her bar stool, leading her outside into the rotting stink of the slums— unwashed bodies, shoddy plumbing, and some kind of weird sulfuric reek.

Breen took her gently by the arms and turned her to face him. The warmest, deepest golden gaze that existed on earth stared down at her. "I've wanted to help you, but I'm just too much of a bonehead to know how. It's why I feel like I've let you down. But..." One corner of his mouth strained outward. "Back while I was hanging from a tree for three nights, I decided not to be a do-nothing guy anymore, so I had to figure it out. And what I came up with is that *I* might not know how to help you, but Karrell does." He gave her arms a little squeeze. "So I'm sorry, but I'm going to have to make you go back there."

Panic iced her blood. "B-Breen..."

He pulled her against him, one arm wrapping around her back, the other hand coming to rest on her cheek, gently pressing the side of her face to the comforting warmth of his chest. He was holding her so she couldn't pull away.

Tears filled her eyes and spilled over. Maybe he knew her pretty well after all.

"I can feel how much you hurt," he whispered. "It's monumental."

She curled her arms into a little cocoon between their bodies and drew in a stuttering breath, filling her nose with his rich, animal scent. It blocked out the sewage smell and made her feel like she was...home. More tears poured.

"You need to go to Karrell and tell her the worst thing that's ever happened to you."

She smashed her eyelids closed. For an instant of flashback the precarious boundary between present and past collapsed—the diesel truck was there, its horn blaring, its eighteen locked-up wheels laying down a strip of rubber a block long. She let out a small cry.

His hold tightened on her. He was so much more powerful than she was. She'd never truly comprehended the full extent of it until now, when his strength was being used to console. "I'll be with you the whole time," he told her. "I know you've basically always been alone your entire life, with no one to watch out for you, but I'm not going to do that to you. Okay? I'm *here*, and not just because I'm physically bonded to you, but because I want to be here." He shifted back, putting her at arm's length and dipping his chin a bit so he could give her a steady look.

She stared at him through the huge, watery pools of her tears and pressed a hand over her heart, feeling the lurch and the double-pound.

BREEN TEXTED KARRELL THEY WERE coming, so when they entered her office, the therapist was already seated and waiting for them.

Charlize stood in the doorway. The muscle fibers in her thighs gnarled into balls of yarn, and suddenly it felt like her nervous system was set up to relay only emergency alerts.

Karrell gave her an encouraging smile. "Why don't you come in and sit down?"

Charlize couldn't move. The therapist was so very motherly in a lot of ways.

Breen took Charlize by the elbow again and escorted her to her regular chair, helping her into it.

He sat next to her and scooted his chair closer.

The silence was thundering. Charlize dropped her hands into her lap and lowered her eyes, raking the tips of her fingers together, over and over. Her cheeks felt crackly from dried tears.

"What's the hardest thing going on for you right now?"

Karrell asked, her voice soothing and deep, like a radio therapist on the three-A.M. shift.

Charlize licked her lips. Her mouth tasted like day-old barbecue ash. "Memories."

"Of your childhood?"

"Yes."

"Your mother was an alcoholic, is that correct?"

"Yes. Still is."

"Your father?"

"Bailed on us when I was seven. Just left his three kids with a woman he knew fuckerized everything."

"I'm sorry." Karrell's voice was still low. "Who was in charge when your mother couldn't be?"

"Me." Tension flared across the bridge of Charlize's nose. "I'm the oldest, so I had to be Miss Responsible."

"That's a lot for a kid to take on." Karrell exhaled softly. "I can understand why you feel like you can't be soft."

"It's more than that. It's..." *Every time I let my guard down, a diesel truck screeches across my memory.*

Karrell waited a moment. "Did something happen shortly after the divorce...when you were eight years old?"

Charlize gripped the armrests. Cold dread seeped into her bones. She shut her eyes.

"In our last session you said you haven't done anything right since you were eight, which doesn't sound like how a Miss Responsible would describe herself."

Charlize slowly opened her eyes, very slowly, like her lids were being operated by an old-fashioned winch. *Inch worm, inch worm, little, scraggly, horrible inch worm...* Karrell was inching toward a place where it was not nice to go.

Karrell's tone never shifted off level and calm. "What happened when you were eight, Charlize?"

Charlize's heart thumped wildly, pumping blood in the wrong direction. Everything was so wrong.

"It's easier to be a rebel than Miss Responsible, isn't it?

It's why you create chaos in your life. Not only because it's what's familiar to you, but because the child in charge is the one who has to clean up vomit and tuck a drunk mother into bed or bail her out of jail. Not the best of roles."

Garish, rhinestone-like dots prickled at the sides of Charlize's vision. Her skin went clammy.

"And constant disasters would also keep you from growing too close to anyone, you know, that someone who will eventually leave you—like your mother did for those three days of hell. Like she always did emotionally. Like your father did. Like Breen did on his mission."

Breen shifted in his seat and rubbed his palms along his thighs.

Stomach acid churned, heaved, and bubbled up, burning the roof of Charlize's mouth. She shoved a fist against her lips.

"Were you abandoned again at eight years old?" Karrell asked. "Is that what happened?"

Charlize dropped her fist. She shook her head. "No." A burgeoning of hot tears ignited an inferno in her nose.

"Tell us what, then." Karrell leaned forward, setting her elbows on the armrests, staring intently. "This memory controls you, Charlize. Vent it and get rid of it for good. You deserve to be happy."

A swallow clotted in her throat midway down. She moved her mouth in soundless horror.

Breen set a palm on the armrest of her chair. He didn't touch her. His hand was just there.

"No," she hissed. "I don't deserve to be happy. I-I don't," she quaked. And then her mouth spoke the abomination.

"I killed my sister."

Chapter Thirty-Six

BREEN STIFFENED IN HIS CHAIR, his radar knotting into such a fibrous lump of pain he nearly groaned.

I killed my sister.

He stretched his chin forward, trying to open his airway wider so he could breathe through the searing agony. "Monumental hurt" might have been a very large understatement. He pressed a fist to the middle of his chest and kneaded the spot. Probably words didn't exist bad enough to describe how much his woman was hurting right now.

Karrell gently put a box of tissues in Charlize's hands. "What happened?"

Charlize clutched the box. "We...we..."

Breen kept his hand on the armrest of Charlize's chair. She seemed to be staring at it.

Charlize's expression glassed over, and she began to speak in a weird monotone. "My brother, sister, and I were playing at a park. I was in charge of them. I was eight, Benjamin, six, and Olivia, four. We were playing a game of freeze tag. I was in a mad chase after my brother—he was impossible to catch. When I finally tagged him, I looked around for Olivia."

Breen's eyebrows felt tight on his forehead. He was watching Charlize carefully while managing to draw in a breath every other try. Even though her voice had that weird, flat quality to it, there was a serpent slither of panicky mania beneath it.

"Olivia had wandered off. She was heading for some flowers across the road, and I hollered at her to stop. I ran after her and kept screaming. Stop! Stop! There were no fences around the park, nothing to keep her from crossing the street, and…" Charlize's blond curls shimmered; she was trembling. "There was…was…" A muffled moan spilled out of her.

Breen felt the muscles in his jaw bunch. He was biting his teeth together.

"There was a truck coming."

Oh, shit.

"I ran after Olivia as fast as I could, *so fast*, but…but… I wasn't fast enough. She…" Charlize lifted her head and looked at the two of them—Breen, then Karrell. Her expression was foggy and confused and too young. "I don't understand what happened. Olivia…she was there, then the truck hit her, and she just…disintegrated."

Karrell's brow knitted.

"How does that happen?" Charlize asked, thin and high. "I mean…there was only blood." She clawed her fingernails across the tissue box. "So much blood."

Breen closed his eyes. His stomach went away. He actually couldn't feel it anymore.

"So you need to stop being nice to me."

He snapped open his eyes and glanced over. And, yeah. Charlize had directed that comment at him.

"Now you know who I am, so you need to *stop*."

He surveyed her eyes, her jaw, the tip of her chin. "Who do you think you are?" he asked.

Charlize hissed air between her teeth. "Olivia died. She *never* came back, and it was because of *me*. Do you hear what I'm saying? Are you listening?"

"Yes."

"I killed my sister."

"No you didn't. Your sister died from an accident. You—"

"Don't!" She lurched to the edge of her chair, the tissue box bobbling on her lap. "I was in charge of Olivia," she ground at him. "Don't you *dare* try to let me off the hook."

He could see Charlize's legs visibly shaking. His own legs felt funny, like his muscles had gone too elastic, and now everything was unstable. "You're asking me to sit here and blame you for a crime you didn't even commit. I won't do that. You're not a murderer."

"I am!" she screamed. "I killed her." She hurled the tissue box at him.

He blocked. The box bounced off his forearm.

Charlize flew out of her chair.

He didn't register she was attacking him until he saw her fingernails curved into claws, and by then his split-second delay cost him. He couldn't stop her forward momentum from doing its thing—her body slammed into his and knocked him over backward. They hit the floor together, the chair shooting out from underneath his ass and zipping across the floor, Charlize bouncing on top of him. Air blasted out of his lungs.

In a frantic churn of legs, Charlize scrambled to get on top of him, and even before she'd locked herself into a full mount, she was flailing a barrage of slaps at his face. Or trying to—she didn't land any. He was too fast for her. Dodging the first two blows, he stole between the next ones and grabbed her wrists.

Cursing, she struggled against his hold, but she couldn't break free.

He had her trapped. She was stuck here in this therapy room, feeling all her shit.

He saw the moment she completely broke. The line of her mouth cracked, hysteria crowded onto her face, then she threw back her head and screamed. It was a long, howling, feral scream full of despair and fury and debilitating remorse, and if he lived to be three hundred, he would never forget that sound. It punched a fist straight through his radar into his heart. He couldn't stop his face from wrenching in abject anguish. *Real men don't cry.*

Fuck you, Dad!

He quick-rolled with Charlize and dumped her onto her back, pinning her hands on either side of her ears. He leaned his weight into her, probably too much, and yelled, "You were just a kid! It wasn't your fault."

Charlize sucked air in at hyperventilation speeds, one breath on top of the other with no break in between— *hahhahhahhah.*

"Where was your fucking mother, anyway, huh? *She* was the one who was supposed to be watching her own damned kids, not you."

Charlize stared up at him, showing him her little girl's eyes, a little girl whose under-the-bed monsters had been the meanest and baddest out there.

A surge of protectiveness pumped through him, spraying grids across his vision. Vengeance lurked like a shadow-beast at the corner of one grid: the male Vârcolac's primal need to hunt down and destroy anything—person, place, or thing— that dared to hurt his mate. Damn him, he was going to kill something out there if he wasn't careful.

Panting, he looked at Karrell. *A little help here, maybe?*

The therapist hadn't moved from her seat. She just sat there, calmly studying the two of them, not offering a single hint about the current state of her thoughts. If it was a common occurrence for Karrell's clients to end up tangled on the carpet during couples counseling, then maybe she needed to reevaluate some of her techniques...not that she didn't already own enough fucking books on the subject.

Without a word, Karrell rose from her chair and walked around to the other side of her desk. She picked up the phone and dialed a couple of numbers.

Breen observed everything she did with hyperfocus. *Beep, beep—ring—click.*

"Donree? Hi, it's Karrell. I saw Hannah Crişan downstairs earlier with her daughter. If they're still around, could you—?

Oh, they're right there? Perfect. Could you please ask them to come to my office right away? Thank you." Karrell hung up and looked at Breen and Charlize. "We have company coming, you two." She sounded like a kindergarten teacher. *Clean up the blocks and the clay, kiddos, it's visitor time!*

What the hell was going on?

Breen hoisted himself to his feet, bringing Charlize up with him.

There was a knock at the waiting room door. Karrell went to answer it.

With an arm fastened around Charlize's waist, Breen kept her locked against his side. They stood beside the therapist's desk and waited, both of them practically vibrating.

Karrell returned, followed by Hannah and her daughter, Kristara. Both mother and child had their golden hair tied into pigtails.

Hannah Crişan had the distinction of being the first Dragon female ever brought into the community. She was also the first to give birth to a living Mixed-blood child, a boy, Ællen, whose successful entrance into the community had given them all a lot of hope for continued Vârcolac survival.

Kristara was Hannah's second child.

After introducing the two new arrivals to Breen and Charlize, the therapist said to Kristara, "Charlize, here, was interested in seeing some of your drawings." She gestured at the sketch pad the young girl held clutched to her chest. Then she explained to Charlize, "Hannah's two eldest children are taking art lessons from Thomal. Ællen creates comic books, and I believe you"—the therapist regarded Kristara warmly—"draw portraits, isn't that right?"

Kristara nodded. She flipped open her sketchpad and stepped forward, showing the top page to Breen and Charlize. "This is Mommy."

It was actually pretty good.

Charlize smiled weakly as Kristara flipped from one page to the next, showing all five of her siblings.

If grayish dots hadn't been jumping across Breen's vision and his heart currently trying to come out his nose, he probably would've really liked the picture show.

"Wow," the therapist enthused. "You have lots of brothers and sisters. How old are you now, Kristara?"

"Eight."

"Eight," the therapist repeated, glancing pointedly at Charlize.

Breen felt a tremor run through her.

"Almost nine." Kristara added, puffing up a little.

"You're getting big." Then the therapist added to Hannah, "Is Kristara doing chores at home now?"

"Oh, absolutely. Kristara's a great helper." Hannah set a hand on her daughter's shoulder. "She washes the dishes with me and takes out the trash."

"Does she babysit her brothers and sisters?" Karrell asked.

"What? Oh, no." Hannah chuckled. "Not yet. She's too young. Maybe in a few more years." She observed her daughter with affection.

Karrell admired Kristara's pictures some more, then thanked the two for coming, and mother and daughter left.

The therapist leaned back against her desk, her arms crossed loosely over her chest. She regarded Charlize solemnly. "Your image of yourself at eight years old is of a girl much older than Kristara, isn't it?"

Charlize's nostrils fluttered. She nodded shakily.

"Guilt has warped your memory into something quite unfair, I think." Karrell pushed off her desk, walked around it, and sat down. "According to the American Academy of Pediatrics, a child shouldn't be left home alone until she's eleven or twelve years old. And that means caring for *herself*, not others." Karrell folded her hands on her desktop. "I realize you were undoubtedly very mature for your age, Charlize, but still, you were a *child*. You should have been able to play a game of freeze tag without any more worries than running down that wild brother of yours." Karrell paused. "Your mother blamed you for Olivia's death, didn't she?"

Charlize was really pale now. She nodded again, shakier.

Breen kept his arm secured around her waist.

"I'm not surprised," Karrell said. "I believe your mother knew on some level that the accident was her fault. Like Breen said, she should have been watching her own children. The horror of her mistake was too much for her to bear, so she put her failure as a mother on you, made *you* feel like the failure, like you weren't good enough. And, unfortunately, you accepted those messages as gospel—understandably, since you were a child. But then do you know what happened? You kept trying to be good enough. Out of guilt. As penance." Karrell's voice quieted. "And to this day, you're still trying. You're still running across that park, Charlize. Literally, you became a marathon runner, and figuratively, you've been running away from—or pushing away—anyone who could make you happy. Because you damn well don't deserve it."

Charlize eyes went very wide, showing a lot of the white.

"You probably also never properly grieved Oliva's death, so loss has remained an extra-difficult concept for you to deal with. Being married to a man who fights for a living has no doubt added to your turmoil." Karrell smiled slightly. "Luckily Breen is good at his job."

Breen swallowed heavily.

Karrell's smiled turned sympathetic. "But don't you think it's time to start seeing this tragedy from an adult's perspective, Charlize, to come to terms with what *actually* happened? Then the memory won't control you. You'll always feel sorrow over what happened, of course, but it won't destroy you. And that would be nice, because I, personally, believe you do deserve to be happy." Karrell sat back.

Charlize didn't answer. She just made a small hiccupping sound and turned toward Breen.

He opened his arms, and she fell into his embrace, buried her face against his chest, and wept.

CHAPTER THIRTY-SEVEN

SOME OF THE BEST IN famous last words:

I checked. It's not loaded.

It's deep enough, don't worry.

Hey, you guys, watch this!

And now a new one for the annals, the BEST of the fucking best:

You're going to want to sit down for this, John.

Ten words. Ultimate destruction.

John aimed a hostile glare at the television set, where a rerun of *How I Met Your Mother* was playing. The guy on the screen, that Ted Mosby architect dude. *Wanna punch him.* John wanted to punch everyone, though. Destroy something, just like his life had been totally annihilated by a hard-up skank who manipulated and used him when he had no idea about the choices his new biology was making.

He sneered his upper lip higher. Looked like the revenge deal he'd struck with MoonRiderOne really *had* pissed off God. Because why else would John have just found his way to a life where he could be healthy and fine, only to be immediately stripped of the one thing he wanted in life: his true love, Toni.

Who he couldn't ever have now.

As in, ever, ever, EVER.

He'd received the news sitting rigid in a spindly parlor chair, his tone going embarrassingly high-pitched and pleading when he'd asked Toni if there was a chance the bond wouldn't take due to his not-fully-vampiric state. Would this—*please*—provide him with an out clause?

Toni offered him the kind of overly-patient smile John had seen doctors use on unruly mental patients. "Maybe."

Meaning, *doubtful.*

He'd held on.

After all, Shaston—a full-blooded vampire—was way worse off than he was, right? Every night of their "bonding week" so far, she'd begged him to sleep in the same bed with her, her face pale, her eyes full of bruises.

Every night, he would let her suffer alone. Unfortunately—and not a good sign—he suffered too, just about gnawing his fists raw while he didn't sleep, plagued with feelings of wrongness and anxiety. He hated the woman who'd ruined him down to his core, marrow, and soul, so the constant pull he felt toward her didn't make sense.

Unless what Toni told him was true, and he and Shaston were physically bonded...as in, permanently. No getting out of it.

Teeth gritted, John squeezed off a few channel changes, one hand locked around the remote control, the other arm crooked beneath his head, propping it against the pillow on his bed. *Selfish and immoral whore.*

Damn her. Just...*damn her.*

The little ho-nasty stepped into his bedroom doorway. Unfortunate timing.

"What?" he growled at her. He was a champion growler now.

She jumped. "Um..." She screwed her fingers into the hem of her T-shirt. "Thomal is downstairs asking for you."

"What does he want?" he snapped.

"I don't know."

John launched himself off the bed, and Shaston scurried away. Their bond prevented him from tanning her hide like he wanted to do, but she still didn't trust him not to hurt her. *Smart girl.* He wouldn't trust him, either. *Damn her all to fuck.*

He tromped downstairs.

Blondie Thomal was waiting in the living room, dressed all in black with a long knife in a hip-holder on his waist. John's heightened vision picked up on the two small scars on his face; a thin one clipping some hair out of his right eyebrow and a thinner one arcing across the slope of his left cheekbone. The man had eaten lemongrass chicken for lunch.

John gave him a sour look. "Yeah?"

Blondie Thomal didn't completely succeed in hiding his surprise.

John was a different man in more ways than on the inside. He was gaining strength and energy at an exponential rate, and in the last three days, he'd packed on at least a good fifteen pounds of muscle. His skin was clear; his vision and mind were sharp; and his hair was turning black—now that he'd "realized his true nature," he was taking after Dear Ol' Bio Dad.

Every day more of his Vârcolac superpowers came online. Lights, noises, scents: all were experienced with un-blunted senses. It could be overwhelming at times, his surroundings as well as this becoming-a-new-being thing. How he felt about it remained a mystery. All of the necessary processing he should probably have been doing was taking a back seat to his need to stew and boil in rage and regret.

"Dr. Jess wants to see you." Thomal rested one hand casually on his belt, not far from the hilt of the long blade. "He'd like to give you a checkup now that you've popped your fangs. Are you able to leave Shaston?"

John's gut howled *no*. "With joy."

"Let's go, then." Thomal *escorted* him.

Yeah, to add insult to John's circumstances, after his sit-down with Toni left his life a nuclear waste, he was put under house arrest in a furnished model home in the community's family neighborhood. He'd done nothing wrong to deserve that. *He* was the victim here. But he supposed if the roles were reversed, he wouldn't have let a man who'd tangled with many of the male members of this hosed place wander wherever he pleased either. Considering, also, that John had spent the last three days doing nothing but stew and boil, he probably wasn't the safest person to be around right now.

John and Thomal walked the whole way in silence—so probably the shouting they heard when they entered the hospital seemed louder than it actually was.

"Shit." Thomal hurtled through a pair of swinging double doors.

John ran after him.

They raced down a long hallway. The bestial shouting was coming from an open door at the end, and there was a yellow alarm light flashing just inside.

A young woman with curly black hair hurried out the door. As soon as she saw Thomal, she waved frantically at him. "Hurry! Jacken's gone insane."

Jacken—*Teeth-Tattooed Asshole!* John picked up speed, racing inside the room just behind Thomal. He slewed to stop, panting, and—what the *fuck*? He couldn't believe what he was seeing.

Teeth-Tattooed Asshole had Toni jammed back against the wall behind her large desk, his inked-up arms planted on either side of her, imprisoning her with muscles that bulged aggressively under his flesh. His hair was a wild mess, as if he'd just rolled out of bed before coming here. *Congratulations again on Jacken being in hibernation.*

"How *dare* you," he snarled, and John had never heard a voice like it—deep and glottal, like it was coming up directly from the sewers of Hell.

Closing her eyes, Toni turned her head aside. Her chin quivered.

The sight thinned John's blood to water, jacked his pulse into a furious rhythm, and hit him with that spring-release feeling in his upper gums he now recognized as his fangs coming out of their chutes.

Heavy bootsteps thundered down the hallway. A second later Nichita entered the office, along with another man, both dressed in similar blackness to Thomal. They shoved past John into the room.

"What's going on?" Nichita demanded.

"I don't know," Thomal retorted. "I just got here. But Jacken's unsheathed on her."

Nichita's lips flattened against his teeth, and his expression darkened.

John edged a step sideways for a better view of Asshole. Sure enough, a set of sharp fangs were spiked down into his mouth.

Toni wasn't so much as fluttering an eyelash.

"Step off, Jacken," Nichita warned. "Right now."

Asshole didn't. The tendons on the side of his jaw were on the verge of bursting through his skin. Then a single tear slipped down Toni's cheek, and he snapped his hands off the wall and jolted back a step. His eyes were as black as someplace nobody would ever want to go.

Toni kept her face turned aside, like she didn't dare risk looking at him.

But Asshole looked at her. *Glared* at her in a pure hellfire way that pushed John's heart into even faster speeds.

"How dare you," Asshole repeated, hissing the words, the muscles along his shoulders standing out. He pivoted sharply, and with fluid, muscular coordination, hefted the big desk and hurled it through a frosted door.

The glass sheered apart with acidic screams, and Toni clutched her palms over her ears and grimaced. The three men in the room surged back from the flying debris.

Booming to the ground inside a courtyard, the large piece of furniture rolled once, then trundled to a halt. Plaster dust swirled.

As the last jarring clatter of brittle hail-fall quieted, Asshole stalked out this new, larger exit he'd made, his broad silhouette parting the fog of dust, then being swallowed up in it.

He was gone.

Toni slid down the wall, her legs collapsing beneath her. Her butt hit the floor, and she hugged her knees, crying softly.

JOHN PROWLED THE LENGTH OF his bedroom, pacing the space in quick, restless strides. He absently patted his breast pocket, searching for a pack of Marlboros. He didn't have any. Smoking wasn't allowed in this bumblefuck town—something about keeping the underground air quality clean. Not that he even craved cigarettes anymore, not since he'd "realized his true nature." He supposed that meant his nicotine fits had never really been about cigarettes in the first place, but were just another disguised craving for blood.

Only out of habit did he want to smoke now, do something with his hands while he tried to figure out what the hell he'd just witnessed at the hospital between Toni and Teeth-Tattooed Asshole.

Thomal had shuttled John out of there and back to this stupid house-prison before he'd been able to get any answers.

Was Toni okay?

Was Asshole currently being drawn and quartered in retribution for what he'd—

"John." The mousey voice came from his doorway.

He whirled on Ho-nasty, his hands curled into fists. "Leave me the fuck alone." He glared at her with eyes that felt like hot coals.

A swallow moved down her throat like knots on a pulley rope. "I-I'm sorry, but there's something I have to tell you." She stepped carefully into the room, and he caught a scent coming off her he didn't recognize: stronger, sweeter, demanding.

It washed a strange, cloudy haze over his vision and momentarily flicked out the lights in his brain, like he'd lapsed into narcolepsy. He shook his head.

"I know this is the last thing you want to hear or…or do, but… I have to tell you." She nibbled the side of her lip. "I tested myself, and I'm ovulating right—"

"Get out!" he roared.

She paled, but didn't leave.

Red smeared like grease paint across his vision. "I mean it, you cow. If you don't—"

"Please, listen to me," she pleaded. "Vârcolac females only ovulate about every six months. I know you hate me, but if you don't impregnate me now, we'll *never* have children. By the time I'm fertile again, you'll be fully vampiric, and then—"

"Hate," he cut in coldly, "is too light a term for what I feel for you."

Ho-nasty's eyelashes flapped.

"You're a vein to me, and that's it. You think I want to fuck that rank pussy of yours? It's attached to a lying, manipulative bitch. A mold spore, a pustule, a maggot."

Ho-nasty's mouth flopped open. Unflattering.

"I guess you should've picked a different man to destroy."

Her throat clicked with what sounded like a half-checked swallow. "I-I tried to find a mate. First Dev couldn't marry me, then the Dragon I was dating last year broke—"

"*What* did you just say? *Dev?*" John laughed: curt, bitter, wintry. "Are you telling me I ended up with Nichita's cast-off for a wife? Oh, the hits just keep on rollin', don't they?"

Her brow clouded. "Can't you…can't you just make the best of this, and…and…?"

"Good God, you can't be *that* naïve, can you?"

She wrung her hands. "You didn't even have a girlfriend before this happened. Why can't you—?" Her sentence ended on a squeak as he stomped toward her.

She scuttled backward, but he lashed out his hands and

grabbed her upper arms in a crushing grip. "I'm in love with *Toni*," he shouted into her face.

"You're…?" Ho-nasty blinked owlishly.

Now that he was closer to her, his dick was hardening. What the *hell* was the matter with him?

"But she…Toni's married to Jacken."

Shock loosened John's hold. *Married?* His fingers slipped down Ho-nasty's arms several inches before he retightened them. "What? You mean…" *No. No way.* "The guy with the tattoos on his forearms?"

Ho-nasty nodded. "They've been married for nearly five years. They have a daughter."

It was as if Ho-nasty hit him in the stomach as violently as she could with a roll of quarters in her fist. "No," he hissed. *No. Fucking. Way* had Toni married that asshole. She had too much taste. Too much good sense. "I saw the two of them together earlier in the hospital. The guy looked like he was about to beat Toni's brains in."

"Oh, no. Jacken would never hurt her. If they were fighting, they were just, you know, having a marital spat."

And John had also seen the two of them together in the hospital when he first arrived. Teeth-Tattooed Asshole had brushed up against Toni, and she hadn't pulled away.

"They love each other."

John snapped his chin up. Ho-nasty had hurled that at him too much like a weapon. He regarded her narrowly. "Where does she live?"

"Who? Toni?"

"Yes, *Toni*, you moron." He needed to talk to her, hear a confirmation about this from her own mouth.

Ho-nasty's forehead wrinkled. "You're not allowed to leave here unescorted, John. You're still under house—ow!"

John clutched her arms down to the bone. "*Where?!*" He shook her hard.

Ho-nasty's lips went blubba-blubba. "Two doors down,"

she cried out as she tried to struggle free.

In the safe house kitchen, Ho-nasty had been stronger than he was. Not anymore.

"B-but Hadley texted me that Toni didn't go home today when she left the hospital. She's at her brother's house. Across the street and three over."

John released Ho-nasty, giving her a good shove, then shouldered past her into the hallway and started for the staircase.

He heard shuffling steps behind him. "Like it or not," Ho-nasty called to his retreating form, "I'm your only choice."

He stopped at the top of the stairs, glowering down the dominoes-like stack of steps. He didn't move.

"If you don't have children with me now, you will never, *ever* have children, John. Do you hear me?"

He turned around, strode back over to Ho-nasty, and backhanded her across the face, hard enough to send her reeling into the wall. *Bam!*

She fell to the floor and whimpered.

A snare drum thumped the inside of his cranium, exploding his skull into two pieces. He staggered backward, hissing in air, so many of his neurons firing punishing messages at him for hurting his mate that he actually had to squint through the frenzied electrical impulses.

He braced his legs wide to find his balance and paused for another breath.

"Yes," he told Ho-nasty, sotto voice. "I hear you."

CHAPTER THIRTY-EIGHT

JOHN PAUSED IN THE DOORWAY leading to Alex Parthen's den and just stood there silently, savoring the view.

Toni was curled up on one end of a maroon couch, a book open on her lap that she wasn't reading. She was staring off into mid-space, a teacup cradled forgotten in her palm. The soft glow of a lamp was picking out the blondest strands in her hair, and John inhaled a deep breath over her unparalleled beauty, drawing air up through his sinuses and fully expanding his lungs.

Holy Mother of God. He nearly dropped to his knees at this, his first experience of Toni with his new senses. How had he never noticed she smelled of sex and sensuality, even now, with a sad look on her face? How had he never seen that her long lashes were tipped with filaments of gold, that the blood running through her healthy carotid beat with such a sure, steady rhythm?

How much more succulent would she seem to him in another week? And another?

He mouthed the word *mine*, and immediately a jellyfish sting blistered his brain. *No*, it admonished, *Shaston*.

His eyes burned, and he grated his teeth together. As cool as his new biology was in some ways, in many other ways, it sucked a bag of dicks.

Toni must have sensed his presence. She turned and blinked her way out of her reverie. "John?" A little frown. "What are you doing here. Are you ill?"

Depends on how you look at it. "No." He walked all the

way into the room.

Toni ran her gaze over his filled-out body and seemed to approve. "Aren't you still required to stay in your house?"

"I needed to see if you're okay. I was in the hospital today when…" He shook his head. "I saw what happened between you and…" He rammed his fingers through his hair. "Jesus, are you really married to that guy, Toni?"

She set down her cup on the coffee table and sighed. "I don't know how to answer such a judgmental question, John."

He threw his arms wide. "Well, hell, I think I'm allowed to be a little judgmental toward the man who beat me out for you."

"It didn't exactly happen that way."

"How *did* it happen, then?"

She glanced down at the open book in her lap. She closed it then set it on the coffee table too.

"We were supposed to go out on a date," he reminded her thickly. "The Fish Market Restaurant. You in a lobster bib. The Beach Boys playing in the background. Any of this striking a memory?"

"John…that was a long time ago." She knuckled one of her eyes. "And I don't have the energy to talk about it right now."

Ire rose in a wave of heat up his nape. "I've been after you for five years, Toni, wondering what the hell happened between us."

"John, I…" She exhaled broadly. "All right, the truth is, you weren't beat out for me because you were never in the running for me in the first place."

Muscles in his stomach divided into taut strips. "Not true. When we kissed there was something between us."

"There was. Lust. I hadn't been with a man in a very long time, and I was drawn to you, yes, more than I had been to a man for a long time. Now I understand it's because you're Vârcolac. But don't let a bout of loneliness and horniness on my part cloud the truth. I never would have loved you, John. I never *will* love you. I love Jacken." She passed a weary hand over her face. "I'm sorry. I didn't realize you'd been carrying a torch for me all these years."

Sympathy—not pity, thank God—twisted her expression. "How do you know you couldn't have loved me?" he asked, his voice going up an annoying octave. "You never even gave me a chance to be something to you."

"I worked cases on and off with you for months, John, and there was never a spark."

He swallowed painfully.

"With Jacken, I knew I loved him in about two days, and he wasn't exactly trying to win me."

His heart felt hot in his chest. *Unacceptable words.* "How," he demanded, numb-lipped, "can you love a man who treats you like what I saw in the hospital?"

She freed a short blast of air. "Jacken was upset, and he had every right to be. I did something…unforgiveable…"

"Jesus Christ, Toni, are you listening to yourself? 'It wasn't his fault, but mine.' That's exactly what a chronically abused woman would say."

"Oh, for Pete's sake." She rose stiffly to her feet. "I'm not abused, I'm…I'm…" Tears shone wetly in her eyes. "I'm pregnant, and…"

The news collapsed his stomach.

"…and Jacken didn't want any more children. I almost died giving birth to our daughter, so he… But…" She shifted backward a step, pressing the back of one knee against the couch, as if she needed the support to remain standing. "He just won't *talk* to me about it. So I finally figured…I don't know…" Her lips trembled. She firmed them until they went white. "Jacken can't stand it when people make decisions out of fear. I see him gnash his teeth whenever Roth does it. So I just thought…if I took the decision out of his hands and got pregnant, then he would eventually be okay with it. But…"

Tears rolled down her cheeks.

John was breathing with more and more difficulty, his lungs buckling under the weight of her sorrow.

"But I blew it." Her voice frayed apart. "God, I blew it so badly."

"You blew it?" He threw back. "Really? How? By wanting to have the man's baby? The bottom-feeder should be *honored*."

"No, you…" She made a frustrated sound. "You don't understand, John. You haven't been a vampire long enough to see how awful it is that I…I used Jacken's Vârcolac nature against him. I made him go into a procreation glaze-out by letting myself ovulate around him when he hadn't agreed to it, and now…" She wiped away tears with a shaky hand, but more fell. "Now he hates me."

"The asshole can go pound sand if he hates you." John grasped Toni's arm, his words coming out pressurized by his tight throat. "You don't have to be with him. *I* love you, and we can—"

"I don't hate you."

John and Toni swiveled their heads toward the doorway in unison.

Teeth-Tattooed Asshole was standing there. Alex Parthen was a slight step behind him, a blond toddler boy swinging from one of his legs.

"Um…" Alex said. "You have a visitor, Toni."

She quickly wiped away more tears.

Teeth-Tattooed Asshole looked at Toni for a long moment.

"I'm so sorry," she said in a clogged voice, her tears starting up again. "I—"

"Later." A nerve jerked in Asshole's cheek. "You and I need to talk, Toni, but not now." He shifted his attention over to John, and the nerve became a full-on, thumping tic. "Waterson and I have to work out a few things first." With dangerous slowness, he tracked his focus down to the hand John had wrapped around Toni's arm. His eyes looked like they were hemorrhaging black.

John's hand caught fire, but he didn't let go. He'd be damned if he would allow this fucker to win again.

"The boxing ring," Asshole ordered. "Bare knuckles. Now."

John's fangs rammed out of their chutes. "Oh, yeah." He grinned widely, flaunting his new arsenal. He could fucking hug the asshole right now. Hug him in savage relief for offering an outlet for the violence stoppered in John's body for weeks. Hell, probably *years*. Hug the man till his ribs crackled and popped like too-thin ice, and important organs ruptured and bled out with all the gross tonnage of the Red Sea. "It would be my extreme fucking pleasure." John stepped away from Toni, his slitted eyes targeted on his enemy. "This has been a long time in coming, sport."

They stalked together out of Alex Parthen's house and headed, side by side, down Main Street, aiming for the mansion where the gym was.

Waves of palpable aggression seethed off both of them.

Bystanders saw their expressions and immediately vanished into shops and alleyways.

One woman snatched up her child and rushed off.

John lengthened his stride. He couldn't get to the boxing ring fast enough. If he thought he'd despised Teeth-Tattooed Asshole before, when the man was Toni's alleged kidnapper and the fucker who humiliated John by knocking him out at Scripps Hospital, now John's blood corroded into acid and his intestines warped into slimy eels. This asshole was Toni's husband and the father of her child—*children*.

"You proud of yourself, skip?" John sneered, his voice all edge.

Asshole's boots pounded the ground.

"I saw what you did to Toni in the hospital." A vein in

John's temple squeezed. 'Round and 'round the drill bit went, digging into deeper layers of hatred. "I've only been a vampire for a week, and even *I* know a man isn't supposed to unsheathe his fangs in anger on the mate he supposedly loves."

A lot of hard, lock-jawed nothing.

"You made her cry."

More heavy silence.

"You're nothing but dog meat compared to her, you know that?" John stopped, grabbed Asshole's arm, and swung him around. "You don't deserve her." *She should be with me!*

They were in the middle of Main Street, civilians everywhere, but John couldn't give a shit. He shoved his enemy. The push was a powerful one, but it still only managed to propel Asshole's densely packed poundage back two measly steps.

The man returned forward those two steps, and—

John landed on his ass with enough PSI of downward thrust to clack his teeth together and jab his fangs into his lower lip. *Fuck!*

He growled, the low, animal rumble sliding out of him for long seconds. He was getting sick and damned tired of these one-punch knockdowns from Asshole. *Hell if you're winning this time, you dick.* John was a different man now. Prying his fangs out of his lip, he lunged to his feet and roared forward. Seizing his nemesis around the waist, he hauled him off the ground and powered him backward. Asshole's knee pistoned up, but John was already driving their combined weight to the ground.

Grunting air, they hit the hard cave floor in motion and rolled across the street together, taking out a delivery guy who was pushing a dolly toward Garwald's Pub. The guy shouted as he went down, the stacked boxes of booze on his dolly tumbling over with a crash. Beer foam fizzed out of the corner of one cardboard box, and John sloshed his elbow through it as he came out on top of his opponent. He took immediate advantage of the dominant position and drilled a right into the side of Asshole's head. He followed with a shot to the man's jaw, then a—

He was hurled off.

He flew through the air for several feet, hit the ground with a jarring thump, and scraped along the rocky floor for several more feet, trashing his jeans. A passerby barely managed to leap over his skidding body.

A woman screamed, then several more.

Jumping up, John filled his lungs, flung back his head, and let out a bellow that reverberated to the top of the stone ceiling. He was supposed to *realize his true nature*, was he? Well, here the fuck he was.

John barreled at Asshole again.

More civilians scattered and yelled.

John light-footed himself into a lethal strike zone, finding a place where he could do the most damage. Then he let rip with the entire stockpile of his rage—of all the years he'd spent thinking he was dying and not knowing why, of losing Toni, and *again*, of having his identity stripped from him along with the father he'd always known, of being given another father, a stranger who wasn't even human, of being saddled forever with a wife he didn't love, and of becoming the type of man who could hit a woman. He fought with all that.

A right to the eye socket.

A left to the nose.

An elbow jabbed to the cheekbone.

Blood wetted his face, and his vision blurred as he took as good as he gave, Teeth-Tattooed Asshole fighting back with whatever carnivorous mess he was on the inside.

The brutality, the animosity, the wrath: it all built and built until they were nothing but brute street fighters, no finesse, no form, just their left hands clamped around the backs of each other's necks while their rights punched furiously at each other. Total obliteration was the goal. John lurched forward into a clinch hold and twisted his body to execute a hip-throw.

Asshole planted his foot to prevent the take-down. Then tucked it back in.

The man hit the ground, and before he could roll or rise, John went NFL kicker on the fucker and rammed his toecap into the man's ribs so hard he felt the splinter of bone through his shoe.

Grimacing red, Asshole surged to his feet, one elbow tucked protectively to his injured side.

John danced in again and—*wham!*

Asshole caught him under the chin with a fist as big as a manhole cover.

The blow slammed John's head back like a crash dummy in full whiplash demo and sent him wheeling backward. He stumbled to a halt and stood swaying on his feet, his vision going all swimmy. *Well.* The bear certainly was a wounded grizzly now. John had better—

"Stop this nonsense. Right now."

John mashed his eyes closed, shifted his eyeballs back and forth against his lids, then reopened them.

The community's police force had formed a ring around him and Asshole.

No big surprise. Screaming civilians, especially women, had a way of alerting security like nothing else could.

The man who'd ordered the ceasefire was a humongous fucking guy with tattoos necklacing his throat. "Half the community's in hiding because of you two jokers," he scolded. "So that's enough."

"It's not enough," John hammered out. He was breathing like he would never manage a full lungful of oxygen again, and his body was rapidly telling him it hadn't been fully ready for what he just put it through. His limbs felt disjointed and rubbery, like he was barely being held together by flabby ligaments. The entire surface area of his face throbbed.

Fine lines speared out from the corners of Asshole's eyes, but his gaze was so flat, John couldn't be sure if those lines were from pain or not. And John needed this man to hurt.

I never would have loved you, John. I never will *love you. I love Jacken.*

"Do you have any fucking clue how many men would kill to have a woman like Toni want to have their children?" Words and air were sawing together through John's teeth. *I would kill for that!* "And you tore her head off for it."

Asshole's tongue circled around the interior of his mouth. He spit blood.

"She didn't deserve what you did to her," John gnashed.

"You don't think he knows that?" Humongous put in. "It's why he just let you give him a beat-down."

John turned in a deliberate motion toward Humongous. His head buzzed like his brain's positively-charged plugs were stuck into negative outlets. *Let me?*

Humongous's eyebrows peaked. "You think you can take Jacken?" He shook his head. "Jacken is leader of the Warrior Class. He can beat *me*. Every hurt you gave him, he allowed. Don't kid yourself."

A knotted ball plunged into the pit of John's stomach, a fist of too many emotions to count, but probably way too many feelings of insignificance than any self-respecting man would care to have. He hadn't even really stomped his enemy's ass.

"All right, party's over." Humongous performed a perfect moving-right-along gesture. "Breen," he said to a guy with hair in his eyes, "take Jacken to the hospital. He should get his ribs wrapped. Waterson, you need a trip to the hospital too?"

John needed to scream. "No." Although probably.

"All right, then. Jeddin, make sure the detective goes home." Humongous gave John a disappointed father look. "And this time, Waterson, mind yourself and stay there."

On the rickety walk back to his house-prison, hatred left John. But since it couldn't have really left him, the only explanation he could figure for the sudden cold calm covering every inch of his body was that the blackness had been assimilated into his very being. He was as one with his hatred now: blood was oil, sinew was copper wiring, bones were steel rods—assimilated, like Star Trek's Borg. As one. Loathing. Him.

John and his escort entered the homey neighborhood, and on the far side John saw a couple of men in carpenter jeans and engineer boots crouched down near an area of the cave blocked off with yellow tape. They were inspecting a machine, reading numbers off it, making notes. Living a normal life. No stewing and boiling. No festering or oozing.

With Jacken, I knew I loved him in about two days.

Don't let a bout of loneliness and horniness on my part cloud the truth.

You were never in the running for me in the first place.

John checked a tooth with his tongue.

It was over now.

I'm pregnant.

Truly and deeply over.

He trudged into his fake house, heard the TV going in his fake living room, and went in there.

His fake wife leapt up from the couch. She eyed him in open fear, her fingers flying to her bruised cheek, then noticed his own battered mug. "My goodness, John, what happened to you? Are you okay?"

He drew in the worst breath of his life. It was over. *There was never a spark…* Completely over.

With a hard yank of his wrist, he unbuckled his belt. "Drop your pants, bend over, and grab your ankles." He stalked forward. "I don't want to see your face while I do this."

❖ ❖ ❖

CAN I HELP AT THE HOSPITAL? I became a Red Cross volunteer when I was living topside, so I have some medical training now.

Hadley jerked a stack of square gauze pads out of a drawer and rolled her eyes at herself. *Why* had she opened her big mouth? If she'd never made that offer, then she never would've become a nurse's aide, never would've been taking Breen's blood pressure when Octav told them about Zalina the bitch witch, never would've found out what her lopsided-3 birthmark truly meant, and so she never would've heard the sentence—*you, my dear, are a changeling*—that robbed her of everything.

Her family.

Her identity—who was she if she didn't even know her own roots?

Her chance at a future mate. Oh, men would still want her, but would they want her for *her*? Or for the magic in her DNA? How could it be real, a relationship based on this magnetic lure thing she had going on? To her, it would be like giving a man a love potion to nab him. She would never know if his feelings for her were genuine. What woman in her right mind would want a man under such circumstances? Yet...

She slapped the gauze pads on a medical tray. What other circumstances did she have to offer? She closed her eyes for a moment. *Please, God, just* please, *let me return to being who I was. I'll work two days a month in an animal shelter and rake leaves at the homes of the underprivileged.*

No answer from above.

Sniffling, she finished stocking the emergency tray with disinfectant, medical tape, and a suture kit. She'd rather be slouched on her couch watching TV and figuring out her next steps in life—or ignoring them—than at the hospital right now. But with Shaston still shut away in her bonding week, Hadley was the only one available to help, and she'd received a text about Jacken and Detective Waterson getting into a colossal fight. One or both would be coming into the ER soon, and probably hurt badly. Vârcolac males didn't fight like some nice guy Norbert at the boxing club, out for a bit of exercise then off for a picnic afterward and a spot of tea. They were territorial and protective males, and when they fought, it was for keeps.

No surprise to hear John Waterson was one of the combatants. Shaston texted Hadley every day about John's temper, and although Hadley didn't condone his brutish behavior, she could relate to all the poor guy was going through.

One day he was a human being, then the next, he wasn't.

One day the man who'd always been Dad was his dad, then the next, he wasn't.

Oh, yeah, *hah*, *boy*, could Hadley relate.

Maybe when John arrived at the ER, she'd ask him how he was dealing with everything. She could use some advice.

Perhaps punching Jacken had helped.

"Hey."

She turned around from the tray of supplies she'd just set next to the exam table.

Breen was entering the room. "Got a customer for you."

Jacken walked in behind Breen, managing on his own locomotion, although, gads, he had to be hurting—his face was a mess.

Without her having to direct him, Jacken eased himself down on the exam bed, the gingerly way he moved very un-Jacken-like.

"Left ribs need X-raying," Breen told her.

"I'll let Dr. Jess know." She walked over to a small corner desk and picked up a clipboard. "Is Detective Waterson coming in?" If Jacken was this bad, John's face probably looked re-pieced together, Picasso-style.

Breen shrugged. "Maybe after the adrenaline wears off." He left.

Hadley started a chart on Jacken, first noting his damaged ribs. "On a scale of one to ten, how would you rate your pain currently?"

Silence.

She glanced up at Jacken.

He'd grabbed a large gauze pad off the metal supply tray and was cleaning blood off his face.

She sighed into the void of continuing silence. The warriors never liked to admit to pain. "Your level of discomfort is something I'll have to report to Dr. Jess."

"It'll be about a three or less once I feed."

She hooked her pen to the metal clip on the chart. How was she supposed to record that? "Is Toni far behind you?"

"I'm here." Toni stepped inside.

Just inside.

Standing by the door, Toni gazed across the three-foot expanse of linoleum separating her husband from her, and the longer she stood there, the wider the space between them seemed to grow. The silence dragged on, and before long, the distance stretched for miles rather than actual feet.

Hadley clasped the clipboard to her breasts and took an awkward step back.

Jacken tossed aside the dirty gauze.

The gesture captured Toni's attention. She looked at the bloody bandage, then looked back at Jacken. "Do you really think I wanted you to do this to yourself?"

Jacken stared across the room, his jaw set.

"I'm so sorry…" Toni began, but Jacken cut her off with a downward chop of his hand.

Toni exhaled a forceful breath. "You need to let me apologize." She licked her lips and tried again. "I know I blew it. I—"

A warning growl erupted from Jacken's chest.

"Dammit," Toni cursed, her voice raw with frustration. "I need to know what's going on with you. Would you please talk to me?"

Jacken's mouth thinned, exposing the sharper parts of his

teeth. "Communication 101 wasn't exactly taught in Oţărât when I was growing up."

"I don't care. Communication is marriage, Jacken. Freaking learn. *Right now.*"

The air seemed to shudder around Jacken. He stayed silent.

"*Talk* to me." Toni looked on the verge of shattering.

Jacken's nostrils pinched. "I can't. Not about this."

"You have to."

Still nothing.

Tears swam into Toni's eyes.

Hadley waited on the balls of her feet, caught up in the tension.

"All right." Toni gave a noisy sniff and crossed to Jacken's bed while she dug into her purse. She pulled out a pill box, opened it, and set two white capsules on the tray attached to his bed. She pointed at them. "What if I told you that if I take those pills, the baby will go away? Then you—"

Roaring, Jacken slammed his fist down on the medicine, the power of his blow disintegrating the pills into dust and sending the tray ripping off its metal arm. It Frisbeed across the room, slammed into the sink, and crashed to the floor.

Heart pounding, Hadley shrank back against the wall.

Gasping, Toni skidded sideways on her heels. "What the hell's the matter with you?" she shouted.

"What are those pills?" Jacken snarled.

"Would you try talking to me for once?" Toni was still yelling.

"*What,*" Jacken yelled back, "are those pills?"

Hadley gripped her clipboard in taut fists. Blood was shooting through her veins way too fast.

"They're ibuprofen." Toni's breathing sounded like she was having trouble managing air through a too-tight windpipe. "I would never hurt our baby, but for Pete's sake, I don't even know how you feel about the danged thing." Her lips quivered. She flung a hand out. "Do you even want it?"

"I want it," Jacken retorted, deep and barrel-chested.

Hadley swallowed several times.

Tears slipped down Toni's face, one after the other…a tide of them.

Jacken looked away. His jaw un-cemented, circled, reset. "Damn you, Toni."

Toni kept crying. "Please talk to me," she whispered.

Jacken's stiff mouth twisted several different directions. It wasn't clear what expression he was either trying to put in place or defend against. Finally he spoke, the tendons along his neck flexing into such gnarled ropes, it must've taken a massive exertion of pressure to force his words out. "I can't lose you."

"Oh, Jacken," Toni uttered. "You *won't*. I've given birth to a Vârcolac baby now, so my body understands what to do, and even if things do go haywire again, Dr. Jess knows what to look for. He'll make sure I—"

"*Toni*," Jacken barked.

Toni's speech startled to a halt.

Hadley couldn't see Jacken's eyes from where she stood, but whatever Toni saw in them made her mouth fall open. "Oh, God," she said in a hoarse whisper. "You're right. I…I have no idea what you went through the night you thought I was dying. It must've been…" She faded off, stared at her husband, shook her head. "I didn't mean to sound cavalier. I deeply apologize."

Hairline fissures broke out all over Jacken's face. His lips went bloodless, then his chest bucked. The four words that came out of his mouth a second time were rocks tumbling in a cement mixer. "I. Can't. Lose. You."

Toni scrubbed a hand over her trembling lips and nodded once. Climbing onto the exam bed, she curled up next to Jacken. "You won't let anything bad happen to me. I know you won't." Setting a hand on his chest, she snuggled her face against his throat and kissed him.

Jacken pressed his eyes closed. "Damn you, wife, you're going to be the death of me." But he spoke this quietly. Turning his head toward Toni, he buried his nose in her hair and cupped a palm to her abdomen.

Hadley felt tears rise, and—She came back to herself with a start. *Dear Lord, I'm intruding.* She slipped quietly from the room.

Softly closing the door, she sagged back against it, still clutching the clipboard. The intimacy she'd just witnessed between Jacken and Toni was exactly what she'd been missing her entire adult life, was exactly why she'd returned to Ţărână—to find a relationship just like it. She still needed and wanted it, but now…

You, my dear, are a changeling.

Nothing was real anymore.

Tears gathered again, stinging her nose. Her heart slid toward the pit of her belly, and, finding no resistance there— nothing but a vast, endless emptiness—it continued into her knees.

She covered her face with one palm and sobbed quietly.

Chapter Thirty-Nine

THE MOON-RIDERS WERE KEPT IN the community hospital for eleven days, not as prisoners, but as convalescing patients, and also to give the chiefs of the town time to arrange the next steps.

Nicolae assumed these "next steps" would involve setting plans in motion to send the Moon-Riders back to Transylvania, but this morning they were gathered for a meeting in the hospital cafeteria—much smaller than the cafeteria on *Grey's Anatomy*—and Dr. Parthen invited them to stay.

Nicolae's jaw dropped nearly to the floor.

They were one people, Dr. Parthen had said, one race. Vârcolac belonged with Vârcolac. And even though their beginning together had been inauspicious—Nicolae didn't know what "inauspicious" meant but figured it had to do with them being bad men toward Son of Nichita—the Moon-Riders would be welcomed into the community in a spirit of forgiveness. The past would be forgotten. None of them would be judged by anything they'd once done, only by how they conducted themselves from this day forth in Ţărână.

Nicolae nearly toppled out of his chair. It was exactly the way he'd always wanted to live—by actions, not ancestry.

He was first in line to take a tour of Ţărână.

It was a town unlike anything he'd ever expected to see.

In all his life, he'd never been outside of the Carpathian Mountains. He only knew of small villages and the forest—the trees and land, hunting and food gathering, and the habits of small creatures—and of the single, very large manor house in the vampires' warded lands that saw to all their needs: cooking, sleeping, convalescing, schooling, work.

He was familiar with other towns only through television. Țărână's primary street called "Main" somewhat resembled the small towns on those shows—colorful, lit-up shops with signs hanging on their fronts—but in most ways Țărână was very different.

First off, it was underground.

The place gave Nicolae a damp, closed-in feeling, and he didn't see how the people here lived apart from the moon so much. He'd been itching for its beauty and power for the past ten days. But even as foreign and claustrophobic as Țărână sometimes felt, it was clear it was a friendly, happy place. A place to find contentment.

As their small tour group—led by a bouncy young Vârcolac named Cleeve—turned right through a tunnel, they came out into a very appealing area. There were many houses painted different, vibrant shades, with white fences in front of them. Nicolae didn't understand the fences. They were too low to the ground to contain cattle effectively, but they were as neat and well-made as everything else.

Nicolae's heart squeezed when he saw children running and playing in front of the homes. *Children!* How amazing was it that these Vârcolac were able to breed? And if the Moon-Riders stayed, they could possibly have families too. Dr. Parthen had promised them the chance, saying the community would teach them things like English and etiquette and sex education.

Nicolae paused in his translation to ask, "What is this? Sex education?"

"We don't believe you Moon-Riders have fully realized this side of yourselves," Dr. Parthen explained. "We'll help you to understand sex fully and to achieve a level of functioning that will allow you to have children...should you find a mate here."

Nicolae's jaw dropped again. There *was* more to sex than kissing. He'd suspected as much, but the mechanics of it had always puzzled him, ever since Miodrag—poor Miodrag, killed years ago by vampire hunters—had reported on a conversation he overhead between two regulars. The act of sex consisted of, apparently, a man fitting his penis inside a woman's vagina.

The group of them exchanged troubled glances. Miodrag must have misheard. Such a thing wasn't feasible. A vagina looked to be suctioned almost completely shut like an anus—Nicolae had seen the un-woman Vika bent over a stream taking a bath once—and a penis sagged and flopped. Impossible to fit one inside the other, unless... Did the vagina swallow the penis down it like a throat? Did it vacuum it inside there?

The idea seemed so absurd and uncomfortable, Nicolae had set it aside. But now he'd experienced the strange pulsing pressure in his penis whenever Hadley was nearby, and he'd changed his mind. Whatever occurred between a penis and a vagina wasn't absurd. It was good, and he wanted to have sex. Very much.

Across the way from their tour group on the far side of this neighborhood, Nicolae spotted Devid Nichita's woman—the woman Dev had fed on in the garage right after he was carried off the bus. She was strolling along with a small girl-child, the baby walking unsteadily on young legs.

The warmth in Nicolae's chest deepened. It was nearly impossible to imagine having babies of his own one day. He'd lived too many years with only extinction in his future—they all had. There was no guarantee, of course, that he would win a mate. He would have to earn one, like every other man here, and there was a great deal of competition in town. But he'd have no chance at all if he went back to Transylvania.

He turned to his brother, who was walking beside him. "<What do you think about staying here?>"

Vasile scowled at the sky...where there was no sky. "<Without a moon, we will lose our power.>"

"<We haven't so far.>" Nicolae just felt like his power ran through him at a lower idle.

"<You would miss it,>" Vasile predicted grimly.

Maybe. The moon, his mountains...yes, probably. "<What I won't miss,>" he countered, "<is living constantly on the verge of attack and death from our enemies in the Patru Puternic.>" He angled toward his brother, walking a little sideways. "<Another thing I definitely won't miss is being bossed around by Chief. This town doesn't follow the old rules of monarchy, Vasile. No more Octav Rázóczi to lay down uncontested law. Here, there is a Council and a court to give us a voice.>"

Vasile grunted. "<So Dr. Parthen said.>"

"<You don't believe it?>"

"<I would be a fool to believe it.>"

The man was stubborn as a plugged-up mule. "<The people in this town have been nice to us. Tell me that hasn't meant something to you.>"

Vasile swatted Nicolae's words aside with an abrupt gesture. "<You want to become one of them? Go ahead, Nicolae. It will work fine, since they plan to warp us into their kind, at any rate.>"

"<Where in the heavens did you get that idea?>"

"<From your translation of this morning's meeting.>"

Now Nicolae made a swat-aside gesture. "<Dr. Parthen only promised to help us adjust to our new life. You're being contrary.>"

Vasile aimed his glower forward and didn't answer.

Nicolae focused forward too.

Devid Nichita's woman was now chatting with a female wearing a red shirt. The girl-child explored a bit ahead of her mother.

"<And what about the chance to bond with a mate?>"

Nicolae pointed out. "<To have children? We never thought such a thing was possible before.>"

"<I still don't. Who are we to catch the interest of a woman?>"

"<In this town, us being part-human means nothing.>" But Nicolae reddened. *The hell if I'm teaching this penis-head anything. Let another donor take him on.* And then there'd been the way Hadley regarded him, with fear and disgust.

"<Women are a trial,>" Vasile pronounced gruffly.

Maybe. But Nicolae was beginning to think, *maybe not.* "<We can finally live as the men we want to be,>" he continued to argue, "<as the men Father always strove for us to be able to become.>" He was really talking himself into this place.

The red-shirted woman left Nichita's mate, waving a friendly goodbye, and a new female entered the neighborhood from another path. This female had very curly blond hair. She'd been in the garage, too, on the day the Moon-Riders arrived—Breen's woman. This curly-haired one also waved at Nichita's woman. She started to call out something, then stopped.

Her expression fell into a look of horror.

Nicolae snapped his attention over to see what she was looking at.

The girl-child had wandered over to a yellow ribbon stretched across an entrance to a different part of the cave, and—*Ungodly hell!* The rock floor was crumbling away beneath her tiny feet.

The baby tottered crazily, fell onto her padded bum, and started to cry.

Nichita's woman hurried forward, then saw what was actually happening—a developing crevasse was opening beneath her daughter. She screamed and ran.

The curly-haired woman tore into a full-out sprint.

"*Fir-ar să fie!*" Nicolae swore, running too, Vasile fast at his side.

Men poured from the surrounding homes—the screams had called them to the trouble—and also shouted.

Up ahead, the curly-haired woman was running faster than Nicolae had ever seen a human go, her sleekly muscled legs stretching out, her arms pumping, knife-hands slicing the air. Her focus was locked onto that little girl with what seemed like mad fear.

Dev Nichita shot past Vasile and Nicolae, his speed powered by parental terror, although…

As swiftly as Dev was moving, he wasn't going to make it in time.

No.

None of them were.

Nicolae gulped down his heart as the chasm crumbled away and swallowed up that poor little girl.

The baby's mother shrieked as, in vain, the curly-haired woman threw herself at the crevasse, skidding on her stomach and knees, one arm reaching for the child.

Dev howled.

In a huffing, hollering clamor, the rest of them pounded up to the hole: the tour group, other Vârcolac males, and—

"Stop," the curly-haired woman panted, her arm thrust down into the dark cavity. "Don't come any closer. There are fissures everywhere. You'll make the hole grow bigger."

The baby's frightened screams echoed up from just below the lip of the chasm.

"Holy fuck, you got her!" Dev was wild-eyed. "You *got* her, Charlize!"

Weeping hysterically, Nichita's woman clasped her hands over her mouth. "Please, don't let go. God, please!"

Veins stuck out all over Charlize's forehead, pounding violently. "I'll go down that hole myself before I let go, Marissa."

Breen's jaw clamped tight enough to damage teeth, and

his eyes lit into a gold like fire.

"I'm trying to bring her up." Charlize grated. "But I'm lying at an awkward angle."

Dev went into a fighter's crouch, like he wanted so much to spring at the dark hole, but didn't dare.

"<There aren't rock fractures surrounding the woman's body.>" Vasile moved swiftly toward Charlize, circling in from behind her. <She's in a safe area.>"

Nicolae hurriedly pointed at Charlize. "No cracks, her. Pull female. Baby come up too."

Breen cut in front of Vasile. "Good idea, Vasile. But I'll do this." Breen grabbed Charlize around the waist and eased her backward.

The baby's shrieks grew louder.

Dev knelt beside Charlize, his panic-darkened gaze aimed at the cavern. Sweat slicked his face and beaded in his beard.

As two hands emerged from the hole—Charlize's clutched around the baby's—Dev leaned forward as far as he could without compromising the unstable edges of the crevasse and wrapped his own large hand around both of theirs.

A final heave brought up the crying baby, covered in dust and with blood smeared across her little thigh.

The mother was right there, scooping the child into her arms and hugging her daughter desperately close.

Dev sank back on his heels and clutched the hair at his temples. "Good God," he croaked.

Nicolae swept the area with a swift glance, confirming that everyone else was safe. His heart wouldn't slow down.

Dev powered to his feet, looking again like a man in command, except when he said, "To the hospital," his voice was still croaky.

Nobody moved right away. Nicolae couldn't speak for the others, but his legs still felt like they were mid-buckle. Dev didn't, either. He stared down at Charlize, who was collapsed back against Breen.

"I..." Dev's jaw convulsed. "I..." He drew a forearm across his sweaty brow. "Your knee is bleeding."

Charlize nodded. Her complexion was waxy, and she was struggling to breathe.

"It's a...it's a good gash." Dev's Adam's apple jumped. "You probably need stitches."

"Go, Dev," Charlize rasped. "Take Maylie to the hospital. Breen and I will meet you there."

Dev nodded. Turned. Turned back around. "I don't have the words right now, Charlize. But I will."

Nicolae and Vasile were swept up in the noisy tide of people hurrying to the hospital, ending up back in the building they'd been so eager to leave earlier today. But they'd been a part of the near-disaster, and it didn't seem right not to keep trying to help wherever they could.

The moment they all burst in the door, the hospital staff leapt into action. Dr. Jess bustled forward, assigning the patients to exam rooms and asking a lot of questions. Mekhel—who'd taken Nicolae's blood many times over the last weeks—readied supplies. Nurse Shaston helped Charlize off with her shoes while Breen supported his woman against his side.

Nicolae stood immobile in the whirl of it all, watching it all, awe-struck. He'd never seen people unite so quickly to help each other, or with such passion. These people obviously cared deeply for one another.

More good feelings washed over him about this place.

A door slammed, jerking Nicolae's attention to the end of a hallway.

Dr. Parthen was charging down the corridor, the edges of her white coat flapping. Rock Jaw Jacken was keeping pace at her side, while Donree scurried after the two of them.

"I want to know what happened," Dr. Parthen blazed. "Țărână's engineers were supposed to be monitoring that area." She cut a gesture behind her. "Get Vlad and his crew out to the scene right away."

"Yes, ma'am." Donree put a cell phone to her ear.

"I'm heading over too," Jacken clipped out, hard and perfunctory. "I'm evacuating the neighborhood until I confirm for sure that the whole fucking place isn't about to come down."

"Good idea." Dr. Parthen nodded shortly.

Jacken strode ahead of her by a couple of paces, then turned around, still walking, but backward. "*You* don't take a single step in that direction." He pointed a finger at her, his focus aimed at her belly. "Not until you've received an all-clear from me."

One side of her mouth edged up. "I won't."

Jacken plowed forward, and Nicolae quickly sidestepped into a patient room to move out of his way.

Nichita's woman—Marissa—was inside with her girl-child, both of them sitting on a table with a white paper sheet on it, the baby on the mother's lap. Marissa had stopped crying, though her cheeks were still wet, but the baby was whimpering. The mother brushed at her daughter to clean the dust off—which seemed silly to Nicolae. The task was impossible.

"Daddy is going to be right here with Buddy Bear," Marissa consoled her child.

Nicolae pulled his brows down briefly. *A bear?*

Someone entered the room behind him, and he stumbled aside, as much from hurrying to get out of the way as from the scent that kicked in his knee joints and grabbed him by the testicles.

He sucked in a bottomless breath.

Hadley.

She hurried to the white paper table, and even though she was rushing, she moved like someone whose body was naturally competent or...attractive...her hips swaying, her shoulders shifting in a graceful way, her buttock muscles gently flexing.

It was a new experience for Nicolae, watching this woman move. Pleasure tingles speared into his groin.

"Oh, my God, Marissa!" Hadley seized the mother's hand. "How are you?"

Marissa teared up again. "I think I've had several heart attacks in the last few minutes."

Nicolae knew the feeling. He might be having one now, peering at the soft chick down on Hadley's nape. Her hair was bundled up on top of her head in a messy clump, exposing her neck. Here was another sight that made Nicolae's penis very excited. And his fangs. Saliva rushed into his mouth, and he suddenly had the oddest urge to build a house for this woman with his own hands then lay a slain deer across the threshold at her feet.

Hold her. Protect her. Taste her.

"Well, everyone's safe now." Hadley lightly chucked the baby under the chin. "And we're going to take great care of you."

Hadley was good with the little one. Nicolae shifted his gaze down to her belly.

Mount her. Claim her. Mate her.

"Would you mind handing me some of those gauze pads, please?"

Nicolae startled. Hadley was talking to him.

She was holding a hand out in his general direction, not even looking at him. Which was probably good. Had she recognized him, she'd probably treat him to one of her fake-friendly smiles. Those weren't pleasurable.

He scanned the cart next to him and picked up what Hadley wanted. Stepping forward, he put the gauze in her hand, his fingers brushing hers, and... His fangs sprang out and locked down while a heavy throb slammed into the area between his legs.

By darkest night. This woman was...she was...

"Thank you," she said.

His heart banged. "Yes."

Hadley went to work cleaning the baby's cut thigh.

Nicolae melted out of the patient room. Once he was back in the hallway, he inhaled two bracing breaths. His hip bones felt strapped too tightly to his body. He closed his eyes for a long moment. *We'll help you to understand sex fully and to achieve a level of functioning that will allow you to have children, should you find a mate here.*

He opened his eyes and hunted for Vasile.

His brother was standing with his back against the corridor wall, carefully watching the activity hubbubbing around him.

Nicolae walked over and came to a stop right in front of him.

Vasile frowned at his mouth. "<Why are your fangs out?>"

"<I'm staying.>"

Vasile gave him a cheerless, resigned look.

He knew.

Nicolae amended his statement, anyway. "<*We're* staying.>"

CHAPTER FORTY

AT TEN O'CLOCK THE NEXT morning John Waterson and Ho-nasty were escorted by a couple of unknown meathead tools to the mansion and dropped off to wait in the Nuclear Parlor—so nicknamed by John because it was where Toni gave him the news that left his life a nuclear ruin.

He planted his ass down hard in a flowered chair. "What the fuck's this about?" he bit out.

"I don't know." Ho-nasty twisted her hands together in her lap. "Maybe I'm being sentenced for the UB today."

"Then why the hell am I here?" Did the community think John would want to bear witness to Ho-nasty's punishment? Revel in it? Maybe he would have if he hadn't been put on a pain train two days ago by Teeth-Tattooed Asshole. He was recovering faster from the beating than his pre-Vârcolac days—oh, the magic of Ho-nasty's blood—but he still seriously would rather be in bed right now.

A half hour ticked by, during which Ho-nasty got more bunched. "This shouldn't be taking so long," she said, her hands refusing to stay still in her lap.

He agreed. It felt like something was up. But if Ho-nasty was looking for someone to do some reassuring back-patting, she'd better not get the wrong idea about his availability for such niceties. Just because he'd let her sleep in the same bed with him the last couple nights didn't mean he'd softened. His only motivation was to prevent her relentless new-bond freakout from knocking his seed loose…if he'd managed to plant any. Other than that, he was still completely *rot in hell* about anything to do with her.

The meathead tools finally arrived and shepherded John and Ho-nasty out of the parlor and into an elevator.

Ho-nasty frowned. "We're not going to the courtroom?"

"The garage," answered a Fabio type, who—come to think on it—John vaguely remembered seeing at Scripps Hospital years ago.

About forty people were already milling around the garage when they arrived. Twenty ugly women and approximately the same number of men, all of them dressed in rough-looking clothes made by someone who'd flunked Home Ec. Everyone in the group had black hair except for one man, who sported a white streak of cowlick on his—

Holy fuck. MoonRiderOne.

John's nerves stood on end.

"Hey, what's going on?" Ho-nasty pointed a rigid finger at several suitcases standing beside a military-gray school bus parked on an enormous elevator platform. "Those are my bags."

And stacked next to Ho-nasty's bags were several cardboard boxes with John's name handwritten on them.

Ice rolled down the back of his neck. He turned toward the higher-ups who were present: Fancy Roth, the lawyer lady, Kimberly Stănescu, and the woman who'd never felt a single spark for him ever, Dr. Toni Parthen.

It was Toni who answered Ho-nasty. "You and John are being sent to Transylvania with those of the Moon-Riders who've decided to return."

John laughed. He had to appreciate the woman's style of giving bad news, no punches pulled.

Ho-nasty's eyes rounded big as cymbals. "What?" she squeaked. "You can't do that."

Roth gave her a flinty stare. "In the due course of community law, your penalty has been decided by the Council, Ms. Dodrescu. You are to be banished from this community for committing an Unauthorized Bite."

"*Banished*!?" Ho-nasty's voice squeaked high enough this time to send auditory follicles running to hide. "But, no. What if…? I might be pregnant. I ovulated, and John and I tried."

Toni blinked slowly and heavily, then consulted the far side garage wall.

The lawyer pressed her eyes with thumb and forefinger.

Ho-nasty kept at it. "I can't be living on a mountain when it's time to have my baby. I'll need proper medical care."

Roth's expression didn't thaw. "Your condition is immaterial to your sentence. It has been decided."

"B-but banishment is too harsh." Ho-nasty whirled on the lawyer lady. "Please, isn't there anything you can do for me?"

"I'm sorry, no," Kimberly said. "You openly admitted to what you did when you returned from the safe house, Shaston. You *are* guilty of committing a UB."

Ho-nasty licked a trembling tongue across her lips. "But when I bit John for the first time, he said he wanted me. Shouldn't that…doesn't it count for something?"

Roth remained resolute. "Before you left the hospital for the safe house, you asked Dr. Jess if Detective Waterson would go vampiric right away. The Council has decided this proves your UB was premeditated."

John turned on Ho-nasty. Had it been?

Her mouth was working like a speared trout's.

Jesus, it had. *Little shitbag.*

"Y-you're just making an example out of me because—"

"Will you shut up?" John snapped. She was such a fucking bore.

A few of the Moon-Riders glanced over. They were in the process of boarding the bus.

Ho-nasty put on a sulky face and hunched her shoulders.

John leveled a look at Toni. "So am I being sent away because I have to go where Shaston goes, and she's being banished? Or am I not welcome here?"

Of course he wasn't welcome. His history with the people of this town was completely fucked. At Scripps Hospital years ago, he'd tried to arrest Teeth-Tattooed Asshole; he'd injured Nichita in a shootout; he'd brought in Nichita's wife, Marissa, as a means to get to Nichita himself; he'd tangled unpleasantly with the lawyer lady on more than one occasion. And as far as recent infractions went, last night he told a married woman—Toni—he was in love with her then knuckle-busted on her husband...and John couldn't say for certain if his every intention hadn't been to kill the asshole.

"You need to learn how to be a vampire," Toni told him softly, obviously choosing not to address the horde of elephants in the room. "Transylvania will be a good place to do that. You and Shaston can start over."

He felt a soggy feeling swell inside his chest, as if his heart was drowning in its own blood. Maybe he should have been able to forge a new life. Occasionally and dimly he could acknowledge that Ho-nasty wasn't the worst of all women he could've been stuck with. Besides letting herself be led astray by desperation, she had some decent human qualities. And if John had been given his shot with Toni, maybe he could've forgiven and forgotten in time.

Try and fail with Toni—Okay. He could accept that. It would've been tough and heart-ripping, but he could have eventually processed through it.

It was being denied any chance at all that was the needle stuck in his craw. He was a man who spent his career fighting for justice, so just sitting back and taking injustice on the chin was too dammed much for him to tolerate. For five long years he'd searched for Toni, never surrendering the fight to save her, never giving up hope...and now it turned out the whole time she hadn't been *kept* from him. No. She'd been busy fucking another man while growing a brood of Asshole-sired children. In the final summation, the unfairness of it was too much stacked against him, and there was no getting around his abhorrence for it.

He could only stand in the oily stench of the garage and stare at Toni, his heart feeling like a wet rag she was wringing out. He would never see her again.

The last of the Moon-Riders clumped up onto the bus. Luggage compartments were closed and secured. Ho-nasty wept quietly at John's side...then another person entered the garage.

From the corner of his vision, John saw the man come to a stop near the wall by the battleship passageway, his hands clasped behind his back, his expression somber...pained, really, if the corners of the man's eyes were inspected closely, which John did when he turned to face him.

Dr. Jess.

John had been in the community for six days now, and in all that time, he never made himself available to meet with this man who was his real father. Stewing and festering took a lot of time and energy, after all. But now he was leaving forever.

So he walked over.

Dr. Jess tried out a smile on him, but it was an awkward, mouth-tangly thing. "I guess this is hello and goodbye," he said.

"Yeah." John put absolutely no feeling whatsoever into the word.

"John, I...I want to say I'm sorry I wasn't able to be in your life. I wanted to be. My Vârcolac wife was never able to give me children, so you're my only offspring, but..." Dr. Jess's throat rippled. "Margaret refused. She wanted to protect you and her family."

"Did she?" Because it seemed to John like his life would've been a helluva lot better if he'd only been *told*. Years wouldn't have been wasted in decrepit illness, his career would still be on track, and maybe, just fucking maybe, he would've had what it took to catch the woman he'd chased for so long.

"Or," he kept on bitterly, "maybe Maggie was just protecting her own cheating ass."

Dr. Jess's eyebrows jumped up briefly. "That, uh, I cannot tell you. But whatever her reasons, Margaret clearly did a fine job of raising you." Dr. Jess managed a better smile now. "You seem like a good man."

John laughed. He thought about turning away, but then leaned forward, close enough to Dr. Jess's ear to offer him a conspiratorial whisper. "I wouldn't hold your breath on that one, chief." He sliced a dark, sideways look at his father.

As one. Loathing. Me.

CHAPTER FORTY-ONE

CHARLIZE WOKE, STRETCHED, ROLLED ONTO her back—and a small wrapped box appeared on her belly.

"Merry Christmas."

She gazed sleepily at a bare-chested Breen, who was propped on an elbow next to her in bed. "Aw, man." She fingered the ribbon on the present. "I didn't get you anything. I'm sorry. I didn't think we'd be spending Christmas together."

Up until her cathartic session with Karrell four days ago, she and Breen had still been living apart, and immediately following the session, she'd been in no state to think about Christmas. The holiday had always been a complete washout for her anyway, the day spent cleaning up regurgitated eggnog and whatever broken ornaments her mother's drunken gestures managed to knock off the tree. Plus her brother would usually be sitting sullenly in a corner, complaining about yet another girlfriend breaking up with him, never bothering to take into account that he'd cheated on her—like he did with all of them.

It's easier to be a rebel than Miss Responsible, isn't it?

Charlize closed her eyes. *Maybe.* But she also felt pretty exhausted from creating chaos.

"Are you okay?" Breen asked quietly.

She opened her eyes and looked into his golden gaze. "Yes." She smiled a little. How had he ever thought he was too much of a bonehead to help her? He'd been nothing but helpful during these last few emotional days.

For the whole first day after her cathartic session, her tears had been on a hair trigger. The slightest thing made her break down—and Breen had been there to hold her through every soggy episode. He took complete care of her, gently steering her around her apartment, making sure she ate, showered, dressed in her pajamas, finally putting her to bed and lying down next to her. Who would've guessed how wonderful it was to have someone look out for *her*?

Day two, the worst of her emotions exorcised, she did what Karrell told her to do: viewed Olivia's death through her eyes of today—an adult's eyes. She doubted she would've been able to do this as effectively if not for the therapist putting eight-year-old Kristara in front of her.

Guilt has warped your memory into something quite unfair, I think.

It wasn't your fault.

You were just a kid!

She *was* just a kid back then. It was true—really, really true.

You deserve to be happy.

She was coming around to accepting this idea, too, and Maylie Nichita had a lot to do with it. Nothing could ever completely compensate for Charlize not having been fast enough to rescue Olivia, but, by God, the day before yesterday she *had* been fast enough. She'd saved little Maylie's life— something she wouldn't have been able to do if she'd been even one millisecond slower. And she would've been slower if she hadn't trained nearly her whole life as a marathon runner. And she wouldn't have trained as a runner if not for what happened to her sister. So in Charlize's heart, she was granting this win to Olivia.

"And your knee?" Breen continued with his check-in. "Doing okay too?"

Her skid-out on the cave floor had earned her eight ugly, crosshatched stitches on her left knee—another thing Breen was being relentless about looking after.

"Yep," she said. "A little sore, but that's all." She should probably down some ibuprofen before heading to the Nichitas' Christmas brunch.

Breen picked up a strand of her hair and wound it around his finger, her curl eagerly following his lead. "So are you going to open your present now or what?"

She mugged a face. "Can't we wait until I have something to give you too?"

His eyes glowed from beneath the inky sweep of his lashes. "It's enough of a present for me to sleep in the same bed with you."

"Ah." She gave him a slumberous look. "But we did more than sleep last night, didn't we?" They'd made love—slowly, gently, tenderly. It'd been the most mind-blowing sex of her life. Who would've guessed her heart could fill with so much warmth and joy, that she had so much love inside herself to give?

He gave his finger a little tug and her curl bobbed off. "We're onto something new here, aren't we?"

She made a contented sound. "Hmm."

"So, uh, for the sake of starting things off with a clean slate. I have to fess up—we could've been having sex all along."

She opened her eyes all the way, "What?"

He grimaced. "Yeah, Toni made up all the shit about us having to be acting like a married couple in order to screw. But don't get mad at her," he rushed to add. "She just did it because she knew I was a bonehead and needed help getting you. If you're going to be mad at anyone, be mad at me for going along with it. Although I would add that I really, really wanted to get you." He paused. "So are you?"

"Mad?" She released a long breath from the depths of her lungs. She couldn't seem to bring herself to be. Breen had really, really wanted her, and it was incredibly sweet. "It seems to me, Breen, that we're two people who were never supposed to end up together, so right now I'm only feeling grateful for all the forces out there that made it happen."

He smiled, his *pitter-pat-there-goes-my-heart* chip peeking out.

Her toes just about curled off her feet. "How did you come by this, anyway?" She tapped his fang. "Your chip?"

Heat flared in his eyes.

Oh, he liked his fangs touched, did he? *Store that one away for later use.*

"Pandra punched me in the mouth," he told her.

She burst out laughing, the jerky movement of her belly bouncing Breen's present off.

"What?" He set the present back on her stomach.

"I don't know. I just wasn't expecting that answer." Her laughter drifted off. "Next chance I get, I'll have to thank her."

His eyebrows eased up. "Why?"

"Your chip was the first thing that made me fall for you."

His brows lifted higher. "Fall?"

"In love."

His smile widened. "Wrap that up in a bow, and you just aced Christmas."

She kept gazing at his mouth, heat stirring in the more tropical regions of her body. "God, you're killing me with that chip." She slid her fingers through his too-long bangs, then pushed back through the rest of his hair, skimming down to the nape of his neck.

She tugged him forward for a kiss, and his mouth came down on hers, lips parted, jaw turned. She sighed from deep in her chest as the lust factor between them instantly spiked high. His kisses always ran heavy on possessive and hungry, and she loved tasting the feral power in him—sexy, knowing and feeling the untamed wildness that lurked beneath the quiet exterior. The erotic movement of his tongue against hers steadily melted her brain to oatmeal, and when his rigid cock prodded her thigh, her inner passage clenched, strongly and eagerly. But...

She nudged his shoulder.

His head came up. His pupils were wide and his fangs long.

"I don't think we can mess around," she said huskily, "and still be on time to the Nichitas' house for Christmas brunch."

"We have time," he said and stole between her thighs.

SNEAKING LATE AND UNNOTICED INTO the Nichitas' festively-decorated living room wasn't going to happen. The moment Charlize walked through the front door, the room exploded in deafening cheers and applause.

She wasn't a woman who blushed easily, but she did now, and with a lot of heat. Smiling gamely at the partygoers, she spoke from the side of her mouth to Breen, "We're late."

Breen's hands dipped into his pockets. He gave her a lopsided smile and shrugged.

Marissa barreled up and threw her arms around Charlize in a strangling hug. "Thank you so much for what you did for our little girl, Charlize. I never got a chance to tell you."

Dev was right behind his wife, wending his way through the crowd, holding Maylie in one arm. The little girl had a small fist loosely tangled in her daddy's shirt, like she knew where the muscle resided in her family, and she wasn't letting go for nuttin'. Not until she felt safe about the world again.

Dev planted his free hand on Breen's chest. "Sorry, Dalakis," he said, pushing him away from Charlize by a few steps. "But you're just going to have to deal with this." Dev hooked the back of Charlize's neck in the crook of his elbow and pulled her against him in a one-armed bear hug. "Still don't have words," he said through her hair into her ear. "Because there aren't any. Just..." He leaned back and looked into her eyes. "Thank you."

She swallowed tautly. "That was perfect, actually." She set a palm lightly on Maylie's back. "How's she doing?"

Dev released Charlize. "Clingy and shaken." He tugged affectionately on his daughter's foot. "But getting better."

Poor kid…although at least at some point Maylie *would* feel safe and sure about her world again. Kids got over stuff when they had loving parents to see them through the hard times.

"Hey," Dev added, "you guys need champagne. Come into the dining room." He strode off.

Marissa appeared in front of Charlize again. "Nice necklace."

"Oh, thanks." Charlize touched the pendant. It was a tiny silver whisk on a silver chain. "Breen's Christmas present to me."

"Is it?" Marissa cast a dancing glance at Breen, then slanted a knowing brow.

"Attention, everyone!" Dev called out. "Time to toast Charlize, savior of our little Maylie."

Charlize peered through an arched entryway leading from the living room into the dining room.

Dev was standing beside a buffet table set with a selection of hors d'oeuvres and several rows of champagne flutes. He gestured Breen and Charlize to come.

They went.

Grabbing a couple of glasses, they turned to face the gathered merrymakers.

"To Charlize!" Dev held up his glass in toast.

More cheers rose.

Dev started to take a sip, but two young boys—a black-haired three-year-old and a blond five-year-old—careened around his legs. He had to maneuver an athletic sidestep to avoid getting knocked into by the boys. "Randon," Dev called after the younger boy, "you and Garez want to chase each other, go out in the backyard. Monkeys."

Breen leaned toward Charlize. "You ever think about having some of those?"

She turned to peer up at Breen, her heart fluttering against her ribs. She'd never considered having children, no...but because she hadn't thought she deserved them. "Have you?"

"Lately." He smiled, all Boyish Breen. "Yeah." He bounced a fistful of her curls in his palm.

She chuckled. The champagne she held gently misted her hand as bubbles rose to the surface of the drink and silently popped. "Lately. I'd say me too."

His gaze growing warm, Breen touched her jawline with the tip of his finger. "You'll make a great mom, Charlize. You're one helluva fighter."

Her lips parted. She didn't get a chance to respond, though.

Marissa came to stand in the archway, holding a chocolate cake on a silver tray. "I made this cake," she announced, "to celebrate Charlize saving Maylie, but now that I'm looking at things, I think maybe this should be a bonding celebration cake for Breen and Charlize." Her eyes twinkled. "They haven't celebrated their bond yet, and, well..." She came forward and set the cake on the buffet, then grinned radiantly at the couple. "You two *are* truly bonded now, aren't you?"

Breen's mouth hitched upward, a mere twitch of a smile for everyone else to see. For her, there was so much more—*all* for her—layer upon layer of the true man.

You just have to agree to try to be in a relationship with me. Just try.

Charlize. No. Come on. That's not what this was about.

I like you, and when I'm inside you it's kind of impossible to ignore.

So, I'm sorry, but I'm going to have to make you go back there.

I'm here, *and not just because I'm physically bonded to you, but because I want to be here.*

You were just a kid! It wasn't your fault!

You'll make a great mom, Charlize.

Happy tears pricked Charlize's eyes. This man of few words had managed to breach a lifetime of dysfunction and defenses with the little he'd said, and now here they were, come full circle.

They'd met while Charlize was on a treadmill, and Breen was the one who'd made her stop running.

Slipping an arm around her husband's waist, she hugged him close, her heart, like the champagne bubbles, overflowing in a continuous cascade of effervescence. "Oh, I'd say we are most definitely truly bonded."

Breen smiled. His chip came out to play. And she was a goner for good.

I need your help!

If you enjoyed MOON-RIDERS, please consider writing a review on your favorite bookseller site. Even if it looks like there are enough reviews, bookseller sites look for "recent activity." New reviews encourage them to decide that a book is still popular, and then they will show it to other, potential readers—and this would really help me out!

Thank you!

✦　✦　✦

COMING SOON!

Book 5 in The Community Series.
WITCH MASTER

After his return to the Romanian warded lands, Octav Rázóczi betrays the San Diego Vârcolac to Zalina, leader of the Warrior Witches, revealing the existence of her hidden daughter, Hadley Wickstrum. Zalina deploys a band of her most powerful witches to obtain Hadley, putting the entire community at risk. Faced with their most uniquely powerful enemy to date, the warriors must rely on the experience of two men who have been newly minted into their ranks, Nicolae and Vasile Lazăr.

Thrust into a life away from the secluded mountains he's always known, Nicolae struggles to adjust while also reveling in the chance to become his own man. Every day his body and mind open to new ways of being with Hadley, the woman he loves. But Hadley is still reeling from the shocking news of her true identity and doesn't recognize the prize she has in Nicolae....not until she's forced to relive a trauma, and Nicolae's knowledge of the wild is the only chance she has of escaping the terrifying nightmare.

Go to the link below to be notified of this book's release.

http://tracytappan.net/vip-moonriders/

ABOUT THE AUTHOR

Tracy Tappan is the best-selling author of gritty romance, her novels spanning genres across paranormal (The Community Series), military romantic suspense (The Wings of Gold Series), and medieval historical (The Baron's War Trilogy). Her debut novel, THE BLOODLINE WAR, won the bronze medal for romance from the Independent Publishers Book Award (IPPY), one of the largest national book contests. The second book in her Community Series, THE PUREST OF THE BREED, was a USA Book News Award finalist. The third book in her Wings of Gold Series, MAN DOWN, won the Reader's Favorite Bronze Medal for Romance and was a 2017 Kindle Book Awards Semi-finalist.

Tracy holds a master's degree in Marriage, Family, Child Counseling (MFCC), loves to play tennis, enjoys a great glass of wine, and talks to her two Labradors like they are humans (admittedly, the wine drinking and the dog talking probably go together).

A native of San Diego, Tracy is married to a former Navy helicopter pilot, who retired after thirty years of service and joined the diplomatic corps. He and Tracy currently live in Rome, Italy. www.tracytappan.com

CPSIA information can be obtained
at www.ICGtesting.com
Printed in the USA
LVOW10s1752260418
574987LV00029B/592/P